# Shadow of the Crescent

Margaret Ball

Galway Publishing

ISBN Paperback: 978-1-947648-28-9
ISBN ebook: 978-1-947648-29-6

Printed in the United States of America
Cover art: Cedar Sanderson
Formatting: Polgarus Studio

# Also by Margaret Ball:

# Shadow of the Crescent

# ~CHAPTER ONE~

*The castle is the key element of the city, just as the head is the key organ of the body —if the head is lost, then so is the body, and in the same way whoever loses his castle also loses his power over the city.*

*-Francesco di Giorgio, <u>Trattati di architettura</u>, quoted in Hollingsworth: <u>Princes of the Renaissance</u>*

~ ~ ~

Caterina was seated by one window of their bedroom in the palazzo, reading two books at once —that is, she was studying a new translation of *The Magical Properties of Stones* while a more respectable book of pious reflections upon the duty of wives lay open in her lap, to be shown just in case her husband happened to ask what she was reading. Girolamo had never actually forbidden her to include magical information in her own book of useful household recipes and experiments, but she knew that he did not like her coming so close to the bounds of what was permitted by the church. Her maid Rosa was occupying the seat under the other window, embroidering a piece of linen while Ercole, her nine-year-old son, played at sorting the colored silks for her and generally created more tangles than he had started with. Girolamo himself was pacing up and down the room, obviously bored. She wished he would go downstairs and have a drink, or go to the stables and commune with his horses, or something

Then the screaming began downstairs in the hall, and the clash of metal

1

upon metal. Girolamo drew his own sword and dashed from the room, telling Caterina to bar the door behind him. She stood at the half-open door, listening to his shouts at the intruders, until the words were broken off by a long bubbling cry.

Then she slammed the door and dropped the heavy bar across it.

Rosa had jumped up when the noises began. Now the partially embroidered cloth, the colored silks and the needle lay at her feet, fanned out across the floor. In a moment of silence the thimble rolled across the floor and fell through the space left by a knot in the wood with an audible chink.

"They are trying to kill my lord," Caterina gasped. *No. They are killing him.* Girolamo had laughed at the talk of disaffection in the city and the suggestion that he and his family should remain in the safety of the old castle, inconvenient and barren though it was. Instead, he had declared that he would enjoy an intimate family evening with his wife and son in the comfort of their well-furnished, richly decorated palazzo in the center of the city. There should have been guards at the outer door; what had happened to them?

Boots thundered up the stairs; a rattle at the door was succeeded by the thump of something heavy against the solid wood.

"Open and no one will be harmed!" shouted a voice that would have been more convincing had it not almost cracked, sounding close to hysteria.

Girolamo had ordered her to bring a casket of her best jewels, saying that the oafs of townsfolk should see that he was not yet reduced to selling his wife's property. Could she do anything with what she had brought with her? Bribe the assassins? That wouldn't work when they could simply take them from her. Well then, at least she could see they did not profit from them. This much, at least, she remembered without the need to consult her personal book of secrets. She had used the same safeguard only a few months earlier, when they lent the jewels to Girolamo's cousin so that Lucrezia could make a good showing at her wedding in Venice.

Under cover of the shouts and thuds from outside, she whispered the words over the open casket, moving her fingers to trace the signs that accompanied them.

"What are you doing, madonna?" Rosa asked.

"Protecting what is mine." The details did not matter; Rosa would not be any happier for knowing that Caterina was invoking a magical protection. Caterina finished weaving the last sign as quickly as she could. The ring that had always been a little too big, even on her thumb, fell into the casket among the other jewels even as she closed the lid, and she looked with dismay at her bare thumb. Was there time to reopen the casket, fumble through the contents and retrieve the ring that had fallen off into the casket, the one that had always been just a little too big even on her thumb? No, they were shouting to bring a battering ram. And the ring would hardly protect her against their swords; it guarded only against subtler attacks.

*A battering ram. Very well-equipped assassins.* She wondered again how much of the town supported them. Well, doubtless she would soon find out –if they left her alive.

Ercole had buried his head in Rosa's skirts. She set the casket down and hurried to the window, thrusting the shutters wide and looking down at the steps of the palazzo. Something like a half-stuffed bolster sprawled there, lying awkwardly half on and half off the steps. A bolster dressed in blue and red? No. That was Girolamo's new doublet of blue silk, the sleeves slashed to reveal what had been cloth-of-silver puffs. Now they were red, and his unseeing eyes stared up at the sky.

*Girolamo.* Her eyes prickled. *No time to mourn him now.* She leaned out of the window and called for help. *Too soft. No one will hear.* Caterina filled her lungs with what might be her last breath and screamed. The incurious citizens did not even come out into the piazza to find out who was screaming, and why. And behind her, the door and its heavy bar splintered.

Caterina braced for death, pushing Ercole behind her. Should she have tried to let him down from the window? But there had been no time –and it was too far –and since they had not answered her screams, perhaps they would not have helped Ercole either.

Stoldo Borghini pushed through the ruined door, irritably slapping at the splinters his wide sleeves collected. So that was who had invaded the palazzo and slain her husband! She might have known it was the Borghini brothers;

they had always been disaffected, feeling that they were excluded from the leadership of the town because they lacked sufficiently noble birth. But they must have gathered support from other townsfolk to have dared this coup. Those rumors of disaffection! She wondered just how unpopular Girolamo's new taxes had been.

"That was unnecessary, Madonna Caterina," he grumbled. "We mean no harm to you or the boy." He glanced at the men entering behind him. "Escort the lady and her son to Casa Borghini."

"For your own safety," he added to Caterina. His eyes slid round the room, brightened when he saw the casket. "The people are disturbed; we must make sure that you are not harmed in the rioting."

There had been no rioting to be seen in the piazza. Caterina thought that most of the people of San Florian were waiting to see how this action of the Borghini would play out. But when she, Ercole and Rosa descended the stairs —with armed guards before and after them —she realized she had been too optimistic. People must have been slipping behind the buildings of the piazza to reach the palazzo inconspicuously.

The hall was filled with people, mostly Borghini supporters, but some whom Girolamo had never suspected and many who would have been beneath his notice. She recognized merchants —minor tradesmen —the baker who had supplied their morning bread - and, of course, all the local ne'er-do-wells. They were rummaging through the hall, each man seizing what he could. One of them turned the dish of lampreys in wine and garlic upside down so that he could tuck the serving dish under his arm; another dropped the white cheese tart on the floor and ground his boot into the sugared crust. *They're certainly not starving.* The *cristallo* goblets from Venice were mostly in splinters, knocked to the floor by careless, greedy hands. One man, a poor commoner from his dress, looked at the forks left lying on the table. "What are these for?"

"Who cares," shouted another, "they're silver!" He snatched up both forks and took a silver serving spoon from the dish that somebody else had already laid hands on. Behind them, two men yanked at the tapestry showing David and the death of Absalom until it fell down over their heads. *Dear God, they would loot our murals of the Assumption of the Blessed Virgin and Bacchus with Ariadne if they could find a way to take the walls they are painted on.* Soon the palazzo would be stripped as bare as the ancient castle that loomed above the town.

Behind her, Stoldo Borghini descended the stairs clumsily, her jewel casket tucked under one broad arm. *Much good that will do you*, she thought with a momentary gleam of malice, and then wondered if that was true. They would be angry when they discovered what she'd done. And if they tortured her – or, worse, threatened Ercole –would she not give in and undo the working? Oh, she should have done something else, something to rout these thieving murderers entirely. She knew the people were unhappy about the new taxes; she had known that the Borghini were always ready to challenge Girolamo's authority. Why had she not been prepared for something like this?

Caterina was still asking herself that question hours later, as she paced back and forth in a dark chamber of the Borghini palazzo. The guards had been polite but uncompromising. Her questions to them had gone unanswered and they had given her no option but to let herself be locked into this airless room. At least they had allowed Ercole to stay with her –and Rosa as well, if only because they had no orders about her maid.

The room had clearly been chosen because the doors and shutters could be locked. Otherwise it was quite unsuitable; low, stuffy and cluttered with bales of wool and fabric corded for transport. Her husband would have said that one had to expect that sort of thing in the Borghini palazzo. Instead of living honorably from the rents on their land or by military service, they lowered themselves to trade, chaffered with low-born merchants and built up the fortunes of their house on the profits from San Florian's wool. Girolamo had always sneered at the Borghini, calling them peasants who had bought a pair of boots and thought that made them gentlemen. Once Caterina had asked if the taxes on commercial transactions cleansed that particular money of the peasant taint; Girolamo had not been pleased. Oh, what did it matter now? All that mattered was that she and Ercole were prisoners.

She thought, from the raised voices that occasionally came through the wall, that the Rocca had not surrendered to the Borghini. Her castellan remained loyal, then. She would reward him —once she got out of this trap — she must make a plan —if only she and Ercole were safe in the Rocca, the fortress that towered over the city, with its miraculous spring of pure water that San Florian himself had struck from the living rock! There she had friends, loyal servants, and her materials. From there it should be possible to mount a resistance to the Borghini takeover. From here? She sank down, exhausted, on a bale of wool. Voices from the hall were rising again. Ercole started to whine that he was thirsty and she shushed him until Rosa came to comfort him. Caterina felt a flash of irritation. At first she thought that at nine, Ercole was too old to cling to a woman's skirts for comfort. Then she realized that she would have liked some of that comfort herself. She fought down panic, locked the memory of Girolamo's murdered body in a box that she would open when it was safe to mourn him. The Borghini had treated them with restraint so far; she did not think that they planned to leave their captives confined in this storage room until they died of thirst. And she needed to hear what they were saying.

She sat close to the wall and listened carefully. Angry shouts overlaid the torrents of words and made it all but impossible for her to follow the debate. Some of their captors spoke of offering the city to Venice in return for recognition; others preferred Florence. But Domenico Borghini's voice overrode the rest and they quieted, grumbling, while he made his argument. It was folly, he argued, for them to side with either Venice or Florence; whichever city they picked, the other would immediately become their enemy and would intrigue on the side of the Rinaldi family. Better, he said, to subject themselves to Rome, to get papal protection. And to strengthen the Borghini claim, he would marry the widow and become guardian of her son, Girolamo's heir.

Rome! Would Pope Sixtus accept the offer? Caterina tried to reason out the tangled threads of inheritance and patronage. Her father had been the rightful lord of San Florian, no one disputed that. But when he fell ill ten years ago, she had known that her position was in danger. A man who died leaving only an illegitimate daughter could expect to see his lands pass to someone else. And he had been in a panic that she did not then quite understand about the possibility of San Florian –and his daughter –falling into the hands of his cousin of Rimini. The new Pope's purchase of San Florian as a gift for his nephew Girolamo had been a solution, and her marriage to Girolamo Rinaldi had been part of that solution, a way to shore up his position by associating him with Caterina's father. *Not to mention a way of getting back the money he had paid for the city, by making it part of the dowry she brought to the marriage.*

At fifteen, Caterina understood that marriage to the thirty-five-year-old Girolamo had been both her duty and her salvation, preventing the takeover of San Florian by Sigismondo of Rimini. And at the same time, she had finally heard about the mysterious deaths of Sigismondo's first two wives; if anything was lacking to reconcile her to a marriage of duty, that information supplied it. She had been grateful to find that Girolamo was not cruel, and –once he had begotten an heir - not particularly interested in the marriage bed. She had been too thin, too dark, probably too plain; his taste ran to lush blond beauties like his latest mistress, La Gonzaga. They had both been reasonably satisfied with the arrangement.

Would Sixtus be angry that Girolamo had been struck down in cold blood? Probably. Angry enough to send a papal army to revenge his so-called nephew? Caterina could not guess. But she did see that accepting the allegiance of Domenico Borghini would be a cheaper way to regain control of San Florian than besieging the city - especially a city guarded by the Rocca San Florian. The Rocca had never been taken by direct attack. Nor had a siege succeeded; the besieging armies ran out of food in the countryside before the inhabitants of the castle had tightened their belts. If the Borghini could get control of the Rocca, Sixtus would probably accept their offer of allegiance. If they could not… The germ of an idea sparkled in her brain, a tiny point of light in the darkness that filled her. She touched the key on the chain she always wore around her neck. If she could just get into the Rocca to use the key… She rubbed her bare thumb without quite realizing what she was doing until Rosa spoke up.

"You shouldn't worry so much about the ring, madonna. Compared to the rest of your jewels, it was no great loss. It wasn't a very pretty ring anyway, with all those marks scratched into the band. And it was always too big for you. I've never understood why you didn't have that emerald reset in something that would fit your hand."

She couldn't risk explaining to Rosa exactly why those scratches were important, let alone why she had never replaced the ring with a smaller, more decorative setting for the big table-cut emerald. "It was my father's ring," she said. "He never had it reset to make it prettier, and I will not change it." *Particularly when removing those runes she calls scratches would rob it of half its power.*

# ~CHAPTER TWO~

*A very simple cipher:*

*Replace each letter of the first word with the succeeding letter; of the second word, with the second letter succeeding; and so on, beginning again if the message contains more than twenty-six words. But it will usually be very short, because doing this is not easy if you have not a table of the letters to refer to.*

*-Caterina Rinaldi's Book of Secrets*

~ ~ ~

Two days later, on a sweltering summer afternoon, the Papal Legate arrived in San Florian. Caterina heard the people cheering and shouting his name. *Bishop Visconti. I remember him; he once visited my father. Will he sell me to the Borghini? Probably; there's no profit in opposing them. Unless the Pope would rather hold San Florian directly rather than through Domenico Borghini. I must at least hint at that when I meet the bishop. If I am allowed to meet him.*

Once again she rued having given in to Girolamo's insistence on dining at the palazzo. In the Rocca she would have been able to ensure that Visconti gave her a favorable hearing. Here all depended on chance and her wits.

Hours later Domenico Borghini summoned her to the hall, more, she thought, to show the Papal Legate that she had not been harmed than to allow her a voice in the negotiations. Perhaps he expected her to stay silent, eyes downcast, accepting whatever fate the men chose for her. *If he had been on better terms with my lord, if Domenico had known us better, he would have had*

9

*me gagged before I could speak to Bishop Visconti. So perhaps it is not so bad that my lord looked down on the Borghini and seldom received them.*

The time spent in waiting had not been wasted; she had thought of a better plan than trying to negotiate with the bishop in Domenico's presence. As soon as the formal greetings were concluded she began to complain in a shrill voice. The room where she had been imprisoned was not fit for a lady to inhabit; if the bishop doubted this, let her maid show him the common storeroom where she had been incarcerated! She would fall ill and probably die if she was denied light and fresh air much longer. Furthermore, the Borghini servants were rude and clumsy, scarcely better than peasants, not that she would have expected much better from such a family. She had been forced to subsist upon coarse food and there had not been enough wine in the water to make it drinkable. If this was how Domenico Borghini treated a lady whom he wished to marry, she would rather beg her bread in the street than submit herself to such a man!

Caterina drew a second breath and continued ranting. *That time Girolamo's cousin Lucrezia visited us wasn't wasted after all; I know how to act the offended lady. For longer than any man can bear to listen.*

Domenico tried to interrupt, simultaneously apologizing for the conditions under which she had been kept, denying that there was anything wrong with the food or the servants, saying that the storeroom was perfectly suitable and besides, there was no other room in the palazzo in which she could be kept safe from the outraged populace, who would otherwise quite likely break into the house and murder her.

"Lies!" she cried out, her voice rising to a wail. "My lord Bishop, you knew my father. The people loved him, and they love me as his daughter. Only let me show myself to them, and you will see that I stand in more danger from these assassins than from any of the common folk." *Apart from the ones who looted my palazzo. But they may not be so bold in the face of a Papal Legate.*

"Since this house is so ill-prepared to treat an honored guest, let me stay with you, my lord Bishop. Surely you have been lodged with the honor befitting your high station?" *I don't ask him to set me free; he doesn't like to commit himself. But there, I will be able to speak with him without the Borghini listening. At the very least he will allow me more liberty than the Borghini would, and if I can persuade him to give me paper and ink…*

Bishop Visconti stroked his heavy chain set with turquoise stones and smiled. "Surely," he said in a deep, strong voice that overrode both Caterina's shrill diatribe and Domenico Borghini's stumbling excuses, "since it is so difficult for you to provide suitable hospitality for the lady, there can be no objection to allowing her to lodge with me in the Porta San Pietro?"

"I should require to set my own guards at the doors," said Domenico.

"Guards? I understood that the lady had agreed to marry you."

*Ha! The idiot overstated his case. A Papal Legate does not suffer fools gladly.*

"Well," Domenico was visibly searching for words. "That is. It is the logical solution. It may be that her mind is temporarily disturbed by the tragic circumstances of her widowhood, but I am sure that she will soon understand the necessity of the marriage. I wish only to protect her from the violence of the uprising. Should she be murdered while enjoying your hospitality, both my family and the Pope would be shamed."

Bishop Visconti sighed and agreed. Clearly there was a limit to his defense of Caterina. Suitable lodgings for a lady, yes; allowing her to escape, no. *He wants the gloss of peace and concord to cover over murder and looting. Doubtless he will likewise be persuaded to officiate at my wedding to this wretch, lending Papal sanction to the Borghini. Unless…*

~ ~ ~

Their new lodgings at the Porta San Pietro were a vast improvement; Bishop Visconti had turned out his personal advisor to give them two light, airy rooms on the highest floor, with windows overlooking the city. Domenico Borghini grumbled about the absence of locks and persuaded the bishop to let him station two guards at the outer door of the suite as well as two more at the entrance to the Porta. He even wanted the windows barred, but Bishop Visconti's secretary said acidly that the bishop had not come to San Florian as a building contractor and anyway, he did not believe that the lady could fly.

Sadly, he was correct about that. Caterina set aside thoughts of immediate escape and requested a private interview with the bishop. He winced slightly even as he agreed; she was careful to moderate her tone, sounding quiet and reasonable and as close to sweet as she could manage. She even half-apologized for her diatribe against the Borghini, saying that she felt sure he could appreciate her distress at being treated so brutally, especially after the murder of her beloved husband.

"Beloved" might have been a slight exaggeration, but it pleased the bishop. And Caterina had no difficulty in producing the tears she had been holding at bay. If the bishop chose to interpret them as appropriate grief for her husband rather than fear for herself and Ercole, he was free to do so.

Sitting with her back to the high arched window overlooking the town, Caterina nibbled on a piece of sugared fruit, sipped wine that had probably come from the cellars of the Palazzo Rinaldi. She watched the bishop's face in the golden light of late afternoon as she put forward an alternative to simply recognizing the Borghini *fait accompli*. "Pope Sixtus has always been fond of his nephew," she pointed out. "Will he simply accept his murder, and even reward the murderers?"

"His Holiness loves all good Christians," the bishop evaded, "and he is charged with the welfare of the entire realm. He has not the luxury of other folk, who can choose to honor the claims of family over those of the state."

"But if it would be good for the realm that San Florian should become one of the Papal States, would it not be even better if this could be accomplished without rewarding foul treachery and murder? And," Caterina added, remembering that the bishop was almost as snobbish about the base-born as her husband had been, "without raising common tradesmen above their station in life?"

The Bishop assumed a look of polite interest. "His Holiness might be willing to consider an alternative arrangement."

"I am but a simple woman," Caterina said, "and I need your advice in this matter. If my lord had died of illness, or in a hunting accident, would not everyone agree that his son Ercole should inherit from him?"

The bishop nodded slowly. "And as regent for your young son, you would naturally seek the protection of Rome."

"Then why can we not agree on just that?"

"Because the town is held by the Borghini, and his Holiness is not going to send an army to retake it. Your late husband, Contessa, squandered this gift of his uncle's and reduced the town to a state of poverty which directly caused this insurrection. Even if Sixtus were willing to throw good money after bad, he would hardly do so now, when his army may be needed to defend the Holy See against the Turk."

Catherine's eyes widened. "The Turk is attacking Rome?"

"Not yet. But he has abandoned the siege of Rhodes to land his troops in Apulia, and Otranto is even now under siege. Who knows what will follow when the Turk has a foothold upon the mainland? Naples has made peace with Florence, and His Holiness has offered to lift the excommunications in Tuscany if Florence will join the defense of Otranto. Your little dispute about inheritance is not worth his attention when the whole of Christendom is threatened.

"An army may still be required, whichever side of this 'little dispute' the Pope supports," Caterina pointed out. "The Borghini hold the town, but not the castle. The Rocca will not be so easy to take."

The bishop fingered the smooth blue turquoises set into his chain; took a sip of wine; twirled the goblet in his fingers and said nothing.

"May I, at least, write to his Holiness?"

"I suppose," the bishop said carefully, "there could be no objection to that. I should, of course, require to read the letter. If you have it ready before I return to Rome tomorrow, I can take it with me."

Once the table had been cleared and writing materials brought, Caterina set to work on writing her most persuasive arguments to the Pope while covertly performing another task. She took her time to underscore the deplorable murder of her husband, the Pope's nephew; would Sixtus not avenge the wrong done to his own family? She reminded the Pope of how much he had paid to set Girolamo Rinaldi in charge of San Florian; would he be willing to hold San Florian through his nephew's killers? The city would be divided so long as her supporters held the castle; the Borghini had been premature in offering San Florian's submission to Rome. She reminded the

Pope that the Rocca San Florian had never yet been taken by siege. It was not hard to pretend to some difficulty in writing the letter; she was at pains to find the right words, underscored some and cross-hatched over others. And whenever the guards standing in the doorway looked away, Caterina slipped a blank sheet of paper out from under the half-finished letter and wrote down her other message in cipher. It was much shorter than the letter to the Pope; polite circumlocutions were not necessary when one was simply giving orders. Once she sensed the guards' eyes upon her and remembered to slow down, sighing and shaking her head like a woman struggling with a task for which she was unfitted by nature. After a moment the guards resumed their conversation. She managed to fold the ciphered text over twice and slip it into her sleeve before announcing that she was finished and handing her letter to one of the guards.

"You don't seal it?" he asked.

Caterina sighed again. "Do I have wax with which to seal anything? And why waste the effort? The bishop will want to read it before he leaves. Probably Domenico Borghini will want to read it. I have written nothing that all the world may not see. *You* two may read it for all I care."

The guards guffawed heartily. "Nay, we're no scholars," said the one holding her letter. He rolled the letter into a loose scroll and left the room.

The remaining guard watched her more closely than before. "Will I take these things away now?" he asked, indicating the writing materials on the table.

"No," Caterina said. "I wish also to send some instructions to my servants in the Rocca."

"I don't think they'll let you plot with your supporters."

Caterina rolled her eyes. "Idiot! Do you have any idea how long I have been wearing this dress? All I want is for somebody to pack up a change of clothing for me."

"Anyone can carry that message, you don't need to write it down."

Caterina stamped her foot. "By Our Lady's mercy, are all men such lackwits! How will they know exactly what I want, unless I write it down? I require certain specific gowns, a fresh pair of sleeves, two fine linen shifts, my comb and mirror, my special rose soap, the bronze hairpins… If you will not let me send a list, then let my maidservant go to fetch the things; she at least will know what is necessary."

The guard raised his hands in a gesture of surrender. "Tomorrow. It is dark now, it is not safe for her on the streets."

"And your masters cannot spare even one man to escort her there and back?"

"Contessa. Tonight, the streets are not safe for *anyone*."

He retreated as far as the door to the outer chamber and entered upon a low-voiced colloquy with his fellow when that man returned from delivering her letter to the bishop.

"Well enough, well enough," said the other man irritably, "That room opens only onto this next one, and as the bishop said, the lady is not likely to fly out the window. Let the child and the servant girl attend her; all we have to do is watch the door. There's no harm in giving them some privacy." He added in a carrying whisper, "After all, her people still hold the Rocca, and if Domenico and Stoldo have some clever plan for taking it, they haven't mentioned it to the rest of us. We don't know who will rule here tomorrow; there's no need to offend anyone."

Caterina wondered if he had been one of the men who hacked her husband's body into a blood-soaked carcass, and if he thought she would find that more or less offensive than a refusal to leave her alone with Ercole and Rosa.

# ~CHAPTER THREE~

*We think of nothing else than how the Italian states may with a unity of purpose resist the terrible power of the Turks... [Now] we have the enemy before our very eyes. He has already been sighted, poised to strike at the province of Apulia with a large fleet... Hear our paternal voice, consider the common peril, and judge for yourself how great is the need to quicken our pace...*

*-Excerpt from papal letter, translated and quoted in Freely, <u>The Grand Turk</u>*

~ ~ ~

News of the war in the south traveled so slowly that the messengers were constantly overtaken by new events. By the time Rome had reacted to the landing of Turkish troops in Apulia, the Turks had laid siege to Otranto and that city had unwisely refused to surrender. The Turkish leader, Gedik Ahmed Pasha, instructed his Italian-speaking envoy Hayrettin Bey to threaten the city with fire and death; the representatives of Otranto politely inquired how this would differ from their fate should they betray their religion and admit the enemy.

While Ferrante of Naples made peace with Florence and alliance with Rome, the Turkish cavalry devastated the land around the city and the Turkish siege guns turned the walls and roofs of Otranto to rubble. The city lay open to Gedik Ahmed Pasha's forces. Guided by the renegade Hayrettin Bey, Turkish troops overran the city, looting houses and churches before setting them on fire, sending the surviving citizens to the central piazza where the janissaries formed a ring of steel around them. Young women and likely-looking children were selected as slaves; a few of the best-dressed citizens were set aside as possibly being worth something in ransom. The rest were systematically beheaded.

A young man in a very shabby doublet, and an older man who had been struck unconscious and who lay with his head in the young man's lap, did not seem to Hayrettin Bey to be worth much either as slaves or for ransom. But as his janissaries finished off the lines of captives in front of them, the young man shouted something that caught Hayrettin's attention.

"Wait!" Hayrettin raised his hand; the slaughter temporarily stopped. "What is that one saying?" He pointed and two janissaries dragged the young man before him, leaving the older one on the ground.

"I said," gasped the young man, "that my father is a great mage who has worked many marvels, and that the sultan will not thank you for throwing away such a resource."

"Ah," said Hayrettin, stroking his beard, "but will an infidel mage serve the Sublime Porte?"

"You yourself, Hayrettin Bey, were not born a Turk. If you would change your coat to save your life, why doubt that another would make the same bargain?"

Hayrettin's thin lips curved in a smile. "Ah, but my enlightenment was the work of Allah through the words of the Prophet (peace be upon him!). Your father, being unconscious, is not able to hear the holy words. How then shall he be converted? And how can he convince me of his special powers?"

"Only send to King Ferrante of Naples, or to the Medici in Florence, and they will tell you that Filippo Cacciote is the wonder of the world, a mage who commands demons and all the powers of the air, who can raise an army of angels and turn a bunch of hovels into a fortified city. On his white horse he can travel the world, going from city to city in a single day."

"This magical white horse, he is lame? For your father does not seem to have benefited from his powers to escape the city."

A flush darkened the young man's face; he pushed a tangle of fair hair out of his eyes and suddenly looked much younger than he had at first appeared.

His height and broad shoulders had misled Hayrettin; he thought now that
the boy could not be older than sixteen or seventeen. He might be made into
a useful slave.

"He was looking for me," he said. "He would not save himself before he
found me –and then it was too late, for one of your fools of soldiers struck
him unconscious. Else we should both have been safely out of your reach by
now."

"Bey," said one of Hayrettin's advisors, "the boy will tell any lie that might
get him a few minutes more of life. Let the janissaries continue."

Hayrettin shrugged. "Lies or not lies, it costs little to wait and see. Take
these two aside and shackle them. The janissaries still have several hundred
infidels to kill." He addressed the young man. "Son of Cacciote –"

"Andrea. Andrea Cacciote."

"Whatever. If your father comes to his senses before my men have finished
their work here, and can demonstrate his powers, and can convince me that for
your sake he will use those powers in service to the Sublime Porte, then you may
live to see another day. If not… you will, at least, be the last to die here."

Andrea sat with his back to a low wall, fanning his father and every once
in a while trying if he would swallow some water. The blood in the piazza
puddled between stones, then covered the lower, most-worn portions of the
paving, then grew thick and sticky in the afternoon sun. The shrieks and
prayers of the victims had mostly ceased by now, as those still alive
surrendered themselves to despair. Some of them looked angrily at Andrea
and Filippo Cacciote and cursed them for renegades.

No one else in the piazza was invited to save his life by turning Turk.

Towards sunset Filippo stirred and mumbled something. Andrea was so
eager to get his father to drink something that he splashed water on his face
and gown. Filippo muttered something else that sounded like "Clumsy fool!"
and opened his eyes. He looked desperately sad when he saw his son's face.
He turned his head, looked at the abbatoir that had been the city's principal
piazza, and tears came to his eyes.

"I tried to get you away," he apologized. "Forgive me; I was afraid to
summon Berith before I drew the circle."

"God be praised!" answered Andrea. "Without that circle, might not the demon have devoured you?"

"Small loss," said Filippo. "It seems we have escaped demons only to fall to Turks. On the whole I have always believed demons to be more reasonable."

"I am not sure about that." Andrea explained how he had persuaded Hayrettin Bey to spare their lives –for now. He looked hopefully at his father.

"I should need my books," Filippo complained.

Proudly, Andrea pointed at a basket propped against the wall. "I persuaded Hayrettin Bey to rescue them before our lodging burned... well, *almost* before our lodging burned... the edges of some pages may be just a little bit charred, but that will not matter, will it?"

Filippo's eyes brightened and he sat up straighter. "No. It will not matter in the least. So, I am to make a demonstration to this renegade, and if he thinks we can be useful, we live? Hmm, let me see, what would impress the fellow? Bring me the book bound in red leather, let me just refresh my memory..."

~ ~ ~

Just outside the town, at moonrise, Filippo stood with Hayrettin Bey and half a dozen janissaries.

"I cannot trace a circle to contain all these people," Filippo complained. "The ground is too broken up here, thanks to your siege guns. We will have to go farther –perhaps to that pasture." He pointed to the east.

"No farther," Hayrettin Bey said. "And you need not include all of my guards. I think you want to make me believe you are tracing something in the ground, and when you get far away enough, you will try to run. You will not escape, of course, but –"

"Would I do something so foolish? When you keep my son hostage in the town?"

The Bey smiled grimly. "I do not know much about you yet. But now I know that your judgment is not good, for only a fool would interrupt me."

Filippo sighed. "A fool –or a master mage, whose words can command demons. Give me a sword."

"Why?"

"To trace the circle, obviously! Did you think I was going to do it with my bare hands? Only steel or iron will work."

Hayrettin Bey said something in Turkish to the janissaries. Four of them drew their swords. Three came forward to stand around the Bey, while the other handed the mage his own sword.

"And the other two?"

"They may stay where they are."

"Oh, very well. If you do not care for your soldiers' lives, why should I?"

Filippo traced a circle around himself and the four Turks and then turned his back to the others to face the rising moon. He chanted, gradually raising his voice until he ended with a shout, "O Lamair, Tatomofon, Rimasor, conjuro vos per sanguinem Jesum Christum. By the most holy name of Tetragrammaton I adjure you to make manifest whatever I shall say and command."

The shadows just outside the circle grew thicker, like three columns of black smoke that blotted out the stars and the moon. Three low, grumbling voices twined together, like stones clashing, like the earth ripping apart.

"Where is our food?"

One of the three janissaries standing around the Bey gasped and bolted out of the circle. The three shadows writhed and elongated themselves until the three guards now outside the circle had been swallowed up in the darkness, as if roiling thunderclouds had fallen to earth and engulfed them. Their shrieks did not last long. When the shadows returned to their columnar shape there was nothing left on the ground but swords and the steel parts of the janissaries' armor. Hayrettin Bey drew a long, shaky breath.

"I adjure you now, by the power and light of the moon and stars, make us to behold tables with a banquet of rich and sweet foods."

Hayrettin Bey sucked in his breath as the shadows wavered and disappeared. In their place were beautiful young boys carrying light tables which they set down around the circle. A wave of their hands, and dishes appeared on the tables. Rich, intoxicating scents filled the air: saffron and honey and cinnamon, lamb and chicken, garlic and oil.

"Three kings will now appear," warned Filippo in a low voice, "inviting you to step out of the circle and join them in feasting. The food is only an illusion. On your life, do not heed them!"

Hayrettin Bey swallowed hard. The smell of the food was making his mouth water. Could it really be all illusion?

As the mage had predicted, the young boys vanished and in their place stood three crowned figures, robed in flowing velvet and wearing heavy jeweled chains. They beckoned towards the people in the circle, and their voices were low and melodious, though afterwards Hayrettin Bey could not remember just what they had said.

He took an involuntary step forward; Filippo grasped his wrist. "Look at the hems of their garments," he said quietly.

Where the velvet robes should have met the ground, there was only black smoke swirling.

"Dispel them!"

Filippo raised a shaky hand and intoned the words that would send the demons away. As the "kings" vanished along with the banquet, he sat abruptly on the ground.

"Can you do anything more useful than creating illusions?"

"Those 'illusions,'" Filippo said tiredly, "have taken the lives of three men tonight."

"Can you raise more demons, and protect my army, and loose the demons upon the opposing forces?"

"The more demons, the more I am drained. Enough to kill an army? They would suck out my life force before the army was destroyed, and then who would save your men from the demons?"

"You're useless, then."

"No," said Filippo, "you are being stupid. Would you send out a handful of soldiers to charge at an entire army? No, you would do something much more clever; what, I do not know, but you doubtless do. No more should you employ a mage for open warfare. You have in your service the greatest necromancer of the age, a master of divination by fire and water, an astrologer and a reader of all secrets –and you would waste my talents and me, by trying to make me destroy the enemy directly? Have you no subtlety?"

"Show me!"

"Show some intelligence!" Filippo snapped. "First your idiot soldiers knock me on the head, then they shove me into a corner for hours with neither food nor drink, then you demand that I conjure up demons for your entertainment! If you wanted to kill me, it would have been kinder to use the sword. Would you send your soldiers into battle starving and hungry and after a long, tiring march?"

"If I were forced to do so," said Hayrettin Bey, "they would obey."

"How fortunate for you. Do you *want* me to continue conjurations when I am so tired that I could easily make a mistake? Does your master reward you for that sort of stupidity?"

If it had been a long day for the infidel mage, it had been longer for Hayrettin Bey. He considered the possible consequences of angering someone who had just proved that he could call demons, and gave in for the moment. "Tomorrow," he said. "Tomorrow, you will have to convince Gedik Ahmed Pasha of your value. Think well! He is not so easily pleased as I am."

# ~CHAPTER FOUR~

*"In Rome the alarm was as great, as if the enemy had already encamped before her very walls... Terror had taken such hold of all minds that even the Pope meditated flight. I was at the time in the Low Countries, in the suite of the Cardinal Legate Giuliano, and I remembered that he was commissioned to prepare what was necessary at Avignon, for Sixtus IV had decided upon taking refuge with the French, if the state of affairs in Italy should become worse."*

Letter from Sigismondo de' Conti, the papal secretary, translated in Freely, <u>The Grand Turk</u>

~ ~ ~

Rosa returned from her errand at the Rocca in mid-morning. The guards demanded to see what was in her bundles. Caterina made a show of irritation, trying to embarrass the men: did they intend to supervise the arrangement of her intimate garments?

"Nothing to be brought in here without a search," one of the men said.

"Perhaps you would like Bishop Visconti to oversee my unpacking?"

"Bishop's gone," said one of them.

"At first light," said the other. "A messenger rode through the night to bring him some bad news."

"What news?"

"Nobody tells the likes of us. But the Bishop turned white and said he had to return to Rome immediately."

"Did he at least take my letter?"

The older man shrugged. "Not for us to ask. We gave it to him last night, is all I can say. Now let's see what's in those bundles of yours. You might be smuggling in weapons for all we know."

"Or poison," the other suggested. "A lady's weapon, poison is."

"Oh, very well," Caterina said. "I *tried* to spare your blushes…"

She and Rosa took a perverse delight in shaking out smocks and underlinen, inviting the guards to examine the rose-scented soap and Caterina's personal face water. "You could do worse than use some of that soap yourselves," Rosa sniffed. "Or do you think soap is poison?"

There was, of course, no contraband in any of the bundles. It was all in Rosa's head.

"Did you deliver the message?" Caterina whispered when the red-faced guards finally retreated to the outer room.

"I was watched," Rosa whispered back. "I could not go in search of Messer Giacomini, so I slipped the paper to the castellan."

Catherine's heart sank. Would Peruzzi even recognize that it was a ciphered message? She knew the castellan was literate, but she also knew that he read even plain Tuscan slowly, sounding out each word and keeping a finger on the text to mark his place. Well, he might not be a scholar, but he was not stupid; he would surely realize that Rosa would not have taken risks to pass him a piece of paper that somebody had been using to practice writing random letters. And the logical person to take it to was Piero Giacomini, who would –she hoped –recognize the cipher at a glance and translate it almost as quickly.

~~~

Domenico Borghini spent much of the morning brooding over the bad news that the messenger had brought to Bishop Vincent. It might have been bad from the Pope's point of view, but it was good, he thought, for his own prospects here in San Florian. No army would come from Rome to support the Rinaldi, regardless of the Pope's private sentiments. Why let the woman delay any longer? He invaded the Porta San Pietro just as Caterina and Rosa finished unpacking. "Come with me," he ordered Caterina.

She backed away from him. "I go nowhere without the protection of the Papal Legate."

"That won't work. You know that he has already left for Rome; he is probably there by now, raising an army to take back Otranto from the Turk."

"Otranto has fallen?" she gasped.

"So the messenger said. You can forget about persuading the pope to rescue you; he has more important things to think about now. And I have had enough of your shilly-shallying. You are to command your castellan to surrender the Rocca at once."

For all that Caterina had planned against this contingency, her heart still sank on hearing the words. Until then she had still enjoyed the faint hope that the bishop would support her claim to San Florian over that of these murderous usurpers. But he would hardly waste troops on San Florian that were needed to recapture Otranto or to protect Rome. Now, it seemed, there was nothing for it but to let the little drama she had imagined play out –and to watch for her chance.

"I need time to put on fresh clothes," she argued.

"You will do well enough as you are."

The guards' hands on her arms were all the argument he needed.

Ercole watched her go, his eyes too big in a face that was growing pinched with worry. Her last sight was of him clinging to Rosa's skirts. She wanted to tell him that at nine he was too big to hide behind a woman. She wanted to tell him to hide anywhere he could, get any protection he could. She wanted to keep him with her forever, even if that meant imprisonment forever. She wanted her freedom.

What she got was a brisk ride to the gate of the Rocca, with armed men around her, with Stoldo Borghini riding beside her and Domenico Borghini himself gripping the reins of her horse. At the gate they dismounted. "Perruzi!" he shouted up. "Your lady would speak with you!"

There was a delay long enough to set everybody fidgeting. *Good. He has understood that he must play for time.* Finally, after Borghini had shouted two more times, the stocky figure of Tommaso Peruzzi appeared on the curtain wall between the two towers of the castle.

Borghini gripped Caterina by the arm. "Go on," he ordered her. "Speak your piece."

Caterina squeezed out a couple of tears. "Peruzzi, they want you to surrender the castle."

"I do not answer to the Borghini," Peruzzi called down, "but to the Rinaldi."

Borghini's grip tightened painfully. "Go on," he said, "order him to surrender."

"What if I should require you to open the Rocca to the Borghini?"

"Lady," Peruzzi said, "such an action would be contrary to the interests of your son."

"Whom do you serve? I am regent for Ercole."

"I have not been informed of that."

Borghini shook Caterina. "What are you two playing at? Tell him to surrender at once! Command him!"

"Perruzi, these men will stop at nothing! They have already murdered my lord, and now I fear for my son's life and my own! If you surrender, they will spare us."

"If I give up the Rocca, your life will not be worth a fig!" Peruzzi shouted back.

Caterina managed more tears and an impressive quiver in her voice. It wasn't hard; all she had to do was remember Ercole's white face as she left him. "You *must* surrender, or our blood will be on your hands!"

"Let me think," Peruzzi called, sounding shaken. "I must consult with my advisors."

He disappeared from the wall, only to return a few minutes later.

"These are my terms," he shouted. "I will never find another post if people believe that I surrendered out of cowardice. Madonna Caterina and her son must come into the castle alone, and she must write a letter explaining that she ordered me to capitulate. Then I will deliver the Rocca to whoever she names."

Stoldo and Domenico stepped aside and conferred in low voices. No one now was holding Caterina, and she looked longingly at the space of white paving stones between her and the gate. If she ran now... *Could I reach the gate before they caught me? Would it open for me? But they have Ercole... No, I need to enter with their permission so that I have time to use my materials before they grow suspicious.*

Domenico shouted at Stoldo. "Don't you understand? We need to settle this as quickly as possible! The bishop could change his mind. He allowed her to write to the Pope yesterday, don't you remember that? The *Pope* could decide against us! He could excommunicate us, he could excommunicate the whole town, where would our supporters be then? He could even send the Papal army!"

"Everyone says the Rocca cannot be taken by siege," Stoldo grumbled.

"Which," Domenico snapped, "is exactly why we need that halfwit of a castellan to surrender it!"

Caterina hadn't thought of the threat of excommunication. She had only thought of the army which the Pope was not going to send. Evidently Bishop Visconti had not spoken as frankly to Domenico Borghini as he had to her; Domenico still thought it possible that she would receive Papal reinforcements. With the Turks in Otranto, she no longer had any hope of that. But she might be able to use Borghini's concern against him... if she could but get into the Rocca.

The argument was evidently over; Domenico stalked over to her. "You may enter the Rocca. Your son remains here as surety that you will return in good time."

"I will need half a day."

"To write *one letter?*"

"I am not accustomed to writing, and the letter must be in my own hand if it is to be believed. And I must first find paper and ink."

Domenico nodded grudgingly. "But this will be a very short letter. You have two hours."

"Four," countered Caterina.

"Three, and that is my final word. Three hours, or the boy dies."

Would three hours be enough for all she must do? It would have to be.

The small door cut into the lefthand gate door opened. Caterina commended her soul and Ercole's to God and walked forward, her knees trembling slightly.

# ~CHAPTER FIVE~

*Aziel is able to make many illusions upon the proper sacrifices and conjuration, but blood must be offered before summoning him. Furthermore, the illusions will last only as long as the one who required them can remain bound to them. A mage who tries to make a vision last forever will die.*

*This I had from the Book of Honorius. Non probatum est because it is a sin to call upon demons.*

*-Caterina Rinaldi's Book of Secrets*

~ ~ ~

Both Tommaso Peruzzi and Piero Giacomini were waiting for her just inside the gate. Caterina felt her strength returning at the sight of Piero's face. Tommaso was loyal by virtue of his office, but Piero had been her friend from childhood. Of course he would have deciphered the letter she sent, outlining what she wanted Peruzzi to do, so he would have been waiting to see her scheme succeed. But neither he nor Peruzzi knew what she hoped to gain from it. He started forward with questions tripping and tumbling from his tongue, but she waved him into silence. "Not now. Go to the dovecote and get me a pigeon. Preferably all white. Bring it to my room, and scratch on the door to tell me when you have the animal." She turned to the left and began climbing the winding stair that led to her workroom at the top of the tower, trusting Piero to understand that she meant that room and not the bedchamber she had shared with Girolamo.

Once she reached the tower room, she took the little key that never left the chain around her neck and unlocked the door. The small book bound in brown leather was still on the shelf where she had left it. Opening the book, she paged through it in search of the information she needed. There it was, between a recipe for brightening the colors of a dyed fabric and an incantation for ridding a place of scorpions.

After locking the door again, from the inside this time, she took a stick of willow charcoal from the pot that held the drawing instruments. She began tracing the circle and the inner diagrams in black, consulting the book frequently to make sure the diagrams were reproduced perfectly. That done, she had just put away the willow stick and picked up the white chalk when there was a scratching at the door. What, so soon?

She glanced out the window and realized that she had lost track of time in her concentration on the diagrams. The sun was low in the sky; she thought that at least one of her three hours was past, if not more.

She unlocked the door and opened it just wide enough to admit the covered basket in which something fluttered and chirped. A whispered inquiry brought the answer that her time was half gone.

And there were still the names to write, the invocations and conjurations to chant, the pigeon to be offered up and the commands to the spirits she raised! She would never complete the work in time.

Setting the basket with its living contents aside, she set to writing the names listed in the book around the edges of the circle. The need for haste conflicted with the importance of getting all these names correctly and legibly written. *No point in this if I do not do it perfectly the first time. There won't be a second chance.* She forced herself to slowness and caution.

Consulting the book again, she saw that she was supposed to be clothed only in white linen, not in a silk gown with an embroidered underskirt, sweat-stained from these days in the summer heat and nights of sleeping in her clothes. *Clean* white linen. More time wasted. If only she had had time to change into some of the clean clothes that Rosa had just brought her! That pig Domenico Borghini, hustling her to the Rocca all sweaty and dirty!

She opened the door a crack, called to Piero, and told him to bring a fresh white shift from the chest in her bedchamber.

Piero's face reddened. He had always been shy of women; Caterina suspected that their childhood friendship had survived to adulthood because she had always been careful not to remind him that she had grown up into one of those frightening creatures. "W-which chest?" he asked.

"The one with the gilded moldings around the edge, and in the center of the lid a painting of the Blessed Virgin." She tried not to snap in her impatience; Piero wouldn't do his task any better for being frightened. But she couldn't help adding, "And hurry!"

To save time, she stripped off her outer garments while he was doing this errand and dropped them in a heap in the corner of the room; the few hooks on the walls here held bundles of dried herbs that were, just now, far more valuable than some stained silk garments. When he returned, she opened the door just wide enough to extend her hand and take the shift from him. She closed and barred the door. Her dirty, sweaty shift joined the little pile of clothes and she pulled the clean, cool linen over her head.

Now, at last, she was ready to start the incantations. She opened the book; the necessary names and charms would be on the next page. Turning the page, she read the first words and her heart sank. "This is to be performed at midnight." Why had she not remembered that? Perhaps because it had been a long time since she copied this conjuration from that book in Rome, and because she had never meant to imperil her soul by actually using it.

She pulled on her underskirt and gown again. The loose seams holding her best pair of sleeves to the body of the gown ripped under the strain. Were there pins anywhere in this room? Of course not. Anyway, she could not attach the sleeves herself; that was Rosa's job, to stitch them on after Caterina had slipped into the gown. One of her shoulders was indecently bare, the green velvet sleeve hanging like a bag. Piero would have to find a cloak for her to borrow, to cover her arms; Domenico Borghini would probably assume she was buying her castellan's loyalty with her body if he saw her shoulder exposed like this.

She stepped out of the room and locked the door, then put the chain around her neck again and tucked the key out of sight. "Piero!" she called. "I must speak with Peruzzi." She ran down the narrow, winding steps and came to a halt, panting, at the doorway opening onto the curtain wall. Tommaso Peruzzi was in the courtyard below. One more flight of stairs.

"The time is almost up," Peruzzi informed her.

"I know. I know. Here is what you must do next."

~ ~ ~

When the Borghini shouted that the three hours they had allotted Caterina were over, and demanded her return, Peruzzi showed himself on the curtain wall. This time he was wearing a steel breastplate and a helmet. "The lady is now *my* prisoner. What will you pay me to redeem her?"

"Surrender the castle, and you will be paid what you deserve."

"That's what I am afraid of," Peruzzi quipped, raising a chuckle from some of Domenico's men. "I should prefer to receive my payment in advance. When I get what I want, I will send Contessa Rinaldi out to you. But not till then."

Domenico's eyes narrowed. "How highly do you value her?"

"Two thousand florins should suffice."

"You know we cannot raise such a sum immediately! What's more, I do not believe you have made the lady your prisoner. I think you are plotting with her to buy time. You might as well save your trouble; there is no rescue coming."

It was a beautiful opening, but Peruzzi did not have the knowledge necessary to exploit it. Caterina joined him. "And when the Pope's army comes to my aid?"

"What makes you imagine that will happen?"

"You know I have written to the Pope. Bishop Visconti himself took the letter."

"And I read it first. I found it singularly unpersuasive."

"Bishop Visconti promised me that the Pope would storm San Florian to avenge the murder of his nephew. Will you gamble that he lied?"

"His Holiness has all of Italy to protect from the Turk. He won't waste men and guns to rescue his nephew's widow. Open the Rocca or lose something even more precious to you!"

Domenico gestured behind him and a guard came to the front, holding a slight figure by the shoulders.

*Of course they would threaten Ercole.*

*If I give in now, neither my life nor his will be worth more than that of the pigeon upstairs.*

She had already, slowly, painfully, reasoned out what would be the best chance for both of them when the inevitable threat was made. There was nothing to be saved, and much to be lost, in surrendering to the rebels' demands. She and Ercole would both be prisoners then, and even if Domenico Borghini did not marry her by force, he would doubtless poison them both in a few months, when the world's attention wandered. She had a much better chance of saving herself and Ercole by fighting the rebels here, in public, for the leaders of every city in Italy to see.

The worst thing she could do, short of surrendering, was to let them know that Ercole could be used as a weapon against her. She prayed that he would understand what she had to do now.

"Go ahead," she taunted Domenico. "If you are not already damned, then you will burn in hell for murdering an innocent child. For myself it does not matter. I am already carrying another heir to San Florian, and I have the equipment to make more!" Her throat burned. She herself would surely be damned if her taunts pushed Domenico into murder.

Thankfully, they seemed to have the opposite effect. He believed her.

So, she saw before tears blinded her eyes, did Ercole. His pinched, shocked face would haunt her nightmares until she could be with him again, comfort him, explain why this pretense of indifference had been necessary.

Domenico and Stoldo were conferring again. She strained her ears but could not make out what they were saying. Ercole had been taken to the back of the group again. Surely that was a good sign?

"You have until dawn tomorrow to surrender yourself and the castle," Domenico finally shouted. "By then it should be obvious even to a stupid woman that there will be no rescue from the Pope."

*God willing, you may change your mind about that.*

Caterina prayed that Ercole would be allowed to be with Rosa tonight.

She could comfort him, take the place of the nurse who had cared for him until the age of seven.

From then until midnight Caterina prayed and committed the lines of the conjuration to memory and stared at the burning candle on her work table. Finally it burned down to the line carved for midnight. Creating timed candles had been a very minor task, requiring no supernatural aid; she had an entire box of them in store. This next charm, by contrast, was far more challenging… well, if she made a mistake, she would have no more worries, would she?

She opened the box, took out the sleeping pigeon, picked up a short, curved knife and stepped carefully over the charcoal lines and into the center of the circle. The pigeon awoke and struggled in her hands.

"*Conjuro te, Aziel, per hoc sanguinim et per verba mea…*"

Gripping the pigeon by the feet, she slashed the curved knife across its throat and shook the bird as the blood spurted out, so that most of it landed on the floor outside the circle. Before the blood could dry, she finished the conjuration and a cold wind swept the room, raising a cloud of dust. The dust swirled and eddied in the air and coalesced into a terrible figure, with the head of a horse and the feet of a lion. The drops of blood on the floor puddled together and vanished into the clawed feet.

"Who are you and how dare you disturb me?" grated an inhuman voice.

"I have paid the price," Caterina said, dry-mouthed. "You are bound to serve me."

"I would know whom I am to serve. I am not to be bound by any common man —or woman."

Caterina consciously stiffened her knees, squared her shoulders and lifted her head. "I am Caterina Rinaldi, Contessa of San Florian, and I have paid your price."

"What do you demand of me in payment for the blood?"

Caterina was shaking with exhaustion; the conjuration had drained her strength. But if she allowed herself to collapse to the floor, the city was lost – and so would she be, if she fell so that any part of her body was outside the protective circle. She stiffened her knees, told Aziel her demands and then recited the words necessary to discharge the demon. But there was no rest for her yet; everyone in the Rocca who could write would have to work through the night to complete her plan.

~~~

Stoldo Borghini slept poorly that night. Domenico had been absolutely certain that Pope Sixtus would not consider San Florian worth the expense of sending an army. But that damned woman had sounded equally certain that Sixtus would support her. And they *had* murdered the Pope's nephew.

And Domenico had been wrong before. He had sounded equally certain that the Rocca would surrender to him when they knew the tyrant Girolamo was dead.

Stoldo was used to following his older brother's lead; Domenico was the smart one, he was the big one. Those had always been the terms of their partnership. But sometimes Stoldo thought Domenico was too smart for his own good. "Sharp enough to cut yourself, boy," their mother had said to him time and again when Domenico's lies caught up with him. Now Domenico was risking his life on the belief that the Pope would not support Caterina Rinaldi. Worse, he was also betting Stoldo's life. And how had they gotten into this mess? By Domenico's assumption that the Rocca would fall to him as easily as the city had done.

Domenico, in the next room, was snoring loudly enough to shake the walls of the Palazzo Borghini. Naturally he was not suffering from any doubts; he always believed in himself right up to the moment when he was proven wrong. Stoldo wished devoutly that they had confined themselves to the wool trade. It might not have been as lucrative after these new taxes, but it had been *safe*.

How could anyone sleep through those rattling snores? Perhaps a walk would help him sleep better. He pulled on his clothes, slipped outside and went to the city wall. Quietly, he climbed to the narrow path at the top of the city walls, turning to the southeast. The darkness outside the walls seemed to him to be alive with soft, furtive movements. Was that the chink of armor he heard? The stealthy steps of attackers approaching the walls?

A flash of lightning ripped the night sky in half and revealed a landscape of nightmare; the light sparkled off cuirasses and the tips of lances, and revealed the shadowy shapes of tents. Stoldo crossed himself and peered to the southwest. The town was not yet completely surrounded. He tiptoed down the steps by which he had ascended and hurried back to the Borghini palazzo. His hands shaking, he lifted the casket he had taken from that woman's room; it almost slipped out of his grasp, and when he caught it, the accursed thing struck a bedpost with a sound loud enough to wake the dead. He heard a mutter from Domenico's room, then the sounds of a body shifting on the bed. Stoldo stood frozen for a moment until the snores resumed; then he left the room and knelt by one of the sleepers in the outer chamber, shaking the man's shoulder gently.

"Up and dress, Zio, quietly, quietly. Domenico's orders," he lied.

The sleep-dazed man did not argue. He did not seem to notice that Domenico was snoring in deep slumber; perhaps he blamed one of his neighbors for the noise. Stoldo hadn't picked Zio for his brains. Domenico himself was evidence enough that brains weren't everything. More to the point, Zio could move quietly and usually obeyed orders without question.

Once outside, Stoldo explained that Domenico was worried that someone might steal the jewels they had liberated from the Palazzo Rinaldi. He had told Stoldo to take one man and the casket and slip out of the town quietly. They were to head south towards Urbino; Domenico would meet them there once this minor business of surrendering the Rocca had been settled.

~ ~ ~

Vico Crevelli was one of the few Borghini allies with military experience, and the main thing he had learned from his years as a condottiere was how to sleep through shouts and thumps and all the stupid noises made by soldiers and drunks. He had felt safe in catching a few minutes of rest; he was lying across the doorway, and anyone who wanted to open the door would have to step on him.

Stealthy movements, on the other hand, signaled to his sleeping brain that something was going on. He woke to the sounds from the room below: rustling clothes, a single thud like wood striking wood, careful steps on the stairs. Then whispering, more steps, the jingling of harness in the courtyard…

He stepped over the sleeping forms of the two exhausted people he was supposed to be guarding and stared out the third-floor window. "Jesu!" he whispered at the sight of the assembled tents on the far side of the city walls, dark shapes in the pre-dawn shadows, but shapes no condottiere could mistake. "So the Pope has chosen his side after all!"

The blasted woman hadn't been lying. The bishop, on the other hand, probably had been lying when he pretended to favor the Borghini over the Rinaldi. It had just been a ruse to let him get away from San Florian and call up the papal army!

All Domenico Borghini's plans had been about achieving surprise; he had expected to slaughter Girolamo Rinaldi and immediately install himself in the Rocca San Florian. When the second part of that plan had failed, it became clear to any intelligent man that Borghini had no idea what to do next. Vico had already been cursing himself for associating with someone he would never have accepted as commander of a troop of condottieri. Now what was he to do? He could see only one way out for him, and that might not work. It would not be possible at all unless he moved quickly, before the others were awake.

He bent and shook the larger of the sleeping pair. "Quiet, on your life!" he whispered. "Get up, get him up, but don't wake anyone else!"

~~~

Dawn brought panic to the city. From every part of the walls, except where the Rocca loomed over the town, the besieging army could be seen. Their swords and lances sparkled in the early sunlight; their horses neighed as if in challenge; their peaked tents covered the landscape. Who knew the Pope commanded such forces? A few people speculated that he had made a treaty with Florence or Venice; most just wondered how they could survive the coming sack of the city. The gates of the Rocca were crowded with townsfolk begging for sanctuary. Vico Crevelli and his companions had been only the first to seek that way out.

Now Vico was disarmed and under guard, protected only by Caterina's comment that she probably would not hang him.

"I brought your son back to you!" he had protested.

"And betrayed your master. Who will ever trust you again? If you escape the rope, Crevelli, I will see you exiled." *At least I have an excuse not to hang this one.*

On Caterina's orders, the archers of the Rocca loosed flights of arrows over the city. The crowds in the street screamed, trampled one another trying to get to shelter, and then… discovered that the arrows had blunted heads and were wrapped in paper scrolls. Little knots of citizens formed around anybody who could read; the priests had never enjoyed such eager attention at Mass or in the confessional.

"The Lady promises that if we do two things, she will not permit the Pope's army to sack the city. Also, she will remit one of the new taxes pronounced by her husband, the demand for a fifth part of the price paid for meat, bread and wine. We must deliver her son to her –No, wait," said one of the priests, squinting at the paper. "That has been crossed out. A note beneath says that she already has her son safe. We must deliver the assassins to her justice, and we must return the property we took from the Palazzo Rinaldi. And these things must be accomplished before vespers."

"Why vespers?" Piero had asked when Caterina first dictated the message to be copied and recopied.

Because maintaining illusions drained a mage's energy. Because just keeping such a massive illusion in place would probably kill her if she tried to keep it going for a second night.

Piero wasn't going to want to hear those explanations.

"There is nothing to be gained by allowing them more time to think it over," she said finally.

Now that message was being shouted out all over the city, while Caterina and Tommaso Peruzzi watched the results from a tower window. At first the crowds seemed to be milling aimlessly in the streets; then they surged towards the southernmost quarter of the city.

Peruzzi swore softly under his breath. "They must be running to the Borghini; unarmed, they can't hope to take the assassins. Shall I order the archers to shoot real arrows?"

"Wait," said Caterina, placing one hand on his arm. "Wait and see."

She was rewarded. Spiked poles and leather jerkins, if there are enough of them and if the bearers are desperate enough, can overcome a few armed men who are confused by a rough awakening. The crowds parted to show three men being dragged towards the castle.

"Domenico Borghini," Caterina said. "And his two closest cronies. Giacomo Albizzi the Florentine and Massacio di Travia! That will suffice; I have no need to decorate the walls of the Rocca with the common men whom the Borghini misled." She frowned and shaded her eyes. "But where is Stoldo?"

"Dead, probably," said Peruzzi cheerfully. "Stoldo never had the guts to stand up to anyone bigger than himself —not that many folk were in that category. I'll wager you he killed himself rather than face your justice."

Caterina shrugged. "If so, he has saved me the cost of a rope."

But they learned from the townspeople who delivered the other three conspirators that Stoldo Borghini was nowhere to be found. One man who lived near the wall said that during the night he had heard horses in the street; eventually the keeper of the south gate confessed that he had opened to let Stoldo and someone else out of the city. He pled that last night he had believed the Borghini to be in charge of the city, and that he would certainly not have let those murderers escape had he known that the gracious lady had reclaimed her inheritance!

Caterina shrugged again. Stoldo had always been stupid, not to mention cowardly when confronted by anyone who might be able to hurt him. She did not think that he would be back. There was nothing for him here now; she intended to confiscate the Borghini goods and keep the profit from their sale. That should go some way towards repairing the loss of the new taxes.

"Let the hangman prepare three nooses," she said, "and let it be known that he keeps a fourth rope in readiness for Stoldo Borghini, should he dare to show his face here again."

"And Crevelli?"

"He *did* bring Ercole safe to me. Exile will do for him. Three bodies should be enough to inspire my loyal people to return to their duty."

She watched the hangings, because Girolamo and her father had both said that a ruler should have the fortitude to see the results of his orders: the bound men hustled into an upper room of the western tower; the ropes put around their necks and fastened to the bars of the windows on the far side; the men thrust struggling out of the unbarred windows on the side facing the city; the three sickening jerks as the ropes tightened, and then the faint squeaking as the dead weights on the ends of the ropes swayed back and forth. Then, somewhat paler than usual, she descended the stairs to put her world back in order. And apart from the way she snapped at Piero when he suggested she should break her fast before setting to work, no one would ever have guessed that she felt sick to her stomach.

# ~CHAPTER SIX~

*Because it reveals truth, the emerald can also protect against malicious and deceptive charms, particularly those which rely upon illusions. The protective power is enhanced if the signs which I draw below are engraved upon the setting.*
  *-Caterina Rinaldi's Book of Secrets*

~ ~ ~

The condottiere who called himself Gian Bracciaforte had allowed his men to pause and rest in the little wood at the crest of the hill. It might not have been the best choice of a resting place, because it overlooked a shabby inn in the shallow valley below, reminding the men that they were hungry and thirsty – and all but penniless. But something had told Gian to stop here, and he had learned to obey the prickling at the back of his neck. It seemed he was always lucky when he paid attention to it. And when it was manifestly wrong and he ignored it –he was not so lucky.

The men were, of course, tempted to take what they wanted from the inn by force. But he trusted enough in his control of them to believe he could renew the march to Urbino before they resorted to violence. Well –his control, and the fact that all of them had pawned their armor to avoid wearing the heavy steel on the march. Sadly, the pittance they had received for the armor had mostly been spent on food and drink, in the optimistic belief that Urbino was only a short march away. And that the condotierre Duke of Urbino would take them into service. And that he would pay for new armor.

They were counting on Gian's luck to see them to success.

He hoped his luck held for the last two items. It hadn't been so good about the march to Urbino; for some reason it had kept urging him toward the east, not away from their goal but certainly no closer to it.

Perhaps, after all, what he thought of as his lucky sixth sense had really been sent not by God but by a demon, first deceiving him with success and then tempting him into a string of bad decisions. It had certainly seemed good, ten years ago, when it warned him to flee before he was arrested for his relatives' failed conspiracy. He had thought himself lucky when, on the strength of having a horse and having had some training in arms, he had persuaded Sforza to enroll him in his force of condottieri. But recently? His decision to follow Carlo Gondi after Sforza's assassination had certainly not worked out well so far. After the brutal sack of Altoviti he had decided that his fifteen-man *posta* would do better to serve under a decent man like Federico da Montefeltro of Urbino. That decision had been supported by the familiar tingling sensation –but look where it had led them.

Perhaps he had only imagined the prodding of his luck. Or perhaps his personal demon had taken advantage of his revulsion at the wholesale slaughter of innocents at Altoviti. He realized, ruefully, that a demon would not have had much difficulty in convincing him. What had seemed a shining opportunity to a boy of sixteen who had never seen war looked very different to an experienced man ten years later. Nights of broken sleep because of rowdy men or the commander changing his mind in the middle of the night. Cities put to the sword for resisting the demands of the army. Drunken gunners wasting ammunition by firing at random. Vital supplies that somehow did not arrive in time. And, since he had taken service with Gondi, the growing realization that the man was not very good at anything more complicated than terrorizing civilians.

To be sure, serving under Federico da Montefeltro would be better. But now that his luck had led him and his men to this damp, inhospitable wood, he no longer felt confident that the duke would take them on. If it had not been for the men for whom he felt responsible, he no longer even greatly desired to join another army. The truth was that he was sick of war and violence.

Suddenly the tingling at the back of his neck returned, just as two mounted men pulled up before the inn. He hadn't been watching as he should; why hadn't his luck alerted him?

*You weren't paying attention,* said the inner voice that sometimes accompanied the tingling. *Those two carry your good fortune. Observe them closely.*

It didn't *sound* like a demonic voice...

Very well. He noted everything he could. Two men; a large one, richly dressed, and a more normal sized one in a leather jerkin. Sweat-soaked, weary horses. They dismounted and the large one took a sack from his horse's saddle bow; not a very large sack, and from the shape of it, disguising something rectangular with sharp corners. A box, then. A valuable box?

The men entered the inn and the sense that he ought to be watching them increased until it was downright painful. He poked Matteo in the side. "I suddenly feel a great thirst."

"We're all thirsty," grumbled Matteo.

"Go back to the others, tell them to wait quietly, and I'll bring some wine back to them." He doubted he had enough coin in his limp purse to buy wine for fourteen men, but the need to get into the inn and see what those two were doing was becoming worse than painful. Perhaps they were going to threaten the innkeeper, and he would drive them away and save the man, and out of gratitude the innkeeper would give all his *posta* not just wine but also a meal.

Or at least some bread.

The newcomers were doing nothing but drinking quietly when Gian entered the inn. The light from a narrow window showed nothing untoward. Gian sat in a corner and tapped a coin on the table until a portly man in a dirty apron came out of the interior door and asked what he wanted.

"Wine."

"My best, messer?"

"Whatever this will buy." He flipped the coin to the man and eventually received a cup of wine. If this was what a *piastre* bought, he definitely did not have enough money to buy wine for all his men.

"At the last inn," he grumbled, "in Sestola, that bought me a bottle."

"Sestola is closer to Altoviti. Their costs for transport are not so high."

There would be no more wine or anything else coming from Altoviti this year, but telling the man that would only encourage him to inflate his prices more. He kept grumbling until Gian sorely longed to tell him what had happened in Altoviti and what might happen here if he didn't shut up and serve them. "Here I have to pay through the nose," the innkeeper complained, "just to get a wagoner to deliver a few casks. And when I get them, most likely half the wine is spoiled by being stored in dirty casks. You have no idea of the difficulties of keeping an inn out here, I would not bother if it were not a public service for travelers like you…"

Gian nodded irritably and waved the man away. All right, so he was not good at bargaining. A condottiere seldom needed that skill for small matters; up to now, Gian had not even needed it to negotiate a contract. That had been the commander's responsibility.

He had better learn before they reached Urbino.

The two men were glancing at him and sniggering quietly. He restrained the impulse to demand —at swordpoint —what they thought was funny. It was difficult; whenever he glanced at them the urge to *do something* got stronger. But he had no excuse to begin a brawl in the house.

"Hey, you!" the larger and better-dressed of the two shouted at the innkeeper. "More wine here, and prepare us beds upstairs! Clean ones!"

"It's too soon to stop," muttered the smaller man.

"Did I ask you to poke your stupid nose into the doings of your betters? The horses have to rest, idiot. Get on with it, man!" he shouted at the innkeeper, who was just standing there.

"I'll see the color of your money first," the man grumbled. "For all I know, you're as beggarly as that one in the corner."

"I'll show you something better than money," said the big one, reaching into the sack they had placed between them and pulling out a casket. A casket with decoratively carved edges and painted top and sides, the last thing Gian would have expected to see in the possession of two unkempt travelers who had ridden their horses to exhaustion.

*Robbers, obviously.*

The little man put a hand on his companion's arm. "Stoldo?"

"Trust me." He flipped open the casket lid and reached inside with two fingers, pulling out a small pad of dark velvet on which something sparkled in the light from the window.

"This brooch would pay for a month's lodging in a good inn," Stoldo said, "but because I'm a generous sort, I'll let you have it for the night's lodging, more wine, and a few florins."

"Where would I find florins?"

"Oh, your sort always have something hidden away."

"It's not real," the innkeeper said, "It's probably a trick to get me to show you where my money is –I mean, where it would be if I had any." He reached out one hand as if to take the brooch and Stoldo moved it away.

"Keep your dirty fingers off it!" he growled. "You'll have it in the morning."

"How do I know you won't sneak off in the night?" The innkeeper snatched at the brooch. As soon as he grasped it, a high, keening sound filled the room and turned into words.

"I was stolen from Caterina Rinaldi of San Florian! Give me back, give me back, give me back!" screamed the ghostly voice.

The innkeeper dropped the brooch and stepped back, making the sign of the cross. "Get out of here and take your demons with you!"

"I *told* you not to touch it!" snapped Stoldo. He rose, pushing the rickety table aside and putting a hand to his sword hilt. "Zio, get behind him!"

"It's just as well, Stoldo. Now he knows that he'll get no good out of trying to rob us." Zio turned to the innkeeper. "We will remove the protective charm in the morning."

"You will, will you? And just which one of you is Caterina Rinaldi?"

Zio stammered for a moment. "Uh, she is lending the jewels to her husband's cousin so that the lady Lucrezia may make a good showing at her wedding. The charm is just to protect us from robbers on the journey."

The innkeeper's eyes narrowed. "She sent just two men, without coin enough to pay their way?"

A woman as scrawny as the innkeeper was fat came to stand beside him.

She had obviously been listening, because her first words were, "And I heard that Lucrezia Rinaldi was married four months ago, in Venice. You're a bit late for the wedding, aren't you? Not to mention heading the wrong way?"

"What do people like you know about the doings of your betters?" Zio demanded.

Stoldo was more straightforward. "If you won't serve us for the jewel, you can serve us for the privilege of not having your bellies sliced open!" His sword came out of the scabbard with a hiss and he lunged at the innkeeper.

Gian was before him. He'd been tense since the altercation began, expecting something like this. His hand had already been at his sword hilt; with one motion he drew his sword and knocked Stoldo's aside. The woman screamed. The innkeeper sat down suddenly on one of the benches. Matteo, sword drawn, rushed into the room. As Stoldo turned on Gian, Matteo slashed at him. The big man turned and took a broad swipe at Matteo. In the eerie clarity of battle when time seemed to stop, Gian noted the blood spilling from Matteo's thigh while he himself lunged forward and ran Stoldo through. The man collapsed, blood bubbling from his mouth.

"I ordered you to stay back!" he told Matteo.

"I was worried about you, boss!" Matteo tried to put weight on his injured leg, hissed in pain and subsided to the floor.

The man called Zio threw the casket down and ran for it. "That stuff was no good to us anyway, and it'll be no good to anybody else!"

"Go after him!" Matteo urged.

Gian shook his head. "Let him get away. There's been enough violence here." The bubbling from Stoldo's mouth had ceased and his sightless eyes were not moving. Had it really been necessary to kill the man? Well, he had been stupid to attack a condottiere. In war, you didn't strike to wound; you killed. Quickly and efficiently. He turned to the innkeeper. "We need to bury this man."

"In this soil, it'll be a day's work. This land grows nothing but stones."

"My men will do it." He glanced at Matteo, who had both hands pressed to his thigh. "My other men. After you give them food and wine; they're tired and hungry now."

The innkeeper showed himself to be less than happy with the turn of events. He complained that his inn was contaminated by demons, looking askance at the gold chains and precious stones spilled out on the dirty floor. He would not only have to bury the big robber; he or his woman would have to scrub away the blood that had been spilled. And now he was expected to serve a gaggle of beggarly strangers without pay!

Matteo spoke up. "And where are *your* wounds, old man? I've shed blood to save you from robbers. I should think you would value your life and your woman's over a round of wine and a decent meal for the men who are going to bury the corpse for you."

A lively round of negotiation ensued, at the end of which Gian, to his amazement, found that the sullen innkeeper had agreed not only to feed his men but also to give them beds for the night and bread and cheese to take with them on the journey to Urbino. Matteo's suggestion that the man might benefit from their lingering at the inn to make sure the other robber did not return with his confederates had, Gian thought, been the clinching argument. Even so, it was just as well that he did not call his other men until after the agreement was settled; the innkeeper might have been less amenable to reason had he realized that he was going to have to feed fifteen men, not four or five.

By the end of the bargaining Matteo was pale with pain and blood loss. "Is there a surgeon within call?" demanded Gian, knowing even before the innkeeper shook his head that there would be no one in such an isolated spot.

"The stable boy is good with horses," the man volunteered.

Matteo grinned up at Gian. "I'd trust you above the stable boy, Messer. I've noticed that men you treat heal quicker than others, even if you do some strange things."

"Habits from my old tu- ah, my mother," Gian said, remembering in time that the man he pretended to be would not have had a noble upbringing involving tutors and fencing masters. As for the boy he had once been –well, Gian-Maria Neroni was presumed dead and had better stay that way. He was Gian Bracciaforte, common soldier, now.

"You and you," he pointed, "move that table into the light, scrub it well, then lift Matteo onto it gently. Try not to hurt him more than necessary, all right?"

Matteo hissed in pain when he was lifted up and dropped onto the table. "Gently" was not a concept familiar to the condottieri.

Once Mateo was positioned and the cloth cut away from his leg, Gian demanded a basin of wine from the innkeeper and washed his hands in it while saying three Aves.

"Is it a magic spell?" asked the innkeeper suspiciously.

"It is only a prayer," said Gian. "Nothing wrong with praying for the mercy of Our Lady, is there?" And no need to mention that the back of his neck prickled painfully whenever he approached a wounded man without performing this little ritual.

He felt a gentle, warm, encouraging tingling now, as he looked over the wound. "Bite on this," he suggested, handing Matteo his own belt. "It's going to sting." Dipping a cup into the basin, he poured wine slowly over the cut in Matteo's thigh. That, at least, was no secret; all the books on healing that he had read since the care of wounds became part of his working life emphasized the importance of keeping the wound clean. This was a shallow cut; Gian thought he could risk closing it once it was rinsed clean of whatever filth might have been on that robber's blade. And at least he would not have to hurt Matteo more by stitching it together with whatever the innkeeper's wife could provide by way of needle and thread.

He laid his hands over the wound and felt the tingling run through his shoulders, down his arms and into his fingers. Three more Aves now, and three Paternosters; it always took at least that long. As the warmth filled his hands, he began to feel tired, but he propped one hip against the table and held his position until he could feel that the cut was no longer open.

"You're a miracle worker!" exclaimed the innkeeper when he lifted his hands.

"Don't say that!" Gian snapped. "There are no miracles here, only cleanliness and the mercy of Our Lord. Not being used to blood, you imagined the wound to be much worse than it was; now you can see that it was only a scratch." *Had* the edges of the cut gaped open? Perhaps he too had been imagining things. He preferred to believe that his success in treating wounds was only due to the fact that men brought him their trivial cuts and scratches, trusting a barber-surgeon for the deeper cuts. He lost less sleep at night when he could convince himself of that.

He demanded a straw pallet for Matteo. Once his friend was comfortable, he reminded the innkeeper of his promise of wine and a good meal for all his band.

"Who's going to clear up *that*?" the man demanded, pointing at the casket and the jewels that had spilled out onto the floor. "I can't run an inn full of shrieking demons!"

"I'll take care of it," Gian said tiredly. "Give me a dishclout."

He knelt and picked up the jewels one by one, trying not to touch them with his bare skin as he dropped them back in the casket. Once a long gold chain swung against his arm and began shrieking, but it stopped as soon as he let it fall into the box. At length nothing was left on the ground but a rather ugly ring with a large table-cut emerald. It wouldn't have been a bad ring if the band had not been marred by a series of scratches forming meaningless, angular shapes. Who on earth could have thought that was decorative?

He realized that he had been staring at the ring for so long that the people around him were beginning to shuffle and whisper. And that he felt the familiar prickling warmth at the back of his neck. Was his telling him to pay attention to the ring?

Very tentatively, Gian poked at the ring with one finger.

No shrieking.

Tensing, he picked it up.

Silence.

He slid it onto the third finger of his left hand, where the emerald flashed and the ugly band was not visible. It seemed to warm to his touch and shape itself to a perfect fit. And still there was no outcry.

Had the spell worn off?

He lifted the casket full of jewels onto the table and sat down to experiment in more comfort while they waited for their food. He discovered that now he could touch any of the jewels without arousing those ghostly voices. But when he persuaded Maso and Battista to try touching them, the high keening wails began and they snatched their hands back, crossing themselves. In the background, the innkeeper querulously demanded whether Gian *had* to play games with demons in his inn. Couldn't he at least take the haunted jewels outside?

It must have something to do with the ring, but what, he could not tell. His luck had prompted him to don the ring –but what good, really, did it do them? He might be able to show the jewels to a potential purchaser, but as soon as the man touched them he would be terrified by the voices. Gian would likely be accused of witchcraft just for possessing the accursed things.

All this, and more, was repeated by the men watching the experiments.

"There's only one logical thing to do," Gian pronounced at last.

"Bury the things?" Maso suggested.

"Attach them all to velvet pads and hope the buyers don't touch them before we get out of town?"

Gian shook his head. "Isn't it obvious?" He looked at the innkeeper, who was anxiously hovering behind the others. "How far from here to San Florian?"

# ~CHAPTER SEVEN~

*To cause the return of stolen goods: Go early in the morning, ere the sun rises, to a juniper tree, and, at sunrise, bend it to the ground, and put a stone upon it. Under this stone and tree lay the skull of a hanged man and speak: Juniper tree, I bend and press thee until the thief shall return my stolen property to its place.*
*-Caterina Rinaldi's Book of Secrets*

~ ~ ~

Before the funeral, Caterina drew Father Benvenuto aside. "I must make my confession to you first," she said. Otherwise she would not be able to take communion at the funeral mass, and who knew what scandal that would inspire?

In the palazzo's private chapel, she knelt and began the familiar words of contrition. That part was easy; finding words to describe what she had actually done was more difficult. Well… not *finding* the words. *Saying* them. Accusing herself of mortal sin. In all her experiments she had strictly refrained from using forbidden magic… until now.

"The army that was outside our walls yesterday…"

"The one that disappeared in the night? I thought there was something strange about that. What do you wish to tell me about that, my daughter?"

"It was an illusion," Caterina said. "I made it appear." She swallowed hard. "I… I employed a demon to make men see a great army, and I fed the demon with innocent blood to keep me safe from it."

The priest gasped. "Who did you kill?"

"Oh, no –I only sacrificed a pigeon," Caterina hastened to clarify. "But it is still –I am not in a state of grace, Father."

Father Benvenuto heaved a sigh. "Did you do this for your personal profit?"

"No! My only wish was to save the city –and my son."

"And could you not have found another way to do that?"

"I wrote to the Pope for aid," Caterina said, "but he is otherwise occupied. No, I could not think of anything else to do."

"Ah, well," said Father Benvenuto, "it was indeed a sin, but God sees your heart and knows that your intentions were pure. And He is pleased that you hastened to confess as soon as the crisis was over. Say three Aves and begin the funeral procession."

Caterina did not feel precisely cleansed of her sin after saying three Aves, but perhaps that night she would find the time to repent more fully and pray for forgiveness.

As she walked behind Girolamo's bier, holding a kerchief soaked in oil of juniper to protect her from the smell that emanated from the body, it occurred to her that neither she nor Father Benvenuto had mentioned the matter of the three hanged men. Well, that was simply exercising her right to do justice in the city, and in no way sinful. Even if the memory made her shudder.

Girolamo should have gone to the grave dressed in the rich fabrics he had favored. But after the way the assassins had hacked at his body it would have been difficult to put clothes on the remains and make him look like a man again instead of a piece of butcher's meat. She and her women had compromised by wrapping the poor, mutilated thing in a length of dark green velvet that Girolamo had given her to make a new gown. They had dropped aromatic herbs in every fold of cloth, but the sickly-sweet smell of decay overpowered the herbs.

The one good thing about the funeral was that Piero Giacomini had to shut up while the priest was speaking. He had done well enough at first, but now that the immediate crisis was over he was reverting to his style of fretting over everything that crossed his mind, trivial or important, curable or inevitable. For instance, it was traditional for a dead ruler to lie in state for three days in his palazzo, and Piero wanted the tradition followed. Sadly, the effect of summer heat on a badly mutilated body that had already been left in the street for several days was not something that any amount of ice or scent could disguise. That was one tradition San Florian was just going to have to do without; the funeral must be held immediately.

Besides, the great hall of the palazzo was hardly suitable for such a display. People were still slipping into the hall and setting down the things they had taken; a silver tray rubbed shoulders with some dirty napkins, two surviving enameled bowls sat insecurely atop a folded tapestry. Caterina had set the palazzo servants to restoring the hall to something of its former glory. They were working with a great show of energy and dedication, possibly ashamed because they had run and hidden when the Borghini killed their lord. Caterina did not blame them; it had been her and Girolamo's responsibility to protect their people, and they had failed.

In any case, the best that could be done in the palazzo would hardly correct all the damage. The chips and dings in the long dining table could be hidden under lengths of fine fabric, but there was no disguising the fact that when she called a council there, she and her advisors would mostly be drinking from wooden cups, sitting in front of a mural of Bacchus and Ariadne with scarred plaster where their faces had been, and looking across the room at a mural of the Blessed Virgin's Assumption into Heaven from which the Virgin's left eye and much of her cloak were missing. Perhaps, later, Caterina would send for a painter from Florence to restore the paintings.

But not until she could afford it.

Once Girolamo's body had been transferred to the coffin and lowered into the new grave in the churchyard, once the earth had pattered down atop the coffin, Caterina had felt something in her relax. *One thing done with. What's next?*

But she couldn't think during the walk back, for Pietro fussed at her all the way back to the Rocca about the perilous state of San Florian's finances. She had been too casual about remitting Girolamo's new tax on the sale of bread, meat and wine.

"But the people hated it!" Caterina protested.

"Since when do we ask the common folk in the street how to rule? Yes, the tax was unpopular, but Count Girolamo would not have announced it if our need had not been dire."

"Would they have turned back to us if I had not revoked the tax?"

"You could have *tried.* There was plenty of time."

There had not, in fact, been time to spare. Caterina had maintained the illusion of an army until nightfall, so that people could believe the army had retreated rather than vanishing into smoky clouds of demons. But by that time she herself had been so drained that she felt almost transparent and feared that her reflection might not show in a mirror. Another twenty-four hours would certainly have killed her.

That was something she probably ought not to explain to Piero. He was happier when she allowed him to live in his world of books and accounts, ignoring the more uncomfortable realities of life. The fact that his childhood playmate had grown up into a woman had been difficult enough for him; she remembered now that during the entire time of her pregnancy he had never once allowed his gaze to drift below her neck. The fact that she was also a mage who had employed demons to rescue the city? Well, she could not hope that he would receive the information with the aplomb of Father Benvenuto. More likely he would evade understanding it unless she made that impossible for him. She would try not to do that, and he would probably try not to ask questions about it.

While Piero twittered on about the city's barren coffers and the crises he would now have to avoid by juggling the accounts, Caterina tried to repress critical thoughts about her dead husband. It was unseemly to think like this on the very way back from burying him, when she should have been mourning his death instead of criticizing his life! Still... She had grown up in San Florian, and there had never been a financial crisis in her father's time. The ordinary revenues of the city should have been more than sufficient to maintain a reasonable lifestyle for Girolamo and his family. The "dire need" Piero had mentioned was simply that Girolamo had let the money trickle through his fingers like water, enriching his mistress in Rome and patronizing artists as though he were Lorenzo the Magnificent. Lorenzo's love of art had weakened even so vast an enterprise as the Medici bank; where had Girolamo gotten the idea that the lord of a very minor city could be a great patron of the arts like a Medici? Regretfully, Caterina put aside the idea of having the pictures on the walls restored. The regent of a hill town whose livelihood came from sheep farming and the wool trade could not afford great art. Perhaps somewhere in the Rocca there were stored some old tapestries, faded or inexpertly darned, that could be hung to conceal the scarred murals.

"And we have searched the Palazzo Borghini without finding your jewels," Piero complained. "If you ask me, Stoldo ran away with them."

"They won't do him much good."

Piero blinked. "They were worth a small fortune!"

Best not to explain to him why she was certain that her jewels would be worthless to Stoldo. It was exactly the kind of thing he would rather not know. "I still pray that they may be returned," she said. She glanced up at the west tower of the Rocca, where the three bodies still dangled from the tower windows to remind the citizens of where their loyalties had better lie. She did not look forward to employing magic that used the skull of a hanged man, but it was reassuring —in a slightly macabre way —to know that one would soon be available, if she needed it.

Piero followed her glance up towards the Rocca, "Certainly prayer is good," he said. "But those new arrivals at the castle gate do not look like good citizens bringing back your possessions."

Indeed, they were a distinctly scruffy lot, all men, hardly well dressed, and sporting an odd bit of armor here and there. Caterina was slightly surprised that Peruzzi had allowed them into the city at all; more surprised that he seemed to be laughing and joking with the fellow on the lead horse.

Even as they walked past the palazzo, two more citizens carrying bundles scurried inside with furtive glances up towards the tower with its grisly fruit. Perhaps they were bringing back her casket? Caterina halted the procession with an upraised hand and stepped inside to look at the table where people had been setting the returned goods. One man very gently unwrapped a Venetian glass goblet whose rim was already deeply chipped; the other one set down the lid to a salt cellar.

With a sigh she resumed the climb to the Rocca. If Stoldo had taken the casket, that charm of hers had not been so clever after all; Stoldo had probably just thrown the jewels away in panic the first time he touched one. And while it was some satisfaction to think that he could not have profited from his theft, it would have been infinitely more satisfying to have the jewels back, if only as surety for a loan that would keep the city going until harvest and shearing time.

She would probably have to sell her wedding dress, a crimson velvet underskirt beneath a gown of gold brocade sewn with almost a thousand pearls, with sapphires and rubies edging the sleeves. It had been laid away for ten years with wormwood and bay leaves in the folds; it was too weighty to wear for any length of time and she thought its stiff, ornate folds looked ridiculous on her slight form. But it would be humiliating to sell it, and even attempting the sale would advertise their dangerous poverty.

As they approached the Rocca, she heard Peruzzi laughing at some jest from the leader of the shabby little group. "You should have called yourself Fortunato, not Bracciaforte, my friend! For a captain of condottieri, you have —"

He broke off and turned to greet Caterina. The man he had been talking to was dressed like a common soldier, but at sight of Caterina he dismounted gracefully, swept off his hat and made a low bow that would not have disgraced a nobleman. Her curiosity was piqued; she had not before met a condottiere with courtly manners. She looked at him closely, seeing light brown hair, inexpertly cut, and a neatly trimmed beard. Tommaso Peruzzi had referred to him as a captain, but he seemed young to be a leader of mercenaries —not much older than she was herself —and something about his lean, mobile face suggested more sensitivity than she had expected of a soldier. The curve of his lips and a twinkle in his brown eyes hinted at a sense of humor.

"Madonna Caterina," Peruzzi said formally now, "allow me to introduce my good friend Gian Bracciaforte, formerly in the service of Milan. He has brought something which you will be happy to receive."

That might be, but Caterina was not such a fool as to invite fifteen unknown condottieri into the Rocca. All except Bracciaforte himself and, perhaps, one companion could wait right there at the gate.

Before she could speak to the new arrival, another unexpected visitor erupted into the courtyard, skirts flying and fair hair shining under a transparent veil. If she had not been looking so annoyed, she might have been beautiful. No. To be fair, she was always beautiful, even when she was in a bad temper. Golden hair, large blue eyes, white skin, enticing curves —no wonder, Caterina thought ruefully, that she expected to get away with any amount of bad temper and bad manners. "It's about time you got back! What are you doing, taking off for hours while your guests wait ungreeted? And why are you living in this wretched barren castle when you have a perfectly good palazzo in the town? Don't you even bother to pretend at a civilized life? You'll have to tell your women to make up the chamber next to yours. And have them start bringing hot water; I want a bath. I'm exhausted from traveling!"

Cousin Lucrezia.

Peruzzi might have called the young man who had just turned up at her door "Fortunato," but Caterina felt quite certain that no one would ever give her that nickname. What evil chance had brought Girolamo's most difficult relative here, today of all days?

"I am sorry you had to wait," she said, drawing on her last reserves of calm. "But you were told, surely, that I was attending my lord's funeral? You have come to a household in mourning, Lucrezia, and we had no notice of your coming. You can hardly expect everything to be run as smoothly as in Ottavio's household." And if Lucrezia wanted princely living, why had she not remained in the Venetian palazzo of the Contarini, the Ca' d'Oro?

Lucrezia opened her mouth to contest this, but Caterina forestalled her. "Is your husband equally unsatisfied with his accommodations?"

"Oh, he isn't here," Lucrezia said. "That selfish bastard! He's rich enough to take his place in society, but would he even try? I was willing to help him entertain brilliantly; I could have got him made one of the Ten, but he didn't care enough to cooperate. All he thinks about is the profits from his dye works and the price of alum since the Pope got control of the Tolfa mines. He even comes home with his fingers stained from the dyes! I've left him. You'll have to get my dowry back from him."

Caterina sighed. Somehow she doubted that Lucrezia could make a case for annulment, or had anything at all to say about her marriage that was more serious than her complaints about the hospitality of San Florian.

"We can talk about that later," she said. She looked towards the inner doorway and caught Rosa's eye. Her maid nodded. Blessed, competent Rosa! "As you say, you are tired from travel. A bath is being prepared for you, and after that perhaps you would like to rest in your chamber for a while."

"Send up some food," Lucrezia said ungraciously before retreating into the hall. "And have someone carry my bags upstairs so my maid can unpack them."

"I'll see what I can do." *I hope the room is not too comfortable. Perhaps she will decide that compared to living in this "uncivilized" castle, her husband is not so bad after all. Shall I tell the cook* not *to make any extra effort?*

But before dealing with these domestic details, she needed to find out why Peruzzi wanted her to receive this young man and his friend. Moving to the door, Caterina saw with relief that Lucrezia was already mounting the stairs. She seated herself at the table and waved the two visitors to take seats across the table from her. The older man, the one carrying a bundle, was limping. *Wounded? Oh, wonderful,* she thought as they introduced themselves. *Not just condottieri, but* unsuccessful *condottieri.*

"If you're looking for work," she said bluntly, "I can't afford to hire soldiers. I recommend you go on to Rimini; Malatesta may be taking on new men."

"We can discuss that later," said Gian Bracciaforte. "My first errand here is to restore something to you." He set the bundle on the table and unwrapped the cloak around it to reveal a gilded and painted casket. As he flipped the lid open, an emerald on his middle finger caught the light and glowed with green fire.

Caterina gasped. "What are you doing with my ring?"

He looked quizzically at her slender hands. "Isn't it too large for you? Or was it your late husband's ring?"

"Mine," said Caterina firmly, "and I want it back."

"First look at what else I am returning to you." He pushed the open casket across the table towards her. A familiar tangle of gold chains, jeweled brooches, earrings and necklaces lay inside, some pieces pinned to bits of velvet and others loose in the box.

Caterina laughed. "Shall I be grateful that you're returning things you cannot sell?"

He did not contest the point.

"I… Matteo?" He looked at his companion.

"We could have buried the jewels," put in the older man. "We could have gone in search of a mage to lift the charm. But because we are honest men, our first and only thought was to return these things to their rightful owner."

*Last thought, more likely. They don't look* that *honest.*

"But if you don't want them back, we can always keep them until we find that mage," Matteo went on, sliding the casket back towards his side of the table.

"You admit they're rightfully mine, and you expect to walk out of here with them?"

"We *expected*," said Matteo, "that the lady of San Fiorino would be appropriately grateful for the return of her property. Not to mention the wound I took in securing that property from the robbers who had it."

"Tell me about those robbers."

The description of the dead man convinced Caterina that it had indeed been Stoldo Borghini. They were less clear about the one who ran away, but it did not matter. Stoldo had been the dangerous one. She had already decided not to revenge herself on the lesser men who had been caught up in the Borghini plot, but she was not displeased to know that at least one of them had exiled himself.

"My gratitude," she said, "extends to a meal and shelter for the night. But I am still not in the business of hiring condottieri. You would do better to try your luck at Rimini or Urbino."

The younger man was rubbing the back of his neck as if it pained him. "Matteo should not ride so far. His wound is not fully healed."

If, as their story went, the brawl at the inn had happened only yesterday, it could not have been much of a wound or he wouldn't have been riding at all.

"And, lady, after what your castellan has told us of recent events, we think you could stand to reinforce your guard with a few more men who have some experience in actual fighting. What do you think will happen when your neighbors learn that San Florian is ruled by a young woman acting as regent for a child? Florence and Rimini and half a dozen others will seek to add San Florian to their own lands," Matteo said.

After some haggling they settled on a compromise that, while it satisfied nobody, at least allowed the appearance of agreement. It seemed that this Bracciaforte fellow was the leader, although, puzzlingly, he allowed his subordinate Matteo to negotiate for him. Peruzzi vouched for the young captain, having served with him under Sforza before he retired to the less demanding job of acting as the Rinaldi castellan. Caterina agreed to hire Bracciaforte and his men as an extra guard for her safety —at somewhat less than half what they would have earned with a proper contract - but also, she pointed out, with their food and shelter provided and no need to actually go to war. She would also pay to replace the armor they had pawned. *"Used armor,"* she emphasized. "You will find enough to suit your needs at a *monte de pieta* - if not here, then in Rimini." They would have to go to a pawnshop anyway, because she had not enough ready money to arm fifteen men. She would have to trade a good gold chain, even so, for their armor; new suits were out of the question. "I'm not going to pay extra just for shiny armor with no dents or scratches," she said firmly. "And there is one other thing. You will return my father's ring."

Gian Bracciaforte looked deeply unhappy, but he started to pull the ring off, then stopped, looking surprised. It seemed to be very tight on his finger. "It - won't come off," he said.

*What a stupid lie, and how easily disproved.* "Oh, I think it will," Caterina said, and took his hand in hers. A strange tingling sensation startled her when she touched his fingers, but she did her best to ignore it while she tugged at the ring. It did seem to be fast to his hand.

Well, there was no need to take the skin off. Her father would have threatened to chop off the finger. Caterina merely mentioned the virtues of soap, and told the fellow that he could return the ring later.

# ~CHAPTER EIGHT~

*"For the conduct of his incessant wars Mehmed required enormous sums of money, which could be raised only in part by tribute, head taxes, debasement of the coinage, and so on. If they wished to raise the enormous sums required of them and at the same time to make a satisfactory profit, the tax farmers selected by the Porte were obliged to gouge the population mercilessly. Similarly, in order to make the required payments to the state and also to realize a profit, the lessees of state enterprises had to drive those who worked for them beyond endurance."*
*-Franz Babinger, <u>Mehmed the Conqueror</u>, tr. Ralph Manheim*

~ ~ ~

After the other petitioners had departed the sultan's divan, his senior advisors remained for certain discussions which were not for lesser folk to hear. They stretched out comfortably on the cushions that ringed the room. Above them, latticed openings alternated with blank walls which Mehmed planned to have decorated by the Italian artist he had sent for.

Karamanli Pasha, the Grand Vizier, and Gedik Ahmed Pasha, the leader of the military, were debating future plans for the Turkish forces. Neither considered the strain on the sultan's purse or the possible advantages of peace.

"The army has already landed at Otranto," Gedik Ahmed Pasha pointed out. "We have raided Brindisi and Taranto, and taken Lecca. The obvious thing is to advance northwards, taking over the Kingdom of Naples. I have already threatened the Neapolitans that if they do not surrender all their southern cities, next spring the sultan himself will march north with an army of a hundred thousand troops equipped with artillery."

"Why do the obvious?" Karamanli Pasha replied before the sultan could speak. "The South is poor, a mere rocky peninsula. Let us withdraw, feint, confuse the enemy, then strike where there are true riches to be gained –at Venice."

"We have just signed a peace treaty with Venice!" protested Gedik Ahmed.

"Bah. A treaty with infidels is nothing but a piece of paper. All the better if they believe in it; we will have the advantage of surprise. *Your* plan would have us fight our way through the armies of Naples and Rome and Florence, all of which have agreed to join in the relief of Otranto."

"How do you know that?"

"I have my sources."

The bickering continued for some minutes without any sign of agreement. Sultan Mehmed II raised his hand and both men fell silent.

"Venice has wealth," he said, "but she also has hundreds of galleys and experience in naval battles. We use our ships to transport soldiers, not to fight independently. And even if we chose to attack from the sea, the lagoon itself is Venice's best defense. They can remove the markers that guide ships through the channels; they can even sink vessels full of stones to block the channels, and then destroy our stranded ships at their leisure. I should not have to remind my advisors of these things."

"What if we attacked by land?" Karamanli Pasha suggested.

"Marching all the way from Otranto?"

"No –from closer to Venice. We could take Rimini, and then –"

"We could not hold Rimini. Its landward defenses were leveled in the time of Sigismondo Malatesta, and his son Roberto is a lazy debauchee who pays no attention to the protection of his city. Easy to take, but also easy to lose."

"I have another place in mind. A short march inland from Rimini there is a place called San Florian. Its castle rises out of the living rock, and is blessed with a spring of clear water that bursts out of that rock. There is little food for an army in the surrounding countryside, and the city has never yet been taken by siege because it is protected by that castle."

"Easy to keep because it is impossible to take?" sneered Gedik Ahmed Pasha. "Who cares for a minor city? My forces will sweep around it."

"Your forces," Karamanli Pasha snapped, "will never make it that far north if you have to fight your way through the armies of all the Italian states!"

"And I suppose you have a better idea?"

"Whereas *you* can do nothing but complain!"

"Peace, toothless Ahmed!" the sultan commanded. "Let me hear what my Grand Vizier has to say —and *don't* interrupt him again."

"What I suggest," Karamanli Pasha said smoothly, "would not have been possible had the noble commander –" he bowed towards his opponent –"not accomplished his great victory at Otranto. We need not risk our armies on the coast roads where Venetian ships can menace them, nor our ships in the labyrinthine channels of the Venetian lagoon; we will stay inland all the way to Venice, and when we reach it, we will take over the city before the Venetians can bring their galleys into the fight. And it is one of your own prisoners, Gedik Ahmed, who will give us the means to a landward base so near Venice that we can easily attack from there."

"You are referring to that Italian dervish?" Gedik Ahmed grumbled. "He has had nothing but excuses for me ever since I allowed Hayrettin to talk me into saving him. He is drained from his previous magic workings –he is seasick –he needs time to recover from the voyage."

"But he has performed great things in Italy. Hayrettin Pasha told me that he himself observed them. As did you, Commander."

Gedik Ahmed Pasha blinked. So Hayrettin was the vizier's source of information about the infidels? He wondered if he should have his subordinate ganched or merely strangled.

"Land this Cacciote fellow on the coast," Karamanli Pasha followed smoothly, "and let him take service with Girolamo Rinaldi of San Florian. Last year my spies reported that Rinaldi squanders the city's revenue on paintings and sculpture to let him play the part of a great patron; without doubt he will also think that it enhances his standing to have a court magician. And Cacciote will easily be able to influence him to leave the castle gates open, or even to invite our advance party into the castle."

"If he does not simply run away the instant he is on land," Gedik Ahmed Pasha grumbled, "and the next thing we hear of him, he will be raising demons from some place like Florence to destroy our troops."

"You brought him back to Istanbul," Karamanli Pasha pointed out. "You must have planned some use for him."

"Yes —to smooth the northward path of my army from Otranto! I would have kept him under guard at all times. I brought him back with me just to make sure he did not use his magic to escape in my absence. I have no intention of setting him back in Italian territory, alone, in the blind faith that he will suddenly be willing to serve our interests."

Karamanli Pasha noted that now Gedik Ahmed admitted the mage had some powers. But he let that pass; he had a more important point to make. "You also brought back his son, did you not? Hayrettin Pasha reports that he is unreasonably attached to the boy. Well," he shrugged, "an only son… one cannot be too surprised. Let Andrea Cacciote remain here, hostage for his father's good faith, and send the father to serve us in the north."

"And how will we know that he is not betraying us?" Gedik Ahmed demanded.

"Dervish Ismail has prepared a means by which we may see what he is doing… and he may see that his son lives, so long as he does our bidding." With a flourish, Karamanli Pasha produced a silver-backed mirror, as large as the palm of a man's hand, from the folds of his robes. "This goes with the mage, that he may report to us by it. We shall explain that if he fails to report regularly, the boy will suffer for it."

Sultan Mehmed nodded slowly. "It is a gamble, but one perhaps worth taking."

"Too much of a risk!" Gedik Ahmed protested.

"Was it also too much of a risk when I took Constantinople?" The sultan's eyes lost focus as he turned inward, reliving that triumph of nearly thirty years ago. Then he shook his head and roused himself. "We conquered the Byzantine infidels, and now we raid along the coast and take what pride we can in capturing little, helpless towns, and take what profit we can by selling their people as slaves. Is this fit for a race of noble warriors? I would like to see one more great victory before I die."

"May that day be many years hence!"

Sultan Mehmed shook his head again. "I do not come of a long-lived line, and this sore on my leg troubles me greatly. Venice –or Naples? The case for taking Naples is clear; I am not so sure about Venice. Let maps be drawn showing exactly what you propose, Vizier. I do not plan campaigns based on vague descriptions. And let me see this infidel dervish and his son; then I will decide if this is the time for the great enterprise."

Gedik Ahmed Pasha knew when to stop arguing. He had made his case; it wouldn't help to point out the possible personal factors that might sway Mehmed to favor the Venice invasion. The sultan's ulcerated leg might impede his enjoyment of some of his usual pleasures, but he still liked looking at beautiful favorites. Once the sultan saw Cacciote's son, that handsome, golden Frankish boy, he would be inclined to any gamble that gave him an excuse to keep the boy close to him. Was it even worthwhile suggesting that the same end could be attained by simply executing the father and enslaving the boy? Probably not. He had opposed the sultan and the grand vizier as much as he dared.

Behind the lattices, the sultan's Serbian stepmother Mara Despina Hatun and his Greek wife Gülbahar Hatun looked at one another in dismay, but they did not dare to speak until they had quietly left the small room and withdrawn to the inner courts of the seraglio. While the sultan's wives had, of course, permission to visit this room and any other parts of the court that were closed to the public, Gülbahar felt it was wiser not to make it absolutely clear to her lord just how often they listened to the deliberations in the Divan. But if she was to protect her son's interests, she had to know what was going on in the outside world!

"Will the treasury support a major war?" she asked Mara Despina.

The sultan's stepmother shook her head. "Whether we attack Venice or Naples, his plan does not serve the dar-al-Islam. Our people are already taxed almost beyond bearing."

"Bayezid would not support a war," Gülbahar said of her son.

"I do not notice that the sultan has requested the advice of his sons," Mara Despina said drily. "Either son."

Gülbahar shook her head impatiently. "Oh, Djem is an idiot, and so is his mother Cicek Hatun. But *my* son Bayezid is wise, and the sultan ought to know what his views are."

"Perhaps it is better he does not know," Mara Despina advised. "Sons who oppose their fathers sometimes find the air of the court unhealthy."

Gülbahar understood and had to agree with the warning, but she was still determined to do what she could to change the sultan's mind. She would consult with Aysin Hatun, who had once been Beatriz Rossi of Venice. And would it be possible to warn the Venetian *bailo* in Galata? There was, of course, no possibility of his entering the seraglio, and written messages were dangerous.

# ~CHAPTER NINE~

*To prepare a spell for later use:*

*Inscribe the diagrams of the conjuration on the object you plan to use. On the first time that the spirits appear, make them swear on this object that they will perform your desires whenever called. Then proceed with the work as described.*

*Probatum est. I have tried this with a minor charm invoking the angel Amaris and binding him to cleanse foul air and make sweet smells when I crushed a certain leaf on which were inscribed the appropriate words and diagrams, and when I crushed the leaf it improved the smell of the privy chamber beyond all expectation. Unfortunately the clean air was not a good protection against moths, and the woolen garments I keep in there for their safety suffered accordingly.*

*-Caterina Rinaldi's Book of Secrets*

~ ~ ~

Determined not to be surprised again, over the next few days Caterina spent some very private time in her workroom. She intended to be able to get away from anyone who attacked her again.

After the conspiracy failed Caterina had taken up carrying a small mirror attached to her belt and a comb tucked into a pocket that Rosa had cleverly stitched in the side seam of her shift. Being unable to comb and braid her hair had been far from her worst problem during her days as a captive, but for some reason the memory lingered. She attached her first spells to those items. What else could she carry on her person at all times? *Jewelry, of course.* But there was hardly space on the settings of her jewels for engraving diagrams, and people would notice if they were all scratched up. Caterina set the problem aside for later consideration.

Her head was aching from engraving the tiny diagrams required for the work. So, she realized belatedly, was her back; so was her neck. She stretched and looked out the window overlooking the herb garden. Ercole was playing at something there, shouting and slashing with his wooden sword. That, at least, was good. She had been worrying because he seemed to want to spend all his time with Rosa since they returned to the Rocca. And *not* thinking about the fact that he seemed stiff and wary around her. She would go and praise him for playing outside and finally getting some fresh air, and maybe they could talk a little; maybe she would be able to explain everything to him. She ran down the stairs. Pausing only to take her battered straw gardening hat from its hook by the door, she stepped from cool shadows to the heat and dazzle of a cloudless summer day. For a moment she was all but blinded; then she pulled the wide-brimmed hat down to shade her eyes and saw that Ercole had not been just playing. He was practicing sword thrusts and feints under the direction of her new captain of the guard.

"Repeat that, and keep your elbow down this time," Gian Bracciaforte suggested. "If you wave your sword in the air like that, you give your opponent plenty of time to make his counter-stroke. Furthermore, it is extremely unpleasant to be stabbed in the armpit."

"Have *you* ever been wounded there?" Ercole asked, letting his sword arm drop to his side as he approached the condottiere.

"No, but one of my men took just such a thrust in battle," Gian said. "A new recruit. He lived… two days? Or was it three? So pay attention next time!"

As Caterina stepped towards them, Gian saw her out of the corner of his eye and leapt to his feet. "Madonna Caterina!" Again the graceful bow, more appropriate to a noble courtier than to the common soldier he claimed to be.

"It is good of you to take the time to amuse Ercole," Caterina said.

"By no means, madonna. He is a promising boy and should be getting regular instruction in swordplay."

Caterina raised her brows. "Do you instruct me in how to bring up the future count of San Florian?"

Gian did not look in the least abashed. "Well, madonna, I was once a boy myself, and no more fond of sitting over a book than is Ercole. Perhaps he would not run away from his tutor so often if he could count on regular lessons in the other matters that a man should learn."

"Perhaps." Piero Giacomini had been trying to teach Ercole basic literacy and how to understand financial accounts, while Father Benvenuto had been charged with his religious instruction. Caterina had to admit that neither Piero Giacomini nor Father Benvenuto was exactly adapted to instructing a restless, scampering, lively boy. But she did not see any present remedy for the situation. She rested one hand on Ercole's head.

"What do you say, Ercole? Will you mind your book better if Messer Bracciaforte is kind enough to instruct you in swordplay after the lesson?"

Ercole hung his head and muttered something that sounded like, "What do *you* care?"

She decided not to hear the impertinent tone. "You are my son and the future count of San Florian. Of course I want you to grow up into a good and gracious man who knows all the arts of the ruler."

"No, you don't! You are going to have a new baby and so you don't care about me any longer. I *heard* you. You would have let that man kill me because all you care about is the new baby!"

It had to come some time or other. Not talking about that bitter exchange was no kind of solution, but she had hoped Ercole would, childlike, forget about it. Instead it seemed that he had tortured himself with continually recalling her words.

Caterina sat down on a shady garden bench. "Ercole. I lied to Borghini! I am not with child, and in any case nothing could ever, ever make me stop loving you. But if Domenico Borghini had known just how much he could torture me through you, he would not have hesitated to hurt you. Do you understand?"

From the way Ercole's lower lip stuck out, he was not prepared to forgive her so easily.

"Your lady mother is right," Gian Bracciaforte said unexpectedly. "When you are a man, Ercole, sometimes you too may be forced to lie to protect the people you love. But perhaps you are too young and silly to understand that now?"

Ercole shook his head violently. "She *said*." But his body relaxed slightly against Caterina's. She slipped an arm around his shoulders and kissed his sweaty temple. "I think it is too hot for you to work at your fighting skills now. Run inside and tell Piero that I said you were to have a honey cake and a half-hour trying to solve one of his puzzles before you must resume your studies."

"Two cakes?"

She laughed. "Don't try to bargain with me, my son! Go on now."

She sat in silence for a moment, looking after Ercole as he scampered indoors. Perhaps she had come one step closer to mending her relations with the boy. How many more steps remained?

The scents of healing herbs rose up in the warmth of the summer sun: rosemary and sage, chamomile and basil in this part of the garden furnished both the kitchens and her experiments. Caterina breathed in the perfumed air and made a mental note that she would have to come here another day to gather some of the herbs whose virtues were strongest at noon; now, in mid-afternoon, their strength would already be waning. Others, of course, had to be gathered at night, under a waxing moon. Those herbs, though, were grown in a separate part of the garden, one that the kitchen staff were forbidden to enter.

"I'm glad you sent the boy inside," Gian said, startling her. "I want to talk to you about him."

But she did not want to talk about Ercole. It was too painful. "Perhaps you want to give back my ring?"

He shook his head and smiled. "It seems to want to stay with me. I've tried soap and oil; nothing helps. But you are quite welcome to try again if you can pull it off."

She believed him. In any case, she did not intend to be found in the garden holding the hand of her base-born captain of the guard.

"The boy is old enough to serve in a noble household," Gian said abruptly, "and I think you should foster him with one."

"To part with him so soon after the dangers we have been through…" Caterina murmured. And who was this Gian Bracciaforte anyway, to lecture her on the proper raising of a noble son? Bracciaforte –Strongarm –it was probably an assumed name. A nobody.

"You are thinking that it is none of my business," Gian went on. Caterina tried not to show how startled she was. Could the fellow read her mind? "But as the captain of your personal guard, it would be remiss of me not to consider all matters that could affect your safety and Ercole's. And having the two of you in the same place doubles the danger. If he were fostered with a noble family in another city, the enemies of San Florian would have twice the work to lay hands on you and the heir. And, especially while they believe your, ah, statements about your present condition, they would know that they must capture both of you to seize power."

Caterina felt her cheeks burning. He might have been tactful enough to pretend he had not overheard her exchange with Ercole.

"I do not know where I could send him," she said finally.

"You have no noble relatives?"

"Oh, yes," Caterina said with slight bitterness. "On my father's side we are related to the Malatestas. You would not recommend that I send him to learn drunkenness and debauchery at Rimini? And though my husband was highly connected, I can hardly send Ercole to the household of Pope Sixtus, which would be as bad if not worse. I observed the pope's tastes for myself when we made that journey to Rome.

And beyond that…I believe you have met Girolamo's cousin Lucrezia. Her husband Ottavio is a merchant, not a member of the nobility; unless I wish to apprentice Ercole to the dye works, there is no place for him there. And in any case Ottavio Contarini will scarcely welcome another member of the Rinaldi family while we shelter his runaway wife."

"If I might make a suggestion…" Gian paused until Caterina nodded for him to proceed.

"His excellency Duke Federico da Montefeltro is a very great and gracious lord, and he has made Urbino a center of culture and the arts."

Caterina raised her eyebrows. "This would be the same great and gracious lord whose condottieri sacked Volterra for Lorenzo de' Medici over the rights to their alum mines?"

"These things happen in war. I have seen similar actions… In any case, both Lorenzo and Federico have repented that and have been absolved. And yes, I still think highly of the duke. As a page at his court, Ercole would acquire both military training and the polish befitting a son of the nobility. If you wished, I could, perhaps, recommend Ercole to the duke's service."

"You were not one of his condottieri, were you?" She could hardly think that a common soldier's introduction would be a good recommendation for Ercole. And she desperately wanted Gian Bracciaforte *not* to be connected with the infamous and bloody sack of Volterra.

"No, my service was with Milan," he reminded her. "My acquaintance with Duke Federico is… of somewhat earlier date. Eleven years, to be precise. But I hope he may remember me."

Eleven years? Caterina frowned slightly. The condottiere looked only slightly older than she herself was; she felt quite sure he was not yet thirty. He could hardly have been in the court of Urbino eleven years ago… unless… Could he have been a page in Federico da Montefeltro's court? Caterina thought furiously. He was very well-spoken; his manners would not have disgraced a court; and she had already decided that Bracciaforte was a made-up name.

"He may remember *you*," she said slowly, "but will he remember Gian Bracciaforte?"

"Forgive me if I do not tell you precisely how I would sign the letter. To recall myself to the duke's memory, I must use a name that is not… healthy… to use these days. I would much prefer to keep it between myself and the duke."

"You're not one of the Pazzi, are you?" Caterina blurted. Lorenzo de' Medici's vengeance upon the conspirators who killed his younger brother had been the talk of San Florian just two years ago.

Gian laughed. "No, I'm not crazy," he punned on the name, using *pazzo*

—insane —instead of *Pazzi*. "It has been much longer than that since the little trouble that sent me on my career as a condottiere. But I should rather not risk reminding… certain people… of my existence. May I write to Duke Federico on your behalf, then?"

"You can write yourself? You do not wish Father Benvenuto to write for you?" *Of course he can write. Obviously he was raised in a higher station of life than he claims now.*

"I should prefer the correspondence to be as private as possible."

"Madonna?" It was Piero Giacomini, peering short-sightedly out into the afternoon dazzle of the sunny garden. Caterina rose.

"There is a… visitor. He wishes to speak with you personally."

"Who is he?"

Piero shook his head. "No one I know, but he was most insistent. He has a… a sort of… I suppose you could call it a letter of introduction, except he seems to be introducing himself." He held out a square piece of paper to Caterina.

"Magister Filippus Faustus Cacciote, fons necromanticorum, astrologus, magus chyromanticus agromanticus pyromanticus in hydra…" she read, translating as she went. "Maestro Filippo Fausto Cacciote, the inspiration of necromancers, palmist, diviner by fire and water, formerly chief magus at the court of Frederick III of the Holy Roman Empire." She laughed. "What a distinguished visitor he claims to be! I will certainly receive him, Piero, if only for entertainment. But I am surprised that you, of all people, would desire me to receive a self-styled necromancer."

"So am I," Piero said. "In fact, I cannot think what came over me. He is riding the worst, spavined, knock-kneed boneshaker of a nag I have ever seen under a gentleman's bottom, and the mule carrying his boxes looks ready to collapse under them. When I was talking with him, somehow that did not seem important, but now… Shall I tell Father Benvenuto to send him away?"

"No, this should be amusing," said Caterina.

As she gathered up her skirts, she was surprised to find Gian Bracciaforte offering his arm. "It is not wise for my lady to meet a stranger without her personal guard," he said.

And so, once again, she entered the great hall of the Rocca with her hand on a man's arm, just as she had so often accompanied Girolamo. But this time she was not there to listen and accede to whatever Girolamo decided. Gian stepped backward, halting two paces behind her, as if to emphasize the difference. She would have to make this decision herself. Well, it should not be difficult; she had neither money nor desire to introduce a strange mage into the household.

The stranger was warming his hands at a small brazier; strange, on such a hot afternoon. Who had brought it to him? Probably the same person who had put a cup of wine on the table beside him. As she entered, he turned away from the glowing coals. A tiny spiral of smoke rose from the brazier and vanished into the shadows. A sharp herbal scent filled the air. Behind her, she heard someone whispering to Gian.

"Madonna." The man bowed low enough, but without the grace that Gian displayed so naturally. *For all the vainglorious boasting, I'll wager his origins were humble enough.* His long black gown was fine enough but bore the marks of travel and insufficient cleaning. He wore no jewels, not even a chain. His long fingers were not callused, but they were bony and awkward looking. *Not someone who works with his hands.*

"You… wished to speak with me?" The smell coming from the brazier bothered her. She felt she needed fresh air to think clearly.

"Madonna," he repeated with another bow, "I have come to offer you my services, to give your court the most precious jewel you could hope to display. With your own court magician, my lady, you will command the respect of all the neighboring states! I can predict the future; I can summon demons to serve you; all things shall be as you will."

"I…" The decision did not, after all, seem so easy. As Cacciote gestured in the air with his awkward, bony hands, the smoke from the brazier divided into dancing columns. Fascinated into staring at them, she seemed to see a glittering future where she mingled with the lords of such places as Urbino and even Florence, where Caterina Rinaldi was the name of a great lady whose opinions and desires were everywhere respected. "Perhaps…"

"A wise decision, my lady! You will not regret employing me."

Gian stirred behind her. "The lady has not yet said that she will employ you." He stepped forward, standing almost between her and Cacciote. "That's a fine gown, *Magister* Cacciote, or at least it once was. But I hear that you are hardly mounted like a gentleman. How do we know you are not some beggarly charlatan, trying to get into the household on false pretences? The Holy Roman Emperor is far away, and I doubt you yourself have ever traveled farther north than Florence."

Filippo Cacciote drew himself upright. "I have seen more of the world than you will ever know, from the Sublime Porte to the abode of the Lapp witches!" His stance only emphasized how poorly the once-fine gown fitted. It was so short that his dusty boots showed under the hem, and its shoulders drooped on either side of the mage's tall, thin body. Clearly it had been made for a different man. *A borrowed gown. Or a secondhand one. But... a mage is not necessarily rich, is he? I am certainly not rich.* It was all too confusing, wasn't it? The obvious thing to do was to offer the man the hospitality of the castle. Then she could lie down and not try to think any more...

Gian's hand closed on her arm, and he put her other hand on top of his so that she felt the emerald ring hard and cold against her palm. Suddenly everything was quite clear.

"Charlatan or mage, I have no need of your services or your demons here!" she snapped. "Get you gone to some court where the ruler does not care for his soul! You might try Roberto Malatesta; if he takes after his sire, he will probably welcome you!"

Cacciote's jaw dropped. *Was he so sure of his welcome here? And why?*

"You have heard the lady," Gian said.

"And I have seen her," Cacciote sneered. "Behold the folly of allowing a woman to rule; she is the prey of the first pretty boy who flatters her! That will make a fine tale for the court of Rimini!"

Gian stepped forward, hand on his sword. "Slander my lady, and I will personally cut your throat. Now get out of here before I have my men beat you!"

The mage scrambled awkwardly backward, paused at the door as if to hurl some further insult, then ran for his horse. Gian glared at him and then doused the brazier with the cup of wine that Cacciote had not drunk.

An outraged shriek came from the stairs. "How dare you!"

Lucrezia, dressed in a tightly girdled red gown that showed off her generous curves, stormed down the last three stairs, berating Caterina and Gian alike. "Here I do my best to show decent hospitality to a guest, bringing him wine and the brazier he asked for, and ordering the kitchen to prepare a meal, all because you were too busy in the garden to take care of your own responsibilities! And now you make an enemy of him and waste all my work!"

"I think he was already an enemy," Caterina said. She recognized the dark red sash, sparkling with gold threads, that wrapped around Lucrezia's waist. And the gilt-embroidered veil of fine, nearly transparent silk that floated over her dark blonde braids. She had last seen both items when she had given them to Rosa to put away after that obscenely expensive feast Girolamo gave for... who had been the guest he was trying to impress that time? Oh, it didn't matter.

Lucrezia noted her glance. "If you'd get my dowry back," she said sharply, "I wouldn't be reduced to borrowing from you! But no, you're too selfish to do anything for other people. First you pretend to be pregnant, and now you spend all your time hiding in that tower room. If you're not careful, Caterina, people will say you are becoming unbalanced. It happens sometimes with aging widows, you know."

# ~CHAPTER TEN~

*Take a square piece of parchment made from the skin of a white lamb, and write in the blood of a white dove the words* SATOR AREPO TENET OPERA ROTAS *in the form of a square.*

*Before the blood is dry, but without blurring the words, sprinkle the parchment with a powder of belladonna and rosemary, so that the virtues of these herbs are absorbed into the writing; the belladonna being gathered by moonlight, and the rosemary at noon. Fold this as shown in the diagram and carry it in the left hand, or inside the left sleeve, to frustrate any attempts to impose upon you by witchcraft whether white or black.*

*-Caterina Rinaldi's Book of Secrets*

~ ~ ~

At first Caterina ignored the discreet scratching on the door of her tower room. What could Piero want now? He had already delivered the pigeon, and she knew he would prefer not to know exactly why she required the bird. It had taken her some time to find the special parchment used for certain charms, and now she was carefully cutting from it the smallest square suitable to her needs. It was late summer; there would be no more lambs for months. She did not want to waste even a fingernail's width of the parchment. But the piece had to be large enough to fold…

"Cannot it wait, Piero?" she called through the door when the scratching turned to a demanding tap-tap-tap.

"'S not Piero," replied a voice much deeper than Piero's. "'S Gian. I need to talk to you."

"Can't it *wait?*"

"No!"

Sighing, Caterina unlocked the door. "What is it, then?"

He held out a hand on which the middle finger was reddened to the knuckle. It looked as if he'd been trying to drag the ring off with his teeth just now. "I've been *trying,*" he said. "I can't get it to come off. I thought maybe you would know some charm…"

Caterina shook her head. "Why would you think that?"

Gian grinned. "My lady, if you *will* enchant your jewels to scream that they are being stolen, and raise mysterious besieging armies that melt away in the middle of the night, do you not think that people will eventually begin to talk?"

Caterina reached for the table to steady herself. She should have known something like this would happen. While Girolamo was alive she had deferred to his wishes and seldom used the recipes in her book of secrets for anything more than removing stains or compounding a special sauce —or, at most, for some very private and small-scale experiments. Since then she had been first desperate, and then, perhaps, careless.

"Don't worry," Gian said. "Your people are very proud of you. Several of them have boasted to me than San Florian has two great protections: the Rocca with its miraculous spring of fresh water, and their Contessa with equally miraculous powers of conjuration. Even Father Benvenuto says that you use your magical knowledge only for good and that he sees no need to involve the Church in the matter."

"How… kind of him," Caterina said faintly. She felt dizzy at Gian's report of how the people viewed her. She had been accustomed to being Count Girolamo's slight, unimpressive wife whom everybody knew he had married just to strengthen his title to the city. Now, it seemed, she was well on her way to becoming Caterina Ristori, powerful mage and defender of her city.

Being the quiet wife in the background had been safer.

But it had also been rather boring.

She sighed and accepted the new reality of her world. "Yes, I do know certain charms. But I do not know of one that will make a ring fly off a man's finger. And even if I did, it would have no effect on this particular ring. Its virtue is that it repels any magic aimed at you."

"Yes, I figured that out when it let me pick up your jewels without their screaming at me. But it didn't get... tight... like this until I... met you. Anyway, the thing is, you need the protection more than I do. I should think you'd recognize that. After, you know, yesterday. You can't exactly hold hands with me all the time in case somebody like that mage tries to bespell you again. Although," he said with a crooked smile, "there is something to be said for that approach –at least as far as I am concerned."

Was he flirting with her? Or just cracking jokes because he was desperately uncomfortable with the situation?

"I need protection," she agreed. "But I have other ways to arrange it. As for the ring..."

She sighed. "I am not sure, now, that we ought to try to remove it. It was always too loose for me, even on my thumb, and it kept falling off. It could have molded itself to my hand, as it has done with you, but that never happened –perhaps because it was made as a man's ring. In any case, I think it *wants* to be with you. And I am not unhappy to know that my personal guard is led by a man who is immune to magical attacks. What if we do manage to remove it, and the next mage bespells you to take off my head?"

"No one could make me do that!"

"I would rather not put it to the test. No, keep the ring... at least for now."

"Is there nothing I can do for you?"

Caterina wanted to snap, "*Yes, go away and leave me alone!*" but she had been too well brought up to say that. "Maybe later," she said. "I am... occupied right now."

Gian withdrew and with relief she returned to the task at hand. She had already trimmed one corner of the lambskin parchment to make a true right corner with straight edges. Now, fold over once to make a perfect square; cut *here* and *here*... She looked at the square shape ready to receive its letters and enjoyed a brief sense of satisfaction before she was interrupted again.

"I don't know why you are always fooling around up here," Lucrezia said. Oh. She had forgotten to lock the door after Gian.

"Is there something I can do for you, Lucrezia?"

"It's not worth asking. You never do anything I want anyway." Lucrezia's eye caught the small, squarish book on the table. "What's this?" She snatched it up just before Caterina could move it away and began riffling through the pages. "Recipes? Oh, and a beauty water for the complexion? Why don't you ever make anything really worthwhile, like that?"

Caterina breathed carefully, one, two, three, and took the book back from Lucrezia. Her cousin tried to hold onto it, but Caterina's fingers were strong from working with metals and leather for her various experiments. "Perhaps," she said with a guilty sense of malice, "because I have never needed such aids for my own complexion." She gazed at the spot –yes, it was a definite spot – on Lucrezia's chin. "But it is said to be very good for ladies with skin problems. You would like me to make up some for you?"

"Just give me the book. I'll do it myself."

"I'm sorry," said Caterina. "I do not lend this book to just anybody."

"How do I know you won't put something in it to make my skin worse?"

"If that's what you think of me, would you trust a recipe I wrote down? Perhaps it's already got the secret ingredient that will make you break out in spots *all over.*"

"Oh!" Lucrezia took a step backwards. "You are a wicked, wicked woman and I will tell Father Benvenuto about you!"

Caterina heard her steps descending the winding stair, sighed with relief and, this time, took care to lock the door securely before returning to her work. Let Lucrezia try to interest Father Benvenuto in a spat over women's beauty secrets! At least it would keep her busy for a while.

And she herself, when next she made confession, would have to accuse herself of wrath and malice. Sometimes she felt that Lucrezia was even more of a danger to her soul than the demons she had raised in defense of San Florian. If only the wretched woman would make it up with her husband! Every dinner since she descended upon them had been the occasion for complaints about her Ottavio, whose principal sins appeared to be that he never noticed what she was wearing, did not include her in important discussions, and didn't even hear half she said. Caterina had tried without success to suggest that men tended to be like that. And since there wasn't anybody else to marry *but* men, Lucrezia might be happier if she accepted Ottavio as he was, just as she had learned to accept Girolamo's infidelities.

She put Lucrezia's marital problems aside and focused on her work. She would have to powder the dried herbs before killing the pigeon, so that she could sprinkle the powder over the parchment as soon as the letters were written. It was a good thing that this charm, like the one she'd put on her jewels to protect them from thieves, could last indefinitely without draining her energy.

A generous pinch of belladonna covered the bottom of the mortar; she stripped three stalks of dried rosemary to sprinkle on over that and frowned at the denuded bundle. How had she used up so much rosemary without even noticing it? Well, not a problem. The rosemary bushes in the herb garden were flourishing; in this climate, you couldn't kill them with a stick. She made a mental note that the next time she was free at noon, she needed to renew her supplies of rosemary and the other herbs which should be gathered at that time.

As she ground the dried herbs to a fine dust, she pondered on the mysteries which were not elucidated in any of the books she'd studied. Why was it that illusions required so much more continuing effort from a mage than these simpler charms of protection? Was it because charms of protection were only activated under direct attack? Or was it because demons were required to create most illusions, and demons were always bent on consuming those who called them up? So that even if you drew your protective circle perfectly, they could come at you another way, working on the link between you that was created when you laid your commands upon them. But she always discharged the demons afterwards, no mage who forgot to do that would survive, so why…

A thought struck her. She could hardly wait to put it into practice. But she had to finish this work. Then she wanted to procure some more pigeons —two, or possibly three, for this great experiment.

Could she go downstairs and tell Piero what she needed without getting trapped into going over the accounts with him? She squared her shoulders. Of course she could. *She* was the regent of San Florian; he was only her financial advisor. It might hurt his feelings, but she could certainly enforce her will for once instead of giving in to his need for attention and reassurance.

Perhaps, afterwards, she could have Piero deliver the dead birds to the kitchen and tell the cook that the countess had a sudden craving for pigeon pie. It didn't seem so bad to kill the birds if you were going to make a legitimate use of them afterwards.

The protective charm was not that difficult to make, but the new one she had thought of required strict and tiring concentration. She used a thin gold sheet that had been intended for alchemical experiments to give her room to engrave all the illusion's diagrams; then she invoked, commanded, and dispelled the demons required to execute it upon her command. She punched a hole to take a hanging link and rolled the sheet into a scroll shape. Hung from a plain gold chain, it could pass as jewelry.

She was exhausted by the time she had done all this and taken the basket of dead pigeons downstairs to be delivered to the kitchen. Would her trick work? She thought that either it would work, or it would fail spectacularly, possibly killing her on the spot. It would have been wiser to try a smaller illusion requiring only one demon... no, it wouldn't. Failure would be her death in any case, whether it came at the claws of one demon or three. If she was going to risk her life, it might as well be for a worthy goal. But she devoutly hoped that it would never come to the test.

# ~CHAPTER ELEVEN~

*Take a quantity of wax and embed in it the hair or other personal parts of the woman you desire; then mold it to the shape of a woman and pierce the heart with a silver needle, saying, "As this needle is fixed, so may the love of this woman be fixed to the love of Roberto Malatesta, that she can neither sleep, nor wake, nor take any ease until she comes to him."*
   *-from the notes of Filippo Cacciote*

~ ~ ~

Filippo Cacciote was dangerously tired by the time he reached Rimini, and sore from bouncing on the back of a nag with a bone-breaking, lopsided gait. But he dared not stop yet. The Turks knew when they had set him on shore at Senigallia; they had at least some idea of how long it should have taken him to reach San Florian from there; and they probably did not make allowances for the fact that they had been too stingy to allow him to buy a good horse or clothes fine enough to impress that stupid, obstinate woman with his stature as a distinguished mage from the court of the Holy Roman Empire. Now he was trapped, afraid to unwrap the charmed mirror that was carefully stowed away in his saddlebags and even more afraid to delay using it. If they did not hear from him soon, they might think he had betrayed them, and Andrea might die. If they did hear from him after his failure at San Florian, and before he could offer them another route to success, Andrea would certainly die.

   He would simply have to accomplish, out of fury and desperation, what should have been a simple task for a mage of his powers. Now, even as he paused to prepare another aromatic leaf with the necessary words and diagrams, this minor work felt as soul-draining as the invocation of a demon. And he still did not know why the same charm had failed on the woman at San Florian, when he had even managed to get a brazier to disseminate the scent as smoke. He could not count on being that lucky every time. Best not to think about it. He needed to exude confidence. More, he needed to get an audience with the lord of Rimini immediately... Better prepare several leaves, one to work on whoever could grant him admission and the rest to make the lord himself understand what valuable services a mage could offer to his court. If he kept crushing the leaves to release their scent, it should have at least as much effect as burning one for the smoke.

The first leaf, crumbled in his hand and waved below the nose of the door guards, got him an audience with Roberto Malatesta. And he never needed a second one. Malatesta had clearly started drinking over dinner and continued into the evening. He was in no condition to evaluate Cacciote's shabby, travel-worn appearance, and he was delighted with the prospect of adding an official magician to his court. "Even the Duke of Urbino has only an astrologer," he said happily, while Cacciote refreshed himself on the cold remnants from dinner and refused a second cup of wine. He would need all his capacities later.

Malatesta had even agreed without question that his court magician would naturally require a private chamber. One did not, he said, waving his goblet and spilling a little wine, one did not ask a man who had been at the elbow of the Holy Roman Emperor to sleep on the benches in the hall!

Cacciote was still tired and aching when Malatesta at last stumbled off to sleep, but there would be little rest for him that night. He had to make his report to the Turks, and it had to be persuasive. He would have to make the gossip he had picked up on the road appear like established fact, and his failure at San Florian as a minor setback of no real concern.

When he brought out the mirror, he saw his son sleeping on a pile of silk-covered cushions. For a moment he simply savored the relief of knowing the boy was still alive; then he set about the task of ensuring that he remained so.

Karamanli Pasha was not well pleased to be awakened at night by the sultan's new boy shaking his shoulder, but he accepted with a little grumbling that Cacciote could hardly use the mirror for communications unless he was assured of privacy. "Is that your chamber in San Florian?" he asked. "They honor you, it seems." Tapestries on the wall, silken bed hangings, a brocaded robe… he was clearly impressed. If only, Cacciote thought sadly, he had indeed been reporting from San Florian! Andrea's life would have been assured.

"Better than San Florian," he said. "I am in Rimini."

Karamanli's brows drew together. "Why are you bothering me now if you are not even in the right city? You have had time enough to do your errand."

"Hear me out," Cacciote said urgently. "Since landing I have learned certain things. This is even better than getting a position in San Florian. Did you know that Sigismondo Malatesta was a cousin to Antonio da Barignani?"

"Neither know nor care," Karamanli said. "All these infidel names sound alike. All I want to know is why you are not in San Florian!"

"Sigismondo Malatesta was the father of Roberto Malatesta, the present lord of Rimini," Cacciote explained carefully, "and Antonio da Barignani was the previous lord of San Florian. Since Antonio had no heir, Sigismondo expected to take over San Florian when Antonio died, but just before that happened the Pope bought San Florian and married his nephew Girolamo Rinaldi to Antonio's illegitimate daughter Caterina."

"Get on with it and tell me why I am up in the middle of the night listening to genealogies of infidels!"

"Because Sigismondo never gave up his claim to San Florian," Cacciote said, "and now his son Roberto is going to take up that claim. Girolamo Rinaldi died recently, and his widow is trying to rule San Florian for her son. Obviously that effort is doomed; a woman won't be able to hold out against the lord of Rimini. If I had taken a position in the present court of San Florian, it would only have benefited you as long as the woman was regent. Roberto will take the city and marry the widow, and by serving him, I provide you not only with access to San Florian, but with the cooperation of the port where you will land your army!"

"You claimed that San Florian was protected by its castle. Now you're telling me that this Roberto can take it by snapping his fingers?"

"He will have," Cacciote said modestly, "my help. And remember that the current ruler of San Florian is only a young, inexperienced woman."

"And why have I not heard of his designs on San Florian from anyone else?"

"He has had other matters to think of since Sigismondo's death. But now I shall bring the case of San Florian to his attention, and soon it will be the thing he desires most in all the world."

"Do not bother me again until you have something better to report than promises," Karamanli Pasha said, and the mirror went dark.

~~~

Cacciote was too tired to prepare a proper spell of compulsion that night, but he was pleased to discover on the next day that it seemed hardly necessary. After he dazzled Malatesta with a demonic invocation that raised an easy illusion –which he dispelled immediately, to preserve his energy –the lord of Rimini was attentive to his every word. Cacciote quickly discovered that the easiest way to guide his new employer's thoughts was to refer to his father Sigismondo's preferences. A little gossip with one of Malatesta's favorites explained the situation.

"He's illegitimate, you know," Niccolo drawled.

"Surely not much of a handicap? The lady of San Florian is also a bastard."

"Yes, but San Florian isn't much more than a pot-hole on the road. It's different with an important place like Rimini. Besides, Sigismondo never recognized Roberto, did you know that? First Sigismondo lost Rimini, then he died and left it to his legitimate son by Isotta degli Atti. Despite the fact that he didn't actually have it to leave at that point. Roberto had to reconquer Rimini for his younger half-brother, and then the degli Atti tried to freeze him out of the government and Roberto had to poison them both. If you ask me, he's still trying to prove to the world that Sigismondo should have recognized him as his heir to begin with."

Armed with that information, Cacciote lost no time in casually dropping a mention of Sigismondo's claim to San Florian into his new lord's ear.

Roberto sighed, complained about the expense and trouble of going to war, but brightened up when Cacciote emphasized that the current regent of San Florian was only a young widow. "I had heard of Girolamo's death," Roberto said, "but I thought his assassins had taken over the city?"

"They seem to have been an incompetent bunch," said Cacciote. "The only way in which they can be said to be 'over the city' is in that their bones are still dangling from the highest tower of the Rocca."

Roberto laughed immoderately at this grisly jest.

"This girl Caterina can hardly hope to keep the city for long," Cacciote prodded, "and who deserves it more than you? The Pope cheated your father out of it; this is your chance to right that wrong."

"Magister," Roberto said, "you may know how to raise demons, but you do not understand how to raise men. It would cost me a small fortune to lay siege to San Florian and to supply the army from here. That's why it has never been taken; it's not worth the effort."

"Your father thought it was important."

"Yes…" Roberto brooded over a dish of sliced ham, fried and dusted with sugar and cinnamon. Suddenly he laughed. "But my father never had the opportunity I have now. Why make war when I can have the city much more easily simply by marrying the widow?"

"But will she marry you?"

Roberto leaned over the table and fixed Cacciote with an unblinking stare. "That," he said cheerfully, "is what I have a court magician for, is it not? It's time you made yourself useful. Illusions and fireworks are very entertaining, but a spell to bring the lady Caterina to me would be much more to the point."

"It may take me a few days to acquire all the materials I shall need," Cacciote hedged.

"Very well, go to the apothecary shop in the city and tell the owner that I said you are to have whatever you need."

"And you'll pay him?"

"That goes without saying," said Roberto impatiently.

In Filippo Cacciote's experience with the nobly born, it was something that needed to be often and explicitly said, but he nodded humbly. It wasn't as if the materials that any apothecary could supply were the most important ingredients. He was still bemused by his failure to make Caterina Rinaldi employ him. It had *almost* worked, he could swear he could *feel* it working, then somehow it had all gone wrong.

This time he needed something that would bind this particular woman to his will, something that nobody from San Florian could interfere with.

"Certain supplies may not be available here in Rimini," he said. "May I send Niccolo to procure them from Cesena? There is an apothecary there who understands the needs of the higher magic."

"Why can't you use what you can get locally? And why Niccolo? I need him here to…" But Roberto couldn't think of anything useful that Niccolo actually did. He was decorative and amusing, but too old to be a page and too lazy to become a soldier. The only reason he was still part of Roberto's court was that his family had not shown any desire to have him back after his service as a page. And that he was amusing. And decorative.

"I would not deprive your lordship of a single fighting man," Filippo said, "and Niccolo, having served as your page, will be able to read my list of requirements." Also, Niccolo had been Roberto Malatesta's envoy to San Florian previously. That woman would probably not accept an invitation from the lord of Rimini, but the delivery of the invitation would get Niccolo an audience with her, and then…

"You will simply have to use your own ingenuity," Cacciote told Niccolo when the young man asked how he was supposed to get hair or nail clippings or anything else of a personal nature from the widow.

~ ~ ~

Niccolo slouched off to the stables, cursing his luck. What kind of miracles did the crazy mage expect from him? Was he supposed to ride all day, then somehow get close to a skittish widow who had just put down an attempted rebellion and who probably didn't trust anybody at all? What's more, he didn't even find her attractive. He'd seen her on previous errands to San Florian; a small, dark woman whose only beauty was in her long, full braids of reddish-brown hair and who held herself as proudly as if the whole world didn't know she was only Antonio da Barignani's bastard daughter. He couldn't imagine flirting with her, and if he did try, she would probably send him about his business.

On the whole, his interview with the countess of San Florian went almost as badly as expected. She received him with cool courtesy, but was never alone with him for a moment. She even requested her captain of the guard to take the letter Cacciote had given him and read it to her. Niccolo was slightly surprised to find the soldier was literate, but that did not concern him. The problem was the woman's extreme caution. If she would not even touch a piece of paper from his hand, how on earth was he to fulfill Cacciote's demands?

He was provided with food, stabling for his horse, and a place to sleep; but there was never the slightest excuse to visit the countess in her private chamber, where he might have been able to tease a tangle of hair out of a comb. In the early morning, still keeping her distance, still watched over by the soldier, she had her personal secretary deliver a courteous response to the invitation Cacciote had invented. Affairs of state prevented her from leaving San Florian at the moment, but she was grateful for Duke Roberto's invitation and hoped that they would ever be able to deal together on a friendly basis.

She hadn't even written the letter herself! Something written in her own hand might have satisfied the mage, but no, it was clear she had dictated the letter to Giacomini.

As he rode out into the cool morning air, Niccolo wondered whether he should even return to Rimini, given that all he had to report was failure. But where else would he go? His father had an excess of sons and had made it clear that placing Niccolo in the household of Rimini was all the provision he meant to make for his future. And if he returned to Rimini, well, leaving San Florian this early meant that he would have time to stop at a certain inn he favored, just outside the city, where both the wine and the women appealed to him. The one called Betta had the same coloring as the Contessa, only allied with more curves and a friendlier attitude. Yes, it would definitely be worth his while to break his journey there.

# ~CHAPTER TWELVE~

*To brighten blonde hair, take a decoction of rhubarb and nettle seeds; add to it an equal quantity of the juice of a lemon, and comb this through the hair with a comb made of ivory or wood. Most efficacious in the light of the sun.*

*Probatum est. I have not had occasion to use this, having brown hair and fearing that this would only make the hint of red in it even worse, but Alessio Piemontese reports that he has seen many ladies lighten their hair to become very fair blondes by this method.*

*-Caterina Rinaldi's Book of Secrets*

~ ~ ~

It was several days before Caterina was able to slip away at noon to renew her supplies of the sun-loving herbs. One minor problem after another kept her too busy to collect the materials for her experiments, while not giving her any sense of achievement. First there had been that very peculiar letter from Roberto Malatesta, and the necessity of dictating a reply that would neither inflame the delicate relationship between Rimini and San Florian nor expose the city's perilous financial state to the lord of Rimini. Then she had been unable to put off any longer Piero Giacomini's demands for a thorough going-over of the accounts.

She had done what she could to reduce their expenses. Her nobly born ladies in waiting had been replaced by girls from the homes of the city's merchants, making all parties happier; the fine ladies did not wish to stay in a town so recently shaken by insurrection, and the city girls were sufficiently grateful for the training in court ways so that they did not demand large stipends. The musicians and artists whom Girolamo had attracted had now been replaced by Gian's soldiers, who likewise did not make excessive demands upon her purse. There were no more lavish entertainments to make San Florian seem like one of the wealthier cities that neighbored them, no implicit competitions with the Medici of Florence or the Montefeltri of Urbino.

But despite all that, there were still too many decisions that Piero could not make by himself. Worse, when she called her councilors together, they were capable of debating the issues indefinitely. What taxes could be remitted, and which absolutely had to be collected? How to balance the demands of the wool merchants with those of the sheep farmers who supplied them? What promised payments could be put off until they had more cash on hand?

Caterina hoped she had navigated all those issues correctly, but only time would tell. If she had made the right decisions, they would make it through the rest of the summer without another popular uprising against the taxes, without actual fighting between the merchants and the farmers, and without the Papal Legate visiting to demand immediate payment of the city's debts to Rome. And with the fall would come harvests, the cycle of trade fairs where the wool merchants could sell their clips and the weavers their finished textiles, possibly even a return on some of Girolamo's investments in trading vessels bound for Turkey with mirrors of bronzed glass, hand-blown goblets from Murano, mechanical clocks and other things of which the Turks were inordinately fond.

She felt she had earned some time for her own pursuits, and she seized on the first sunny day after a series of cool, cloudy ones to make her long-deferred visit to the herb garden. It was annoying to discover that her straw gardening hat had mysteriously disappeared from its hook beside the door. Probably Rosa had taken it with a plan to replace or refurbish the thing; she was always unhappy when any of Caterina's clothes were shabby, even an old hat which she never wore except in the garden. But if she went back upstairs to demand that Rosa give it back, somebody was sure to find her with some new problem that only the countess could solve. And she wasn't going to be out for long. And who would even notice if the sun turned her skin a little darker than the ideal milk-white shade of a noble lady's complexion?

*Gian Bracciaforte*, said a sardonic voice at the back of her mind.

Caterina shook her head. Girolamo was just buried; how could she already be thinking about a personal relationship with any other man, let alone a lowborn one who worked for her? It was the kind of thing that Lucrezia would characterize as "an aging widow growing peculiar." Anyway, she had enough to deal with already; the last thing she needed was another man cluttering up her life!

She lingered over the herb bushes, cutting what she needed slowly and carefully and keeping the various herbs separated by fine linen cloths. There was, she told herself, absolutely no hurry. So what if her face was in the sun for a few minutes? She wasn't an idiot like Lucrezia, forever worrying about her appearance. She was a sensible widow with a son to bring up and a city to care for… and…

It was an extremely bright day and the sun beat down on her bare head. Without the wide-brimmed straw hat to shade her eyes, she was almost blinded by the brilliant light, and her head began to ache before she had half finished collecting the herbs she wanted. The long braids coiled around her head seemed heavier than usual; the hairpins that held them were sharp points of pain digging into her scalp. Stubbornly she went on cutting, breathing in the resinous tang of rosemary, the dusty sweetness of sage, the sharp bright mint smell that she always imagined as being green like the sea. Then, feeling suddenly dizzy, she sat down abruptly on a garden bench and only just avoided spilling the cuttings out of her basket.

"You should be indoors," said a cool, reserved voice with a definite Florentine accent.

Caterina couldn't agree more.

"Shall I call your maid to help you?" Gian asked.

"No –it's nothing –I just lost my balance for a moment." Caterina stood up too quickly, swayed, felt an arm supporting her briefly. As soon as she was steady on her feet, Gian released her. "Allow me," he said, and this time presented his arm for her to lean on while she made her way into the cool darkness of the interior.

"Sit here," he commanded. Caterina blinked. They were in the hall. Yes, sitting down again was definitely a good idea; she was not feeling quite ready to take the stairs up to her workroom with the basket of herb cuttings.

"It's all Rosa's fault," she said. "She *will* whisk away anything of mine that she thinks is too shabby for my station. But I did think she would have allowed me to keep my old gardening hat."

"I do not think she took it," said Gian. "The reason I came looking for you in the garden was because Rosa was fluttering around, complaining that somebody should take your hat out to you before you got sunburnt, and that she couldn't find it anywhere." He paused. "Well…that was one reason, anyway." He rose, took a cup from a servant and set it before her, together with two letters. The one on top was unsealed and bore the device of a crown over a shield, the crest of Urbino. "The wine is watered," he said. "You need something cool to drink."

Caterina was almost thirsty enough to gulp the entire contents of the goblet. It was a real effort to sip discreetly, like a lady. Sweaty and unsteady from her time in the sun, she did not feel much like a lady just now.

And Gian had had some other reason for seeking her out. She suppressed a sigh. New problems?

"Two messengers have arrived. Both are waiting for an answer." Gian tapped the top letter. "This was addressed to me; the Duke of Urbino will be pleased to accept Ercole into his household. With your permission, I shall take the boy to Urbino as soon as possible. Every hour that you and he are in the same place makes me more concerned, particularly with the pressure from Rimini."

"From Rimini!" She thought she had dealt with that when she turned away that boy from Malatesta's court.

"Ah, that would be the other messenger. I have not read the letter, but the bearer told me that it is of the greatest importance to Roberto Malatesta that you should come to Rimini so that he can celebrate your new status as the regent of San Florian."

Caterina broke the seal and looked through the letter. "It is almost a threat," she said. "He says that he would be extremely reluctant to see any dissension between San Florian and Rimini, which have always been united. I think he is trying to establish that San Florian properly belongs to Rimini. Perhaps I had better accept his invitation, so that I can make clear to him that San Florian is and will remain an independent city."

"By no means!" Gian exclaimed. "And particularly not when I am not here. You cannot risk yourself thus."

"But if Ercole is safe in Urbino?"

"That might deter Malatesta from killing you or taking you prisoner, but not from marrying you out of hand. Then he could claim that he has the guardianship of Ercole."

"He would marry me by force?" Naturally she would not consent to the marriage, any more than she would have consented to Domenico Borghini's plans. But Caterina had a sick feeling that her will would not count for much, once Malatesta had her in Rimini. Women had been married despite their objections before, and the usual attitude of society was that marriage was more honorable than rape and the woman might as well accept her lot.

"I don't know whether he depends on his charming manner or on the force of his soldiers. But I think you should not try to find out."

"I'll temporize," Catherine decided. "I shall tell him again that the affairs of the city require my presence, and this time I'll invite him to dine here."

"Not until I get back from Urbino."

"No, of course not. I shall propose a formal banquet two weeks from now, and I'll say that I need the time to prepare an entertainment suitable for such a distinguished visitor."

Gian nodded. "That gives us time to think. One question: what if he brings a very large armed escort? He commands a large troop of condottieri, at least tenfold more than my fourteen men. Can you think of a tactful way to say that they would not be welcome? He might not be willing to invest the time and money to besiege the Rocca, but once his men are inside…"

"I depend upon Peruzzi not to let them into the Rocca," Caterina said. "And… I will try to think of some tactful way to prevent his bringing a small army in the first place. I can always hint that the city cannot lodge many people, and if he brings more than… oh, half a dozen men… they might have to camp in the east pasture. The one with all the rocks, where only the goats are allowed to graze." Or would that be too rude? She badly wanted to rest in a shady place for a little longer before trying to compose a letter that would keep Malatesta reasonably happy without offering him any concessions.

"I shall dictate the letter to Piero," she decided. That pretty, peacocking boy who had delivered Malatesta's previous invitation had boasted to the servants that *his* lord now had his own court magician. She had the protective charm tucked inside her left sleeve, but it might still be wise not to give Malatesta something written in her own hand.

Gian rose and bowed. "I expect Piero is at his accounts, as usual. I'll send him to you."

"No, I'll go to him." That might not be consonant with her dignity, but if Piero was in the strongroom, that would be a much better place to compose a tricky letter than here in the great hall where anybody could interrupt or overhear them.

As if to underline the wisdom of that decision, Lucrezia came running down the stairs even as Caterina rose. "Look at my hair!" she cried. "Isn't it beautiful? I've been combing lemon juice through it in the sunlight, and already it's much brighter."

She twirled around, displaying her rippling locks.

"It does look lighter," Caterina agreed. "But how did you manage to sit in the sun at this time of day without getting sunburnt?"

"Oh, I've learned a thing or two from the Venetians," Lucrezia said happily. "You wear a wide-brimmed hat without a crown, you see, and take your hair through the opening and spread it out all over, and the brim of the hat shades your complexion from the sun." She waved a straw hat. "See?"

It was certainly crownless now. It was also what remained of Caterina's gardening hat.

"And it didn't cost you a thing," Lucrezia said, "for I just cut up a shabby old hat I found lying around, instead of sending to Venice for a specially made one."

# -CHAPTER THIRTEEN-

*A very excellent way to prepare a peacock for a feast:*

*The head and legs should be first cut off; then the skin may be peeled off in one piece, together with the feathers. Let the body be roasted slowly with cloves and nutmeg, taking care to keep it moist by wrapping it in fine linen saturated with honey. The wrappings may be removed and the skin, head and legs put back afterwards, and the feathers dusted with gold powder or, if that is too expensive, with cinnamon.*

*Cousin Lucrezia recommends this recipe, but I have neither the gold, the peacock, nor the inclination to attempt it.*

*-Caterina Rinaldi's Book of Secrets*

~ ~ ~

"I don't understand this letter," Roberto Malatesta complained. "What does she mean, my previous invitation? This is the first letter I've sent to anybody in San Florian since... well, before Girolamo's assassination."

Filippo Cacciote shrugged his shoulders under his splendid new gown of black silk brocade. He saw no reason to tell Malatesta that he had procured some of Caterina's hair for the love charm by sending Niccolo with an invented invitation to the lady. If she had accepted that one, he would have taken credit for it and would have been spared the effort of working the charm, which required him to stay up for three consecutive nights and to avoid mentioning any holy names during that time. Since she did not, he had

had to tire himself making the image that incorporated her hair and calling up the appropriate demons to strike her with so great a desire that she could neither sleep nor rest until she came to Roberto Malatesta.

"Who knows what a woman thinks, or even if she thinks?" he said. "Perhaps she is referring to some correspondence of yours with Girolamo. Or perhaps, under the influence of my charm, she is imagining that you are being more attentive than you are."

"If so," said Malatesta angrily, "it is all the result I have gotten so far from your work! She temporizes, she pleads pressure of affairs and the disordered state of San Florian, she suggests that I should visit her instead –but not for two weeks, because it will take her that long to prepare a banquet worthy of my magnificence!"

"Obviously the charm *is* working," said Cacciote. "Remember that she is only a woman, and is doubtless constrained by the will of her advisors. Since they will not approve of her coming here, she seeks to bring you to her to satisfy her great yearning for you. And because she is desperate to please you, she plans a great banquet with which to receive you –which is no more than your due as lord of Rimini."

He thought he had persuaded Malatesta. Inwardly he felt some concern. The demons he had summoned had promised on blood and iron to work his will on the woman whose hair was embedded in the image. She should have come directly to Rimini, no matter what her advisors said. She certainly should not have been willing to put off meeting with Malatesta for two weeks!

Ah well, perhaps even the great desire which the demons had laid upon her was not enough to enable her to go against her councilors. Even that could be turned to his favor! After suffering the pangs of insatiable desire for two weeks, the woman would be ready to fall into Malatesta's arms.

～～～

Caterina was, of course, not privy to the mage's thoughts. But she was certainly ready to fall somewhere –preferably onto a nice soft bed in some mountain retreat with a cool climate - after two weeks of preparation for a formal banquet in the palazzo. Lucrezia insisted on helping with the work, but as Lucrezia's idea of help consisted mainly of saying that there weren't enough different dishes planned, or recommending some delicacy involving unavailable or out-of-season ingredients, Caterina could have done with a little less help. The one useful thing Lucrezia had done was to find an artist who was willing to repair the murals in the palazzo for his meals, his lodging and a horse.

"And you wouldn't have had such a bargain," Gentile Bellini said frankly, "if I weren't sick to death of that mule, and if I didn't need to rest so that I can show myself to best advantage on my return to Venice." He had been visiting the court of Naples when he received a message from the Ten urgently requiring his return. King Ferrante of Naples, already bad-tempered because of the reverses he'd received in attempting to recapture Otranto from the Turks, had flatly refused to pay the court painter for his work on a royal portrait that the man was obliged to leave only half done. So Bellini's journey back to Venice had not been quite as comfortable as he would have liked.

Caterina took refuge from the ordered chaos in the palazzo kitchen to sit in the hall and watch Bellini at work. The chatty, gossipy little man combined deft strokes of the paintbrush with a lively tongue that painted a picture of the court of Naples in words. His conversation became even more interesting when he drifted into speculations about the politics of the peninsula.

"To tell you the truth, Madonna Caterina, I was not entirely sorry to leave Naples –ah, apart from the agony of a great artist compelled to leave his work unfinished," Bellini said. "Not to mention unreimbursed –ah well, Ferrante will have to pay me to return and complete the portrait, and I rather think my prices just went up. But just now, Naples is war-mad. Half the inhabitants have fled for fear of the Turk marching north from Otranto, and the other half are boasting about how they will drive the Turk out of the peninsula for good!" He squinted sideways at the Virgin's face. "Hmm, the left eye still needs a highlight... here!" He dabbed a minute spot of white onto the eye and, like a miracle, the Virgin suddenly seemed like a living woman looking back at them from the wall. "And a few, I suppose," he added, "have actually joined Ferrante's army... but none of them have come back yet. I do not know why the Ten commanded my return to Venice, but..."

"Can they command you?" Caterina asked. "I thought Venice was a free republic."

Bellini shrugged. "Oh, very free, but it is not healthy to displease the oligarchs. And I am, after all, the official portrait painter for the Doges... although I have already painted Giovanni Mocenigo. I suppose one of the council has a commission for me. It will sound well enough, when I spread it about town that whoever actually requested my return was willing to send all the way to Naples to get me rather than commissioning an inferior artist –for all the other artists in Venice *are* my inferiors, you understand. At any rate, I would rather be painting in Venice than listening to war fever in Naples. I need more blue for the Virgin's cloak; you must send to Florence for lapis lazuli."

Caterina suppressed a sigh. She might not be having to pay Bellini directly for his work, but the little man's insistence on using only the best materials was straining a budget already stressed from buying spices and sugar for the banquet. It was fortunate that the looters had not had time to steal all the wine in the cellars of the Palazzo Rinaldi, or she would have had to sell off some of her jewelry to host this feast. As it was, she would probably need to send Gian to Florence with a ring or some links of gold to pay for the lapis lazuli.

And Gian was not back from Urbino yet...

She put aside that niggling worry and tried to take a serious interest in Bellini's gossip. "Why are you so sure that people in Venice won't be worried about the Turks?"

"Contessa! Only last year we concluded a treaty of peace with the Sublime Porte. Who can blame Venice for making peace after fifteen years of exhausting her men and her fortune in fighting off Turkish attacks on our coastal cities, with, I might mention, absolutely no help from the other Italian states? Now, for a change, we Venetians are perhaps the only people who have no need to fear the Turks. And it is perfectly all right with us to let the others, Naples and Rome and even Milan, take up the burden for a while!"

Caterina could hardly argue with that. She was devoutly grateful that San Florian was too far inland to fear the lightning-quick raids by which the Turks had taken so many little coastal towns over the last ten years. As the Turks encroached farther and farther up the Adriatic coast, it was no surprise that the Venetians had at last resorted to buying the Turks off in return for peace. But in peaceful little San Florian, the only reason anybody even thought about the Turks was because Lucrezia had suggested that a Turkish pudding with rice and white raisins would be a good choice for one of the sweet dishes at the banquet. It was unfortunate that San Florian was so far north that rice was a luxury good. But the pudding could, perhaps, be served in very small bowls…?

"I've thought of another thing," Lucrezia greeted her when Caterina made her way back to the kitchens. "Why don't we serve some peacocks cooked and stuffed as though they were alive? I saw them once at a Papal banquet in Rome and everybody was most impressed! We could dust the feathers with spices, or gild them…"

Caterina already felt as though this banquet was requiring her to sprinkle the entire kitchen with gold dust or, worse, saffron. "Unfortunately," she said, "we have no peacocks in San Florian."

"You could send to Rome…"

"There's hardly time." And in any case, she wasn't about to waste money on showy birds which her father had condemned as far too scrawny and gamey to be worth eating. She had already arranged to serve capons in wine with peppercorns and garlic and a pigeon pie in puff pastry, and the cook had promised to end the meal with a subtlety consisting of an entire castle made of sugared pastry and meringues. She had also planned on a dish of eels with cinnamon and marzipan, and one of venison sausages fried in butter. Together with the usual plates of salads and plain roast meats, and the Turkish rice pudding which Lucrezia was to oversee, that would have to do.

Lucrezia pouted. "I'm only trying to help you impress the man!"

"If you want to impress Roberto Malatesta," said a familiar voice behind her, "do not worry about the food, just keep the wine flowing freely."

*Gian.*

Caterina half closed her eyes against the rush of relief that pervaded her whole being. Hearing Gian's voice, knowing he was back in San Florian, was –it was a drink of cool water on this sultry September day. No, it was like –

like putting off her silk dress and linen smock to swim naked in the river.

*What a* peculiar *thought. As if I'd ever done such a thing!* The closest she'd come even to thinking about it had been in her childhood, on a summer day as hot as this one when she was crossing the bridge and saw some peasant boys stripping off and jumping into the water. She had envied them, but all too soon her nurse had hustled her away, clucking at the impropriety of the lord's little daughter watching naked boys.

"How did you leave Ercole?" she asked. *A much safer topic.*

Gian chuckled. "Playing at ball with three other little pages, and driving their tutor to distraction."

Well, that was better than hearing that he was crying for her, wasn't it? "I thought the court at Urbino was supposed to civilize him."

"It may," Gian said judiciously, "take more than three or four days to achieve that."

"Well –I am very glad you are back," Caterina said. That sounded too personal. She added immediately, "Because I need you to do an errand for me in Florence."

Gian glanced at the cook and the assistants and Lucrezia, all standing stock-still and looking interested.

"Perhaps," he said, "we could discuss that elsewhere, so as not to distract your staff from their work."

"Oh. Yes. Of course."

"If he's going to Florence," Lucrezia said, "he can get me some white silk for a new pair of sleeves."

"We can discuss that later," said Caterina. "Messer Bracciaforte, will you attend me in the counting-room? You need not come, Lucrezia," she added to forestall her cousin's motion towards them. "We are only going to be going over Piero's accounts. It would bore you extremely."

Caterina noticed that Gian was looking very unhappy. His sidelong glances at Piero suggested part of the problem. She gave Piero leave to withdraw and shut the door after him.

"What is it?" she demanded. "Is there something wrong at Urbino? Is Ercole not safe there?"

"Oh, *he* is safe," said Gian unhappily. "But I… encountered… somebody I would rather not have met there." He tried to laugh. "I had thought that the passage of ten years, together with my beard, would have been sufficient change in my appearance. But it seems that I have only grown into the image of my late uncle."

"Who was your uncle, and why is it a problem that you look like him?" Caterina was annoyed. If there was a problem at Urbino, why couldn't Gian tell her straight out?"

Gian sighed, rubbed one finger over the emerald in his ring, and seemed to come to some sort of a decision. His shoulders straightened as though he were bracing himself for some disaster. "I probably should have told you long since. The uncle whom I have the misfortune to resemble was Diotisalvi Neroni. I was born Gian-Maria Neroni."

Caterina gasped. "One of *those* Neronis? I thought they were all –"

"Dead? I am sure that is what Lorenzo de' Medici intended for the family that tried to assassinate his father."

"But you weren't part of the conspiracy, were you? I don't really know much about it," Caterina apologized. "I had other things to think about at the time. My father was dying that year, and he was afraid that his cousin of Malatesta would try to marry me to substantiate his claim on San Florian. I was afraid, too."

"What, Sigismondo Malatesta the Wife-Killer?" Gian exclaimed in shock.

"I am not absolutely sure that epithet is justified. He had only lost two wives at that time, and it was never proved that they had both been poisoned. But my father did not want to risk that I would be the third in that series. There was also a problem of consanguinity, but by the time the pope ruled on that it might have been too late for me. The pope's purchase of San Florian and my marriage to his nephew were my father's attempt to protect me."

"I can see why the doings in Florence escaped your attention," Gian agreed. "But for me… well, I was sixteen, and I also had other things to think about, like riding and swordsmanship and avoiding my tutor's insistence on Latin composition as a necessary skill for a gentleman. I didn't even know anything about Florentine politics; I was just returned from serving in the court of Urbino as a page. I didn't pay attention to my father and my uncle whispering in the corners until it was almost too late. They tried to ambush Piero de' Medici outside the town when he was returning from his country estate, but Leonardo thwarted the plot and saved his father's life. Suddenly it was very unhealthy to be a Neroni, especially in Florence. I fled to Milan, changed my name, and took service as a condottiere under the Sforza. Later, after Galeazzo Maria Sforza was assassinated, I followed my captain Carlo Gondi and sought service elsewhere. The rest you know."

"What happened to your father and uncle?"

"Uncle Diotisalvi also fled in time, but died in exile some years later. My father... did not leave quickly enough."

"And you are still afraid of Florence?"

"To the best of my knowledge," Gian said dryly, "Lorenzo de' Medici has never rescinded his decree of death for any member of the Neroni family caught in Florence. And as our estates were confiscated and given to Medici supporters, I have had no reason to take the risk of returning. The man who recognized me at Urbino," he added, "was Paolo Uberti, who profited from our downfall. I think he was not pleased to discover that there was still a Neroni alive, but we did not exactly discuss the matter."

Caterina shook her head. "I wish you had told me earlier."

"Yes. I have been lying to you. Do you wish me to leave your service?"

"No! But if I had known, I would not have told that painter that you would go to Florence to get him some more lapis lazuli for the Virgin's robe. I thought, you see, that I could trust you to sell one of my rings quietly. Now I shall have to make Piero find the money some other way."

"Couldn't he sell the jewelry for you?"

Caterina smiled grimly. "He could indeed, and he might even get a tenth part of what it is worth —assuming he was not robbed on the way to Florence!"

"Well," said Gian, "I think you are being robbed without the trouble of going to Florence. How many days until the feast? Even if I did procure more lapis, the painter would scarcely have time to prepare it for use on your walls. He is probably trying to trick you into supplying his future needs."

This seemed, sadly, all too likely.

# ~CHAPTER FOURTEEN~

*To remove wine or other stains that contain no grease from silk: soak the fabric where it is stained, and for several inches around the stain, in the best verjuice, and it will be cleaned.*

*Probatum est. By this treatment I have restored my lord's favorite doublet after an accident with his wine cup.*

*-Caterina Rinaldi's Book of Secrets*

~ ~ ~

Niccolo's chestnut mare got him in trouble on the way to San Florian.

"I thought you prided yourself on your horsemanship!" Roberto Malatesta grumbled, the third time that the mare ignored Niccolo's yanks on the bridle to shoulder her way forward, next to his own horse.

"The mare used to be sensible!" Niccolo protested. "But for the last couple of weeks she's been acting possessed. You can hardly expect me to combat demons with spurs and bridle."

The mare underlined his point by whinnying and shoving up against Malatesta's leg.

"Well, take her back to the stables and find a mount that is not a demon in disguise," Roberto snapped. "And catch up with us when you have done so."

Niccolo had to yank on the bridle and use his whip to get the mare turned around and riding away from the festive group. He was beginning to think that his idea for satisfying the mage had not been quite so brilliant after all. When he'd arrived at his favorite inn only to be told that Betta of the long chestnut hair had gone to live with her mother in Milan, he'd panicked. It seemed better to come back with anything rather than confessing total failure, and anyway, he didn't believe in love charms operating at a distance; the mage was clearly exaggerating his powers.

Well, he hadn't believed in them then.

The mare made one or two energetic attempts to throw him and finally, subdued by whip and spurs, settled down to a grudging plod away from the object of her devotion.

Filippo Cacciote, riding discreetly behind the lord of Rimini, breathed a prayer of thanks when Niccolo left the group. He had been much too ready to accept the long hairs Niccolo had delivered wrapped in a scrap of silk. He should have known there was something wrong with them: too coarse, too bright. Well, now he knew why his love spell had failed to bring that woman to Rimini. And Niccolo would pay for the trick he'd played on him. Some time.

Assuming he survived their upcoming arrival in San Florian and the greeting from a stupid woman who not only thought she could rule a city, but who was not the slightest bit in love with Roberto Malatesta. He should have used his energy to put a really strong compulsion and favor spell on Malatesta instead of wasting his powers on love magic.

～～～

After spending the morning whisking from place to place in the palazzo, making sure that the banquet dishes were being prepared properly and that the rooms for Malatesta and his followers were appropriately grand, Caterina was more than willing to sit still in the hall and wait for her visitors. Fortunately Malatesta had agreed to bring only a small armed guard who could, he said, be housed in the city; he asked lodging only for himself and two members of his court.

She looked around the hall with no small measure of satisfaction. The murals so recently repaired by that Venetian painter looked even better than they had before the damages incurred in the looting; the little man's vanity was, perhaps, not undeserved. It would have been nice if she had had the money to have him add a *Procession of the Magi* with Girolamo as the leading wise man –a salutary reminder to her people about the folly of rebellion, that would have been, and a tasteful tribute to her late husband - but at least the walls were decently covered. She had taken out some lengths of plain and flowered silk that Girolamo had given her for dresses and had them tacked up to cover most of the bare spots. There had not been quite as much fabric as she'd thought; she'd meant to cover the last spot with some honey-colored brocade, but hadn't been able to find it. They'd had to make do with a faded tapestry that had previously been relegated to the attics.

She hoped her guests would not throw their food around and get stains on the finest piece, a dark red brocade embellished with gold embroidered dragons. That stuff could still make her a fine dress for the winter season, once the visitors from Rimini left, so she had placed it as far as possible from the dining tables. The muddy brown silk, on the other hand, was hung in the place of greatest danger, directly behind where Malatesta would be sitting. Many of Girolamo's gifts of fabric were in colors so unbecoming to her that she could bear the prospect of their getting spotted and wine-stained with equanimity.

She also wondered where Lucrezia was. She had expected her cousin, so bored by the quiet life in San Florian, would be eager to meet the visitors. But even now, as she heard a stir in the piazza and the jingling of harnesses, Lucrezia was not to be seen.

A page threw the palazzo doors open and announced, "Roberto Malatesta, Lord of Rimini!" and Roberto strutted into the hall, a middle-aged peacock in the crimson and white of Rimini, followed by two courtiers.

*The necromancer, and that vain page. Oh, this is not good.*

She heard steps on the staircase behind her, and the rustle of silk. "Welcome to San Florian, my lord," said a sweet voice. Caterina turned and saw her cousin, dressed in a new gown of honey-colored brocade that picked up and emphasized the gold of her hair.

Roberto Malatesta swept off his cap and executed a clumsy bow. "My lady, I have been grossly deceived by rumor."

Lucrezia laughed lightly. "Indeed? How?"

"I was led to believe that the lady of San Florian was not as beautiful as the angels and the sky."

Lucrezia laughed again. "You have been twice deceived, my lord. I am not the countess, but only her poor relation Lucrezia Rinaldi. You should direct your greetings toward my cousin."

Roberto finally looked at the woman sitting at the table. If this Lucrezia looked like an angel come to earth, the lady of San Florino looked like an old-fashioned painting not quite come to life. Her small oval face and slender frame were overshadowed by stiff garments heavy with embroidery and by jewelry that must have been designed for a larger woman: the principal ornament was a heavy gold chain ridiculously weighed down by an outsize scroll-shaped gold pendant nearly three inches long.

She did not look, he noted, the least bit happy to see him. That damned mage's love spell had been a total failure.

Caterina forced herself to endure the long, impertinent gaze without shrinking. At last she found her voice. "Allow me to introduce my cousin, Lucrezia *Contarini*. Her marriage is of so recent date, she sometimes forgets her new name."

Lucrezia swept past Caterina with a swish of silken skirts and seated herself by Malatesta. "Oh, that will not last. The marriage was a mistake; I am certain that the Pope will grant me an annulment." She darted a poisonous glance at Caterina. "The only issue is the retrieval of my dowry. Until that is done, I am truly a poor relation. Even my dress I owe to my cousin's charity."

Caterina supposed that was a reasonable translation of *I took this length of silk away from the servants decorating the walls and had it cut and stitched into a dress before Caterina found out.*

If she had known how much help Lucrezia was to be in entertaining the guests, she would have happily given her cousin any length of fabric from her chests —well —maybe not the red brocade figured with gold dragons, but anything else. For once, instead of carping and complaining, Lucrezia was exercising all her glamour to fascinate the lord of Rimini. And she could indeed be enchanting; for the first time Caterina understood why Ottavio

Contarini had been so bowled over as to take her in marriage despite the smallness of her dowry. She had not only beauty, but charm, when she chose to exercise it. She teased Malatesta, laughed at him, pretended to prefer the handsome Niccolo –and then, when his brow grew stormy, apologized so prettily that they were better friends than before.

Caterina looked wistfully down the length of the table. Seated just below the guests were the highest-ranking men in San Florian, the nobly born gentlemen who served on her council and who represented the city's interests to other states. Then came advisors like Piero Giacomini and, below even them, the captain of her guard. There had been some difficult discussion about even admitting a man with a common name like Bracciaforte to the banquet; was it not an insult to the lord of Rimini to expect him to share a table, no matter how long, with one so lowborn? Caterina had cut off the discussion with the flat statement that she would not sit in the same room with Roberto Malatesta without the head of her personal guard. No Gian Bracciaforte, she had said, no banquet, and her councilors could apologize to Malatesta.

But the low-ranking people at the foot of the table seemed to be having a lot more *fun* than she was, stuck up here between a sour-faced mage and a drunken lord. Oh well, she would just have to make the best of it.

"You are hardly eating, Maestro Cacciote," Caterina said to the mage. Despite his fine new black satin gown and the new rings on his fingers, the man looked as bilious as though he had been offered dogs' meat instead of a perfectly good dish of eels. "If the eels are not to your taste, perhaps you will take a morsel of the pigeon pie?"

The brittle puff pastry covering the stewed pigeons shattered under the mage's knife and strewed his black gown with a blizzard of little pastry flakes. He gave Caterina a venomous glance, as though she had somehow caused the accident.

"You would do better to exert yourself to please my master," he said in an undertone.

"I think my cousin is doing that quite adequately."

On the other side of the table, Malatesta was now inviting Lucrezia to visit him in Rimini for the purpose of choosing some fabrics which, he said, were set aside for her to select as a wedding present.

Lucrezia laughed sweetly. "You are a dangerous man, Roberto Malatesta. How you flatter and trick us poor females! Confess it, you had no notion who I was, nor that I had a husband in Venice, before this evening."

"I am infinitely richer for learning the first," said Roberto, "and poorer, alas! for the second."

"Fortunately," said Lucrezia, "the second will not much longer be true. My cousin has been dilatory in presenting my case to the Holy See, but as soon as she does so the Pope will certainly grant me an annulment. He was misled about Contarini's status; the man has not ambition enough to rise above his origins as a moneygrubbing merchant. I was supposed to marry a man who could be one of the Ten, not a dyer with stained fingers!"

As Gian had recommended, the wine flowed freely throughout the meal. By the time the castle of sugared pastry and marzipan was served, Caterina's guests were beyond appreciating the pastry cook's masterpiece, and she herself was more than ready to retire. Added to the predictable headache was a strange feeling of heat in her left arm. She rested that hand in her lap and toyed with some scraps while the visitors broke up the pastry, munching on battlements and feasting on delicately pointed turrets.

When she was finally able to excuse herself, Roberto Malatesta was close to falling asleep in a puddle of spilt wine and crumbling pastry. But when Caterina stood, he lurched to his feet and attempted a gracious bow to his hostess, and announced that he would drink to her hospitality. Raising a brimming goblet to his lips, he swayed backward, then forwards, and then collapsed across the table. The goblet sprang from his outflung arm, flew across the room in a graceful arc, and spattered against the red silk brocade on the far wall.

# ~CHAPTER FIFTEEN~

*And, in truth, fortresses are unserviceable in every way, since they may be lost either by the treachery of those to whom you commit their defence, or by the overwhelming strength of an assailant, or else by famine.*
*-Machiavelli, <u>Discourses on Livy</u>*

~ ~ ~

"I don't like it," Gian said abruptly.

Caterina looked up from her book. "What do you have against the secrets of Albertus Magnus?" she inquired, startled. She had already learned several useful things from this new acquisition, such as a way to cure a child of the cough by hanging a sponge around his neck, and a potion with the virtue to protect anyone from being burned by hot iron.

"Not the *book*," Gian said impatiently. "The *situation*. It's all very well for you to let your cousin ride over to Rimini until she spends more time there than she does here, but I should like to know what she's doing when she is with Malatesta."

Caterina thought she had a pretty good idea of what Lucrezia was doing, and Ottavio Contarini would certainly be unhappy if he found out about it, but she did not think that was her problem to solve. And life in San Florian was much more peaceful now that Lucrezia was occupied elsewhere. Besides –

"I do not think I can stop her," she pointed out. "She brought her own horse, her own maidservant and at least a few of her own clothes when she left Contarini's house."

"You could at least tell her that she is behaving scandalously!"

"Oh," said Caterina demurely, "is that what you think she's doing in Rimini? So do I, actually. But I do not see that anything would be improved by having a fight with her about it. And I am not sure I would stop her if I could –though that, I suppose, is a sin which I shall have to confess. You must agree that it is convenient to have two of my biggest problems keeping one another busy. Roberto Malatesta has stopped bothering me since Lucrezia began visiting him. She must have made him forget about his idea that San Florian should be his."

"I hope that is true," said Gian. "I wish I knew exactly what is going on in Rimini with those two."

"You would probably," Caterina said, "be extremely embarrassed if you had a magic mirror to show you what they do together. So it is as well that I do not propose to make one."

Gian took a turn about the room. "I don't like it," he repeated, rubbing the back of his neck. "Something is making my lucky angel unhappy, and I think it has to do with Lucrezia."

Caterina took the opportunity to distract him with a renewed debate on whether his luck was of angelic or demonic origin, and the subject of Lucrezia was dropped for the moment.

~~~

Lucrezia twirled around and around until she was entirely wrapped in the shimmering green taffeta.

"A sea goddess," Roberto Malatesta applauded. "I knew when I saw it that it would be criminal to let that silk clothe anyone but you."

Lucrezia pouted slightly. "In Venice," she said, "only the doge marries the sea, and he is an old man. As for Ottavio, if he looked at this taffeta he would not ask if I wanted it –he would ask how much the alum to fix the color had cost!"

"Need we remember your tiresome husband?" Roberto took the trailing end of the green silk and tugged slightly.

"I wish I could forget him! But I have not got my annulment yet." Lucrezia rose on her toes and let Roberto's pull on the silk turn her around and around until, dizzy and completely nude, she collapsed on the billowing green taffeta and smiled up at him.

"I mean to make you forget all about him," Roberto promised, and took her in his arms.

"Will you speak to the Pope for me?"

"Don't make demands," he said thickly. "I don't like demands."

Later, when they were sharing a carafe of wine chilled by blocks of snow brought from the mountains, he revisited the subject.

"We work well together, you and I," he said, stroking Lucrezia's flanks.

She tittered. "If you call *that* work…"

"No. I call it… anticipating the reward."

"You mean that you'll help me get my annulment?"

"Help me get San Florian," Roberto said, "and I promise to see you free of that boring Venetian merchant, one way or another."

Lucrezia pretended to shiver. "Ohhh… you do like to get your own way, don't you? But why should I help you take San Florian away from my stupid cousin?"

"Because she is only a woman, and somebody else is bound to take over the city, and you would like it to be a friend of yours?" Roberto suggested. "Or because it is mine by right, and I was cheated of my inheritance when her father died?" His hand slid up, passed over her breasts and paused at her throat. "Or because you want to return to San Florian as beautiful as when you left it? Think, silly girl. You are mine now —and I don't let what is mine defy me."

This time Lucrezia's shivers were unfeigned. "I don't believe you," she said. "You would not be cruel to *me*, 'Berto?"

"Not as long as you are mine," he said. "And if you are mine, then you will help me to what else is rightfully mine, and then… Ottavio Contarini will no longer be a problem for you."

"I knew you would help me!"

"As much as you will help me."

"But what can I do about San Florian? Caterina keeps a tight hand on power, and that mercenary she raised up from nowhere is always on guard."

"Oh? Has she taken him as a lover?"

Lucrezia giggled. "Oh, I didn't mean *that*. She is too much a little prude for that, and in any case…" she ran her fingers lovingly through her own unbound blonde locks, "I don't think he has ever seen her in that light."

"It would be a miracle if he could see her at all, next to you," Roberto said. "But if he is not with her at night, all the better."

"I don't see why…"

"You don't need to know all the details. You have only to play your part."

Roberto told her exactly what to do and how to do it. Lucrezia pouted and complained that he was asking too much, but a show of anger on his part got her to promise whatever he asked. "It is only because you love me so much that you get angry," she said, willing her words to be true.

"Of course, my angel. I love you so dearly that I long to lay both Rimini and San Florian at your feet."

~ ~ ~

"You see," Caterina told Gian a few days later, "you were worried about nothing. Lucrezia has been much easier to live with since she started visiting Rimini. All she needed was a handsome *cavaliere servente* to flatter her. If I'd realized that earlier, *you* could have…"

"No, I could not!" Gian interrupted her forcefully. Then he tried to make a joke out of it, "Gian Bracciaforte is not nearly highborn enough to set his eyes upon the lady. She would probably have asked you to hang me for insolence."

Caterina paused in her work. She was cutting another square from the lambskin parchment, and the task deserved her full attention –but it was more fun to tease the captain of her personal guard.

"Gian Bracciaforte may be beneath her notice, but what about Gian-Maria…"

"Don't!" They were seated in Caterina's tower workroom, she at the table and he straddling a bench. Now he got up and closed the door. "It is bad enough that one of the Uberti recognized me. If they hear that I am living here under my own name…"

"Yes, what if they do? You have not gone back to Florence; Leonardo has no grounds to seek your death."

"But Paolo Uberti has reasons to wish for it. I think he will feel less secure in his enjoyment of my estate now that he knows there is still a Neroni living. As for Lorenzo... ten years ago one of my father's friends who had been involved in the conspiracy managed to flee as far as Constantinople. Leonardo actually negotiated with the Turks to get him back to Florence and hang him. Just because he said any Neroni who returns to Florence is subject to the death penalty does not mean he won't kill any of us he finds out about, no matter where we are."

"Could you not go to Paolo Uberti and explain that you do not mean to contest the estates?"

"He would not believe me. Besides," Gian said, "it is not entirely true. As a boy I was in no position to do anything but run away. Now..."

"With a command of fourteen men," Caterina pointed out, "you are not exactly in a position to challenge a powerful Florentine family –particularly when even setting foot in Florence might be your death sentence!" She took up her sharp little knife and cut another perfect square from the parchment. There might be enough left for two more such squares. She hoped that would be enough.

Gian sighed heavily. "You are right. I still have no hope of regaining our lands. But... do you know, even now I dream about our country villa, with its cool arbor shaded by grapevines. We made wine from the grapes in the fields, but the ones hanging down through the rafters of the arbor were there for anyone who wished to pluck and eat. The air smelled sweeter there than anywhere else... And lately... there are other dreams which a Neroni might aspire to, but which are unthinkable for Gian of the made-up name, unsuccessful condottiere."

His eyes lingered on her face and, to her annoyance, Caterina felt a blush rising to her cheeks. The man had an annoying knack of making her forget that she was a sensible widow, regent to a young son, with no intention whatsoever of risking that son to a stepfather's mercies.

*I would not need to fear Gian.*

*Can you ever really know what a man is thinking? They are such queer creatures. What if Gian could use Ercole to help him regain his Florentine estates?*

It was an unpleasant line of thought. Caterina turned the discussion into a joke. "If you would like," she said sweetly, "I could recommend you to Lucrezia's notice."

Gian made the sign of the horns. "Angels forbid! I am very well as I am. Why are you making a new charm against magical attacks?"

She had not thought he noticed what she was doing, or that he would understand it. She slipped the first charm out of her sleeve.

"I think the power of this one may be close to exhausted." The brown writing on the formerly white parchment was all but obliterated; unfolded, the center of the square showed almost black, the corners brown, as though it had been held too close to a flame.

Gian crossed himself. "Roberto's pet mage?"

"I think so, yes. I first noticed it darkening after that banquet. Since then it has grown hot and darkened farther every few days."

"What does your book say about that?"

"Nothing. I have the instructions for how to make and wear the charm, nothing more. But it seemed wise to prepare a fresh one."

Gian touched the big, flawed emerald in the ring that refused to leave his finger. "There was an emerald brooch in your jewel casket. No mystical runes, but does not the emerald itself convey some protection against magic?"

"I never liked that brooch; it's an ugly design, and much too heavy for my taste. I had thought of selling it."

"I wish you would wear it anyway," said Gian.

~ ~ ~

There were three long days to go before the full moon, and Lucrezia found them extremely boring. But she did not want to go back to Rimini when dear Roberto was counting on her to follow his instructions here in San Florian, so she spent her days in embroidering a new veil with some gold thread she'd found in Caterina's sewing chest, and her nights in fevered fantasies of the future in which she was free of her Venetian husband and she and Roberto could be together always.

The only thing she had to do for the first two of those days was to send a little wine to the gate guards —not enough to make them drunk —with a message that Caterina's cousin was thinking of them and wished to relieve their boredom.

On the third night, when the moon was just beginning to show itself as a golden glow on the horizon, she poured the contents of the vial Roberto's mage had given her into the wine before sending her maid down to the gate with the usual message. She wondered if the soldiers would taste the extract of poppy that was to put them to sleep. Probably not; men like that didn't savor their drink, they gulped it down like greedy animals.

She herself did not sleep. She sent her maid to bed but sat up, watching the moon rise over the castle. One thing you had to say for this antiquated castle, she thought wryly; it was easy to find a place to wait where you were in no danger of nodding off. After a while, the bare stone of the seat built into the window made her bones ache as if she were an old woman. Get a cushion? No, she dared not become too comfortable for fear of missing her next task.

~ ~ ~

Elsewhere in the Rocca, other sleepers stirred and mumbled under the pale light of the rising moon. The well-born tossed in their beds; the servants stirred and rustled among the rushes on the floor. Only Caterina Rinaldi sat up, like Lucrezia, waiting for she knew not what. Lucrezia had been… strange… all that day; constantly glancing sidewise at Caterina, then giving a small secret smile. She must be up to something. But Lucrezia's concerns were invariably petty. It was hardly worth losing sleep just to wonder if she had stolen some finery out of Caterina's chests, or had started a flirtation with some handsome but ineligible man like one of Gian's soldiers.

The moon was high. A sensible woman would undress and get some sleep before the demands of the new day broke upon her. A sensible woman would close the shutters against the flood of silvery light; it must be the moonlight that was making her restless. Still Caterina sat up, fingering the chain that held her gold scroll pendant and thinking that any minute now she would wake Rosa and begin the process of removing her jewelry, cutting loose her sleeves, then putting off the rest of her dress. Any minute now…

On the floor below, Gian Bracciaforte stirred in his bed and opened his eyes to the white light of the full moon pouring in the window. He had been granted his own chamber in the Rocca to give him standing with the castle servants and his own men, but he was not entirely comfortable with the gift. A good captain should be with his men, should know what was going on with them, should hear what they joked about and what they avoided saying. Tonight, for some reason, that need seemed urgent. The back of his neck was tingling to the point of pain; it did not ease up until, sighing, he got up and pulled on his clothes. Perhaps his luck would be satisfied if he just checked up on the gate guards…

He stopped in the hall. The outer ward was full of stealthy noises, bits of metal jingling, hushed steps… the sound of armed men on the move. Gian slipped to the narrow window beside the door and peered out. The moonlight showed him two men on the ground and the small door in the gate standing open, men coming quietly through, far more men than he had; there must have been fifty already in the outer ward, and there were more coming through all the time. If the two on the ground were his, what could he and the remaining twelve others do in response to this invasion?

Years of life as a condottiere prompted the obvious answer.

Matteo, sleeping heavily on a bench in the hall, woke quietly when Gian shook his shoulder, came instantly to full awareness and nodded to indicate his understanding of Gian's finger laid across his lips. Gian spoke very low, directly into Matteo's ear. "A traitor –an army assembling in the outer ward –too late to stop them. You will go to them and offer your services. Make them think you and the other men were already bored and dissatisfied and that you would be only too happy to join a real army again."

Matteo raised himself on one elbow. "Are you coming with me, boss?"

"No."

"If you have some stupid idea of sacrificing yourself for your honor- "

"No, but I have something else to do."

He was on the move again before the words sank in, tiptoeing up the stairs while the prickling in the back of his neck warmed and hummed, *yes this way yes yes hurry…*

Caterina jumped when her bedroom door swung quietly open.

"Good," Gian said with a glance at her, "you're still dressed. Come with me."

"Where?"

"This way, but quietly!"

She did not think to question him.

They reached the hall, where Matteo was waking up the other men, and Gian drew her out the back way into the Rocca's small herb garden. There was a perilous flight of narrow steps hacked into the rock, hardly more than ledges enhanced with a bit of chisel work, connecting the garden with the stables below. In the time of Caterina's grandfather, she had been told, the stable boys brought fertilizer to the garden up this way in order to spare the gentry the sight and smell of baskets of manure being carried through the hall. But that custom had been abandoned after a boy slipped, fell, and was crippled for life. Her grandfather had decided that he would rather smell horse droppings than risk any more drains on his purse from pensions to injured servants.

Now Gian was urging her down those same stairs. She gritted her teeth, kilted up her full skirts and followed him. She could feel every crack, ridge, and pebble through her thin-soled indoor slippers. All the better! She would rather get her feet bruised than slip and break her neck. And if Gian thought they needed to get down these narrow steps by moonlight rather than face whatever was behind them, the need must be urgent indeed.

"Wait,' he breathed as they slipped into the stables. With quick, economical motions he saddled his horse. He looked at the next horse, then tensed as the sounds of men and armor reached him. Caterina realized that there was not time to saddle another horse, and raised her arms to help him lift her up. A moment later he was in the saddle before her. She put her arms around his waist and pressed her face to his back, and almost fell off in shock. Something totally unfamiliar seemed to have taken over her body, something sweet and intoxicating, a sense of pleasure unlike anything she'd known before.

*I shouldn't be feeling this way.*

*I can't let go; I'd fall.*

*Oh, if this is what Girolamo felt with his mistresses, how can I blame him for seeking joy?*

Gian walked the horse, ever so slowly, out the open stable door and around to the long sloping way down to the city. But partway down, he nudged the horse onto the steep hillside and away from the city walls. They had to go even more slowly now, as the horse picked its way through rough grass and stones. At the base of the hill they rejoined the road northwards. Gian eased the horse into a canter. "Go on, Bungler," he whispered. "Make what speed you can while the moonlight lasts."

"*Bungler?*" Caterina repeated.

Gian laughed. "I named my first horse Balius, after Achilles' steed. After the teasing I took for that act of monumental egotism, I have been careful to give my horses unassuming names. Granted, with this one I may have overdone it… Can you keep your seat if we gallop?"

The gallop, while it lasted, at least served to take her mind off the other sensations that plagued her.

# ~CHAPTER SIXTEEN~

*To obtain a spirit in the form of a horse:*
*On a Tuesday you should go to a secret place, taking with you a new bridle*
*and a nail. Draw a circle with the nail...*
*-Caterina Rinaldi's Book of Secrets*

~ ~ ~

Torches blazed against the dying moonlight; small groups of soldiers hurried this way and that through the passageways of the Rocca and herded the suddenly awakened inhabitants into a corner of the great hall. Only Lucrezia had the boldness to leave the little group. She walked up to Roberto Malatesta and would have kissed him, but he thrust her away. "Not now, Lucrezia! Where is your cousin? Did you warn her to flee?"

"My love, I would never betray you! She must have been warned by the black arts."

"Or by that commoner she made captain of her guard," Roberto grumbled. "I notice he too is nowhere to be found. That's small loss; his men are so disheartened that they want to change sides and serve me. But the woman? That's another pair of sleeves. You!" he barked at Filippo Cacciote. "Why did you not ward the Rocca so that she could not escape?"

"I did not know that the woman was important to you," Cacciote said. "I thought it was the Rocca that you desired, and behold, I have given it to you, and at no cost!" Unless you counted the two gate guards whom Lucrezia had poisoned. The silly woman had actually believed that the vial he gave her contained nothing worse than a strong solution of opium. As if he would risk the guards awakening!

"Fool! Do I want to defend this stinking rock against the Pope's armies? I heard he sent them on behalf of his nephew's widow after they killed her husband. They didn't even need to fight, they just showed themselves and the city surrendered. If she gets away and raises her people against us, who's to say he will not favor her again? I need to marry her to cement my claim!"

Lucrezia shrieked. "Marry her? Marry *her*? But it's me you love, 'Berto!" She burst into loud sobs.

"What does marriage have to do with it, you stupid woman? You never let your own marriage stand between us; my taking Caterina Rinaldi to wife will not impede my ability to enjoy your favors."

"But –but –you were going to get rid of my husband! And marry me! And we were going to rule together!"

Roberto casually backhanded her. She staggered back a couple of steps and her mouth opened in a cry of disbelief.

"Shut that woman up and get her out of my way," Roberto ordered one of his soldiers. "I can't *think* for her noise!" As the man clapped a hand over Lucrezia's mouth and pushed her towards the wall, he turned back to his other soldiers. "They've fled, but they cannot have gone far. I'll catch up with them before morning. You, you, you," he pointed at a dozen men, "come with me. The rest of you stay here, secure the Rocca and tell the city it is under new leadership."

"The horses are tired," objected one of the men he'd chosen to come with him.

"Take fresh ones out of the stables here!" Roberto snapped. "God's bowels, do I have to spell out every detail for you pismires? I want to be on the road to Urbino before the moon sets!"

"Maybe not," said Filippo Cacciote, prudently staying back out of Roberto's reach. "What if they have not fled to Urbino?"

"They must have done so. That woman is on such good terms with the Duke of Urbino that she has fostered her son with him. Where else would she look for support?"

"She might be desperate enough to offer San Florian to Florence… or even to Venice… in return for support against you."

Roberto yanked at his beard. "Stop confusing me! All right, if you are so wise, divine their path, but do not be all night about it!"

Florence was the closest city where they might take refuge, but Cacciote had never heard that San Florian had particularly good ties with the Medici. Most likely they were indeed heading south for Urbino, but it would cost only a few minutes to make sure. Filippo Cacciote sketched a map on the table with the dregs from a wine cup. He suspended a ring from Caterina's abandoned jewels by a hair found on her pillow, and three times he saw the ring sway to the northeast.

"Venice," he said firmly. "They are making for Venice."

~~~

Bungler went lame on a stretch of rough road between two villages. Gian dismounted and knelt, felt the bad leg and looked unhappy. "Old fellow, you've served me well in battle and on the road; why did you have to betray me now?" He looked up at Caterina. "Can you stay on if I lead him?"

"Of course I could," said Caterina, sliding down off the horse's back, "but that would be bad for his leg. I don't want to see a good horse ruined."

"Better him than us," said Gian.

"Just wait a minute." Caterina drew a small, squarish book out of the bosom of her gown and squinted at it. "This is hard to read by moonlight. Let's get off the road and out of sight first?"

There were several clumps of trees and bushes in the rocky, uncultivated land to the west of the road. One of them was even large enough to conceal their horse.

Caterina ignored Gian for a few minutes, moving her lips slowly with her nose almost on the written words. "Oh. That one takes three days…"

"Whatever you're thinking about doing," Gian said with restraint, "I do not think we have three days to do it in. It will not have taken Malatesta long to discover that you're gone. Our only real hope is that he thinks we have gone south to Urbino, and doesn't even bother looking for us in the north."

"I am thinking about making a horse appear," Caterina informed him, "but unfortunately this spell requires three days to complete. I may have another one... oh, no, it requires a bridle that has never been used, and it can only be done on a Tuesday."

"Oh," said Gian, "I think I can make a horse appear in somewhat less time than that. Wait here!" He took Bungler's reins and was gone before Caterina could ask him what he had in mind. She hoped his luck would keep him safe.

The night grew darker as she waited; the moon was setting now. She could not have read instructions from her Book of Secrets even if she had been able to find a spell. What a pity that she did not have one ready prepared against this eventuality! Somehow, in all her preparations to elude another pursuit, the mundane usefulness of being able to produce a spare horse had escaped her.

She sat so still that every rustle in the bushes sounded like a soldier from Rimini, rising out of the earth to capture or kill her. She sat so long that her legs began to cramp under her and a traitorous part of her mind began to scream *Run away! Get up and run away! He's not coming back! Don't just sit here and wait to be killed!*

If Gian had betrayed her, she thought bleakly, she might as well give herself over to Malatesta's henchmen. If Gian had betrayed the trust she placed in him, she was an idiot who had no business trying to rule. In any case, she should not have run. She should have stayed in the Rocca, where she might have been able to protect her people from the worst excesses of the usurper. What was happening to Tommaso Peruzzi right now? Piero Giacomini? Lucrezia? Rosa?

*You can't walk back, can you? So you might as well wait. And try to hope.*

When she heard the unmistakable sound of horses drawing near, she was so stiff that she nearly fell when she jumped up. *Whatever it is, I will face it standing.*

"It" turned out to be Gian, seated bareback on a lean, rawboned bay mare and leading a second horse with his saddle on it. Caterina felt just mildly silly about all the terrors her dramatic imagination had concocted. Of course she hadn't really thought Gian would betray her. She had just been indulging her bad habit of trying to predict the worst possible outcome to any situation, in the hope that she would feel able to bear whatever happened.

"How did you do that?" she demanded.

"Very quietly," Gian said with a grin. "At last some of my military experience comes in handy. I may not be able to conjure up demons, but I am able to find a couple of horses." He gave his mount a friendly slap on the neck. "I suppose it would have been too much to expect a couple of *good* horses in this wilderness."

"You just happened to find a stable. That was unlocked and unguarded. And that housed two horses. That made no noise when you led them away."

"That's the nature of my luck," Gian agreed. "It guided me to the right place. Although I would claim some skill entered into it as well. And it would have been nice if there'd been a spare saddle in the stable... although I shouldn't complain; at least there was a bridle for this fellow."

"So your luck encourages stealing?"

"No such thing," Gian protested. "I left my Bungler in the stable. He's a serious horse, a gentleman's horse, trained for war; worth a dozen of peasant nags like these. If the farmer has any sense, he'll sell Bungler discreetly and keep quiet about the exchange."

"What if Malatesta's men hear about your horse turning up at a farm north of San Florian?"

"We had better," Gian said, "be in Venice before that particular piece of gossip reaches them."

But the farm horses, although well enough behaved, did not have the stamina for more than a few minutes at a trot, and there was no question of galloping them. "Trained for pulling loads, not for speed," Gian grumbled. "And half starved! I half wish I had kept Bungler after all. He could have kept up with us indefinitely at this pace if he didn't have to carry anybody."

"It's too dark now to go any faster anyway," Caterina said. The last light of the moon shone across the road before them, turning pebbles and tufts of grass into monstrous elongated shadows and hiding dangerous ruts.

"Tell that to the fellows behind us. *They* brought spare mounts."

Caterina caught her breath. When she was silent, listening as hard as she could, she could just hear the sounds of a group of riders behind them. They were closing rapidly.

She caught up the mirror that hung from her belt, tugged it loose, turned in the saddle and threw it down in the road behind them.

~ ~ ~

Roberto Malatesta yanked at his horse's reins just in time to prevent it from riding straight into the lake that covered the road. "Where did this come from?"

"Must have been a storm," the nearest soldier suggested. The sky was clear now, but who was to say it had been so a few hours earlier? This had to be the result of heavy rains flooding the road.

"Fools of peasants," Roberto grumbled, "they don't even maintain ditches to control the flooding after a rainstorm. How deep is it?"

One of his men dismounted, picked up a pebble and threw it as far as he could. The rock sank without a sound... and sank... and sank.

"The road must dip low here," Roberto decided. "Very well, we'll go around it. That woman must have had to do the same thing, so we won't lose time by the detour. I'll wager we pick up her tracks along the verge."

The moon had all but set; it was too dark to test his theory. They rode on in silence, the horses picking their way delicately over rough country full of bushes and rabbit holes. To their right, the countryside was dark and silent; to their left, the lake was a dark mirror of the night sky, full of trembling stars. Suddenly it vanished, leaving them in darkness and far from the road.

"*Merda!*" Roberto swore. "Wizardry!" He should have brought his mage, but he hadn't wanted to be slowed down by an inexperienced rider, nor to hear the mage whining about the pace and the length of the ride. Who would have thought the woman had a mage of her own? No wonder she favored the captain of her guard so much. This had to be his work.

They lost precious time finding the road again, and they had hardly gone a league before they were halted again, this time by a sinister forest of bare trees whose thorny branches twined together like a wall. The lead riders' horses shied, terrified by the sudden appearance of this wood where a moment before there had been nothing but the road and the fields on either side.

"Don't pull up!" Roberto shouted. "You cowards, it's nothing but more wizardry!"

"It feels very real," said one of the leading men. He had drawn his sword to hack away the branches in front of his face; now it was wedged in the thorny tree and resisting all his attempts to withdraw it.

"So does a dream," growled Roberto. "Am I leading men? Or children who cry about their nightmares?" He lowered his head and spurred his horse to charge headlong into the wood.

The horse balked. It stood, legs stiff, head thrown back, while Roberto laid into it with his whip. Neither whip nor spurs seemed to frighten it as much as the shadowy shapes before it. When the wood began to come alive with little wandering lights between the trees, several of Roberto's men retreated to a safer distance.

"Fools!" Roberto snapped. "I tell you, it's not real! When I catch up with that woman's pet mage, I'll hang him in a cage from the top of the Rocca."

The man whose sword had been caught by the trees crossed himself furtively as the wood dissolved. Roberto's horse suddenly discovered the power of motion, and the group galloped on.

Most of the group.

The three men at the back looked at one another and silently turned back. They had hired on to fight men, not wizards and demons. If their lord never came back from this ill-omened excursion, they would have to find a new contract. And if he did come back, having discovered their desertion... It seemed a good time to start looking for that new contract. One heard that the condottiere duke in Urbino was always looking to expand his forces...

~ ~ ~

Caterina's heart sank when she heard the sound of galloping behind them once again. The comb had not delayed the pursuit nearly as long as the mirror; she had been too tired to maintain the illusion. And she could not pause to look for more solutions, even if it had not been too dark to read her book. There was no help for it; she would have to deploy the spell which she had hoped never to use, the one encapsulated in the longest scrolled pendant on her necklace. The one which had never been tested; the one that would see her torn apart by demons if she had guessed wrong.

"Wait," she hissed at Gian.

He paused and waited for her to come up beside him.

"You should get off the road," he said in a low voice. "Hide in the bushes. I will delay them. I can tell them I fled on my own account and I suppose you to be in Urbino by now."

"They will kill you."

"Maybe not."

Caterina leaned towards him. "I have one thing left to try, but it won't work unless you kiss me first." She was not going to risk death by demons before she found out what it was like to kiss somebody she actually loved.

It should have been ludicrous and awkward, two people who had barely even touched leaning from horseback to press their lips together.

It wasn't.

It was fire and glory and joy, and it made her even more reluctant to leave this world. But she had to risk all to give them a chance of survival. Breaking away from Gian, she tugged at the scroll-shaped pendant she had prepared in advance for the worst emergency. Infuriatingly, the link that joined it to the chain held. She yanked it again and the chain itself came loose, collapsing over her hand. She threw the whole thing, chain and pendant, behind them, calling out the names of the demons whom she had tried to trap within the illusion.

~ ~ ~

Suddenly the pursuers heard the sound of men and horses advancing, the clanks and thuds and shouts of an entire army on the march. They were coming from the eastern side of the road. Roberto swore. "That must be the papal army! But how did they learn of our move so soon? I haven't even held San Florian for a full night! The wizard must have told them!"

The eight men remaining with him looked at each other with faces that were pallid in the darkness. If the Pope had indeed been warned by wizardry that his city was conquered, if he had been able to muster his army on such short notice, what hope was there for them?

A flight of arrows hissed overhead, and a hundred voices shouted, "You cannot escape your death today!"

"Back!" cried one of Roberto's chosen men, and they fled back down the road they had traversed. There was no point in trying to please their lord by capturing the woman when he was about to die, and even less point in dying with him. If they could but gain the safety of the Rocca they might be able to hold out against this army.

"Cowards! Traitors! Your mothers were whores!" Roberto shouted after them. "It's only another illusion!"

This time the arrows were aimed lower, hissing right past his face. If the army was an illusion, it was an extremely good one. Best to take himself out of the way until it dissolved like the lake and the thorny forest. Robert spurred his horse northwards. If those whoreson soldiers didn't have the guts to follow him, he would take the woman by himself. First he would capture her captain-mage and shackle him in iron to prevent any more illusions, and then he would make the two of them follow him with ropes around their necks.

The army followed him, drawing ever closer. But there was a walled castle just ahead, and the gates swung open as he approached, mutely offering sanctuary. Robert slashed his whip across the horse's flanks to force it to one last burst of speed, heard its hooves drumming on the wooden drawbridge, and drew it up, foam-flecked and panting, inside a beautiful courtyard lit by torches and wreathed with sweet-smelling flowers.

Behind him, the gates swung shut.

# ~CHAPTER SEVENTEEN~

*Italy hath a generation of empiricks called monti banchi for mounting banckes or litle scaffolds. They proclame their wares upon these scaffolds, and to drawe concourse of people they have a zani or foole with a visard on his face, and sometymes a woman, to make comicall sporte. The people cast their hand kerchers with mony to them, and they cast them backe with wares tyed in them. The wares they sell are commonly distilled waters and divers oyntments for burning aches and stitches and the like, but espetially for the itch and scabbs, more vendible than the rest. Many of them have some very good secrets, but generally they are all cheaters.*
*-Fynes Moryson, An Itinerary Containing His Ten Yeeres Travell Through the Twelve Dominions of Germany, Bohmerland, Sweitzerland, Netherland, Denmarke, Poland, Italy, Turkey, France, England, Scotland and Ireland*

~~~

While the bulk of the Turkish army remained at Otranto, a separate force landed much farther north, in Friuli, at the head of the Adriatic. Under the *sanjakbey* of Bosnia, Iskender Bey, they struck deep into Friuli. Geronimo Novello, the Venetian commander, lost both his life and a decisive battle to the Turks, leaving the Turkish forces less than forty miles from Venice. They plundered and destroyed as far inland as the Piave river; during the day the Venetians watched the smoke of burning villages from the rooftops of their palaces, and at night the northeastern horizon was reddened by the Turkish fires. For once the Ten moved quickly, assembling a force of infantry and cavalry to march to the relief of Friuli. At the same time they sent messages to the Venetian *bailo* at Constantinople, urging him to remind the sultan that the district of Friuli was a Venetian possession and that the sultan was therefore breaking the newly-signed peace treaty.

~ ~ ~

Cousin Lucrezia had described Venice as a center of gaiety and pleasurable entertainments, contrasting it unfavorably with the dull life of little San Florian. To travel-stained and weary travelers, without money in their purses or friends to call upon for aid, the city presented a less glowing aspect; it seemed to be a maze of stinking canals bordered by narrow walkways and crossed by little hump-backed bridges, both built of very hard stone.

Gian had planned to sell their borrowed horses upon arrival, giving them enough ready cash to procure not only lodgings and food, but clean clothes in the style befitting his lady's rank. But the horses were in such poor condition that he got barely enough for their immediate needs.

"I think you were cheated," Caterina said. "The horses weren't *that* bad."

"Yes, they were," said Gian. "But it's true," he sighed, "I am not a very good bargainer."

"Isn't that difficult for a man of your profession?" The very name *condottiere* meant, literally, "contractor."

"Well. All I ever had to do was follow the terms agreed upon, and fight our employer's enemies when it couldn't be avoided. My commander was always in charge of the negotiations." Gian sighed. "A pity that he wasn't nearly as good at battles as he was at squeezing money out of a client. After a while we got the name of a force that cost more than it was worth... Well, that doesn't matter. We will ask around; a city this size must employ a large force of condottieri, and it will go hard if there are not some among them who have served with me and who will give us lodging and credit."

His initial inquiries were discouraging. Everyone he asked told the same tale: the Turks were in Friuli, all the fighting men Venice could scrounge up had gone to defend the province, "and," finished more than one interlocutor, "I'm leaving Venice myself, today, before it becomes the next jewel in the Turk's turban!"

"If I'd known how many people want to get out of Venice," Gian grumbled, "I could have sold our horses to two of them for a better price."

"We still have this," said Caterina, touching the folds of cloth beneath which the emerald brooch lay concealed.

"And you," said Gian, "are still the target of that murderer Roberto Malatesta, with his pet mage! How else did they know to pursue us along the Venice road? Even though we got away, don't you think they will still be after us? God knows what devilish attacks the mage may attempt. I read what your Albertus Magnus had to say about the virtues of emeralds against magic. You're not taking that brooch off."

From somewhere ahead of them there came the strains of music, the sound of laughter, the enticing smell of sausages roasting. "It must be a feast day," Caterina hazarded as they turned towards the sounds and smells.

Gian grinned, looking suddenly younger than he had since their midnight flight began. "No. I think it's the grand piazza –the Piazza San Marco. I've been told that it never sleeps."

*Neither do we*, Caterina thought through the haze of her exhaustion. She would not complain to Gian, but at the moment she would have been willing to trade the entire contents of his purse just to lie down in a quiet corner and sleep.

Across one of the ubiquitous hump-backed foot bridges, and down one more narrow footpath, and the Piazza San Marco opened before them, with the green waters of the Grand Canal shimmering like a narrow sea at its far side. Some of the Venetians might be shivering with fear of the Turk and planning to sneak out of town, but there were still plenty left to enjoy a bright autumn day in the style of the Most Serene City. Near the steps of the basilica a group of fiddlers made music for a woman dancing on a rope; beside them, a pilgrim begged alms for the conversion of the Turkish infidels. Beyond that a man in scarlet held up two ropes, one in each fist. No, not ropes –they were living snakes, twisting and writhing in the air. Caterina shuddered and averted her eyes as he opened his mouth wide and moved one of the snakes' heads toward his face.

There were plenty of other sights to enjoy. Here, a miniature pointed tent of damask shaded a table on which a man was shuffling three overturned goblets with gestures too quick to follow, while a country fellow in undyed wool threw down his coins; there, a puppeteer shouted out the lines of a bawdy ballad while he made a little woman of wood and satin dance in time to the verses. Close by them was a narrow stage where a fair-haired man in sweeping robes of figured green silk gestured widely and proclaimed himself Luigi il Capello d'Oro, the world's greatest living empiric. He boasted of the efficacy of his marvelous elixir, guaranteed to cure any and all ailments up to and including death itself, could it but be administered in time. The Grand Turk himself had been cured by this elixir!

The crowd applauded this announcement. A nearby competitor, on a somewhat smaller stage, jeered at Il Capello d'Oro and tried to drown out the high points of his peroration by beating a drum and urging his assistant to blow the largest horn. A woman with a lute scowled at the noisy medico and directed her masked servants to move her chair farther away from him. Caterina stared shamelessly at her; she thought she had never seen anything so beautiful as this black-haired woman in a low-cut crimson dress, with her high-heeled red shoes and her hair dressed with dozens of little tinkling bells. As if aware of her gaze, the lute player raised her head, looked directly back at Caterina and gave her a little smile, as if inviting her to come closer.

Caterina took a step forward, but Gian's hand closed on her arm. "*You* do not talk to women like *that*," he said firmly.

"Oh, is she a… But how do you know? Do you know her?" It would be a jest of the blackest sort if Gian's only acquaintance in Venice turned out to be a prostitute.

"I don't need to," Gian said. "That is how all *meretrici* dress, with high-heeled shoes and bells in their hair. It's the law, so that no one shall mistake them for honest women. Have you never been anywhere?"

"I went to Rome once, to meet Girolamo's uncle. The Pope." *And to sit alone, trying to look as if I did not mind, while Girolamo sported with Madelena Gonzaga.*

"Oh, well, you probably wouldn't have seen any prostitutes in the Vatican," Gian allowed.

"I wouldn't say that," Caterina murmured, thinking of La Gonzaga.

"Not official ones, anyway, like this woman in red."

"I expect," Caterina said demurely, "that this one is very successful. She is so beautiful —more beautiful even than Lucrezia."

While they were talking, there was a bustle behind them that caught Caterina's attention. She turned to see a formerly bare white-painted platform being decorated with a canopy of gold-fringed dark blue velvet at the back. Painted canvases hung on the velvet background, some showing coats of arms, others depicting learned physicians in conference, and still others frankly bawdy. Suddenly a tall, white-haired man in a long gown of black velvet, with a heavy gold chain around his neck, parted the blue curtains and strode to the center of the stage. Gian gasped and Caterina smiled to herself. So even her worldly-wise captain was not above being surprised!

Musicians had been filing around the sides of the stage; now, to a blast of trumpets and drums, the man in black raised both his arms for quiet and began speaking. "People of Venice! Today you are privileged to hear the greatest physician of the age. The deeds of Agostino Foscari, Il Scampamorte, the Death-Defying, have been praised in the courts of France and England, Milan and Naples, in the Holy Roman Empire and in the lands of the Turk, for all nations have benefited from the secrets of medicine which I now bring home to Venice, my beloved native city. I —"

He had been glancing over the gathering crowd as he spoke; now his eyes fell upon Gian and Caterina and he paused for just a moment.

"My musicians and dancers will now entertain you while I prepare to display my miracles of healing."

Caterina felt almost sure that was not what he had been going to say. But the musicians took up the hint and struck up a lively tune, and two gaily dressed midgets were lifted up to the stage to begin strutting and prancing while the great physician retreated back behind the blue velvet curtains. A small mountain of a man with a face to frighten children tapped Gian's shoulder and gestured for him and Caterina to follow him behind the stage. There was a small curtained-off area there, where a young woman with a sour expression was lacing herself into a pair of men's hose beneath a tunic too short and tight for modesty. Agostino Foscari ignored her and swept forward to envelop Gian in a tempestuous embrace.

"Bracciaforte! So you came out of the affair at Altoviti all right! And you're better dressed than a condottiere has any right to be. You must have fallen upon flowers, as the saying goes!"

"Not quite so much," Gian said. "I was, in fact, almost ready to pawn my doublet for a meal."

Foscari's bushy white brows went up. "What's this? Have you been having attacks of conscience again? Haven't I told you that a conscience is only a liability for a man of your profession?" He bowed to Caterina. "Madonna, in the name of our future friendship —for anyone who travels with Bracciaforte I count as a friend - I must advise you that this man should follow the ways of peace to make his fortune. No barber-surgeon in Italy can boast of such good results as he has shown, just by treating his wounded on the battlefield with no special tools and no unguents, nothing but simples and common sense. And yet the silly fellow persists in wounding others and risking himself, just because he thinks that soldiering is a noble profession and surgery a common one."

"At the moment I should be grateful for any honest work," Gian said.

"Then you have come in a good hour!" Foscari drew back slightly and looked him over from head to toe. "And there is a story here! I, Agostino Foscari, I can sense it! Well dressed, but hungry as a young wolf, and accompanied by a noble lady who seems about to drop from weariness —I must hear it all, and at leisure! You know my house, beside the church of San Silvestro? Oh, no, you do not know Venice. Well, ask at the Rialto for the House of the Crocodile and anyone can show you the way." He took a narrow gold ring from one finger. "Show my servants this ring, and tell them I said that you were to be lodged and fed in the best style. After I finish this day's work I shall return home; you will be rested by then, and I want to hear everything!" He turned back towards the stage, but added over his shoulder, "And stay within doors until my return; it would not do for you to be seen by too many people!"

"Do you suppose he meant Malatesta's men?" Caterina asked as they left the piazza.

Gian frowned. "Could they have reached here so soon?"

"I think not," said Caterina. "The last illusion was a lasting one; it does not require my essence to maintain it."

"Indeed! I thought that was impossible."

"It was an idea I had. Only I was not sure… it might have worked as I intended, or it might have failed completely. In which case the demons would have taken me as soon as I invoked it."

"Does that mean I shall have to wait until we are threatened by demons before you give me another kiss?"

Caterina smiled at the memory. "Maybe you should ask your luck about that," she evaded.

Gian automatically rubbed the back of his neck. "Well, it's not warning me away from Venice, so I don't think there's any danger of my being recognized here as a Neroni. But if he didn't mean Malatesta, and he didn't mean the Medici, just who *doesn't* he want to see me?"

The charlatan's house was modest compared to the palazzi lining the Grand Canal, but it was sturdy and comfortable enough to seem palatial to Catherine after the flight from San Florian. Granted, the entrance was somewhat intimidating. Foscari's reference to the House of the Crocodile had not been in the least metaphorical; an eleven-foot stuffed reptile was mounted just over the door. But the servant who opened the door to them was all smiles at the sight of his master's ring, and ushered them into a large front room with shelves and drawers on all the walls. Bundles of herbs hung from the ceiling and bottles of oil stood atop the shelves, and a customer was looking through a tray of sharks' teeth. While the servant withdrew to see to a meal and a room for them, Caterina wandered round the room, fascinated by the wealth of medical and magical supplies. Her own workroom had never been half so well furnished! But she did not envy Foscari's tastes in decoration. A yellowing horn that tapered in a spiral to a sharp point, a stuffed lizard with a scorpion's tail, and a three-foot spiny fish skeleton with monstrous fanged jaws were displayed on the walls. Two of the three would have given her nightmares, and she thought the unicorn's horn should have been locked away from thieves.

"My dear lady, no one steals from Il Scampamorte," Foscari told her when they shared a meal in the late evening.

"Oh, do you have all these things charmed against thievery? Does not that make it difficult if someone wishes to buy something while you are out? Surely your servant is not competent to lift the charm."

Foscari's bushy white brows flew up. "I have never heard of such a charm. I meant only that I am so respected in Venice that my house and goods are quite safe. What did *you* mean?"

"I am sorry. I meant —I have heard of such charms —and I thought a gentleman of your great learning would have…"

Foscari's eyes remained fixed on her face. "We must speak of this again," he said when she stumbled into silence. "But first, there is a matter for me to settle with your companion." He turned to Gian. "Did you hear how brazenly that quack, that false empiric who calls himself the Golden-Haired, lied? Curing the Grand Turk, indeed! I suspect he has never so much as been in the Middle Sea, much less all the way to Constantinople, and he has certainly never had an audience with the sultan! But he draws in the gullible with such exotic claims, and I —well, I require something even more exotic to draw them back to me!"

"What, are not dancing midgets, a pretty girl in doublet and hose, and your other entertainments enough to command attention?"

Foscari waved one hand dismissively. "Oh, I can still draw the eyes of the masses. But that quack draws their money. They would rather throw away good *scudi* on colored water that comes, they think, with the recommendation of the Grand Turk, than heal themselves of every ailment with my incomparable elixir! In short, I need an actual Turk to put the lie to him and draw their attention back to me —so you see, my dear Bracciaforte, why I said that you were come in a good hour!"

Caterina was totally bemused. "But he's not…"

"Madonna," said Foscari, "in our business, what *is* matters less than what is *believed*." He bestowed a benevolent smile on Gian. "You told me once that your knowledge of Turkish might come in handy some day; neither of us, I think, guessed that it would be through me that you benefited! You shall dress *alla Turchescha* —I think I have a turban in the storeroom, and one can always purchase a curved sword from the theatrical suppliers —and, as a Turk who has seen the light and accepted Christ as his savior, you can testify to the many great and curious secrets of Turkish medicine which I have learned."

"When did you learn Turkish?" Caterina blurted out.

"A long time ago," Gian said. "When I was a boy serving in Urbino, there came a Turkish *converso* to court seeking alms, and Duke Federico paid him to tutor me and two other pages in the language. For, he said, the only treasure which cannot be taken from one is knowledge."

"And you see how right he was!" Foscari beamed.

"No, I don't," said Gian. "That was twelve years ago. I've forgotten most of what I learned, for a condottiere does not spend much time chatting with the enemy. And in any case I was never fluent enough to pass as a Turk among Turks."

"But I am not asking you to do that," said Foscari, sounding very reasonable. "I am only asking you to pass as a Turk among Venetians —a very different pair of sleeves! And that is why I wanted to get you out of sight as quickly as possible. You can hardly appear as Yusuf the Turk if you have been wandering the city as Gian Bracciaforte."

Gian frowned. "Has it occurred to you that the Turks are not especially popular in Venice at the moment? The business in Friuli —"

"A Turkish warrior would not serve my purpose at all," said Foscari. "But a Turk who has seen the light of Christ, and who is willing to impart all the secrets of the East to the faithful, will be a tremendous draw. Trust me for that!"

He turned to Caterina. "And you, Countess, can also lend your talents to my little business. Betta —the girl who parades around in tight hose —catches the commoners' eyes, but she cannot pass for a noble lady. You will credit my secret unguents for your beauty, and the little boxes will fly into the hands of gentlemen whose wives will send them to make the purchase!"

"Beauty?" Caterina repeated, disbelieving. "Me?" It seemed to her extremely unlikely that anyone would pay good money to look like her. He needed Lucrezia!

"Madonna, with all respect, I think that you have never studied the art of presenting yourself to best advantage. Whoever gave you that mustard-colored gown should be hanged. He should rather have given you jewels to show off the curve of your cheek and the shine of your eyes. Presently we shall investigate my storeroom and find something better for you. In the meantime, let me urge you to take a little more of the roast quail, and wash it down with this white Trebbiano. The wine will restore your strength and color."

After the meal, Gian put a hand on Caterina's arm as she rose to follow Agostino Foscari. "You don't have to do this."

"What, should I sit back and embroider while you work to keep us both?"

"That's different. You're a noble lady. It's not right that you should be displaying yourself in a bawdy street show."

"Dear boy," Foscari's voice boomed from the hall, "there is nothing tawdry about the excellent and improving demonstrations which I devise to entertain my customers."

"I said *bawdy!*" Gian shouted.

"Nor that neither! Now let the lady see what costumes I can offer her, and let her make her own decision!"

Once Caterina had begun looking through the contents of the big chests in Foscari's storeroom, she felt that she would be quite well able to sustain whatever part he wished her to play if she could do it in a matching skirt and bodice of yellow silk with gold lace, paired with cloth-of-gold sleeves. Or there was a wine-red damask dress, just the color of the red brocade Roberto Malatesta had stained at the banquet, with a flesh-pink underdress of transparent sendal embroidered in silver.

"That one is much too low-cut," Gian grumbled about the yellow silk.

"Well, this one isn't," said Caterina. "Look, the undershift goes all the way up to my throat." She held the pink sendal shift up against her body.

"Worse," said Gian. "It will make people think you are naked to the nipples on first sight, and then they will think about nothing else."

"Hopefully," Caterina said, "they'll think about how their wives would look in such garments, and then they will buy them a present –like Dottore Foscari's unguent, or even my own beauty water, for which I have an infallible recipe."

"And what if you're recognized?"

"As you pointed out," said Caterina, "I've never *been* anywhere. So who's to recognize me? Besides, I will look quite different in these clothes, and with my hair loose." She glanced at Foscari. "Could you find me a mirror and a comb? I... lost... mine in our flight."

"You're not wearing your hair loose," Gian said, "you're not wearing those extremely improper clothes, and you're not exhibiting yourself in public on a mountebank's stage! I forbid it!"

Caterina gave him a smile modeled on one of Lucrezia's nauseatingly sweet expressions. "And you, dear sir, are not my husband and have no authority to forbid me to do anything!"

The resulting fight raged up and down the stairs of Agostino Foscari's house and brought the admiring attention of his neighbors to these newcomers who had such a way with words. The old widow who lodged across the square said that they sounded exactly like the nobility, and she should know, having served in the household of the old Doge fifty years ago!

# ~CHAPTER EIGHTEEN~

*To destroy an illusion, it is usually sufficient to call upon the holy name of Christ. But he who does that had best fast for three days beforehand, confess himself before attempting the work, and otherwise ensure that he is in a state of grace; for the slightest sin will provide an opening through which the demons of the illusion may devour him.*

*-from the notes of Filippo Cacciote*

~ ~ ~

Roberto Malatesta was haunted by a nagging feeling that he ought to be somewhere else, doing... he was not sure what... but something very important. Oh well –that was the nature of life when you were the lord of a great city like... what was its name again? No, he was lord of *two* cities...

To hell with it! Ruling was a hard and lonely calling, and a man was entitled to relax now and then and enjoy the hospitality of good neighbors like these. True, he could not quite recall having heard of a great castle like this on the Venice road, but there was no need to cudgel his memory. The castle obviously existed, and his host would doubtless introduce himself whenever he appeared. And there was no hurry about that either, for Roberto had seldom been better entertained than here. The servants all seemed to be slim creatures with big dark eyes and great hanging loops of dark hair twined with crystals, dressed in gowns of silk so light and fine that a man could almost see every detail of their lovely bodies... except that they kept moving, and the light kept changing. In a minute he would get up and grab one of them and explore her body at leisure… if only he were not so hungry and thirsty! He thought he had been eating and drinking for hours, feasting on the most delicious viands and the finest wines, and yet his belly was empty and his throat was dry. Clearly he had only been in the castle for a few minutes!

One of the dark-eyed sylphs filled his goblet; he snatched it up and drank thirstily, then grabbed a roast leg of fowl and gnawed the rich, moist meat. A fine place, this, and some compensation for that barren rock called San Florian. Why even go back there, to live on sour wine and tough mutton and to put up with the screeching of Lucrezia? The girls here were much more to his taste; they did not speak at all. Neither did the pages who were continually bringing in more and finer dishes, peacocks dusted with gold and marzipan knights and little houses of blanched almonds set in a tracery of sugar. And somehow his trencher was already laden with all these delicacies! Roberto lounged in his chair and listened to someone playing the lute, someone else singing a sweet wordless song, while he bit the head off a marzipan bishop. He would get up when he was ready…

~ ~ ~

A small, unhappy group gathered in one of the few private rooms of the Rocca San Florian. It had been two days since Roberto Malatesta conquered the castle and immediately left in pursuit of the Rinaldi woman. It had been two very long days since anyone had heard a word about the fortunes of Malatesta and the dozen soldiers who had accompanied him on that midnight pursuit. Luca Portinari, his castellan, was fretting over leaving Rimini practically undefended; he wanted to send three-quarters of his men back to that city.

"Can you hold the Rocca with only three dozen men?" the mage asked.

"Now that we're in, I could hold it with a dozen," Portinari said. "At least, I could if you would give me permission to hang Peruzzi and a few other obstinate fellows."

"My lord Roberto has the right of justice here," Niccolo Bianchi objected.

"He won't have any rights at all if we lose him Rimini through concentrating too much on this place!" Portinari replied. "Look, it's obvious what has to be done. Hang a few as an example to the rest, march Bracciaforte's turncoat soldiers back to Rimini where they'll be seriously outnumbered in case they rethink their oaths to us, leave a few people here to keep the castle and find out where the city's money is. If a collection of beggarly peasants and sheep farmers *has* any money. If you'd let me rack that Giacomini, I'd know by now whether the place is worth keeping."

Filippo Cacciote concealed a shudder. These brutes were all alike; their first, last and only solution to any problem was violence. And once you let them start torturing their betters, who knew where it would end?

"As my lord's advisor," he said, "I must strongly recommend against abandoning the Rocca. It is not a matter of mere money; San Florian is his by right of inheritance, and he will not give it up lightly."

"I still say, a touch of the rack..." Portinari grumbled.

"There does not," Cacciote pointed out, "appear to be a rack in this castle. It was hard enough finding a store room to lock up the malcontents."

The impromptu meeting broke up like all the others, with nothing decided. Nobody wanted to risk making a decision in Malatesta's absence, and in any case he had not named anyone to be in charge until his return. Of course, he had been expecting to return almost at once. How had that woman managed to lead him on a merry chase for so long?

Cacciote retired to the room he had claimed as his own and considered his options. They were not attractive. Naturally Malatesta's soldiers ought to look to him, the wisest man in the castle, for leadership. They did not seem to have grasped that point. Meanwhile, the Turks were impatient for results. And he dared not communicate with them now, when all hung in the balance until Malatesta returned. They might fail to grasp the nuances of the situation. They might decide, in fact, that *he* had failed them —and then what would happen to Andrea? At all costs he must keep them believing that they needed him and that he could deliver what he wanted.

But if he dared not turn the mirror to Andrea in Constantinople for fear of the Turks' impatience, he could temporarily refocus it on someone else. And he had been collecting little things in preparation for working a highly personal charm. Hairs taken from Roberto Malatesta's bed, nail parings wrapped in silk, even a drop of blood from an evening when he had cut his finger at table and wiped it on a napkin which Cacciote later made off with – all these things had been intended to add force to a charm of compulsion. But he could spare a few for the more immediate problem.

He laid two short hairs on the back of the mirror, added a few teased-out threads from the napkin, and intoned the requisite words while he lit the tangle with a candle and watched it shrivel into ashes. When he turned the mirror face up again, his shoulders relaxed from a tension he had hardly been conscious of. There was his target… but what in the name of ten thousand demons was he doing?

Flames in the background lit the scene: not exactly torches, not exactly candles, but seemingly free-floating tongues of fire. The stocky figure in the mirror seemed to be seated on air; he reached forward exactly as if he was picking up a goblet from a table, tilted his head back as if to drain it, then grabbed at an invisible something and began biting the air in front of his hand.

An illusion –and a powerful one! Cacciote scowled at the mirror. He had actually been in the presence of that soldier who seemed to control the widow, not just once but twice, yet he had not sensed such latent power in the man. Well, if he had maintained an illusory castle with a phantom banquet for nearly two days, he must be close to dying of exhaustion by now. The prudent thing would be to wait until the illusion faded of its own accord and Malatesta returned; bad things sometimes happened to people who broke such spells. Best of all, once the soldier had killed himself to keep the illusion going, the widow would be without guidance. She would probably welcome Malatesta's protection then.

Only, how far had she fled while Malatesta was trapped in the fantastic castle?

Cacciote's sleep was troubled with dreams of demons and monsters, and worse, of Malatesta returning in a towering temper because he had not caught the woman after all.

~~~

In the morning, Cacciote's mirror showed no significant change. A light rain was falling, and had been for some time; Malatesta's clothes were sodden, but he did not seem to notice. He was still trying to stuff himself with illusory dainties.

"You'd think even that idiot would notice that he's not the slightest bit drunk after downing goblet after goblet of imaginary wine!" Cacciote grumbled. But he was seriously worried now. Malatesta's face was thin and pinched. What if the illusion lasted so long that the man starved to death or got sick from being cold and wet? Even more urgently, how much longer could he last with nothing to drink?

With great reluctance, Cacciote concluded that he could not afford to wait any longer on events. He would have to go and free Malatesta from the illusion himself. It would be an uncomfortable and risky business... but...

He began to smile as an obvious way to mitigate the risk presented itself.

"I do not see why it must be a secret," young Niccolo complained after Cacciote found him and told him what they were going to do.

"It is a matter of demons," Cacciote said, "and there are, sadly, unenlightened folk who would tar us with the same brush as the evil wizard who called up the demons, did they know our errand! Besides, do you want to share the credit for rescuing your lord with a bunch of common soldiers? We shall leave quietly and return triumphant, and Malatesta will owe you a great debt of gratitude for saving him from the hellish tricks of that wizard. I should not be surprised if he made you castellan of the Rocca after this. Now go and saddle a couple of horses."

"Shouldn't I saddle one for my lord also?"

"Oh... yes, yes, you should." There was always the possibility that Niccolo would survive breaking the illusion. And Cacciote had already decided that they couldn't count on Malatesta's own horse being nearby; not being privy to the illusory feast, the animal might have wandered off anywhere by now.

"What if he wants to continue chasing the woman?"

"Well, then, he can use the horse we are bringing him for that." It wasn't likely that Malatesta would be in any condition to pursue his quarry after three days with nothing to eat or drink, but Cacciote was tired of explaining things. "Now go on, and be sure to pick a nice gentle nag for me! At my age I can't bounce around like you young folk."

After the first league on the grey gelding with the bone-crunching trot and the back-breaking canter, Cacciote was perfectly reconciled to the sacrifice of Niccolo to save his master. Not that it had troubled him very much before. There had been that matter of the hairs from the chestnut mare that Niccolo had passed off as being taken from the comb of Caterina Rinaldi. If Malatesta had figured out that Cacciote had accidentally bespelled a horse into falling in love with him, he would be a dead man now. As it was, he preferred to see somebody else die.

# ~CHAPTER NINETEEN~

*Upon the third day take the silver and cast it in the prepared form, then quench it in the urine of a virgin boy. Make a hole in the silver to receive the blood and hair of the intended target, and close up the hole with earth taken from the grave of one who died unshriven. Then say, "By this image, may so-and-so desire nothing better than to do my will."*

*The notes of Filippo Cacciote*

~ ~ ~

The Roberto Malatesta who returned to San Florian was not exactly a broken man, but his state of health was bad enough that winter had set in before he was able to think about resuming his pursuit of Caterina Rinaldi. By this time, though, it was far too late to get her back simply by riding hard with a dozen men to kill the soldier and take her prisoner. By now, as the mage's improvised pendulum confirmed, she was in Venice.

Somewhere in Venice.

The pendulum was maddeningly imprecise.

"There must be fifty thousand people in Venice," Malatesta grumbled.

"Closer to a hundred thousand," Cacciote said.

"And *you* –" Malatesta broke off in a fit of coughing. "You got Niccolo killed, the only person I could send who might have a hope of recognizing the woman!"

Cacciote was sorry to see that it still rankled with Malatesta that his rescue from the enchanted castle had been achieved at the cost of Niccolo's death, despite the very lovely story that he had told him to explain how it came about through no fault of his. In Cacciote's version, both he and Niccolo had been surrounded by a strong protective circle that should have shielded them from the demons that were released upon the breaking of the enchantment. "But so great was young Niccolo's anguish upon seeing you so vilely imprisoned, that he forgot all caution and ran forward to your side, crossing himself and calling upon Christ Jesus. This, of course, freed the demons, and even as the illusion faded they swooped down upon Niccolo –three of them there were, monstrous creatures with the claws of griffons and the heads of dragons. The boy was lost before I could utter a single word to protect him, and so great was my horror and astonishment at the sight that I lost consciousness for a time."

The part about the demons was true, anyway, and Cacciote had no need to simulate the terror he had felt at the sight. As for just why young Niccolo had not been in the protective circle, and just who had told him that he could break the enchantment by calling upon the holy name, and who had failed to warn him about the demons –well, there was no need to trouble his lordship with these unimportant details. Cacciote felt he had performed heroically enough to obviate the minor loss of that obnoxious young man - it had been no easy task to get the exhausted Malatesta onto a horse and to keep him from falling off all the way back to San Florian –but he had an uncomfortable feeling that Malatesta would not see it that way.

"Lucrezia Contarini would recognize her," Cacciote said. So would he, but he hoped that would not occur to the weak, irritable man who lay half reclining on a couch laden with pillows.

Malatesta shook his head. "I thought of that. She absolutely refuses to go to Venice. She says that if I force her to do that, she will just go back to her husband."

"Would he take her back?"

"She certainly thinks so. She describes him as a lovesick old fool and claims she can wind him around her little finger just by crying and claiming she was forced to leave –though how she expects to persuade the man that Caterina

Rinaldi could force her to come to San Florian is beyond me –but then, a sufficiently enamoured man will doubtless believe whatever he wishes to if it comes from the woman who holds his heart in thrall. I myself," said Malatesta, "have never been such a fool, but I have seen others like that."

Cacciote held the private opinion that Malatesta was immune to this particular disorder by virtue of having no heart. But that was not important now, not compared to the brilliant idea he had just had. "Have her write to the husband then, saying she longs to return to him, but Caterina left her in charge of San Florian and she does not wish to betray her trust. She will return to Venice as soon as Caterina is back here. That should inspire him to send the widow back."

"If she has gone to Contarini for refuge…"

"Where else could she go? Lucrezia says she has never been to Venice and has no friends or family there. And she is doubtless telling Contarini all sorts of lies about Lucrezia betraying him with me. This letter will both counter that malicious gossip and get the woman back here to marry me."

Roberto Malatesta had an interesting definition of "malicious gossip." It was fortunate, Cacciote reflected, that Lucrezia's husband in Venice did not possess an enchanted mirror like the one he kept close by him; actually seeing Lucrezia's behavior with Malatesta would have made it exceedingly difficult for him to persuade himself that she was an unfortunate, mistreated, sadly wronged victim. There was just one problem remaining.

"The lady Lucrezia will, of course, have to dictate the letter to someone else," he mentioned. "I have seen her writing. It is no better than the minimum required of any noble lady. We want to be sure her husband can read the letter."

"All the better," said Malatesta. "There is no need to involve her at all. *I* will dictate the letter, and you will take it down. Thus we can be sure it says exactly what we wish. Do not fail to mention that she is having the letter written by someone else, just in case the husband is familiar with her hand."

The eagerly awaited response from Venice was not long in coming. Sadly, it was not accompanied by Caterina Rinaldi.

"Lucrezia, my heart's heart, I have been in agony wondering what can have happened to you," Malatesta read with disgust. "Why did you not write to me before? You are too kind to your cousin, and she is showing no consideration for you. She has not even called upon me, and I have no idea how to find her. Surely someone else can take charge of this little town and free you to return. I cannot leave Venice at this time due to affairs of state and the Turkish problem, so you must demand an escort to keep you safe upon the road. I remain in all eagerness to hear from you or, better, to bathe myself in the light of your countenance once again,

"Your loving Ottavio."

Malatesta crumpled up the letter and threw it to the floor. "A waste of good paper! Apart from confirming that the husband is every bit as besotted as Lucrezia claimed, it gets us no closer. Why has the widow not been in contact with Ottavio Contarini? Was Lucrezia lying? *Does* she have other friends in Venice?"

"If she did," the mage said slowly, "they would surely be from her own class, members of Venice's forty great families. But if any of them had received her she would surely have become known to society by now, and Contarini would at least have heard something of her, even if he had not met her."

"Did she flee with a purse of gold, then, that she can subsist unnoticed and unseen?"

"She had not time for that," Cacciote assured him. "She did not even take her jewels."

"Jewels…" Roberto said slowly. "There was something about those jewels. Lucrezia was prattling to me about them once, but she did not seem to know exactly what was wrong with them. I think –I need to know! We might be able to use them!"

His excitement brought on a return of the dry, hacking cough that shook his entire body. "Have you no elixir –to cure –this damned cough?" he demanded between convulsions.

"My liege, I have invoked the angels of healing on your behalf," Cacciote said, quite truthfully. Malatesta ill was easier to deal with, but his death would be disastrous. The lord's soldiers would not obey him, and he could hardly place a spell of compulsion on seven or eight score men at once. God only knew who would wind up in control of San Florian, but whoever it was would probably not be satisfactory to the damned infidels who held his son hostage.

But it was a delicate matter to keep Malatesta alive while also keeping him too ill to make trouble. A soothing syrup for his cough would relieve the symptoms while doing nothing about the underlying cause, and it would cost him little to prepare it. Better yet, if he claimed that he required time and solitude for the preparation, he could work the enchantment of compulsion that he had been putting off for too long. And he could use the excuse of the Great Elixir to procure the ingredients he had hitherto lacked for the other spell. "I shall prepare the greatest of elixirs, my Aqua Mirabile et Divina, at once. I shall require certain ingredients that are not to be had in the workroom –leaf gold, silver, the urine of a virgin youth, and the milk of a woman who is suckling a child - and three days of solitude."

"Procure those things and get on with it, then," snapped Malatesta irritably. "But first send for that worthless scholar, Piero Giacomini. He was hand in glove with the Rinaldi woman; if anyone knows of some shady secret about her jewels, it would be him."

Unfortunately, it turned out that Giacomini, like most of Caterina's other loyal supporters, had slipped out of the castle once he was no longer locked up. The guards had been paying too much attention to people trying to get into the Rocca, and had not really troubled themselves about people leaving it. Malatesta sent for Lucrezia and spent the better part of a morning finding out exactly what was strange about Caterina's jewels. The information, once he had teased it out of her digressions and emotional outbursts, pleased him mightily. A pity his mage was locked up for three days making the elixir that was to heal him; he needed to discuss his new idea with the man.

# ~CHAPTER TWENTY~

*The most exotic names combined the hint of far-off lands and medical traditions with confessional otherness. Domenico Antonio Franchi, maker and pedlar of a Balsamo della Porta Ottomana (Balm of the Sublime Porte), capitalized on the fact that he was a 'Turco fatto cristiano', a convert to Christianity and resident in Naples.*

    *-Gentilcore, <u>Medical Charlatanism in early modern Italy</u>*

~ ~ ~

To Venice, winter brought the withdrawal of the Turks from Friuli, repeated assurances of friendship from the Sublime Porte and the remission for that year of the payment they had agreed to make to the Turks in return for peace. There was even a rumor that Iskender Bey had been recalled to Constantinople and beheaded for his initiative in attacking Venetian territory. That might or might not be true, but he was certainly no longer *sanjakbey* of Bosnia. Venice returned to her regular preoccupations of money-making and amusement, and business in the Piazza San Marco flourished in the cold months from December to Carnival.

Gian's appearance under the pseudonym of Yusuf the Turk, and dressed *alla Turchetta*, or at least as like a Turk as the Venetians expected, drew attention and purchasers to Agostino Foscari's white-painted stage. In extremely full blue pants tucked into red boots, with a wide red sash around his waist and all but covering his shirt, his hair concealed under a turban bearing a peacock feather, Gian looked suitably exotic. And with, in addition, his beard dyed black and trimmed to a neat point and his mustache waxed into a furious crescent, Gian stopped worrying about being recognized as a member of the outlawed Neroni family. His success in healing all manner of wounds and open sores sold a great many little bottles of Foscari's Miraculous Oil. If the oil did not work quite so well when applied at home, that only brought the sufferers back to Yusuf to have him apply the oil with his own hands, which almost always yielded satisfactory results.

Foscari's rivals, though doing business quite successfully on their own stages, grumbled continuously about the Turk's stealing customers. Men who had been quite satisfied to apply Blessed Balsam or Unguent of Serpents to their cuts and scrapes were now crowding Foscari's stage and buying so much of his Miraculous Oil that the empiric's supplies regularly sold out before the close of the day.

"I haven't prepared so much of the healing oil in years," gloated Foscari to Gian and Caterina as he cooked up another batch of oil with madder and alum to give it an impressive purple hue, and mixed with powdered mandrake root for its universal healing effects. "And not only I, but the apothecary shops, the *speziali,* are profiting by my success. I have been three times to the Phoenix for more mandrake, and now that apothecary's supplies are exhausted and I shall have to pay the extortionate prices at the Golden Eagle."

"You could always powder some other root," Caterina suggested, looking around at the herbs, bark and dried roots that decorated the walls of Foscari's front room.

"Contessa! I, Agostino Foscari, cheat my customers? Never!"

Caterina decided it would not be tactful to mention the demonstration of eating serpents' flesh to protect against snakebite, or the fact that the Balsam of Mecca, supposedly brought by Yusuf the Turk from the lands of the infidels, was in fact identical with a healing unguent that Foscari had previously sold as Balsam of Gilead.

Gian was, as usual, looking worried. She drew him aside to find out what he was fretting about this time.

"This mummery may be making Foscari wealthy by his standards," he said in a lowered voice, casting a glance at the empiric, "but we shall hardly gain enough by it to raise an army to retake San Florian."

Caterina considered the matter. Did she, in fact, wish to retake San Florian? By now, rumors of what was happening there had become a matter of common chitchat in this city renowned for its near-instantaneous spreading of news. She knew that Piero Giacomini and Tommaso Peruzzi had slipped out of the castle and had taken refuge with friends in the town, as had Rosa and most of the others who had remained loyal to her. As long as Ercole was safe in Urbino, was it really her duty to return?

She supposed it was. In any case, she and Ercole would never be truly safe as long as Roberto Malatesta thought he could cement his claim to the city by forcing her into marriage. Only marriage to a powerful man like the Duke of Urbino could protect her, and she had not the slightest desire to marry the old duke even if he would have had her.

"If you can think of a way to raise a small fortune," she said with some asperity, "pray do not hesitate to inform me of it! But for now, I must mend this costume."

She repaired the rent in the yellow silk bodice, tacked its trimming of gold lace more firmly in place, and considered without enthusiasm the virtues of letting its seams out. The thing had fit her perfectly well when she first donned it, but she seemed to be putting on weight in certain areas since they had begun their new career. Agostino Foscari no longer insisted on her wearing the band that pushed her breasts up to a degree that Gian condemned as indecent; she looked plenty indecent just wearing the costume as originally designed. It was happiness, she supposed guiltily. This interlude of play-acting, of putting aside the responsibility of ruling and the decorum of well-born ladies, had been more fun than anything she had hitherto experienced.

But that was only true because she did look on it as an interlude, an escape for a few months from the burdens of her position. She could not leave Ercole motherless and squander his inheritance by running away indefinitely.

～～～

In San Florian, Caterina's friends and advisors were doing what they could to safeguard Ercole's inheritance. It wasn't much –they had no real power and scarcely any money –but since Roberto Malatesta showed no interest in the city beyond occasional demands for cash, the people naturally turned to those they had always known as council members. After the first few tense days, when the city's leading merchants waited to see if the usurper would confiscate their estates, the city settled down to a nearly normal life.

When first Piero Giacomini, and then Tommaso Peruzzi, slipped out of the Rocca, Councilman Cosimo Michele offered them his hospitality. Thereafter the (technically nonexistent) city council met quietly in an upper story of the Palazzo Michele and managed the city's issues through a combination of reason, debate, very small sums of money, and appeals to an authority they no longer, technically, had. Everyone understood that should they fail to settle their issues in the Palazzo Michele, they might have to take them to the Rocca for Roberto Malatesta's judgment. And since nobody in San Florian was eager to be noticed by Roberto Malatesta, the system worked reasonably well… for the moment.

That did not mean that meetings were interesting, or productive, or anything more than an increasingly doomed attempt to keep the city of San Florian from falling apart during the enforced absence of the heir and his mother.

"Maso Trevi accuses Rospo Forza's grandmother of putting the evil eye on his herd of sheep and causing them to fall to their deaths over a cliff," Piero Giacomini summarized with a sigh after an excessively long and tedious discussion. "Rospo Forza claims that the sheep were going of their own accord to the cliffs beyond the east pasture and he has no way to stop them sneaking off there. Furthermore, since the higher part of the east pasture rightfully belongs to him through his grandmother's brother, Trevi should be fined for allowing his herd to graze there. The rest of the complaints are similar –stupid peasants being stupid peasants. Oh, and just to make it all more interesting, if the usurper Malatesta finds out we are not only still in San Florian but daring to sit in judgment on these crucially important matters, he will probably hang us. Tell me again why I didn't just get out of San Florian and go to visit my cousins in Tolfa as soon as I escaped the Rocca?"

"Because it is our duty to safeguard the Contessa's inheritance for her," said Tommaso Peruzzi.

"That was logical when you first escaped," said their host, Cosimo Michele. "We did not know her plans, and some of us hoped she had gone to raise an army to take back the city and the Rocca. But now..."

"Some of us," said Peruzzi, "still hope that! No one fights in the winter. When the spring campaigning season starts, we shall see some action. We only need to hold things together until then. Now, about these wineshop brawls between the Donati and the Espositi..."

~ ~ ~

Caterina told herself to stop wondering what was going on in San Florian. It wasn't as if she could do anything about it right now! Better to concentrate on what she *could* do... even if it was only dancing in a much-mended yellow silk gown that, yes, definitely needed the seams let out. At least her performances were contributing to their success. And so were her real skills. There were so many women who wanted a private conversation with her that Foscari had prepared a curtained stall beside the main stage where women could slip in to consult her after the dancing. With the benefit of her Book of Secrets Caterina had been able to help women suffering from a host of minor ills that modesty forbade their mentioning to a male physician.

Some of the consultations, though, were anything but reassuring.

"Today," she told Gian one evening, "I had a client who wanted me to "cure" an inconvenient pregnancy. Yesterday there was one who thought I would give her a poison to get rid of her husband. And last week –" she shuddered at the memory –"there was a frightful hag who claimed she needed the fat of a newborn child to make her flying ointment with which she rode through the sky to consort with demons."

"Have you told Agostino?"

"Not yet. I've always been able to get rid of such folk without his help – and in the last case, I sent the old witch away with a flea in her ear! As if I would encourage her in associating with demons!"

Gian cleared his throat, cautiously. "Of course you would never do something so evil as sacrificing a newborn child. But –forgive me –I had the distinct impression that demons were involved in that last illusion you raised

155

to help us get away. The enchanted castle, the illusory army —was all that the work of angels? You *did* mention demons at the time..."

"Oh, that," Caterina said. "It's all right. I did not do it to hurt anybody, only to protect us. And I have already confessed about using the demons, repented, and obtained absolution."

"You mean there's a priest in the city who knows about us?" Gian paled.

"No, silly. I'm not that stupid! I found a wandering friar, a pardoner who was just about to leave Venice to try his luck at the trade fair in Padua. He was in such a hurry to leave that he did not even want to wait and hear my confession, but after I purchased an indulgence from him for forgiveness of necromancy he wanted to hear the whole story."

# ~CHAPTER TWENTY-ONE~

*Once, when at the commencement of a campaign one of his chief officers asked him what were the main objects of his operations, Mahomet answered sharply, 'If a hair of my beard knew them, I would pluck it out and cast it into the fire.' No one could tell what throne was menaced by the host that now gathered at the Sultan's bidding.*

*-Creasy, <u>The Crescent in the West</u>*

~ ~ ~

As a mild winter was succeeded by an early spring, Agostino Foscari put off his usual round of travel to Milan and the surrounding towns of the North. Carnival in Venice that year had earned him a veritable fortune, enough that he felt no need to milk the people of other cities just yet. And in any case business was simply too good in Venice for him to leave the city yet, and his house too comfortable to exchange for the inevitable cold and damp of traveling in early spring! Perhaps later, if the Venetians tired of getting their wounds healed by "Yusuf il Turco" or if the season turned so hot as to be uncomfortable, he would seek the snows of the north. For now, he had just introduced a novelty to his stage performance, and he was eager to see how the new attraction of little plays performed by his troupe worked to draw the crowds.

In the first of Foscari's playlets, Caterina acted the part of a heavily pregnant noble lady who was unable to give birth until the dwarf Raimundo, posing as a physician, administered a treatment which caused lascivious urges in her. When he announced that the remedy for her condition was for someone to put another child in her to push the first one out, the rest of his speech was drowned by the cheering of volunteers from the audience. His rivals' stages had been all but deserted as the silver poured into his hands in return for the Balsam of Luxury, guaranteed to give the purchasers' wives or mistresses the same urges that Raimundo had created in the noble lady.

"They loved it!" gloated Agostino after that day's work.

Unfortunately, Gian did not share his glowing opinion of the play. He announced that he would never have permitted Caterina to take part if he had known how improper it was going to be, and that she was not going to portray that character again —or any other character of Foscari's indecent imagining. And this fight he won, because Caterina herself had felt embarrassed at acting like that on a stage. She had never behaved like that even in the privacy of a bedroom! She had been, at best, obedient and dutiful to Girolamo.

And despite their sharing a room, she had had no opportunity to find out whether it would be any different with Gian. On the very first night he had taken one of the mattresses stacked high on the wonderfully comfortable bed and placed it on the floor between the bed and the door, announcing that he would sleep there, the better to prevent anyone's entering to attack her by night. And he had never even hinted at changing that arrangement.

Well. After all, they were not married. Nor would they be, not while she was still afraid of being discovered by Roberto Malatesta; a husband who was a barrier to Malatesta's marrying her himself would not outlive their capture. And anyway, why should she think that Gian wanted to marry her?

"You expect to get all the benefits of marriage without paying any of the cost," she grumbled after he put his foot down over the bawdy play.

Gian's jaw dropped. "The devil I do! Have I ever failed to respect your virtue?"

"I mean," Caterina clarified, "you boss me around just like a husband."

"Well, somebody has to take care of you, Contessina-from-the-Country! If I don't watch over you, you do crazy things like telling your most dangerous secrets to wandering pardoners!"

"I didn't tell him who I was! You're being unfair and unreasonable again!"

"*Again?*"

The fight provided some relief to overstrained minds and spirits, as well as being as good as a play to the rest of the household. But when it was over, Caterina let out the dark red damask gown for Betta and coached her in the mannerisms of a noble lady.

Takings from subsequent performances were much reduced, and Foscari complained that it was hard enough making up plays for two dwarves, two women, a manservant and a Turk without having his aesthetic decisions overruled by said Turk. "Then hire some more actors," Gian said.

Agostino sighed. "Dear boy, you can't buy the look of the true nobility. You may think of your little Contessa as a country nobody, but you can't deny she was raised a lady. Betta can never in a hundred years imitate what she does so naturally, and neither can anybody else I could hire… oh, all right, all right! I won't ask her to act again!"

"That," said Gian smugly, "is just what I've been telling you. I am glad it has finally sunk in."

～～～

Spring brought more work for the unofficial city council of San Florian. With the sheep turned out to graze the hillsides, the number of grazing rights quarrels tripled. And with the evenings warm enough for most people to resume taking their evening walk around the piazza, so did the number of complaints about rogues alienating the affections of married women, rascals shocking decent women with their lascivious antics and jokes, less decent women tempting husbands away from their wives, and most of all, about boys and girls forming attachments that ran counter to the plans of their families.

"On the whole," Piero Giacomini grumbled, "I think the sheep are easier to manage."

"Good," said Peruzzi promptly, "then you can go and investigate this perpetual quarrel about the east pasture. Who owns the grazing rights up the mountain from the east pasture, and whose sheep are actually going up there, and what's all this new fuss about sheep being lured up there to break their necks?"

"It is not necessary to lure sheep to break their necks," said the very respectable and very overweight Onofrio Fabbri, who had once, before most of the present council was born, and before he married a rich merchant's only daughter, been a barefoot shepherd boy. "Sheep devote most of their ingenuity to finding new ways to kill themselves. Fortunately, they do not have much ingenuity, or we would not have a woolen business. But I certainly do not have the figure to go clambering around the cliffs beyond the east pasture. You had better do it, Giacomini."

With resignation, Piero Giacomini realized that he had just talked himself into a long, cold, and tiring scramble among the volcanic rocks that tumbled down to the edge of the grazing lands east of the city.

~ ~ ~

As Venice recovered from the excesses of Carnival, Turkey awoke from the winter cold in which all sensible folk stayed at home surrounded by braziers to take the chill from the air. The streets of Constantinople came alive again with the calls of peddlers and tradesmen; the covered bazaar bustled with activity; and on the shores of the Bosporus, the sultan's horsetails were raised up on high poles to signal the gathering of his army.

"Where do they go?" people wondered. "Will they try to take another Italian city? Or an island? Or do they mean simply to raid the little towns on the shores of the Adriatic for slaves and gold?"

That last option, suggesting less expense and even some potential profit, was widely favored by the common people. But then, they were notoriously selfish and narrow-minded. They cared more about bread for their own families than about the sultan's desire for one last glorious war of conquest.

The option of minor but profitable raids was not even under discussion within the walls of Topkapi, though the sultan's ministers sounded him as tactfully as they could on his intentions for the spring campaign. Venice? Naples? Another attempt on Rhodes?

"You will know when the time is ripe!" Mehmed snapped at one of them. He was already in a bad mood; the ulcer on his leg had reopened, and they had been tactfully suggesting that he should not take the field at all for this campaign. "By

Allah, have I not said that if my beard knew my plans for this war, I would pluck it out and cast the hairs into the fire? And if it were your beard that knew, I would not bother to pluck it, but would simply burn your head with it!"

A carefully cultivated network of gossipers, peddlers and beggars carried that threat to Battista Gritti, the Venetian agent in Galata, and the *bailo* in turn passed it on to his masters in Venice. He had to be very careful what he wrote, for the agents of the Sublime Porte certainly read his letters before allowing them to be sent on. They had even told him not to try sending messages in cipher, because they found it difficult if not impossible to break the Venetian ciphers. That they were willing to admit as much made him more, not less, cautious. But he rather thought that Mahmud II would be pleased to keep the Venetians on tenterhooks with this bit of information.

~~~

Antonio da Treviso, head of Venice's unofficial but extremely efficient spy service, brought the *bailo's* letter to the next meeting of the Ten, together with certain deductions he had made from the uncommonly peculiar wording of the rest of the letter.

"That the Grand Turk is preparing to make war again is beyond question," he assured the other members of the ruling council. "They did not even try to prevent Gritti from sending us this letter with the information that the horsetails have been planted and the army is gathering. But the object of the war is a secret so closely guarded that even the sultan's highest advisors in Topkapi do not know it."

"Perhaps they want us to know of the war plans so that we may be provoked into unwary action," suggested the newest member of the Council of Ten, Ottavio Contarini.

"Like what?" demanded Marco Dandolo. "Naturally we shall keep our own forces close to Venice, rather than sending them south to help the Kingdom of Naples, until we know the Grand Turk's plans. That is simple prudence."

"If the Turk plans to strike at Naples, that is exactly what he wants –for us to withhold our support for the Kingdom."

"He is most likely going to try for Rhodes again," said another. "Never mind our condottieri —we need to be setting our galleys in good order and sending them out into the Middle Sea, so that they can destroy the Turkish ships before they can land the army at Rhodes."

Some wrangling ensued before Giovanni Mocenigo, Doge of Venice, overruled them all with his deep, commanding voice.

"What we need," he said, "is more information. Messer da Treviso, you had some thoughts in the matter?"

There were some frowns and mutterings at this; the rest of the Council felt Antonio da Treviso had been stealing a march on them by consulting privately with the Doge before this meeting. Nevertheless, they fell silent under Mocenigo's steely eye and waited to hear what da Treviso had to say.

"After retailing the Grand Turk's insistence on secrecy and his refusal to inform even his closest advisors," da Treviso said carefully, "Gritti writes of certain other matters which an ill-informed reader might suppose to be only his private concerns. But I am of the opinion that he intends to convey certain information to us in a form which the Turks who read his letters will not recognize. Take this passage here, where he says that as the leader of his people, he begs us to send him a physician who speaks Turkish."

"If he's sick, let him return here as soon as we can appoint another *bailo*," said Dandolo. "Is that all?"

"Reading between the lines," explained da Treviso, "I believe that the words 'the leader of his people,' are meant to hint that it is the Grand Turk himself who is ailing. Gritti is not given to referring to himself so bombastically; not only is it entirely inappropriate, but styling himself so would be usurping the role of the Doge, and he would hardly do so in an official communication to the Ten. And in the next sentence, he refers to a recurring ailment which has all but crippled him. Gritti is perfectly healthy and has never been seriously ill. But we know that Mehmed was troubled by an ulcerated leg last year; it was said to be better, but such things seldom heal completely. It may have broken open again. So, again, I believe him to be referring to Mehmed and not to himself. In that case, the request for a Turkish-speaking physician means that such a one might be able to gain an entrée with the sultan and learn more about his plans."

"Deduction, inference, guesswork! You spies build an entire castle from two bricks and an iron latch," grumbled Dandolo.

"If Gritti really wanted a physician for his own problems," da Treviso insisted," why would he ask for one who speaks Turkish? And then - and this *must* have a hidden meaning - he says that his wife is also unwell, and wishes very much that she knew of a woman herbalist whom she could consult without offending her modesty."

"Nothing strange in that," Dandolo said dismissively. "My own wife prefers to see only a midwife in her times of confinement, and my personal physician consults with her only in great need and from behind a curtain."

Antonio da Treviso sketched a bow in Dandolo's direction. "Ah, but the purity and propriety of Benedetta Dandolo are well known. The case is different here. Gritti, as we all know, left his virtuous wife here at home and took Lucia Fiore to warm his bed in Galata. La Fiore is not –ah –particularly known for her modesty."

As the lady in question had been a rope dancer in the Piazza San Marco before Gritti successfully bid for her exclusive services, nobody was inclined to question this statement. Perhaps there was something to da Treviso's deductions after all!

"But I do not see how this benefits us, even if you are right," Contarini claimed. "Unless you have recently recruited to your service a Turkish physician and some low-life woman who ekes out a living selling simples to the simple-minded?"

Everyone laughed, and da Treviso's cheekbones flushed dark. "When I do," he snapped, "I assure you, Messer Contarini, that you will be the first to know!"

And so the meeting ended without his informing the Ten that he did at least have, shaking the outer edges of his web as a particularly juicy fly blunders into a spider's trap, the story of a converted Turk who claimed to be something of a healer. Until Gritti's letter, the gossip about this new performer in the Piazza San Marco had been merely an odd fact to be filed with the rest of the thousands of bits of information stored in da Treviso's memory palace. Now… it might be something more, and if the man was at all suitable, how he would enjoy the look on Contarini's face!

# ~CHAPTER TWENTY-TWO~

*"It is not necessary to lure sheep to break their necks. Sheep devote most of their ingenuity to finding new ways to kill themselves. Fortunately, they do not have much ingenuity, or we would not have a woolen business."*
  *-Onofrio Fabbri, member of the San Florian City Council*

~ ~ ~

Piero brooded sourly on the vicissitudes of fate as he trudged up the muddy path leading to the east pasture. He was a learned man, a scholar of the University of Bologna, and also an extremely good accountant. Since his return to San Florian after studying at the university he had always held a respectable position in the young Contessa's council, the kind of position that involved a dignified long velvet robe, a chain of office, and a comfortable study where he could store the city's financial records and go over the accounts in peace. Never in his career plans had he seen himself shivering in borrowed hose and doublet under a wholly inadequate cloak, plodding uphill along a path so sorry that his shoes were totally caked with half-frozen mud. And for what? To look at sheep? One sheep looked exactly like another, did it not? For two piastres he would turn around right now, make his way back down to the city and tell the councilors that yes, there were sheep in the east pasture, and he was not a shepherd and he neither knew nor cared whose animals they were!

But he had been cursed with an outsize sense of responsibility. And even if Caterina had disappeared, she was still Contessa of San Florian, he was still her man, and to some extent —if only because their wool was taxed by the city —these were her sheep. And since he could hardly be more cold and bored and miserable than he was right now, he might as well…

God's body and blood! There went one of the accursed animals now, an ewe heavy in late pregnancy, apparently determined to give birth to her lamb in the highest, rockiest, coldest spot in all San Florian. Piero sprang forward to grab her; the idiot sheep rolled her eyes, scurried away and went right over one of the ledges that formed the natural boundary of the east pasture.

By the time he had climbed high enough to look down, the ewe was lying dead on a rock outcropping a good thirty feet below him. A talented mountaineer might have been able to make his way down the sheer cliff to the body; a brilliant shepherd might, just might, be able to save the lamb she carried in her belly. Or not. Being neither a mountaineer nor a shepherd, Piero had no choice but to write the sheep off as a total loss. Frustrated, he kicked the slippery rocks over which the stupid ewe had fallen, and hurt his toes.

Not far away, another sheep was venturing up among the rocky outcroppings. Piero stayed very still and watched. This sheep, not having been spooked by an idiot accountant trying to grab it, was taking its time. It stepped daintily among the rocks, occasionally putting its head down and sniffing the earth. Then, apparently having found a place to its satisfaction, it began licking one of the whitish rocks that poked out of the ground.

Piero stared; frowned; then, very slowly, bent down and picked up one of the loose rocks at his feet. It was grayish-white, with a pitted surface. He dampened one finger, touched the rock, then tasted his finger. Salt —that was what was attracting the animals —and, more important, an astringent quality that anyone who had spent time near a dye works could not fail to recognize. Alum!

Hurrying back down the hill, he sent for the peasants who had started the quarrel about the east pasture, stripped off his borrowed workingman's clothes and pulled on his velvet gown without even waiting to wash the spatters of mud off his legs. By the time the first of the men he wanted to talk to had been found and brought to the Palazzo Michele, Piero was sitting behind a long table, with ink and parchment ready to hand, looking like a gentleman —or at least like a lawyer.

"I find it is true that there is something attracting the sheep up to the cliffs beyond the east pasture," he said.

"My lord, I did nothing!" protested Rospo Forza.

"I did not accuse you," said Piero. "But you claim it is your land, and so the rocks sticking out of it are your rocks, and they have a salty taste, and that salt is attracting your neighbor's sheep, and they fall over the cliffs and get killed. So it seems to me that you must not only make restitution, but see to it that no more sheep are killed there."

"How can I do that? The rocks are part of the land. I did not put them there and I certainly cannot move them!"

"I am afraid a good, solid fence is the only practical solution."

The man paled. "No, no, I will pay for the dead sheep, but I cannot afford to build a fence!"

"Nor can I countenance leaving this hazard unattended." Piero let that sink in, watched the man's fingers twitch as he tried to figure up how he could build a fence at the lowest possible cost, then dangled the prospect of relief before him. "There is one thing…"

"Yes?"

"The maps of the area are not as precise as I should like. The cliff itself, being adjacent to the Rocca, is the property of San Florian. The east pasture is divided between you and Maso Trevi, is it not?"

"Yes, yes, so he should share in the cost of the fence!"

"Perhaps… or perhaps not. If it can be shown that everything beyond the high point of the hill is part of the Rocca, then it would be the city of San Florian that must bear the expense of the fence. It is our duty," Piero said, "to protect you, the people of San Florian, from dangers that arise from our land."

It took the rest of the day to get hold of Maso Trevi, who had been out on the hills with his sheep. And then it was necessary to write down both men's statements about the ownership of the high end of the east pasture, to make sure they agreed in every particular, and to get them to make their marks before witnesses. Piero considered it time well spent.

"Congratulations," said Cosimo Michele. "You have spent a whole day and used up a quantity of parchment, and for what? To make absolutely sure that the city of San Florian is responsible for building this fence! And where do you think to find the money for that?"

"From Tolfa," Piero said dreamily. "I must write to my cousin in Tolfa…" He imagined Caterina's delight when he told her of this discovery. That mercenary soldier she thought so much of hadn't been able to save San Florian for her. But there was just a possibility, now, that the mere bookish accountant would be able to buy it back for her. If only he knew how to get in touch with her!

*~ ~ ~*

Gian paced the entry hall of the Palazzo Treviso, trying to stifle the natural anxiety of a man who had been summoned by a member of the Ten without being told the reason. True, the four men who had been sent for him had said that he was not under arrest.

They had also said that if he knew what was good for him, he would obey the summons at once and without resistance. And so here he was, cumbered by the trappings of what Agostino Foscari conceived to be Turkish costume, and with no weapon but the cheap curved sword that Foscari insisted he wear instead of his own proper blade! But neither of these things troubled him so much as the memory of Caterina's white face as he was led away. If he did not come back, who would take care of her?

After an agonizing wait, the master of Palazzo Treviso himself appeared, all cordiality, inviting Gian to come within and take a cup of malmsey with him.

This was not particularly reassuring. All the world knew that Antonio da Treviso was the head of the Most Serene City's far-flung web of spies and gossips. Friendly overtures from such a man were exactly like a spider's invitation to walk into its parlor, and Gian felt like a very clumsy fly. How much did da Treviso already know about him? That he was not actually a Turk would not have been difficult for the spymaster to discover, but he did not think that Antonio da Treviso troubled himself personally with minor charges of misrepresentation in an empiric's booth. All the entertainers in the Piazza San Marco lied constantly about matters large and small; an edict requiring truth from them would have shut down the Piazza and deprived Venetians of their cherished free entertainment.

What if da Treviso had penetrated deeper into Gian's disguise, and knew not only that "Yusuf il Turco" was really plain Gian Bracciaforte, but that Bracciaforte was not-so-plain Gian-Maria Neroni? If the man planned to sell him back to the Medici, though, why not just take him prisoner and send him to Florence? Why treat him like a guest and offer him what turned out to be exceedingly good malmsey?

Gian was astonished to find da Treviso not only acting friendly, but addressing him as "Ser Yusuf." Had the man taken his performance on Foscari's stage for literal truth? It seemed so, for da Treviso's questions seemed aimed not at his antecedents but rather at probing the validity of "Yusuf's" conversion to Christianity.

"I am a faithful son of the Church, Messer da Treviso," he said, "and I do not take it kindly that you question my sincerity."

"Doubtless," said da Treviso, "your confessor here in Venice can testify in support of this? And the church where you hear Mass?"

Gian flushed. He had been somewhat neglectful on certain points of Christian observance. Not being as trustful as Caterina about priests' honoring the seal of the confessional, he had felt it wiser not to confess himself to anybody in Venice. And since to receive the Host at Mass was a very bad sin if you were unconfessed and unshriven, he had also failed in attendance there. "I am afraid that an empiric's booth is not the best of places for a true Christian," he said at last.

"But I need to *know*," da Treviso insisted. "If you have truly given up the false faith of your compatriots, if you are indeed a true son of the church, then you have a unique opportunity to repay the Most Serene City for her generosity in receiving and sheltering you. You could serve us in Constantinople! But I cannot offer you this chance until I am assured that you will not revert to your old religion."

The vaunted spy service did not seem to be as impressive as gossip made it out to be. Gian decided that his best hope now was truthfulness.

Up to a point.

"Does the illustrious signor believe that I am really a Turk?" he asked. "If so, the play-acting I have been doing in the Piazza San Marco has been more successful than I imagined. Sir, I am as Italian as yourself. I am *and have always been* a faithful son of the Church. The character of "Yusuf il Turco" is an invention to entertain Dottore Foscari's customers, nothing more."

Da Treviso scowled and drew some papers out of a leather case. "You have been heard to make Turkish invocations over those whom you healed," he said irritably. "I have here their testimony. Do you deny that you said to one man with a badly ulcerated leg…" He frowned over the writing before him. "Something that sounded like 'Kushlar rim ciocce ior gun varzh.' Is that not Turkish? What does it mean?"

Gian sighed. He had definitely been putting too much into the character of Yusuf. "Oh, it's Turkish, all right," he said. "And it means, 'My birds are very tired.'"

"What about this rhyming chant?" da Treviso demanded, squinting at another paper. "'Turungiu kitabi okuyorum, Turungiu kedi goeziyorum, Turungiu atlarim varzh.' Confess it, Turungiu is the name of the Turkish demon you are invoking!"

"Turungiu simply means 'orange' in Turkish. That 'chant' says, 'I am reading the orange book, I see the orange cat, I have orange horses.'" Gian leaned forward to stave off a pointless demand for yet more translations. "Messer, as a boy I encountered a Turkish renegade who taught me a few words of the language. And since no one in Venice seems to speak any Turkish at all, I have been using those words to impress the idiots who want to believe in 'Yusuf il Turco.' But you cannot send me to Constantinople to spy for you! I do not have nearly enough of the language to do that."

"You could still be useful."

"I am not going to Constantinople. I would *not* be useful there, and I have interests of my own here in Venice." Gian stood up. "Look elsewhere for your renegade Turk, Messer da Treviso."

~ ~ ~

After the bogus Turk left, da Treviso drummed his fingers on the tabletop and cursed his own precipitate action. His desire to make a fool of Contarini had betrayed him into the sort of haste that would have been justly punished in one of his underlings. At a minimum, he should have sent these so-called magical incantations to the proper department for translation; he might not have any people in his service who could speak Turkish fluently, but there were two secretaries with a limited ability to decipher any Turkish information the spies happened to get hold of.

He had the relevant papers copied and sent them to both secretaries, warning each one not to tell the other about the request, so that he could check their translations against what that insolent play-actor had claimed the words meant.

The results were depressingly in agreement. One secretary was not sure what "goeziyorum" meant, the other hedged about the proper translation of "kushla rim," but their theories of what had been said accorded well enough with this Yusuf's version. He cursed himself for not having done this elementary check first. But "Turungiu" had sounded so like the kind of name a demon would have…!

Still. His spies at the Piazza San Marco seemed convinced not only of Yusuf's Turkish identity, but of his ability to perform semi-miraculous cures of ulcers and open wounds. Perhaps they were more accurate on the second matter than they had been on the first.

Da Treviso brought in the one who had been most insistent that Yusuf was a Turk, and had one of his personal guard hold the man's arm while another slashed it open with a dagger. "Now go to Yusuf the Turk, at the stage of Agostino Il Scampamorte. Tell him —oh, that you were injured in a street fight over a girl's favors - and pay whatever he asks for healing," da Treviso instructed, tossing the man a purse heavy with gold. "You can keep the rest."

"For that kind of money," the fellow said, "you can cut my arm every day of the year, Messer!" He got his cut bound up and went off, wincing only slightly and jingling the purse in his good hand.

If this Yusuf could really heal open wounds with only an application of the empiric's purple oil, he might still be useful in Constantinople. After all, Gritti had not requested a Turkish physician, but only one who understood Turkish. And one who could heal the recurrent ulcer on Mahmud's leg – assuming that to be his problem - would surely gain high favor in Topkapi and would have every chance to find out the sultan's war plans.

It was just a matter of finding the right lever to use with this obstinate not-really-a-Turk. Da Treviso summoned two of his most competent gentlemen, one to watch the stage where Agostino Foscari and "Yusuf il Turco" performed and one to spy on the empiric's household. Before he spoke with Yusuf again he would not only be sure of his facts; he would also have figured out how to compel the man to serve Venice as he ought.

# ~CHAPTER TWENTY-THREE~

*"As soon as a coin in the coffer rings, a soul from Purgatory springs."*
*-attributed to Johan Tetzel, seller of indulgences.*

~ ~ ~

Fra Salvezza's travels were constrained by no commands from the Franciscan order of mendicant friars, for despite his long brown robe tied with a rope, his dusty sandals and his rosary of wooden beads, the Franciscans would have been very surprised to learn of his existence. He had left Padua early after an unpleasant encounter with some representatives of the Most Serene Republic of Venice, and, vowing not to revisit any others of the cities owing allegiance to Venice, had wandered through the smaller towns of the Romagna. San Florian had not even been on his mental list of potential targets, being too small and too poor to support many rich fools willing to pay for the salvation he offered. But he had happened to be passing nearby after an unsatisfactory tour through Imola, Forli and Faenza, and upon learning that the lord of Rimini was currently in residence at his minor possession of San Florian he had thought it worthwhile to pay the little town a visit. His informant had mentioned that Roberto Malatesta suffered from a persistent cough, and great men with incurable illnesses often found a renewed interest in salvation that could be quite profitable to a man armed with the right tools. Fra Salvezza patted the leather pouch containing his collection of indulgences and requested the hospitality of San Florian for the night. When one of

Malatesta's servants invited him to dine at the castle, he began to see golden florins dancing in the air.

So far, that beautiful vision had failed to materialize. Inquiries in the town had given him high hopes, for it seemed that not only was Malatesta suffering from a lingering illness, but he was a very great sinner who was in desperate need of the redemption which Fra Salvezza could dispense. The poisoning of his brothers and stepmother, the mysterious death of one of his mistresses, and even the taking of San Florian by trickery and force were merely the lowlights of a most amoral career.

The problem was that Malatesta seemed entirely unconcerned with the concepts of repentance, redemption and salvation. Fra Salvezza brought out some of his improving stories about sinners rescued at the last minute from the flames of hellfire by virtue of one of his indulgences; Malatesta merely yawned and told him to shut up unless he had some more entertaining conversational fare.

Well, there was that poor deluded woman who'd bought an indulgence from him just before he began this latest round of travel; he could turn that into an amusing story about the foibles of women —and end with some reflections on the value of his authentic Papal indulgences.

"Usually these insane women are old hags with no other way to get attention," he said, "but this one was young and pretty —and quite, quite mad. She would have it that she had sinned by compelling demons to build an enchanted castle in which to trap some man who was pursuing her!" Fra Salvezza paused and was gratified to see the effect of this opening on Malatesta. The lord of Rimini and San Florian was sitting more nearly upright than Fra Salvezza had yet seen him, and his eyes burned with either fever or interest. Hoping it was excitement and not illness, the pardoner expatiated on the charms of the crazy woman. "She was not really so beautiful as to attract a determined pursuit," he said judiciously, "being dark-haired and of a slim build. Nothing comparable to the effulgent beauty of your lady, if I dare say so." Fra Salvezza bowed to the lovely woman who sat at the head of the table beside Malatesta, a vision of golden glory from the fair braids woven with pearls to the shimmering dress of honey-colored silk brocade. "But as the madwoman was dressed in the shameless style of her trade —I did mention, did I not, that she was in the service of one of those mountebanks who peddle cures in the Piazza San Marco? —being, as I say, quite improperly dressed in a gown with a very tight and very low-cut bodice, and with such glossy masses of brownish-red hair in braids looped low to show beneath her veil, she was… well, not unattractive."

"Serving a mountebank!" exclaimed Malatesta. "Which one?"

Why did the man fix on the least interesting feature of his story? "I did not ask," replied Fra Salvezza, "for that had no connection with her fancied sins. You see, I knew she could not really have done what she claimed. Even a master mage who tried it would have had to take the greatest care to shield himself from the powerful demons required to create the illusion, and a woman would have had no idea even how to begin such an enchantment. Doubtless she had got the idea from one of the plays or ballads so popular in the Piazza, and had brooded on it until she was convinced it was real, and her doing. As if a woman could have such control over demons! It was like claiming that my mule had called up the Archangel Michael!" He laughed heartily. "But to spare the poor creature further suffering, I sold her an indulgence for the sin of necromancy and did not even ask more than such a one could pay. My noble clients, of course, are far too dignified to haggle, and they pay me at a rate consonant with their dignity, so I could well afford to be charitable to this poor creature."

To his chagrin, the lord of Rimini did not even notice this powerful hint, but returned to interrogating him about the madwoman. Why did he call her a lady? How exactly was she dressed? Did she say what role she played in the service of the mountebank? Was Fra Salvezza *sure* she had never mentioned just which of the empirics she worked for?"

"I called her a lady because of her bearing and speech, which were more suited to a court than to an empiric's stage in the Piazza. Her dress was dark green silk, and of good quality, and gold-embroidered," Fra Salvezza said, searching his memory for details that had seemed unimportant at the time, "but she wore no jewels, so she must have been telling the truth about her employment. If she had been, as I first thought, the wife or mistress of some wealthy Venetian, she would have had at least some gold chains and rings to show off his generosity. But she must have served one of the more important empirics, for the common wandering sort of mountebank does not dress his women so well. Let me see... oh, probably it was the Blond Boy –Il Capello d'Oro –for he too is very elegant, appearing in a long robe of green figured silk. But it might have been Il Scampamorte or even Il Mangiabissi. The others," he said dismissively, "are not successful enough to support a gently born woman, even a mad one."

~~~

Malatesta's first impulse, in his delight at finally getting onto Caterina's trail, was to reward Fra Salvezza with a purse of gold florins. Given the paucity of cash in San Florian, this was quickly reduced to a purse with Florentine florins, Venetian ducats, and a lone Hungarian forint sprinkled on top of a larger quantity of silver lire. Once again Malatesta regretted not having tortured Caterina's secretary Piero Giacomini before the man slipped out of the Rocca. He kept the accounts of the city –he must know where the money was hidden! But his men had turned the Rocca inside out without discovering more than a few paltry handfuls of coins. Oh, well –the reward was more than the wandering pardoner deserved, and Malatesta wasn't even going to ask for an indulgence in return. He didn't trust a God who would forgive sins like his for cash.

His mistake had been in dispensing the pardoner's reward immediately, in the glow of satisfaction at having at last found Caterina. He had intended to send the friar right back to Venice, to point out Caterina to his men, but the slippery fellow left the castle before dawn with no hint as to where he was bound next.

His next idea was to enlist the mage in identifying Caterina. If the idiot woman was actually showing her face –and, to judge from Fra Salvezza's story, much of the rest of her –in the Piazza San Marco, it should be child's play for Cacciote to identify her. He would send the mage with half a dozen men, enough to carry the woman off quietly without arousing any outcry.

"An excellent plan," said Cacciote when it was broached to him, "but you… cannot… spare… me… from your service at the castle."

The slow, emphatic speech seemed to burn into Malatesta's brain. "I cannot… spare… you," he repeated, feeling his tongue unusually thick in his mouth.

"But I can write another letter as from Lucrezia, that will get her back here without even the need for violence."

"You can write another letter as from Lucrezia. But what will it say?"

"Oh, that Lucrezia repents of her alliance with you, that you have been mistreating her vilely…"

"I have not!" Roberto exploded. True, he had backhanded her the other day and knocked her to the floor, but that was only what a woman could expect when she dared to nag her lord. He had certainly been keeping the idiotic female happy in bed, and that was all women really cared about.

"Of course you have not," Cacciote said, "but we are not concerned with the truth here, are we? We are composing lies that will persuade the little Countess to return, and you have thought of a very good one here."

"Yes… I thought… of it," said Roberto slowly. "What else?"

"Oh, that she will open the Rocca to Caterina's men, and they will take over the castle and everything will be as it was before. And to make sure the widow believes this, we will send some of her jewels with the letter, as Lucrezia's apology."

"Not the pearls," Roberto said. "I don't wish to hear Lucrezia's screeches if we try to take those back."

"No, of course not the pearls," Cacciote agreed. "They are much too valuable. The ruby tiara with matching earrings and necklace should be enough to make the widow forget any questions she may have." He had spent more than one evening looking through the contents of Caterina's jewel boxes, trying to figure out which items he could safely dispose of to swell his own purse. "And the sapphire filigree pendant, and a few chains and some rings, and perhaps a pearl brooch." If by some ill chance Malatesta learned that a few of these items had not actually reached Caterina in Venice, why, the soldiers sent with them would be the obvious suspects. But most likely he would never hear about them.

"I still think it would have been a good plan to enchant the jewels to identify her."

"Hardly necessary," replied Cacciote, not mentioning that he had no idea what charm had first been used to protect Caterina's jewels from thieves, much less how to modify it so that the jewels would cry out only when Caterina herself touched them. "And unwise. Talking jewels would draw attention that we do not need. They might even get her arrested for witchcraft, and it would be extremely hard to extricate her from a Venetian prison."

"Un...wise," Roberto repeated. "Yes, of course. I see that now."

And he had, most conveniently, forgotten Cacciote's earlier excuse that such a charm could hardly be useful in locating one woman out of the multitudes in Venice; it could take a man all his life to show a ring to every one of the fifty thousand living there, and long before he identified Caterina he would probably show it to the wrong person and get his throat slit for the ring.

Now the task was so much simpler that there was no need to play tricks with the jewels; Malatesta's men had only to observe life in the Piazza to figure out which noted mountebank had in his troupe a brown-haired woman who spoke like a lady. Even they should be up to so simple a task. And now that he had invoked the charm of compulsion, Cacciote could ensure that Malatesta did not send him along to make the identification. He really should have worked that charm much earlier; a pity that the ingredients were so hard to get!

Once the letter was sent off, Malatesta's impatience for results kept him from resting and kept the members of his household on edge. The lingering cough was developing quite nicely in Cacciote's opinion, being tiring enough to keep Malatesta reasonably quiet while clearly not life-threatening. But now the pardoner's broad hints about the value of indulgences had set Malatesta to thinking about his latter end.

"I am still a young man," he said angrily to Cacciote. "I cannot endure being shackled by this damned cough! I want to ride, to hunt, to invite my neighbors to banquets..." He broke off to cough.

"Patience," Cacciote advised him. "You are already much better. Now that the weather is warm, you will recover much faster."

"I wish I felt like it," Malatesta said. "Are you sure, mage, that I am not tottering to my deathbed?"

"As you just said," Cacciote reminded him, "you are still young and virile! Nobody questions that!"

"Sometimes I question it myself. Prepare my horoscope."

"What?"

"I know that you necromancers have secret arts by which to divine the future. Go and find out the day of my death and tell it me, that I may cease brooding over this damned chest-cough!"

"The day of your death? That is an exceedingly difficult and perilous divination," Cacciote protested. He infused in his voice a little of the compulsion spell that helped him keep the lord of Rimini under control. "You... do not need... the exact date... for it is surely many years in the future."

"Not... the exact... date..." Malatesta repeated. "But you must be able to give me some clue!"

Cacciote had no intention of exhausting himself by working a death-divination. But he collected the materials necessary to make an impressive display for Malatesta. Two nights later, the lord's body servants helped Malatesta to sit in an upright chair in one of the tower rooms and then withdrew, leaving him alone with his court mage. Cacciote drew a protective circle around them both and then called up a number of minor fire spirits. At the same time he released the bottles which he had previously filled with voices and music. They did not, of course, say anything comprehensible; that would have been too difficult to fake. But the breathy melodies and the flickering, varicolored flames had the desired effect upon his dupe, and Malatesta did not complain when Cacciote told him that he had only been able to get a partial answer to the question.

"To learn a precise date," he said, truthfully, "would require me to call upon demons of such power and evil will that the Pope himself would hardly be safe in their presence. But what we have learned tonight should relieve your mind. The wind spirits sang that you will not die until three days after I myself do –and I am an exceptionally healthy man, not to mention having access to life-prolonging secrets which I gladly share with you!"

He felt quite proud of this "divination." Malatesta showed an alarming tendency to break free of the compulsion spell from time to time; this prophecy should help to insure Cacciote's own life during those perilous moments. The lord of Rimini would henceforth be as careful of Cacciote's well-being as of his own.

# ~CHAPTER TWENTY-FOUR~

*Some of these dishonest mountebanks undertake to suck water out of the ear, which they fill with a tube from their mouth, and hold the other end to the ear; and so spurting the water out of their mouths, pretend it came from the ear. Others pretend to get out worms, which grow in the ear, or roots of the teeth. Others can extract frogs from the under part of the tongue; and by lancing make an incision, into which they clap in the frog, and so take it out.*
*-Abu Bekr Mohammed Ibn Zacariya ar-Razi, commonly called Rhazes*

~ ~ ~

The competition between the healers who peddled their wares in the Piazza San Marco was usually good-humored enough, but on this particular day the Signoria had, with the approval of the Ten, announced a new tax on all transactions in the Piazza. The prospect of giving up the sixth part of every ducat received made the practitioners irritable and unusually dedicated to seeing that their own sales were not injured by those of the frauds and criminals who dared to compete with them. Even Agostino Foscari was moved to bitter invective against Capello d'Oro's shameless attempt to steal away the customers who had been drawn to Yusuf il Turco.

"Everyone knows," he thundered in response to Capello d'Oro's questioning of the real identity of 'Foscari's pet Turk,' "yes, even in Milan and Naples they know that the Golden-Haired is ignorant and vicious. He would do best to go back to his home town of Florence, where the vice he practices is so much in vogue that the Pope has threatened the entire city with excommunication for tolerating it! Why do you think no women act upon his stage? He has eyes only for pretty boys!"

"Attacking my personal life," Capello d'Oro shot back, "does nothing to conceal the lies and cheating of that quack who calls himself the Death-Defying! Not only are his attempts at alchemy unsuccessful, but he has lowered himself to the occupation of a pimp. His house is full of courtesans and outright prostitutes who get the attention of the masses by posing half-naked upon his stage!"

"A true scholar has no need to pay attention to such lousy slanders," Foscari thundered back. "My translation from the Arabic of al-Razi contains secrets of medicine which Golden Boy can never divine. What's more, my translation from the Greek of Ptolemy's Geography is a handbook for travelers everywhere - "

"May God help them," Capello d'Oro interrupted, "for it is riddled with errors so great that a man seeking to travel from here to the Holy Roman Empire is like to find himself adrift in the Middle Sea!"

"Golden Boy speaks of matters which he understands as well as my horse!" retorted Foscari. "Furthermore, not only are his recipes more like poisons than potions, but he seeks to defraud the ignorant even further by secretly inserting a bone or even a tiny frog into an open wound and then making a show of withdrawing it, as though that were what had prevented healing all along!"

While the two men settled down happily to a protracted slanging match, Caterina made herself inconspicuous inside the curtained booth where she met with women who desired a private consultation, but who were afraid to come to a house guarded by a monstrous crocodile. She had no desire to be dragged up on the stage to testify to the cures she had wrought, and even less to be called a whore by Capello d'Oro. Gian might enjoy joining the war of words by shouting things in what he claimed to be Turkish —which sounded like the barking of dogs to her untrained ear —but she wished devoutly that she had not come to the Piazza on the day the empirics had decided to enjoy a good fight.

A man's hand twitched the curtain aside.

"This space is only for my female clients!" Caterina snapped. Where was Foscari's manservant Topolino when she needed him? She was not afraid - she could always run out of the back of the curtained enclosure and onto the stage where hundreds of eyes would see any attack on her —but she was annoyed, for escaping an intruder that way would plunge her right into the middle of the vulgar quarrel she was avoiding now.

"I have a letter from a lady, madonna," the strange man said softly. "A lady whom you know well and will be happy to hear from." He extended a hand that held nothing more threatening than a leather tube with a rolled-up sheet of paper protruding from its open end.

Caterina perused the letter with growing pleasure, accepted the accompanying gifts, and called to Foscari's manservant to escort her home. She was not going to remain in the Piazza with these things in her possession, nor was she about to risk walking alone through Venice's crowded streets with them!

"My men and I would be pleased to escort you home, Contessa," said the gentlemanly-looking one who had given her the letter and the casket. He raised the curtain slightly and indicated five more men, looking more like common soldiers, awaiting him just outside.

"Then you and your men *and* Topolino shall accompany me," Caterina decreed, slightly distracted as usual by the irony of calling Foscari's hulking manservant "Little Mouse." Men could be so cruel in the nicknames they gave one another! She supposed that Topolino was lucky his friends hadn't picked on something even worse, like "Pretty Boy."

While Caterina was collecting her medical supplies, the soldiers conferred softly.

"Boss, why don't we just knock her over the head and carry her off?" one of them asked.

"In the middle of the Piazza San Marco? Are you crazy? Do you want to experience a Venetian prison? We'll wait until we're alone with her. Besides, she's cooperating right now. It'll be easier if she continues to cooperate until we're well out of town."

That continued to be the plan, since "alone" was not really a concept that applied to Venice in the middle of a pleasant day. Boatmen delivering fresh vegetables to local markets leaned on their oars and gossiped with servant girls sent to throw the household's garbage into the nearest canal. Women gathered around the wells in the little squares shouted slightly improper suggestions to apprentices on their masters' business, and the apprentices rightly interpreted these as invitations to stop and flirt. Peddlers added their cries to the general hubbub, as did tavern keepers who leaned over their open half-doors and suggested that hard-working citizens were entitled to a shady seat and a cup of wine.

And at least half of these people recognized Caterina and greeted "the little healer" warmly.

"See?" the leader elbowed his second-in-command behind Caterina's back. "We do it quietly, nobody gets hurt, nobody goes to jail. We can tie her up after we get out of the city." With any luck, the hulking man whom Caterina had called "Little Mouse" was one of the mountebank's servants and would not come with them. Any two of his men could take out the big servant, but why risk getting hurt if it wasn't necessary?

Once safely at the House of the Crocodile, Caterina told the messenger that he and his men should wait outside while she made her preparations. She would send Topolino out to them with bread and cheese to sustain them while they waited.

"And wine," she added, seeing the crestfallen faces of the men from San Florian. "And, naturally, wine." But not, she thought privately, the strong, sweet wines imported from Zara and Cyprus. The cheapest local vintage, thin and sour, was good enough for these men. But one had to give them something if they were to wait until Gian and Dottore Foscari returned home. She hoped her friends would soon tire of verbal brawling in the Piazza and would pack up, to go back to work another day when the mood was more settled.

The wish turned out, for once, to be father to the fact; it was only mid-afternoon when the rest of Foscari's troupe returned to the house, tired, hungry, but cheered by the certainty that they had insulted Capello d'Oro far worse than he had slandered them. Caterina could barely contain her excitement until they had eaten and she could draw Gian back into the room they shared.

"I need to talk to you," Gian said before she had even begun. "There are soldiers watching the house, did you know?"

"Oh, yes," Caterina said happily. "They are from San Florian."

"*Porca miseria!*" Gian cursed. "Where's my sword –the real one, not this worthless stage property?"

"It's all right," Caterina hastened to assure him. "They are only here to protect me and the jewels. I have even provided them with food and drink while they wait for me to make my arrangements for the journey. And now that you're here - "

Forgetful of courtesy, Gian sat down on the room's single chair. "I seem to have entered in the middle of the play. I think," he said, breathing hard, "you had better begin at the beginning."

Glowing with happiness, Caterina showed him the letter from Lucrezia and the collection of jewels which had accompanied it. "She is not really a bad person," she told Gian, "only a little…"

"Self-centered?" Gian suggested. "Short-sighted? Untrustworthy?"

"She is *family*," Caterina said firmly, "and she has now seen enough of Roberto Malatesta to convince her of her errors. Apparently he is as unpleasant as his father Sigismondo the Wife-Killer was, if not quite so lethal; I do not wonder that she is eager to get free of him. She wants me to come back to San Florian; she says she can let us into the Rocca secretly, and that most of Malatesta's men have returned to Rimini so it will not take a very large force to secure the castle. And with the jewels she has sent in token of her honesty, we can easily hire enough condottieri to do that."

"We cannot possibly get enough to fund an army to besiege the castle."

Caterina ignored this complaint as irrelevant. "Look, this pendant of sapphires set in gold filigree would alone buy us a dozen men! And if we go by way of Rimini, and collect Matteo and the rest of your original group from there –"

"We still would not have nearly enough for a siege! I thought you could count better than that!"

"We shan't need to besiege the city," Caterina said. "I told you, Lucrezia will let us into the Rocca."

"And you trust her to do that?" Gian sprang up and paced around the room. "Have you run mad?"

"Why not? She's done it before," Caterina pointed out.

"Yes," said Gian with heavy sarcasm, "Nothing inclines me to trust someone more than the knowledge that they've betrayed me in the past." He rubbed the back of his neck irritably. His luck didn't need to keep pestering him with warnings; the folly of Caterina's plan was clear to the meanest intelligence. But the tingling only grew in scope and intensity, sweeping up the back of his head and making the hairs stand on end. What must he do? The first thing was to get rid of the soldiers watching the house from outside. Of course they were Malatesta's men, not Lucrezia's, and they were there to take Caterina back to San Florian by force if necessary. Gian had absolutely no doubt about that, especially when his luck was so insistently warning him of approaching danger. But how to dispel them? Gian was under no illusions about his ability to take out half a dozen armed men. Maybe with Topolino's help? No, the big servant might look frightening, but he was no fighter.

Perhaps Foscari could think of a trick? A frightening stage illusion? No, he was more expert at making people laugh than scaring them. Caterina could probably have come up with something, but as long as she kidded herself that these men were from a repentant Lucrezia she wouldn't cooperate. What else could he do? Well… Caterina had already mentioned giving those damned soldiers food and drink when they arrived at the house. By now they were probably ready for more wine. And this time the thin, cheap stuff kept for lower-class visitors wouldn't do. It would have to be Foscari's best malmsey, with its rich, deep taste.

# ~CHAPTER TWENTY-FIVE~

*The manufacture and sale of poisons was only one small part of the activities of an extensive underworld that specialized in the supply of services that could not be offered by the established church and state. This community... numbered among its members wise women, astrologers, alchemists, confidence men, witches, shady apothecaries, and back-street abortionists who between them told fortunes and cast horoscopes, sold love potions and lucky charms, cured toothache, and offered to dispose of unwanted babies and unwanted husbands.*

*-Philip Wexler, Toxicology in the Middle Ages and Renaissance*

~ ~ ~

"You're sure it won't kill them?" Gian insisted anxiously. He might have risked killing one man and tipping the body into a canal, but half a dozen dead bodies outside the house just might be pushing his luck. The back of his head was positively throbbing with warning. Kill all those men, and he'd find himself marched away to a Venetian prison. Besides, murder by poisoning was a coward's way.

His neck burned as if he'd laid a stinging nettle on it. He rubbed it and looked closely at Foscari, trying to gauge the man's sincerity.

"My dear boy," Foscari said irritably, "has it not occurred to you that a collection of corpses in front of my house would be extremely bad for business? Of course I'm not going to give you a poison. This is a simple decoction of Blessed Thistle and Star of Bethlehem. Either would serve our purpose; both, especially when mixed with alcohol, are infallible. And the effects are indistinguishable from those of overindulgence in wine and spirits –something to which soldiers are known to be prone! Only wait a few minutes after those greedy dogs have gulped down my excellent malmsey, and they will be quite incapable of interfering when you spirit your little countess away. They probably will not even notice her, if you dress her like a serving woman and throw a hooded cape over her."

It all sounded good; but now the prickles were running up and down his spine. After Topolino went out with the malmsey Gian peered between the shutters, waiting anxiously for the effects Foscari had promised. It would be no good unless all of them drank at the same time.

"I had the foresight to pour all three bottles into a leather skin," Foscari said smugly. "Of course they'll all swill it down as fast as possible; no one will be such a fool as to wait and let his fellows drink up the whole skinful."

He was right about that. And very soon after the skin of wine had been emptied, the vomiting and groaning started.

"Madonna, for the love of God, *hurry!*" Gian whispered through the closed door. "This is our time to get away."

A slim figure all but drowned in a bunchy skirt and bodice emerged. "Betta's clothes are a little big for me," Caterina apologized. "And since she can't wear mine –"

Whatever she had been going to say was drowned out by a thunderous hammering on the door. Gian groaned. One of Malatesta's men must have been more abstemious than they thought.

He peered through the shutters again. The soldiers from San Florian were moaning, trying to stand up, and vomiting all over the stones of the courtyard, too miserable even to aim at the gutter.

The men banging on the front door were dressed in the blue and gold of Venice.

With half-armor.

And swords.

"Let them in, Topolino," groaned Foscari, "before they break the door down."

There were a dozen armed men surrounding a shabby woman with the wide, milky eyes of the blind. Behind her was a hideous old woman.

"That's her!" the old hag screeched, pointing at Caterina. "She sold my daughter a potion that she said would expel the baby from her womb before her husband found out about it, but instead it killed my poor daughter! Poisoner!"

"Poisoner!" echoed a well-dressed lady who had hung back for a moment. "She offered me a potion to rid myself of my husband, when all I wanted was to regain his affection!"

Foscari stepped between Caterina and her accusers, raising his hands for a moment's silence. "These are obviously false accusations laid by my jealous competitors. Only ask that fraud who calls himself Il Capello d'Oro –"

"She can tell it to the inquisitors," snapped the leader of the guard. "Come along, my girl." He dodged around Foscari and caught Caterina by the arm. Gian instinctively reached for his sword, but found nothing except the hilt of the cheap tin "Turkish saber" with which Foscari had outfitted him.

"Aiii!" screamed the blind woman. "There are demons here, I can feel them! Take away the necromancer!" And her finger pointed directly at Caterina.

"Not while I live!" For lack of anything better, Gian pulled out the cheap "saber" and…

The prickling at the back of his head turned into shooting pains, and then the world went dark.

~ ~ ~

When he opened his eyes, the light was like a dagger stabbing through them. So he closed them again. A moment later he sat up, his head whirling, and vomited. He noticed without much interest that someone had kindly placed a bowl in front of him.

Then his memory returned.

"Caterina!" He scrambled to his feet. The room spun around him and he leaned on a cabinet. "They took her. What –where is she –we have to find her!"

"I know exactly where she is," said Foscari, "and we can hardly do anything about it until you are able to stand. Here." He guided Gian to a chair and pressed a cool, damp cloth to his forehead. It eased a pain he hadn't really noticed until then.

Foscari's cherished curiosity, the skeleton made by joining that of a spiny fish to the jaws of a wolf, lay in pieces on the floor.

"They took Caterina," Gian repeated stupidly. "And wrecked your house?"

"Ah, not exactly," Foscari said. "In a moment of excitement, I —ah —well, I threw the skeleton at them. It didn't help, of course. I should have thrown something heavier."

"I am glad you did not," Gian said. His brains seemed to be returning. "I should be in sad case indeed if you were locked up as well as Caterina. We have no other friend in Venice."

Foscari cleared his throat. "As to that… I am thinking that it is time I set out for Milan. I usually visit the northern fairs in spring, but I had been delaying my departure this year because business was so good in Venice." He looked sadly down at the shattered skeleton. "I think that, for a while, I had best not try my luck in the Piazza San Marco. I was collecting my supplies and packing when you regained consciousness."

Gian groaned.

"Of course I was not going to leave without saying goodbye to you, my boy!" Foscari said. "What's more, you are welcome to stay in the House of the Crocodile as long as you like. I am afraid that Topolino and Betta, not to mention my midgets, must accompany me. But you will easily find some good woman to come in and cook and scrub for you. I am leaving," he said proudly, "almost all of the countess's jewels, which I found in her room while looking for spare clothes for Betta. If you were so rich, Gian, what were you and she doing working for an empiric in the Piazza? Was I part of some plan which you did not share with me?"

"We weren't rich," Gian tried to explain. "The jewels —she only got them this morning —the soldiers from San Florian brought them."

"Indeed! Do your enemies always bring such fine gifts?"

Where are they now?"

"The jewels, or the soldiers?"

"Both."

"The jewels are in the casket where I found them," Foscari said, "all except one little, little ring which I borrowed to defray my expenses in this sudden move. And the men of San Florian have been locked up in the common jail for being disgusting drunks and spewing all over the street in the middle of the afternoon."

"Not with Caterina!" Another shred of memory came back. "They spoke of inquisitors. Did the Church take her?"

"Worse, I fear. The inquisitors have been known to free those who can convince them of their innocence. It was Antonio da Treviso's own bodyguard who took her away." Foscari regarded Gian with a touch of pity. "I am afraid that the spymaster of Venice has your lady. Few escape his interest without being drawn into one of his tortuous plots; he is one of the Ten, you know. Do you not think you would do better to join me on the road to Milan?"

Gian was somewhat more impolite about that suggestion than became a man speaking to his only friend in a city of a hundred thousand, but Foscari made allowances for the natural intemperance of a man in love. He had not guessed that it had gone so deep with Gian —and if it had, why the devil was he still sleeping on the floor? He'd seen how the little countess looked at his friend, and he would have laid a gold florin to three silver scudi that she wouldn't kick him out of her bed.

Not that she'd have the chance to, now that she was well and truly caught in one of the spymaster's webs. Foscari did not wish to hurry Gian, but he really wanted to be well out of Venice before da Treviso thought of a way in which he, too, could be useful to the city's intelligence services.

~~~

Gian was admitted at once when he presented himself at da Treviso's house. This time he was not dressed like a fool in Foscari's idea of Turkish garb, but in the black velvet doublet which he had worn as the captain of Caterina's personal bodyguard, with his good sword in the scabbard that hung from his left hip. Da Treviso's servants relieved him of the sword, of course, but afterwards they politely showed him into the cool, comfortable room where he had been received previously, with its tapestried hangings of Biblical scenes, its painted table holding jugs of wine, and its high-backed chairs.

"Where is she?" Gian demanded as soon as da Treviso entered.

Da Treviso regarded him for a long minute, looking him up and down. "Last time I received a Turkish mountebank; this time, it seems, I have the honor to speak with a gentleman. All the better. Let us try, if we can, to conduct this business without rude demands."

"Caterina?"

"Your woman? She is quite, quite safe, and will remain so. I had already prepared a room in the upper story of my house for her. My servants will attend to her every comfort."

"A room," said Gian, "with a door that locks from the outside, I suspect."

"Not quite suitable for a palazzo belonging to someone of my eminence," da Treviso agreed smoothly, "but the exigencies of my service to Venice occasionally require inducing someone to stay with me who otherwise might be tempted to leave. Now *you*, I am persuaded, will be cooperative in all ways —seeing that the lady's well-being depends on it. My people assure me that the attachment between you two is quite charming. Why have you never married her?"

Gian felt his face warming. "Is that any of your business?"

"Everything that goes on in Venice is my business," da Treviso said, "including what does *not* go on. Now explain why you have not married the lady. Is she your light-of-love?"

Gian was half out of his chair, right hand reaching across his body for a sword-hilt that was not there, before he remembered his position and Caterina's.

"The lady," he said, "is as far above me as a star in the night sky is above a tallow candle."

"But you are," da Treviso pursued, "most sincerely attached to her."

"I am her loyal servant."

"Loyal enough to do what is necessary to set her free?"

"And what might that be?"

"Have you so soon forgotten our last meeting? I require a Turkish-speaking physician whom I can recommend to the Sublime Porte as a token of the great esteem and mutual regard of our two states."

"I cannot go to Constantinople and leave her as your prisoner!"

"I do not see that you would have a great deal of choice in the matter," purred da Treviso, "but, fortunately, that is not what I am proposing. The physician of my choice will travel with a woman skilled in the use of simples for healing women's complaints."

"Your –Caterina, is it? Strange, that is not the name she has been using in the Piazza. Well, whatever the name, she has attracted considerable interest by her successes with women. Formerly barren women sing her praises, wives seeking to amend a husband's neglect call upon her, and she is said to have cured a host of the lesser-known and disgusting ailments of which females complain. The two of you will travel, at my expense, to Constantinople. There, our *bailo* will recommend you to the notice of the sultan."

"And Caterina?"

"Will find some way to enter the seraglio, bearing either healing potions or luxury goods for the sultan's wives –whichever works. I have reason to believe that there is a formerly Venetian lady there who still entertains some fondness for her natal city, and who may be able to inform us of the Sublime Porte's plans for their spring campaign." Da Treviso stroked his beard, delicately shook out his lace cuffs, and favored Gian with a benign smile. "She was once Beatriz Rossi, but is now known, I believe, as Aysin Hatun."

"And you will free Caterina if we agree?"

"The lady," Da Treviso said, "will be awaiting you on board the merchantman which is to take you both to Constantinople. She will be freed from her very slight and not at all burdensome confinement as soon as the lagoon of Venice disappears beyond the horizon."

# ~CHAPTER TWENTY-SIX~

*From the marble gods they make limestone; the bronze figures are recast into cannon; the bronze pedestals of the statues are cast into coins; the lofty columns are cut up to make building stones with which to erect mosques or tile the floors of Turkish baths.*

*Pierre Gilles, translated and quoted in Babinger, <u>Mehmed the Conqueror and His Time</u>*

~ ~ ~

Entering the waters of the Golden Horn, the carrack swept around the city of Constantinople and the palace of Topkapi. The green hill with its white walls, its courtyards and gates, its halls and outbuildings and separate palaces within the great compound, rose before them. The residence that Mehmed II had begun building more than twenty years previously was still under construction. Most of the walls gleamed white with new paint and plaster, and were overtopped with narrow walkways along crenellated parapets that could provide shelter to defending archers. Those walls, the high bulbous towers of the minarets, and the gates upon gates within the palace complex proclaimed the consequence of the Sublime Porte for all to see.

To their right, on the other side of the water, was their immediate destination: the suburb of Galata, which had become the unofficial sanctuary of Christian merchants and ambassadors in Constantinople. Here the Venetian *bailo* had his residence, as did the Genoese ambassador and those of

Rome and France. The leading merchant dynasties of Florence and Milan, Venice and Amalfi and Genoa kept representatives in Galata; the Patriarch of Constantinople, installed by Mehmed II after his conquest of the city to manage the Orthodox Christian community, lived in Galata; twelve Catholic counselors administered the affairs of the Catholic churches. And, of course, there were taverns on every street. Apart from the prohibition on the ringing of church bells, the suburb might almost have been an Italian city.

"It looks like one of our hill towns –a very prosperous one," said Caterina, looking up the hill at the straight streets, the red-roofed stone houses and the sprinkling of churches.

Something in her tone caught Gian's ear. "You disapprove?"

"No… I am sure it is very nice, and I am more than ready to get off this ship. But having come so far, I had expected something more…" She fumbled for words. "…more *different*! I mean, Constantinople is the home of the Grand Turk! I…"

"You wanted something more exotic," Gian guessed. "Well, if you get into the seraglio as da Treviso wants, that should be exotic enough for anybody!"

Caterina sighed happily. "*No one* in San Florian has ever seen Constantinople, let alone Topkapi Palace, and certainly not the seraglio! I do hope the gifts we have brought will get me an invitation to visit there."

"And I," said Gian somewhat more seriously, "hope that you come out again!" The concept of letting Caterina go into a walled world strictly forbidden to intact men was one that had been giving him nightmares all the way from Venice. What could he do if she never came out? What if the sultan, struck by Caterina's beauty, decided to keep her for himself?

At least he was not feeling any ominous tingling or prickling at the moment. His lucky angel seemed to be as contented as Caterina was disappointed with the Italianate suburb of Galata.

For fear of breakage or other damages, they refrained from unpacking the gifts and merchandise sent by da Treviso until they reached the compound of the Venetian *bailo*. Better to pay the extra fees for lugging the boxes and bales than to take any chances with the contents.

Battista Gritti exploded into the courtyard as soon as the little cavalcade of travel-stained people and overladen donkeys appeared. "Where have you been? I expected you over a week ago!"

Gian considered pointing out that the swift, narrow brigantines employed by da Treviso to carry important messages to and from Venice were bound to reach Constantinople faster than the round-built carrack, heavy with European manufactured goods, that had brought him and Caterina here. But why bother? Gritti must know that already. The family was something important in Venice –he could not remember, now, just where he'd heard the name –but any wealthy Venetian had to be aware of the constraints that limited the movement of their merchant ships, from storms to piracy.

"I did not know there was any urgency about our arrival," he said, not quite as an apology.

"*Urgency!* When I –" Gritti looked about him at the very interested porters who were, as slowly as possible, removing the baggage from the donkeys and setting it down in the courtyard.

"Never mind," he said hastily, "let us discuss the matter indoors. You must be tired after your journey. Will you and the lady take a glass of wine with me?"

"Are you allowed to have wine here? I thought Muslims did not drink!" Caterina exclaimed. She had spent much of the voyage picking the brains of the sailors about the ways of this strange world they were going to.

"But Christians do," said Gritti with a smile. "And so, in my experience, do Turks –at least, a good many of them come over the water from Constantinople proper to give custom to our Galata taverns like the Stone Steps and the Constant Traveler. If you would care to join us, ah, Madonna…"

He paused gracefully and Gian, remembering himself, made formal introductions.

"You seem to be in a hurry," he said. "But I should like to reassure myself that our gifts to the Sublime Porte have arrived undamaged."

"I suppose we have time for that," Gritti acknowledged without explaining what the hurry was about.

Over twists of sweet spiced bread and cups of golden Bulgarian misket wine, they unpacked the gifts and trade goods sent by da Treviso. The bulk of the carrack's cargo, sent by private merchants, consisted of Flemish woolens and other dull but useful goods, but da Treviso had spared no expense to catch the eyes of the ladies of the seraglio. There were lengths of silk velvet falling in heavy, graceful folds; veils and dress lengths of the very fine crinkled silk called by the Turks *bürümcük* and by the Italians *plissettato*; red silk brocades bright with gold and silver threads. But all these were outshone when they came to remove the glassware from its straw-filled boxes. Bowls and goblets, beads and mirrors, a covered drinking cup with two handles shaped like dragons and a plethora of enameled saucers covered the table with sparkling light and color. A string of turban-shaped beads made up of twisted layers of translucent gold-flecked glass was set aside as a gift, as was a second string of brightly colored tubular beads that looked like massed gold and blue flowers on a red background. Caterina added to this pile a convex mirror cleverly framed in the twisted latticework that had recently become popular among the glassworkers of Murano. At the other end of the table, two goblets from the Barovier workshop were among the finest of the goods being withheld in the hope of getting an invitation to display them in the seraglio. The stems and bases of the goblets were clear as rock crystal, while the bowls were bright with enameled hunting scenes against a lapis background.

"We had a pair of goblets of *cristallo* once," Caterina said wistfully, eyeing these treasures, "just clear glass, with no picture-work, but my husband valued them highly." So had the merchant who'd sold them to Girolamo for more money than she had ever guessed you could spend just for something to drink out of. "They were broken when the palazzo was looted."

"These will be even more highly valued," said Gritti, "for the Turks have no idea how to do this work. They keep trying to lure away some of our Murano glassworkers to teach them the secrets of *cristallo* and *latticino*."

"But of course good Venetians cannot be tempted by Turkish bribes," Caterina suggested politely.

"That is a matter for Antonio da Treviso's department. The last two artisans who tried to take employment away from Murano were fished out of the canals," Gritti said. "That –ah –encourages the others to remain loyal. In any case the Turks would require not just these secrets, but all the expertise of the glass houses, from the building and management of the kilns to the secret of powdering and applying colors. They would have to bribe away an entire company of workers!"

He spoke proudly, and Gian remembered where he had heard the name of Gritti before. They had married into one of the great glassmaking houses of Murano. Doubtless this Battista Gritti knew what he was talking about. Although, equally doubtless, he had been reared as an aristocrat and not as a glass worker. An actual glass worker would have been far too valuable to be sent as an ambassador...

Gian picked up the string of gold-flecked glass beads. "Would these, and the mirror, be appropriate to send as gifts to the sultan's ladies? And, hmm, perhaps one length each of *plissettato* and silk brocade? We do not wish to insult the ladies, but we must also hold something back so that they will invite Contessa Rinaldi to show the remaining goods." This had been da Treviso's idea; he was not altogether sure that he had correctly interpreted the *bailo's* hints about a woman herbalist for the seraglio, but he was absolutely certain that Caterina had to get in there somehow to speak face to face with the woman who had been Beatriz Rossi.

"We can discuss that tomorrow," Gritti said. "For now, you need to put on something more impressive, preferably a physician's robe –you *did* bring appropriate clothing, did you not? And while you are doing that, I shall get a boat to take you across the water. The countess and I can organize the trade goods and gifts while we wait for your return."

"Where," Gian inquired mildly, "am I going?"

"Oh. Did I not explain? I was so worried that you would not arrive in time. Da Treviso's letter led me to expect you last week... You have an appointment in Topkapi this evening, you see. The sultan is most eager to see a new physician with new cures."

"You do understand that I am not actually a physician?"

"All the better," said Gritti, "that means you have not yet killed anybody with your nostrums –you *do* have nostrums, do you not? The Miraculous Oil that you were hawking in Venice, and suchlike cures?"

"Cures for what?"

But Gritti was vague on this point. Everyone knew the sultan was not in good health. Everyone knew that it was debatable whether he would be able to accompany the army on the coming campaign. Everyone and his brother and his brother's laundress knew what ailed the sultan; the trouble was that they all knew different things. It was either a blockage of the intestines, or a recurrence of last year's ulcerated leg, or an infected wound, or a quartan fever, or something else.

"It would be nice," Gian grumbled to Caterina before Gritti hurried him off, "to know exactly *what* I am supposed to be curing."

# ~CHAPTER TWENTY-SEVEN~

*Sura 113: Daybreak*
*Say: I seek refuge with the Lord of the Dawn,*
*From the mischief of created things;*
*From the mischief of Darkness as it overspreads;*
*From the mischief of those who practice secret arts;*
*And from the mischief of the envious one as he practices envy.*

*-Translation of the Koran by Abdullah Yusuf Ali*

The sultan's intelligence service was nearly as good as that of the Venetians. Before the Venetian carrack had been unloaded Karamanli Pasha was already conferring with Cicek Hatun, mother of the sultan's younger son Djem, about the meaning of this new arrival. The two parties sat on opposite sides of a delicately carved wooden lattice that allowed the passage of sound and a sprinkling of light but did not permit the pasha's eyes even a glimpse of Cicek Hatun's face. On his side of the lattice, two janissaries stood out of earshot at the far end of the conference room; on hers, she was attended by two recently acquired slave girls who had not yet learned Turkish. Thus they conferred in the perfect propriety required for a lady of the seraglio, and yet with the perfect privacy desirable for people speaking on the subjects that concerned them.

"There are already too many Venetians creeping around Topkapi Serai," Cicek Hatun complained. "First the sultan makes a pet of that hostage boy who was captured at Otranto; then Venice sends that painter to decorate the walls of the palace with images of courtiers and men in battle, which is not only unnecessary but *haram*. Now they have sent a physician to get access to the sultan's private rooms! They are clearly seeking to get influence, probably to dissuade him from his plan to conquer Venice next."

Karamanli frowned. "They may even succeed. He has had maps and plans of campaign drawn up, but he has always been impulsive. He might suddenly declare that we are to take Naples or even Alexandria, and never mind the disaster that would be for the army's masters of logistics."

"Venice would be the best target," Cicek Hatun insisted. "He desires another great victory. The fall of Venice would shake the world of the infidels nearly as much as did the conquest of Constantinople."

"I agree, but I do not think the Venetian influence in the serai is as great as you fear. The fair-haired hostage is a Frank, to be sure, but I do not think he is necessarily a Venetian. Most of the Venetians and Genoese that I have seen are as dark as Turks. From Andrea's looks, I would guess that he hails from the northern part of the Frankish lands, where there are many people with golden hair. In any case he has no influence with Mehmed; he is just a pretty boy whom it pleases the sultan to use for a crutch when he hobbles anywhere. As for the painter —I have heard him prattling when the sultan allows him to remain to share a meal. Trust me, in all matters not concerning drawing and color he is just an idiot."

"And the physician?"

"I do not know about him yet," Karamanli admitted. "But I shall consult with Dervish Ismail, who understands both medicine and the dark arts far better than any crude Frank. If he cannot himself cure Mehmed, he can at least ensure that this foreign physician does not gain credit for any cure."

"You had best make speed," said Cicek Hatun sharply. "The Frank is to be received this very night. And if he has some trick of Western magic to ease Mehmed, you and your dervish will be the ones who get no credit."

~ ~ ~

The journey to the sultan's side might have been, and probably was, designed to unnerve foreign visitors to the court. An escort of janissaries marched Gian back down the hill of Galata to the harbor, where a boat was waiting to convey them to the opposite shore. There Gian mounted a horse of uncertain temperament which he had to guide through the narrow, winding streets of the old city. He had thought that most of old Constantinople had been burned down at the time of the Turkish conquest. Now he could have wished that a bit more of the city had suffered that fate. There was just one straight road to the outer gate of Topkapi, and the janissary who rode beside him gave him to understand that of non-Muslims, only foreign ambassadors were allowed to use it. All other accursed Franks had to make their way through a twisting maze of back streets, the riders bending their heads to pass below the overhanging porches and rooms that hung out over the street from the second story of each house.

Well, at least his Turkish was good enough to understand not only the rules, but the subtle malice behind them.

The darkening streets were quieter than those of an Italian city where evening walks were the main amusement for most of the population, but they were far from deserted. Women called to one another from the overhanging windows; a child's thin cry rose and was immediately silenced with a lullaby. Men chatted on the streets, reluctantly moving away to give passage-room to the two men on horseback and the following escort of marching janissaries. A seller of sweetmeats called out the description of his wares in a monotonous chant.

The evening air was sweet with the perfume of strange flowers, and oil lamps flickered in windows like fiery spirits sent to mislead the unwary.

But the back of Gian's neck was, for once, not tingling. This and this alone allowed him to keep his countenance firm and undismayed as he was escorted past a massive building to face a high, arched portal. On either side of the arch were columns with niches in which ugly rounded, shriveled objects were incongruously displayed, just visible in the fading twilight.

"The Sublime Porte," said the one janissary who had ridden beside Gian and condescended to speak to him in Italian. He raised his curved sword and pointed at one of the desiccated shapes in a right-hand niche. "The former Kadi of Anatolia. He usurped the rights of the sultan by administering his own justice to lawbreakers. So end those who displease the sultan." The blade lowered to point out the head directly below the kadi's. "The former *sanjakbey* of Bosnia, Iskender Bey. He broke the peace treaty with Venice by raiding into Friuli, which displeased the sultan." The crescent blade swung left, pointing at something slightly more recognizable as a severed head; the eyes had not yet been pecked out. "The former Defterdar of the City. He failed to deliver all of the royal rents which he collected, and..."

"Let me guess," Gian said, trying out his rusty Turkish. "This displeased the sultan."

The janissary's eyes widened. "So. You do not only understand, you speak?"

"My Turkish is not very good," Gian confessed.

"No! For a Frank, you speak very well! *Çok iyi konuşuyorsun!* The sultan will be pleased."

"That is good," said Gian. "Much better, clearly, than displeasing him."

The janissary bellowed with laughter and slapped Gian on the back. "Come, then. We have only to ride through this next courtyard."

He meant, Gian discovered, not that the tortuous journey to the sultan was almost over, but just that the *riding* part was almost over. After they passed through a courtyard bright with lamps and crowded with separate white-walled buildings, through air cooled by falling water from the fountains that had been set in every possible open space, they came to a second gate, this one flanked by two towers. Torchlight reflected the ornamental Arabic calligraphy in gold that covered every flat surface; a distinct improvement, Gian felt, over the decorations of the previous gate. "Bab-us-Selam," the janissary said. "The Gate of Salutation. We dismount now; only the sultan himself is allowed to ride through here." He clapped his hands and two boys in silken tunics ran forward to take charge of the horses.

This next court seemed to be a garden bordered by high, colonnaded walls where shadows flickered in the light of the torches that illumined the paths. They walked through groves of cypress trees and past yet more fountains singing in the evening stillness. A gazelle, drinking from one of the pools, raised her head, stared wide-eyed at the men and bounded away from them. Gian's long physician's robe brushed over patches of herbs, releasing the scents of sage and mint, lavender and rosemary into the night air.

A cluster of square buildings at the northwest corner of the courtyard broke the symmetry of the design. The janissary beside Gian stopped.

"The Divan of Sultan Mehmed, Conqueror of Constantinople, Monarch of the Terraqueous Orb, Lord of the Horizon, Sultan of the Two Continents, Emperor of the Two Seas, Kayser-i-Rum, the Shadow of Allah," he said. "Enter with respect. When you are given leave to depart, ask for me –Ozman Kapikulu. I will see that you return safely." He stepped back into the darkness beyond the torches. Gian crossed himself and walked through the delicately carved doorway in front of him.

Candles and wall torches drove out the night from this square room, its walls lined with low cushioned benches, the wall niches holding vessels of beaten copper and silver that caught the firelight and sent it forth again in gleaming rays. Between the niches, gold and silver thread flashed from hanging tapestries, and clusters of pearls dangled from their ends. A stout, black-bearded man of middle years reclined on the couch directly in front of Gian. To his right, a fair-haired boy held a gracefully curving silver pitcher; to the left, a white-robed and white-turbaned figure moved in the shadows.

To Gian's surprise, the man who was the center of all this magnificence spoke to him first –and in Italian. "So, Frank. Are you the latest gift sent me by the Venetians?"

"I would not claim such a distinction," said Gian. He devoutly hoped that the sultan did not really think he was a slave whom the Venetians had given him. No, there was no premonitory prickling at the back of his head. This was just a gambit, then, an attempt to rattle him. "It is the hope of my masters that, insh'Allah, some small part of my experience as a physician may help to assuage the sufferings of the Lord of the Horizon. I am grateful and flattered that the Emperor of the Two Seas condescends to speak Italian with me."

The boy with the silver pitcher laughed softly. "My lord speaks Arabic to God, Turkish to gentlemen, Persian to his physician, and Italian to foreign unbelievers like us. Truly there is no one like my lord for delight in learning and desire for wisdom."

The sultan stared at Gian, ignoring the boy's flattery. His eyes were sharp, black, almost like black glass beads in the flickering candlelight that illumined his face. "You, a Frank, call upon Allah?"

"There is but one God," Gian said. "Our two peoples can agree on that much."

The sultan laughed. "Well and tactfully said!"

"*Kafir,*" muttered the white-robed man.

"Finish your work, Dervish Ismail," the sultan snapped. "I commanded you here to ease my ills, not to fight with my other servants." He gestured to Gian. "Sit here, and wait your turn."

Gian sat on his knees as the boy had done. Hands folded in his lap, he watched in respectful silence while the dervish chanted, blew on scraps of paper, rolled up the papers and gave them to the sultan to swallow. Was the sultan's trouble a digestive difficulty? And even if it was, why should eating bits of paper help him? This was no better than the cheap mountebanks' tricks which Foscari had so despised –preferring as he did to engage in *expensive* tricks.

The low-voiced chanting woke a long-buried memory in Gian, a memory that belonged to the days when, as a page boy at Urbino, he had been set to learn from the Turkish renegade at Duke Federico's court. The man had claimed to know the entire Koran by heart, and while he had not attempted to force the pages to master Arabic as well as Turkish, he had recited certain passages so often that they had sunk into Gian's memory –there to vanish, he would have thought, without a trace. But now he found himself understanding the dervish's words. It was one of the shorter chapters, he thought, and it had to do with protection against wizardry.

"From the mischief of created things;

"from the mischief of darkness as it overspreads;

"from the mischief of those who practice secret arts;

"I seek refuge with the Lord of the Dawn," the dervish chanted. On the third repetition, he knelt beside the sultan and bent over his right leg. The sultan groaned and drew aside the loose robe that had been covering him, and groaned again as the dervish bent low and blew upon the leg between the knee and the ankle. *A wound then,* Gian thought. *Or something of the sort.* That was a good sign. He had no idea what to do for an intestinal blockage. But cuts and wounds were surely the same here as on a battlefield.

"It does not ease me —it does not ease me," the sultan complained in Turkish, twitching the hem of his robe.

"It is the Sura of Daybreak," the dervish said. "It would work better at dawn."

"Then come back at dawn and try again!" The sultan switched back to Italian. "You, Frank, can you do better?"

Gian rose, took three steps forward, and knelt again. "Hold up the light, boy!" the sultan commanded, and the fair-haired boy set his silver pitcher on a low table and lifted a branch of three candles to illumine the wound.

Gian's heart sank. This was no simple cut to be healed just by anointing it with Foscari's purple oil and laying his hands on it; it was a swollen mass that had broken the skin in several places, releasing a vile-smelling, dark green discharge. Around the open sores, the skin was dark red and stiff. The entire leg, from knee to ankle, was swollen and the skin was tight. He had heard of men suffering ulcers like this but had never treated one; condottieri tended not to live long enough to develop such ailments.

"I do not wish to cause my lord more pain," he hedged.

"The path to good health is thorny," the sultan said. "Go on. If you have a healing elixir, apply it. I will probably not behead you, even if the application hurts me." He took up a cup from the low table beside him and drained the contents.

"*Haram,*" whispered the dervish.

The sultan glared at him. "I do not recall asking your opinion," he snapped. "As you have so far failed to relieve my pain, you need not criticize any other measures I take, whether it is a glass of wine or the help of an unbeliever! It is not as if I were an opium addict like my worthless son! Well?" he turned back to Gian. "What are you waiting for?"

Gian drew the little bottle of Foscari's Miraculous Oil from the bosom of his robe and held it in the candlelight so that everyone could admire its rich purple color. Then he uncorked the bottle and let fall three drops on each of the three openings where the ulcer had burst through the skin. Waiting a minute in the hope that the powders mixed into the Miraculous Oil would slightly numb the sultan's flesh, he laid his hands with infinite caution upon the broken and inflamed skin. The luck-angel at the back of his neck was humming as it did when he healed wounds upon the battlefield.

The sultan sighed. "That is better… much better."

Gian, lifting his hands, was not as happy as the sultan. He could still see the angry mass of the ulcer. All he had accomplished was to numb the pain a little, and to encourage a tissue-thin growth of skin at the edges of the open sores.

"There is much yet to do," he said. "I need to consult –to consult my books of wisdom," he stumbled, remembering at the last minute that it would hardly do to say he wished to get the advice of a woman. "And I must have access to my medicinal supplies to prepare a healing poultice. I could return tomorrow…"

"There will be no need of his heathen remedies tomorrow," said the dervish, speaking so low and quickly that Gian could barely understand the words, "for the Sura of the Daybreak will cure all. I shall pray without ceasing until the dawn, and then I will attend my lord again, when the cure is certain."

"Do that," said the Kayser-i-Rum and the Sultan of the Two Continents. "And let the Frankish physician also attend me tomorrow. Boy!" And, groaning again, he got to his feet with the help of the fair-haired boy. "Help me to my bedchamber." He leaned heavily on the boy, who looked back at Gian as if he wished, but dared not, to say something before leading his master to bed.

# ~CHAPTER TWENTY-EIGHT~

*The idea of the sacred and mysterious character of letters has given rise to a belief that each one has its special Djin appointed by Allah to wait upon it, and who may be invoked either severally or collectively.*
   *- Garnett: The Women of Turkey and their Folklore*

~ ~ ~

"My lord is excessively troubled by affairs of state," the Frankish boy said softly, "and this aggravates the pain of his wound. With my lord's permission, might one so lowly as I arrange some entertainment to relieve my lord of his cares for an hour?"

"What do you have in mind, that wine will not do better? And do *not* suggest opium. After seeing how it has turned my idiot older son into a useless writer of bad poetry, I have no intention of poisoning myself with the stuff!"

Andrea Cacciote smiled. "Only a little, little amusement that has this virtue: unlike either wine or opium, it does no harm, only good. The ladies of the seraglio have been enjoying a series of Karagöz puppet shows, and this night I have thought of a very funny scene to add to one of the plays. Allow me to explain it to the puppet master, and then, instead of remaining in the *haremlik*, the blind puppeteer could come to the *selamlik* for an evening –perhaps as soon as tomorrow night." He explained what he had in mind. The sultan laughed and slapped the thigh of his good leg. "It should be amusing, indeed. But let us see how the foreigner's medicine works first.

Then he shall watch Karagöz with the puppet you mentioned –and we shall watch him!"

~ ~ ~

Dervish Ismail retired to his private rooms after the fiasco of the Frankish physician. The man was lucky; his coming had coincided with a very, very small remission in the sultan's pain. But by dawn the Lord of the Horizon would be in pain again. And if the Sura of Daybreak was insufficient to heal him, there were other and darker powers that could be called upon. But he needed time and privacy to make the calculations for this work.

By the light of a candle carved with sacred signs he wrote out the letters of Sultan Mehmed's name, assigning to each one its proper value. These numbers he multiplied together, and then performing a similar process with the name of a jinn, he made certain calculations involving adding and subtracting the cubes and squares of these numbers until at last a number of no more than two digits remained. The first, second, even the fifth name thus used failed to give a usable result. Finally, on the eleventh attempt, he established that the name-number of the ifrit Damriat, upon being combined with the sultan's name-number, reduced to an eight –which was the number corresponding to the letter *dal*.

The inference was unmistakable. The name of an angel such as Jibrael or Uzrail would have been preferable, but the Slaves of the Letter could not be compelled against the evidence of the numbers. The ifrit it must be, then, and one of the most powerful of that breed.

The shadows in the corners of the room moved strangely in the wavering candlelight. There was a sound of little teeth clashing, of little paws with long nails scampering across the stone. Dervish Ismail longed to dispel these manifestations by crying out, "Iron! Iron!" and throwing certain nails which he possessed into the corners. But he had *invited* Damriat, and with Damriat came his creatures.

In a low, shaking voice Ismail stated his desire: just that the sultan should be cured of all his ailments upon the next recital of the sura "Daybreak."

"We do not love the words of your Book," said a voice that seemed to emanate from the stones of the wall, as though they were clashing and grinding together to produce speech that was very far from human.

"Then let it be done in the fullness of the day," Ismail said, "dependent not upon holy words, but on Damriat's own power!"

"Will that content you, man of clay?"

"Beyond anything," said Ismail. At that moment, the only thing which he desired more than the ifrit's departure was the satisfaction of knowing that he, and not the insolent kafir, had healed the sultan's grievous wound.

"Be it as you will," the voice ground out like a millstone crushing bones, "the Kayser-i-Rum shall be healed."

A wind from nowhere swept through the enclosed room; the candle went out, and horribly soft, damp filaments clung to Ismail's face. He scrubbed his eyes clear with the heels of his hands, and, shaking, went to find a new light for his candle.

~ ~ ~

Gian's luck did not torment him with prickling hints of danger the next day. But that, he considered sourly, might have been simply because it was not necessary. He could tell for himself how much trouble he was in.

He and Caterina had sat up late the night before, consulting her Book of Secrets for charms, poultices, anything that might help to augment the very slight healing Gian had achieved. What little he himself knew of treatments for such a serious ailment suffered from two major problems: it was entirely second-hand, and the very beginning of the treatment would almost certainly cause the sultan severe pain. What need of angelic warnings, when Gian had only to close his eyes to see the sunken eyes and desiccated heads of those who had displeased the sultan?

"Cleaning the wound and removal of the dead flesh, elevation of the leg, and hot compresses to encourage blood flow are the first steps," Caterina summarized their collective knowledge. "After that, a dressing of fine silk soaked in honey may serve to protect the wound while the skin heals. The problem is-"

"That after I have caused the sultan unspeakable agony by washing his wound with quintessence of wine and cutting away the dead flesh," Gian said, "I am not likely to live to apply that or any other dressing."

"Did you not say that yesterday he endured pain for the sake of healing?"

"Yes, but that was nothing to what this will cause him," said Gian gloomily. "I have seen a young, strong man cry out when I used *aqua ardens* to cleanse his wound –and I have never seen a wound in such bad condition as this! Have you no charms to reduce the pain?"

Caterina shook her head. "If he will take opium beforehand… or nightshade, but that is dangerous and I do not think you should risk trying to procure it; you might be accused of trying to poison him. It will have to be opium, and a generous portion."

"He does not approve of opium."

"Then," Caterina said, "you had better not risk the debridement. There are poultices you can apply without cleansing the raw flesh. This," she pointed to the open pages of her book, "says that the leaves of bugloss, bruised and mixed with hog's grease –"

"No chance of finding pig fat among the Muslims," Gian said. "Do you think olive oil would work as well?"

Caterina shrugged. "I do not believe that anything will work if the dead and rotting flesh is not first cleared away," she said, "so we may as well pick whatever treatment will buy a little time. This is said to alleviate some pain. You will have to find out if the herb is even available in Constantinople. It grows well at home, but here…"

This time, when Ozman Kapikulu arrived to escort him to the palace, Gian was armed with a list of herbs and other supplies to request, and the knowledge of three holy invocations to take away pain. Even the use of those was not without danger; who knew if the sultan, or that slit-eyed dervish who had been slinking around the room last night, would take offence at Gian's invoking the sacred words of his own religion? Well, perhaps he could murmur the charms very, very quietly. He might even mumble a little. It seemed reasonable to suppose that Christ had better hearing than the aging sultan.

This time he was received in a white-walled room with tall windows in each corner, framed by slender pillars that reached toward the ceiling in an elaborate filigree of carved vines and leaves. A short man in a paint-stained robe was standing beside one wall, carefully applying colors as indicated by the thin black lines outlining a battle scene. He had covered perhaps three-fourths of the wall; half-naked men with swelling muscles, a sword in the air, the terrified rolling eyes of a falling horse seemed to spring out like living presences. Gian wrenched his eyes away from the interesting doings of the painter, made obeisance to the sultan and began his list of necessary supplies.

"Bugloss?" repeated a slender, black-bearded man who had been sitting with the sultan when Gian entered. "Okis —no —oxtongue, is it?" His Italian was thickly accented, but quite understandable.

Gian shrugged helplessly. Caterina had not said anything about oxen. "This *bugloss* is a Greek word, meaning oxtongue," the man informed him, "for the herb which we call *gavisban* in Persian, or *havadjiva* in Turkish."

"I am dying in great pain," the sultan grumbled, "and you wish to talk etymology, Hamideddin?"

"The sultan will naturally wish us not to make any mistake with the ingredients," the other man said deferentially, adding something in a language unfamiliar to Gian. He turned back to Gian. "Light green leaves covered with down —blue flowers —the roots make a red dye? You are fortunate; it is grown in the kitchen-garden of the serai for the value of those roots. I have never heard of using it as a poultice, but I am always happy to learn of new cures. A boy shall be sent at once to gather a crate —no, box —oh yes, a *basket* of the leaves. Will you instruct one of the cooks in their preparation?"

Gian was only too happy to be escorted down to one of the palace kitchens, away from that room where the sultan's pain and the foul smell of his ulcer lay like the oily shadows of demons over the clean air from the windows. He was slightly less happy that his escort was the sultan's talkative friend, but at least the man's pleasure in hearing his own voice prevented his asking too many searching questions of Gian about the preparation and virtues of a poultice he had only learned about last night.

"I am Hamideddin of Lari, in Persia," the man introduced himself, "but Italian is our best common language, I think. Unless you would prefer Persian or Turkish?"

"By no means!" said Gian. "I have no Persian at all, and my Turkish is not good. Your courtesy is my good fortune."

"I have," said the Persian, "become, sadly, accustomed to meeting with people who do not speak my language. It pleases the sultan to think that he is such a master of languages that he can speak Persian with me, but truthfully, he speaks little and understands less. You will forgive me if I throw in a simple Persian phrase occasionally when talking with him; it is foolish to omit a small thing which pleases him. But among ourselves no deception is necessary. Italian will serve our purposes well enough."

While the fresh-picked leaves were being pounded into a paste and mixed with olive oil, then slowly heated to release their healing essence, Gian learned that his companion was the sultan's official physician and a man of some standing at court. Unlike the learned doctors of the Italian universities, the mountebanks of the Piazza San Marco, the barber-surgeons who accompanied mercenary troops, or the dervish who sat in shadows and scowled at Gian, al-Lari seemed to harbor no jealousy of potential competitors. His view was that they were all men of learning and men of good will who could share information about the medical world for the good of all.

It was, Gian considered, a wonderfully civilized attitude. Persians were evidently sophisticated people without vulgar prejudices. The only problem was that he had no medical knowledge to share.

"I regret," he said after al-Lari had asked whether Italian physicians followed the theories of Rhazes, "that I am not sufficiently learned to discuss these matters with you. The truth is, Dottore al-Lari, that I am an ignorant man, no physician but merely a barber-surgeon with only the smattering of healing knowledge I have gained from working in the army. At best, I can say that I have been extremely lucky in helping wounded men before now, and that I devoutly hope the sultan will benefit from my good luck like others before him."

"Insh'Allah," said al-Lari.

# ~CHAPTER TWENTY-NINE~

*The mother of the heir hath continually, at her gate, a guard of thirty or forty eunuchs, and so do all the other Sultanas, who are never seen by any men but by the Grand Seignor only, and the eunuchs.*
*-Ottavio Bon, The Sultan's Seraglio, edited by Godfrey Goodwin from the seventeenth-century edition of John Wither*

~ ~ ~

The invitation from Mara Despina Hatun arrived shortly after the janissaries had taken Gian back to Topkapi. It was delivered by a smooth-faced, soft-spoken, rather pudgy young man who bowed to Battista Gritti, bowed to Caterina, and would probably have bowed to the Greek girl provided by Gritti as Caterina's maid if a gesture from the *bailo* had not stopped him. He gave the note to Gritti's dragoman, who translated it into the sort of Italian, liberally studded with Turkish and Arabic words, that was the principal means of communication for Europeans in the city. The essence of the note was that Mara Despina had been very pleased with the gifts of glassware and fabric and wished to see more of the newly arrived goods, if there happened to be a woman in Gritti's employ who could bring them into the seraglio.

Caterina drew a little aside from the dragoman and asked Gritti, in an undertone, just who this Mara Despina Hatun might be. She had thought that her assignment was to make contact with a certain Aysin Hatun; was this a different name for the same woman?

"No, Mara Despina is only the most powerful woman in the seraglio, being the stepmother of the present sultan," Gritti said, smiling in satisfaction. "You could not ask for a better sponsor!"

But the escort sent for Caterina had to wait while Gritti made certain arrangements of his own. He was not as worried as Gian about sending Caterina into the seraglio, but he was also not totally unconcerned. Had she been a commoner his concern might have been less. But she had been introduced to him as Contessa of San Florian. Although he was not exactly clear on just where San Florian was, presumably it was a possession of Venice. And in his experience the Contessa of even a small Venetian city was likely to have powerful relatives who would be seriously annoyed if a lady of their family vanished into the Grand Turk's harem.

Pleading the difficulty of transporting such a mass of fabrics and glassware, he made a selection of the remaining goods —enough to show their quality, but only a small percentage of what had been set aside to sell in the seraglio. He collected short cuts of silk velvet to show off all the colors of the full dress lengths, a handful of floating, transparent *plissettato* veils but not the matching yardage for clothing, a cushion cover of red silk brocade with gold embroidery. The fabrics were wrapped around samples of the Venetian glassware for sale. Last, and most carefully, he packed just one of the *cristallo* goblets from the Barovier workshop, with its enameled hunting scene against an ultramarine background.

"This is hardly more than we already sent as gifts," Caterina pointed out.

"But each of these items is a sample to show the quality of what remains behind," Gritti said. "You can set prices based on the quality of these goods, and the bales of fabric and boxes of glassware can be sent *after* you return."

"I appreciate your caution," Caterina said, "but I should find it more reassuring if you sent some of the embassy guards with me."

"I shall," said Gritti, "as far as they are allowed to go."

She understood him later that morning, when after passing under an arch ornamented with grisly rotting heads and a second arch bright with elaborate calligraphic designs traced in gold, after walking through a garden as large as a deer park where gazelles grazed among the cypresses and drank from the shining fountains, after passing through a series of rooms ornamented with painted flowers and velvet cushions, they reached a low door where two men stepped forward and crossed their spears to bar the opening.

"We must wait for you here," said the dragoman in his strangely accented Italian. "Only those such as this one may enter." He flicked his fingers in the direction of the soft-bodied young man who had brought the invitation.

"It is the law of the seraglio," whispered Agnella, the Greek girl.

There were more men like the messenger waiting on the far side of the gate, men of all ages, but all beardless and all dressed in long silk and velvet robes, and Caterina began to understand. With eunuchs pacing before and behind her and on either side, with slightly less well-dressed eunuchs carrying her boxes of samples, she entered the part of Topkapi that even Battista Gritti would never see.

It was not so different from the public rooms she had already passed through, but arranged with even more taste and delicacy, even richer furnishings. Latticed windows allowed light to sprinkle in delicate patterns upon marble floors and silk carpets; cushions rich with gold and silver embroidery were heaped against the walls; low tables of wood inset with bright stones and shimmering mother of pearl held cups of beaten copper with silver rims. Around the junctures of wall and ceiling, gardens of painted plaster flowers bloomed.

Finally the escort of eunuchs paused in front of a brightly striped curtain, indicating that she and Agnella were to put aside the curtain and go in. Caterina saw a long room furnished only with carpets and cushions until one reached the far end of the room. There a bevy of girls dressed in very fine, full white breeches and jackets of brilliantly colored silk brocade clustered around an older, but still handsome, woman seated on a high cushioned chair. One of the girls plucked a round-bellied stringed instrument to produce a haunting melody while another sang a counterpoint in words Caterina could not understand. Two others played with a white kitten, while a fifth girl knelt over a small brazier, carefully stirring something that smelt hot and sweet and thick, and a sixth sat idly, hands in her lap, watching the cooking.

But as Caterina and Agnella entered, the girls fell silent and drew aside, leaving bare a narrow carpet leading to the feet of the aging, sharp-featured woman in the chair; a carpet so brightly figured with flowers that Caterina could have imagined herself walking above a garden.

In such splendor, who would be impressed by her samples of Venetian work?

She reminded herself that it did not matter. She was not here to make money for Venice, but to perform a more important and much more dangerous task.

"*Gel,*" said the woman on the chair, beckoning with one finger so that Caterina guessed the meaning and walked forward.

"Ah!" the woman said. "*Türkçe konuşur musun?*"

Caterina shook her head, uncomprehending. "I do not understand," she apologized. "I speak only Italian. And –well, Arabic I can read, but do not speak." She had never thought, back when she was puzzling out the secrets of Al-Razi's writings, that the strange sounds associated with the curving shapes of the letters would ever matter to her.

"It is well," the woman said. "I myself, Mara Despina Hatun who was once Mara Branković, I who have in my veins the blood of the great Byzantine houses of Palaiologos and Cantacuzene, in my father's household at Toplica I spoke only Greek and Serbian. But in the palace of my husband, and now in that of my stepson, I have learned to speak Turkish, Arabic, Persian and Italian. I merely wished to find out whether you were a Turkish impostor posing as a Venetian."

Caterina shook her head again. Why, she wondered, would anybody go to the trouble of such an imposture?

The woman's sudden smile lit up her dark, rather severe face with its pronounced features. "You will learn, little one, that everyone at court lies about something. If you are not lying about your nationality, then doubtless you are lying about something else. I do hope, however, that you were telling the truth about the quality of the goods you bring for sale."

Caterina swallowed, her throat suddenly dry. If Mara Despina Hatun meant to share Turkish military secrets, naturally she would not do so in the presence of all her... her... ladies-in-waiting? Junior wives? Whatever the girls were. Very well, she would talk like the merchant she pretended to be and… wait for an opening, she supposed. "The gifts we sent were only a few examples of Venetian manufactures, my lady. Today I have brought with me samples of what we have to sell, and I think that you will be pleased with what you see. Our *plissettato,* for instance, would make far lighter, finer veils for your girls than what they wear now." The girls clustered on either side of the Hatun wore little round caps embroidered with pearls, from which dangled veils made of the same white linen as their breeches. Her Venetian silk gauze would be a far more suitable frame for the girls' pretty faces.

While the sultan's stepmother had been interrogating Caterina, her escort of eunuchs had carried in the boxes she had brought from the embassy, set them down in a crescent around the chair, and silently withdrawn. Caterina stepped forward to the box with turquoise-painted swirls carved around its edge, opened the lid and drew out a small bundle: one of the fine gold-embroidered silk gauze veils, wrapped around a *cristallo* bottle enameled with red and blue flowers.

The girls exclaimed in pleasure and jostled one another to get at the box's contents. "Careful!" Caterina warned. "There are very valuable pieces of glass within."

No one answered her, but clearly they understood, for they slowed down and lifted out the contents very gently. One after another the gauze veils were unwrapped, until four Venetian glass bottles stood on the table beside the sultana's chair: the enameled one, a tall curving one covered with swirling white lines, one with gold rings set into the neck, and one made entirely of the coppery gold-flecked glass called *avventurina.* Mara Despina picked up this last bottle and turned it over and over again, holding it in a beam of sunlight that made the gold specks shimmer and dance, while the girls quarreled over the silk veils.

"*Bürümcük!*" one exclaimed. "But so fine!" another said in Italian. "I must have this one, it has flowers embroidered, and my name-of-the-seraglio is Cicek, Flower!"

"And your name in Sicilian was Peasant Fool!" retorted one of the girls who had not managed to get her hands on a veil. "The mother of the sultan's younger son is also named Flower. She will probably take it from you, worthless one!"

Caterina had packed four veils, each embroidered in a different pattern. And there were six girls. Shrill quarreling disturbed the peace of the hall until Mara Despina clapped her hands and the girls fell silent.

"Silence, greedy children! If I decide to do business with this little Frankish peddler, I am sure she has enough *bürümcük* to supply each of you with a veil."

"We have two full bolts of... beremjek?" Caterina tried to pronounce the Turkish word. "But the rest is not yet embroidered and hemmed for veils. We thought that the ladies of the seraglio might wish to wear some of it as, as..." Agnella had told her that the Turkish ladies wore fine white shirts under their velvet and brocade dresses, but had not mentioned the name of the garment. "Like that?" She gestured at the lady's shirt, framed in a dark velvet gown that was open to the waist and then gathered tightly by four diamond buttons above a gold-embroidered belt. The long sleeves of the gown were tight to the elbow and then fell open, framing the white lace that cascaded from the sleeves of the undershirt.

"*Gömlek?*" Mara Despina suggested, touching her shirt. "You have enough to make *gömlekler* as well?"

"Enough for you and the other great ladies of the seraglio," Caterina said, "but it is not inexpensive." And for a woman of Mara Despina's age, a transparent gauze shirt under which the lady's bosom would be clearly visible might not be the best possible fashion choice. But perhaps the standards of the seraglio were different.

"We can talk of money later," said Mara Despina. "Do not sell any of your *bürümcük* elsewhere."

*Not bloody likely*, thought Caterina, restraining a smile. *The whole point of bringing a fortune in fabrics and glassware was to get me into this place. Only, what do I do next? How do I get away from this crowd, and how do I get speech with Aysin Hatun?*"

The sultan's stepmother provided the immediate answer. She set down the copper-colored bottle, clapped her hands again, and the girls looked up as though waiting for instructions.

"I have had enough of your chatter," she said –unfairly, Caterina thought, since the girls had been completely silent since the first reproof. "You have my permission to go into the garden and play at ball. Only, first, tell Aysin Hatun that I desire her to attend me here. She will, I know, be interested to see these things from her former home, and perhaps she can tell me if there are any flaws in their manufacture."

# ~CHAPTER THIRTY ~

*But the puppets Karagoz and Hacivet depend on the third, rogue, element for their comedies: a gaggle of ladies, the unworldly Sufi, a blustering janissary, or a Frank.*
    *-Goodwin: <u>Lords of the Horizons</u>*

~~~

On his return to the sultan's room, Gian found Mehmed in an extremely bad mood, complaining bitterly of his sufferings. He had dismissed the painter, saying that the smell of the paints made him sick; he had thrown a cup of cooling sherbet across the room, and his attendant was just now cleaning up the sticky mess.

Gian dared not apply the poultice of bugloss to the sultan's leg until the simmering mass of crushed leaves spread on the linen bandage had cooled down. It might be slightly more effective hot than lukewarm, but given that he did not believe it would be of any use at all when applied to an uncleansed and undrained wound, that likely made no difference.

He felt ashamed of using a less than optimal treatment just for his own safety. He would not have dealt so with one of his comrades who needed healing for a serious wound.

On the other hand, none of the other condottieri had had the power to behead him if his surgical treatments caused them pain. They certainly had not made jokes about the possibility.

*A man is served as well or as ill as he treats his servants.* Gian tried to put his conscience at rest, tried to comfort himself with the absence of any warnings or guidance from his luck-angel, and joined the sultan and al-Lari in idle conversation while they waited for the poultice to cool. There was some talk of a play which they expected to see after dinner, something the sultan anticipated with hearty guffaws while al-Lari was more reserved.

"You know Karagöz, Frank?" the sultan demanded.

Gian confessed his ignorance. "Is he an actor?"

The sultan laughed again. "One might say so. But he who knows not Karagöz, can never understand Turks!"

"It is a shadow play," al-Lari explained.

"A *what?*" For a moment Gian remembered how his nurse had comforted him, when as a very small boy he had been sent to bed with a single candle. She used to manipulate her hands in front of the candle to make the shadow of a rabbit. It had been a very tall rabbit, with a twitching nose... But even the blond boy who attended the sultan was much too old for something like that; surely these grown men were not amused by such childish games!

"Forgive me, I do not know what you call it in Italian. A... a puppet show? But you do not see the puppets, only their shadows."

Gian surreptitiously felt the poultice. It was still hot enough to irritate sensitive skin. He would have to go on discussing children's games and puppet shows for a few more minutes.

"Please explain," he said with a show of more interest than he actually felt.

Al-Lari went into greater detail. The puppets in a Karagöz show were made of camel leather, dyed in brilliant colors and scraped to near-transparency. The puppeteer manipulated them with long sticks, sitting behind a white sheet, with lamps and candles set so that the light shone through the translucent puppets and made them appear as jewel-toned images on the sheet.

It was actually an interesting technique, and one that Gian had never encountered in Italy. He would not have minded learning more about the technical aspects of the production, but the sultan kept interrupting with comments about the principal characters, Karagöz and his friend Hacivet, and the extremely funny jests they made.

Gian gathered that, at least to the sultan, the best part of the play was when the puppeteer manipulated Karagöz's outsize penis to beat Hacivet or some other character.

It was hard enough to keep up the conversation while the sultan kept interrupting al-Lari, and almost impossible when Dervish Ismail resumed whispering from his corner. Gian had the irrational feeling that the shadows in the corner where the dervish crouched were growing and spreading, covering the entire room. And yet there were no clouds outside; the flowers in the gardens had been open to the spring sun, the herbs releasing their scents into the air, when he returned with Hamideddin al-Lari from the palace kitchens.

But the room felt dark and chilly.

At last the poultice was cool enough to apply. Gian knelt in front of the seated sultan and waited for him to bare his leg; then, with infinite care and gentleness, he laid the linen cloth with its mass of herbs and oil over the ulcer. The room seemed to grow even darker as he performed the task, and he imagined –surely it was imagination? –grinding sounds from the corners, as though stones spoke.

"*In nomine Jesu*," he whispered.

The stones ground louder, drowning out the furtive prayer. Perhaps he was acquiring a luck-demon to go with his luck-angel.

That would be an interesting theological problem… if he lived long enough to consult a Christian priest in the matter.

The sultan inhaled sharply, and the shadows seemed to swirl away into nothingness. "*Bismillah!*"

"I have hurt you?" Gian inquired, ready to snatch up the poultice. Or perhaps it would be better to leave the poultice in place and simply run. How far would he get before he was cut down?

"No…" the sultan said on a long exhalation. "It… it has *stopped* hurting. Remove the poultice –let me see!"

The flesh where the poultice had lain was pale and flabby, but the angry red color was gone; new skin covered over what had been open sores; the stinking green pus must have been absorbed into the paste of leaves and olive oil. What Gian saw now was merely the leg of an overweight, middle-aged man who did not take enough exercise; not an attractive sight, perhaps, except in contrast to what he had expected.

The sultan touched the center of the pale area with trembling fingers. "*Alhamdulillah!*" he exclaimed. "Nothing hurts! Frank, you shall have as much gold as you can carry for this cure. Better –you shall be my personal physician!"

At a sudden, unguarded movement from Hamideddin al-Lari, the sultan turned to him. "What? Can the Lord of the Two Continents, the Master of the Two Seas, not have two personal physicians?"

The sultan was almost intoxicated with delight, and the room was full of sunlight again. "Andrea! Help me to stand!" He took a turn around the room leaning on the Frankish boy's shoulder, and then walked unaided. "Praise to Allah, the beneficent, the merciful!" he said over and over. "And praise to His servant, this infidel to whom Allah has gifted the secret of healing! Frank, it is grievous to me that you, who have healed me, will nevertheless assuredly burn in Jehannum. Will you not make *shahada* and become a Muslim, and ensure your afterlife in the green gardens where fountains run perpetually and beautiful virgins attend your every need?"

"If that is heaven," Gian said, "it appears to me that the sultan already inhabits it. He must be favored indeed of Allah who lives in this earthly paradise!"

"And you," decreed the sultan, "shall live here with me. Infidel or no infidel, I cannot do without you, master of healing!"

Gian thought that if his luck-angel had been on the job, it might have warned him about this outcome. Well, the sultan would surely allow him to leave the palace long enough to gather his personal property from the embassy. And once outside the precincts of Topkapi, he had only to find Catherine and take the first ship leaving Constantinople.

They would hardly be able to call on Battista Gritti's dragoman to make the arrangements, though; Venice would want him to stay and gather information. Venice did not particularly care whose life was at risk to get that information... Perhaps Ozman Kapikulu might help them?

It became clear that there would be no chance to get out of Constantinople today in any case. The sultan was already planning his afternoon. First the hammam; then a dinner which was now to become a feast of rejoicing; and after that they would enjoy the Karagöz show.

*Wonderful. I get to hang around here all day so that I can see a puppet beating another puppet with its penis. And what then?*

At least the malevolent dervish with his constant hissing of verses from the Koran had slipped away during the general rejoicing.

~ ~ ~

The shadows that had departed the sultan's divan followed the dervish, grew and coalesced around him as he chanted the words of invocation.

"Damriat, you have cheated me!" the dervish complained over the squeaking and chittering of the ifrit's little followers.

"You desired me to heal the sultan and behold, it is done," ground out the voice of stones.

"But that cursed infidel, that Frankish nobody, has all the credit!"

"You did not specify who was to receive the credit. I was bound to obey your words, man of clay, not the secret wishes of your heart. Now you are paid and I –I am freed!"

The stones laughed and the shadows dissolved as the dervish cursed.

~ ~ ~

The sultan chose to dine in privacy that night, accompanied only by his two personal physicians and his boy of the inner chamber, although the room where they ate could easily have accommodated all the advisors of the Divan as well. In fact, Hamideddin told Gian, that was usually the case. A lattice-covered door at the far end of the room apparently led to the kitchen, because a small parade of page boys in bright silk came through there bearing a panoply of aromatic dishes, arranged them on a tapestry-covered low table in front of the diners, and backed out of the room to vanish into the darkness behind the service door. The sultan took his favorite morsels, urged others on the physicians and said grandly that they might as well please themselves, as whatever they did not eat would be given to the poor as part of his thanksgiving for this miraculous healing.

"Pomegranate rice," Hamideddin identified one dish for Gian. "And this is roast partridge —that you eat also in Italy, yes? This, here, is one of the sultan's favorites —a pilaf of pistachios and crushed almonds. We will probably see a similar treat among the sweets to be served afterwards, only then the nuts will be wrapped in flaky pastry and the whole soaked in honey."

The kitchens were evidently some distance away, and the food was served in silver dishes that absorbed any remaining heat. Gian wondered idly if the sultan ever enjoyed the luxury of a hot meal. Despite having different specialties of the sultan's chef pressed upon him, Gian restrained himself to plain boiled rice and a skewer of roasted lamb chunks, followed by a cool and refreshing soup made from sour milk and sweetened with sugar. He had no intention of dulling his senses by gorging on strange foods while he was still looking for a way to escape the sultan's hospitality.

After the passage of an interminable time during which the sultan made inroads into half the dishes served, the pages were permitted to enter and take away the food and the red and black tapestry that had covered the table, now spotted with meat juices and drops of soup. A new cloth, this one of blue silk embroidered with flowers, was spread over the table, and the boys brought gold bowls of water and smaller, porcelain bowls filled with a soft soap. The diners washed their hands and dried them on long linen towels that were stiff with embroidery for six inches at either end. Mother-of-pearl spoons with emerald-set handles appeared, with bowls of sherbets and plates of pastry-wrapped sweets, and the feasting resumed.

There was one strange incongruity in all this display of wealth. While Gian and Hamideddin al-Lari took their food from silver bowls and ate it off gold plates rimmed with rubies, the sultan dined from plain ceramic ware of a curious light green color. And before he took a bite of anything, he laid the food down on the green plate and stared at it for a few seconds. Later, Gian thought, perhaps he would get the Persian to explain this odd custom. If there *was* a later. If this obscene feast for the benefit of three people ever ended.

The preparations for the shadow play began as soon the sultan had finished his last sweet dish, a sherbet of crushed rose petals topped with a lattice of sugar syrup poured out into strings and browned under fire. As soon as the table was cleared again, all but two of the pages retired through the kitchen passage. The two who remained set up a tall frame halfway across the room and attached a white sheet a good six feet square to the frame, held taut by cords at the corners and more cords midway between them. They disappeared behind the screen; there were the sounds of things being brought into the room and unpacked, and Gian heard one of the pages telling someone to take his hand and sit just here, where all his puppets and poles were arranged ready for him. Then the door behind the screen was shut with a firm and final click. Lamplight sprang to life behind the sheet while the candles on Gian's side of the room were quenched, leaving the three men sitting in darkness.

A second lamp was lit behind the sheet, then a third, and then the shadow of a brightly colored figure leapt upon the screen.

"Karagöz?" Gian inquired.

"No, that one is Hacivat!" the sultan snapped. "Shut up and listen!"

The puppet's head wobbled back and forth as it intoned an interminable prayer to Allah for the cure of some unspecified ailment. Meanwhile another, larger puppet ambled upon the scene; listened for a moment; slid down the screen to a recumbent position; then emitted thunderous snores which drowned out the prayer.

"*That* is Karagöz," the sultan said, laughing at Hacivat's mimed anger over the interruption.

After this hilarious opening the play wound on its way. It had to do with Hacivat's impotence and his search for a cure. First he turned to a tantalizingly veiled wise-woman who seemed to be having some success until her veil slipped to reveal a hideous face. Next he turned to a horse-doctor, but vomited up the potion which turned out to be the one the horse-doctor used to cure worms. When Hacivat was reduced to total despair, Karagöz promised to find a great physician from foreign lands who would cure his friend. Gian was put on guard by the sultan's tense expectancy, and did not react when the great physician turned out to be a comically ugly figure, capering in a ridiculous style and dressed in an almost exact copy of Gian's own physician's robe and cap.

The sultan looked slightly disappointed, but cheered up when the puppet ceased dancing to emit a long screed about his miraculous cures and grateful patients. The broken Turkish was, Gian supposed, very entertaining to those who spoke the language fluently. But he was startled when, in mid-speech, the puppet switched from Turkish to French.

"I have cured all," the puppet declaimed, "who came to me at the hour of midnight, who came to me through the Gate of the Cool Fountain, who came to me at the Kiosk of the Tiles!"

"Speak Turkish!" shouted the sultan, hammering on the table with his cup of green porcelain. "Or even Italian! What good is a play that no one can understand?" He threw his cup at Andrea. "Did you write this nonsense?"

Andrea's eyes rolled wildly, giving him a momentary resemblance to the dying horse on the half-painted mural. "My lord, I do not even know what he is saying! Is it even a real language, or is it some invention of the puppet master's? It sounds like the twittering of birds!"

The physician puppet resumed saying idiotic things in Turkish. After it proclaimed that "He who is sick cannot be said to be well," and "A man who is walking is not yet dead," it declared that Hacivat's impotence was caused by "an ailment at the opposite end of the body." An outsize hammer and chisel appeared on the screen, and the puppet announced its intention of knocking out the teeth in Hacivat's head, one after another, until the tooth that was causing the evil was gone.

At this, Karagöz leapt to Hacivat's defense. Accusing the physician of being a mere quack who caused suffering rather than relieving it, he belabored him first with his hands, then with his bald head, then with his engorged penis, until the puppet wailed for mercy and abruptly exited the stage. The sultan laughed merrily throughout this denouement.

"What do you think of our Karagöz?" he demanded of Gian while the puppeteer packed up his materials.

"Most amusing."

"And that speech the physician puppet made —what language was he speaking, anyway? Another of your infidel tongues? Andrea was right, it sounded more like the twittering of birds than like proper human speech."

"I have no more idea than you," said Gian. "As no doubt you know, we Franks have many different tongues –Alemanic, Ingilizi, Ispanyic –and I know only my native Italian."

Actually, thanks to a campaign involving Sforza's support of Louis the Cunning, Gian's French was quite good. But he had a strong suspicion that the puppet's choice of that language had been dictated by the fact that, unlike Italian, it was not known to the sultan or even to Hamideddin. And while the sultan's boy re-lit the candles and Mehmed and Hamideddin discussed the finer points of the farce, Gian silently committed those few French words to his memory. The hour of midnight –the Gate of the Cool Fountain –the Kiosk of the Tiles!

"Andrea! Boy!" Mehmed shouted, interrupting Gian's train of thought. "Go and tell the puppet master that it is my wish he should use only civilized languages in his plays! A little bit of Italian I could accept, but all this barbarian chatter destroys the sense and fun of the show!"

The boy nodded and slipped behind the taut white sheet that screened off half the room. He did not come back immediately. Gian noticed, without thinking anything of it, that he couldn't hear the discussion presumably going on behind that curtain. The sultan seemed to convey his orders by shouts, but his servant evidently preferred a tactful murmur.

Then Andrea reappeared, with a white, shocked face that made him look even younger than the sixteen or seventeen years Gian had guessed to be his age. His hands were stained with something dark.

"My lord," he stammered, "some –someone –some evil one must have come through the lattice door behind the screen, with a knife, and - "

"Impossible!" the sultan snapped, turning almost as pale as the boy. "Were not the serving boys ordered to withdraw and not to return until sent for?"

"It –I do not think –it was any of the pages. It had to be someone taller, because - "

"It is impossible that anyone else used that passageway!" the sultan insisted.

"Difficult, at least." Hamideddin al-Lari modified. He turned to Gian. "The other end of the corridor is always guarded." He frowned as he watched the shaken Andrea trying to scrub his hands clean on a tunic of priceless purple silk. "Is supposed to be always guarded," he corrected.

That the lattice door was now swinging open, that someone with a knife had penetrated this close to the sultan, were the matters that most exercised the sultan, the Persian physician, and the soldiers and advisors who came in answer to Mehmed's calls. Only Gian, somewhat left out of the discussion conducted by many voices in extremely fast Turkish, stepped around the white screen and contemplated the huddled mass that stained the carpet. Who, he wondered, having come to assassinate the sultan, would instead have contented himself with stabbing a blind puppeteer?

# ~CHAPTER THIRTY-ONE~

*Sura 6. 95*

*He it is that cleaveth the daybreak from the dark: He makes the night for rest and tranquility and the sun and moon for the reckoning of time: such is the judgment and ordering of the Exalted in Power, the Omniscient.*

*-Translation of the Koran by Abdullah Yusuf Ali*

~~~

In the hubbub caused by the discovery that the sultan's rooms had been invaded, no one had time to consider the sultan's new Italian physician until long after midnight. When Ozman Kapikulu finally presented himself to escort Gian back to Galata, the first faint light of dawn was already showing as a dim glow behind the black silhouettes of the cypress trees. No rendezvous would be possible that night, and Ozman's janissaries stayed so close around them that Gian dared not ask about the places the puppet master had mentioned before he was stabbed. Unless –

"*Fransizca biliyorsun?*" he asked quietly at a point where the narrowness of the street had forced the marching janissaries to fall behind the two riders. "Do you know French?"

It was a lucky guess. Ozman replied in that language and explained that he had enjoyed the support of a powerful woman who desired him to have the best education possible.

"When the *devşirme* took me, I was a barefoot child who knew only

Serbian, and could not read even that. But when they were debating where to place me, someone mentioned that I was from Toplica, and this came to the ears of the ladies in the seraglio."

He said this as though it explained everything.

"Toplica?" Gian repeated. He had never heard of the place, but supposed it was some Serbian village.

Ozman looked surprised. "The Branković have a summer home there. Mara Despina Hatun, the wife of the previous sultan, remembers it fondly. And for the sake of those memories, she arranged for me to be one of the boys accepted in the palace school. There they found that I had a gift for languages. I was taught not only Arabic and Turkish, but also French, Persian, and Italian, as well as algebra and accounting and the art of letter-writing."

"That sounds like preparation for a place in the government," Gian said. "Are all janissaries so well educated?"

Ozman laughed. "No, most of my fellows never had to undergo so much education. And I, when I was old enough to escape the school, desired only to be a soldier. Mara Despina Hatun was disappointed, but she understood and did not withdraw her favor. She could see that I had not the temperament to sit all day in an office, making marks on paper and splitting words with would-be philosophers."

"Nor had I," Gian said warmly, and he felt another bond of friendship with the janissary.

"To show you that I still have the Hatun's favor," said Ozman proudly, "I need only mention that on this very evening she sent for me personally and requested that I watch over you."

"Me! Why?"

"She did not say. I believe, though, that she is very pleased with some gifts of silk and glassware that came with a mention of your name."

That, if true, would make their mission much easier. And it emboldened Gian to ask if Ozman was familiar with a place called the Gate of the Cool Fountain and another called the Kiosk of the Tiles.

"The Gate of the Cool Fountain," Ozman said, "leads to the Tiled Kiosk. This is one of the most beautiful buildings in all Constantinople, being extensively decorated with tiles of green, turquoise and blue. You should definitely visit it while you are in attendance on the sultan."

"I have heard," Gian said, "that it is especially beautiful after dark –at midnight, perhaps."

"Sometimes the sultan or some of his favorites will go there by night to watch the moon rise," Ozman agreed.

"I should like to see that."

"*Yarin*," Ozman said. "Tomorrow."

And it was already tomorrow; before the boat had crossed over to Galata, there was enough light in the sky to distinguish a black thread from a white one, and the calls of the muezzins summoned the sleeping city of Constantinople to morning prayer.

Gian had not thought to meet with anyone in the embassy immediately; he was almost too tired to yawn, and much too tired to make a sensible accounting of all that had happened since he had been shown into the sultan's presence so many hours ago. But Caterina was awake and waiting for him, pale with fatigue and anxiety. "We began to think you were never coming back!"

Gian noticed that anxiety had not kept Battista Gritti awake.

"What happened?" Caterina demanded.

"As you see," Gian told her, "the sultan has not yet beheaded me. And that poultice you recommended to me worked better than it had any right to do." He recounted the story of the extraordinary cure.

"God worked a miracle to save your life," Caterina decided. "We must pay for masses of thanksgiving to be said in all the Christian churches of Galata."

"I am not ungrateful," said Gian wearily, "but it might be premature to celebrate. The situation is still rather complicated." He told her about the rest of his extremely long day, right down to the moment when Ozman Kapikulu had more or less confirmed that he would help Gian to the meeting at the Tiled Kiosk.

"Well then," Caterina said cheerfully, "you will go to this kiosk and learn whatever your mysterious informant has to tell you, and when I go back to the seraglio I will learn what Aysin Hatun has to say, and…"

"*Back* to the seraglio?" Gian interrupted. "*Back*?" One of his few comforts during this excruciatingly long day had been the thought of Caterina safe in Galata, surrounded by decent Christian folk –and now he was being told that this had been just a delusion? He felt furiously angry with her. Could the woman not stay out of danger for just one day?

"Why, yes," Caterina said, "the sultan's stepmother Mara Despina Hatun sent for me to show our trade goods shortly after you left." She told Gian how the initial meeting had gone, right down to the point where Aysin had been summoned.

That helped to explain the Hatun's request to Ozman Kapikulu. It wasn't the silk that had so favorably impressed her –it was Caterina.

"Then you have already spoken with this Venetian renegade woman," said Gian, feeling so relieved that he might even contribute to those masses of thanksgiving Caterina wanted, "and there is no need for you to return. Excellent! You must take the next ship for Venice; I will tell Gritti to arrange it, and to see that you have a proper escort."

"You expect me to leave without you?"

"Contessa. Caterina. It is *not safe* here. Did you not understand what I told you? A man has just been murdered for giving me information about a meeting."

"But you are staying to use that information."

"Yes, but *you* need not –"

"On the contrary," Caterina interrupted him, "I am expected back at the seraglio day after tomorrow. Today, when Mara Despina summoned Aysin Hatun, she got more than she had asked for. The mothers of the sultan's two sons also came to finger my samples. Gülbahar, Bayezid's mother, had some concerns about our prices. But Djem's mother, Cicek, is ready to pay anything within reason for more goblets from the Barovier workshop, only they must be decorated only with flowers to refer to her name –Cicek means flower, I learned that much. She will not buy the ones with hunting scenes, because she says that in Islam it is *haram* –forbidden –to portray the human figure."

"It is?" said Gian, momentarily distracted. "And yet the sultan is having a battle scene painted in his divan."

"I think that Cicek Hatun, who converted to Islam to marry the sultan, is more observant of the rules than the sultan himself," Caterina said. "She also mentioned that it is *haram* to drink wine, as the sailors on the carrack told us. Messer Gritti confirmed that. And yet did you not say that the sultan took wine to relieve the pain of his wound?"

"I suppose," Gian said thoughtfully, "a Turkish visitor to our country might be somewhat confused, if he tried to deduce the rules of the Christian religion from the behavior of actual Christians… Never mind that, it's not important. Who cares how much this Flower Hatun would pay for Barovier's goblets? Anybody would think that our only interest was in getting back from the Turks a small fraction of the money Venice paid them for peace. Get to the point! Have you forgotten why the Venetian spymaster arrested you and forced you to accompany me?"

"Now that's unfair. You wanted me to tell you everything!"

"Well, now I want you to tell me about the important part. *What did this Aysin Hatun have to say?*"

"That's what I have been trying to tell you!" Caterina exclaimed. "I've learned nothing from her yet, for there were too many people there today. She could hardly discuss the sultan's secrets in front of his stepmother and his two senior wives, could she? I am to return day after tomorrow, with my book of remedies, for a private consultation with her. I think," Caterina said, "she really does require the services of a healer. She looked –oh, not well. There were lines of pain and sleeplessness upon her face. I shall pray for her tonight. Maybe God will send another miracle of healing."

"I think you should go back to Venice *now*," Gian repeated.

"Don't be silly! Are you going to wrap a veil around your face, cram your feet into silk slippers and tiptoe into the seraglio? I can speak with Aysin Hatun; you can't."

"It's not worth the danger to you," Gian said, "not now that they've started killing people."

"Venice is not exactly all that safe for me either," Caterina pointed out, "not while Roberto Malatesta holds San Florian and thinks to cement his possession of the city by marrying me."

"I thought," Gian said snidely, "that you trusted your dear cousin Lucrezia to support you in getting back control of San Florian."

"That," said Caterina, "was weeks ago. She has had plenty of time to change her mind."

At least, Gian thought vaguely before exhaustion toppled him into sleep, at least Caterina had let go of that crazy notion of trusting Lucrezia, so they wouldn't have to have that fight again. With any luck, he wouldn't even have to think about San Florian until they had finished this mission and returned to Italy.

~ ~ ~

The Tiled Kiosk was not actually in the best of positions for watching the moon rise, but then, that was not actually Gian's reason for making this midnight visit. He had been in attendance on Sultan Mehmed from noon until sunset, but had escaped after the evening meal on the plea of requiring exercise after eating so many rich meals in a row. Too, he had said, there were some books of his in Galata which might help him to devise a plan whereby the sultan could escape a recurrence of his painful ulcer.

These excuses had freed him to walk through the grounds of Topkapi, escorted by Ozman Kapikulu, long before the hour of meeting. Gian welcomed the quiet and the darkness, the peace of taking long strides past rippling, laughing fountains and startled gazelles, the sweet scents of flowers and herbs mingling on the night air. But he was not unhappy when Ozman touched his arm and indicated a turnoff from the path they had been following.

The Gate of the Cool Fountain led to a cross-shaped building overlooking the Bosporus. The interior was quite dark; Gian lingered in the colonnaded porch, watching the reflected moonlight shimmering on the water. Ozman had, as was his habit, quietly vanished into the darkness of the gardens.

A shadow moved among shadows; the moonlight fell on a fair head, a novelty in this country. Gian's heart sank.

"Did the sultan send you to bring me back to his rooms?" he asked in an undertone.

The boy called Andrea smiled and shook his head. "No, it was I who sent you here, that we might speak away from my lord's presence. Is it not well done?"

"Very adroit," said Gian in French, watching Andrea's face. Yes, the boy understood him. Gian rapidly rearranged most of the ideas foremost in his head. If this meeting had been Andrea's idea, and if he spoke French, then it must have been he who coached the puppeteer in words that would have been meaningless to the blind man who spoke them. It seemed, to Gian, an excessively convoluted way of getting private speech with him. But then, what did he know of the contradictions and convolutions within Topkapi?

And had it also been Andrea who so quickly, so deftly disposed of the puppet master? Gian remembered, with a shudder of revulsion, the way Andrea had tried to scrub the blood from his hands.

Up to now he had not thought much about the boy: a Christian captive, he'd thought, in very comfortable servitude; a child who was making the best of his lot.

A very cold-blooded child, it seemed.

"What did you wish to tell me?" he asked.

"First," said Andrea, "you must promise to help me get away from here."

"And exactly how do you imagine I can do that?" Gian wasn't even sure he could get himself free of the entangling alliances of Topkapi. It would be ten, a hundred times harder to remove one of the sultan's slaves.

"You will think of something. You must!"

"If you can tell me something that is useful to Venice, then I am sure the *bailo* will be happy to exert his influence in your favor."

Andrea sighed, shrugged and sat down on the top step. "I know that which should buy both life and fortune for whoever tells it to the Venetians. I am not sure I should trade it for no more than the half-promise of help. But... well, better you, I suppose, than that chattering idiot of a Venetian painter. *Someone* should be warned... Do you know how I came to be here?"

Gian had assumed that Andrea, like Ozman, had been taken in the *devşirme* –the regular tribute of the brightest and handsomest boys in the Christian lands ruled over by the Turks. He waited to be told, and after a few moments' silence the story spilled from Andrea's lips. The capture of Otranto —the clever way he had saved his father's life from the bloodthirsty Turks — the agreement that he should be kept here in Constantinople, hostage to his father's accomplishing a certain task in Italy for the Turks. "But he has done what they wanted, many months ago, and still they keep me here. It's not fair!"

*Wonderful. The kid is not just a slave, not just a favorite of the sultan's, but a hostage for his father's good behavior. And he expects me to get him out of here.*

"If you want help from Venice," Gian said, "what do you have to offer Venice? Because I do not think that a tale of mages and demons will interest the *bailo*."

"Even when the mage has been tasked with getting hold of San Florian for the Turks?"

Gian stiffened. "What do you know of San Florian?"

"Not very much," Andrea confessed. "But that is what Karamanli Pasha wanted my father to do. First he was supposed just to go to this San Florian place, get the lord of the city to take him on as his court magician, and then use his arts to control the lord so that he would open the city when the Turks were ready. Then it got complicated… this lord, somebody Rinaldi, was killed just before my father got there, and the widow was a sour-faced bitch who had no proper respect for my father's great learning."

Gian's fists clenched, but he did not interrupt the boy's naïve stream of words. "So then my father went to Rimini and got hired as court magician there, and persuaded the lord of Rimini that he was entitled to San Florian, and then, I am not sure exactly how, he helped this man…"

"Roberto Malatesta?"

"I think that was the name… Anyway, my father helped this Malatesta get control of the city and the castle, and now he is just waiting for the Turks to send their army, and…"

"How do you know all this?" Gian was beginning to think that the Turkish spy service must be an order of magnitude better than Venice's, if the doings of a place like San Florian were so well known in Constantinople.

Andrea explained that he and his father communicated by means of an enchanted mirror. "But he dares not use it often, for fear that the Italians will catch him at it. And nothing has happened now for *months*," he whined, "and why won't they release me? I am afraid that the sultan will kill me when the army marches. It is only a matter of days now, perhaps hours; the horsetails have been raised and the soldiers are assembling. The sultan has named the members of his household who are to accompany him - and I am not among them!"

"If he depends upon your father to deliver him San Florian," said Gian, "it would be insane to kill you before the fortress is already in his hands."

"Yes, well, the sultan is not always all that well balanced," Andrea said gloomily. "Anyway, it is just as bad if he leaves me here, a prisoner, and I am killed after his army possesses this San Florian place and they don't need me any more." He looked up at Gian. "But *you* can tell the *bailo* everything, and then you will help me to escape the sultan, and then he will no longer be able to force my father to help him take San Florian and Venice will owe me a great debt of gratitude."

Gian could see a few problems with this naïve analysis. One was that Venice was apparently expected to pay this 'great debt of gratitude' in advance; another, that there was no certainty that Roberto Malatesta would not surrender to the Turks whether or not some self-styled magician was controlling him. But the most immediate difficulty was –

"Why," he asked, "do the Turks want San Florian? And why should Venice be more concerned about this than Florence, or Rome, or even Naples? Venice has a treaty of peace with the Turk. Not so these other states."

"I don't *know*," wailed Andrea. "They tell me nothing! But I think it must have to do with Venice, because of what the sultan said when my father reported that he had complete control over Roberto Malatesta and the city of San Florian."

"And this was?"

"That –that the Doge of Venice could leave off marrying the sea each year, for now it was the Turks' turn!"

That put a different complexion on things. But it still might not be possible to buy Andrea's freedom. Occasionally Christian captives were successfully ransomed, but those tended to be the old or infirm, who could be of no use to the Sublime Porte. A bright, handsome boy who was both favored by the sultan, and a hostage to the Turk's war plans, would not be easily ransomed. Gian promised to do his best for the boy, but refrained from confessing his fears of failure.

# ~CHAPTER THIRTY-TWO~

*If you want to make cinnabar, take sulphur, break it up on a dry stone, and add to it two equal parts of mercury, weighed out on the scales. When you have mixed them carefully, put them into a glass jar. Cover it all over with clay, block up the mouth so that no fumes can escape, and put it near the fire to dry. Then bury it in blazing coals and as soon as it begins to get hot, you will hear a crashing inside, as the mercury unites with the blazing sulphur. When the noise stops, immediately remove the jar, open it, and take out the pigment.*

*-Theophilus, <u>De Diversis Artibus</u>, tr. John Hawthorne*

Gian paced up and down the hall that ran the entire length of the ground floor of Battista Gritti's Galata house. He was not good at passively waiting. And he took no comfort from the entire absence of warnings or guidance from his luck-angel; perhaps it did not even care what might be happening to Caterina in that abode of infidels! Perhaps it only warned him about matters concerning him personally.

"But everything that concerns her is also my concern," he muttered, pounding his fist into the palm of his other hand. "If only I could *see* –"

"It is not," his companion said cheerfully, "as if she had been carried away by demons, you know. The Turks are a civilized people. And the Grand Turk has no shortage of women in his seraglio; why should he detain your woman? You forget, we have met. She is well enough to look at, I grant you, but not of such a beauty as to drive the sultan mad with desire –particularly not when, as now, his mind is all bent on war, not women."

Caterina's oval face and fine eyes, framed with that wealth of reddish-brown braids, rose before Gian as the painter spoke. How, he thought, could anyone look at her and fail to see that here was so much more than beauty? That boy Andrea had described the painter as a chattering idiot. Andrea had been absolutely right about that; now the man was twittering on about how he wished he had been able to persuade Caterina's cousin to sit for him, for Lucrezia would have been such a Blessed Virgin as would have shone in glory from the canvas and made Bellini's name!

"I should not have thought that the official portraitist of the Doges had any need for additional fame," Gian interrupted the man's prattlings about Lucrezia. "An artist so well known that the Grand Turk himself requested you to come to Constantinople and paint his portrait!"

Gentile Bellini smiled at this tribute to his reputation. "As to that," he said, "the Ten were naturally eager to send their finest artist to fulfil this part of the sultan's request, since they were obliged to excuse themselves from satisfying the other part."

"Oh? What was that?" Not that Gian cared, but he was willing to snatch at anything that might distract him from counting the hours since Caterina had left the safety of the embassy.

"He wanted one of our bronze-founders to teach his people the way of casting the new cannon," Bellini said. "Naturally they were not about to hand over a military secret that is not even known to Naples or Rome yet! The Turk will have to be satisfied with iron guns. So the Ten made excuses: this man was ill, that one away on a diplomatic mission… and to soften the refusal, they sent *me* to be his portraitist! Not that I have made very much progress," he said ruefully. "It is hard enough to get the sultan to sit still in the normal way of things. And now that he is restored to health and preparing for war, it is all but impossible. I shall probably have to take my sketches back to Venice and finish the work there."

"You have other projects in Topkapi, though. That mural in the Divan –"

"The conquest of Constantinople? A masterpiece," Bellini said, "wasted on these infidels. Half of them look only to complain that their god forbids them to paint the images of men –as if God would not wish us to glorify His creation of men as well as all else that He has made!" He snorted. "And the other half are worse, having no understanding of the laws of composition. Those who fought on that day with the sultan keep nagging me to put in this detail or that from the battle, as though a great picture were nothing more than a laundry-list of who smote whom with what kind of sword! Sit *down*, won't you?" he added irritably. "Your woman will not return any faster though you should wear a threadbare path on Gritti's carpet! And I want to relax and enjoy my meal. It is not often that I get to eat without worrying about poisons."

"I did not think that poisons were so popular in Constantinople," said Gian, throwing himself down on a couch at the end of the table. He himself had no appetite.

"It is more a matter of Venice than of Constantinople," the painter said. "Did you not know that the Ten have sent to Gritti, telling him to make me poison the sultan?"

"You too?" exclaimed Gian. Poison had been the first thing Battista Gritti thought of when Gian made his report about the midnight meeting; though the Venetian *bailo* had not seemed to be sure whether he wanted Gian to dispose of the sultan or of his hostage. Gian, however, found the idea of poisoning a child –even a murderous child –even more distasteful than that of killing the sultan.

"Gritti does not think logically. I made the mistake of telling him that I had come over to Galata to get more cinnabar made for me, because it is illegal to make it in Constantinople; it requires the heating of sulfur and mercury together, and those who are careless and breathe in the fumes do not live long. I had to explain to him that the sultan does not attend my workshop –he likes watching the paintings take form, but he has no patience for the details of the craft. And even if he were to watch me create cinnabar, how could I cause him to inhale the fumes without poisoning myself at the same time? And then he asked if I could not just put mercury in the sultan's food!"

"Could you?"

"I explained to the *bailo* that I have no idea whether that would work or how long it would take," Gentile Bellini said, "and then he pressed this upon me." He drew a small blue bottle out of the bosom of his shirt. "I believe it is venom of scorpions mixed with black henbane."

"And are you planning to use it?"

Bellini laughed. "There is a limit to my loyalty to Venice, and that line is drawn just where my head joins my shoulders. No one can possibly poison the sultan's food. Look at the precautions he takes! Every dish that is set before him is tasted by a slave in the kitchens, and a different slave is chosen for the task each day. Then, he eats no food that is not served on a dish of celadon-glazed ware, which is well known to change color in the presence of poison. And that ugly domed ring on his right forefinger is filled with the shavings of unicorn's horn, which infallibly counteracts all poisons. Even if I could somehow evade all the precautions and kill him, I probably would not try. The price of being caught is too great. Besides, murder is a sin... Are you going to try it? Do you want to take the bottle?" Bellini juggled the small bottle from hand to hand. Gian wished he would put it away again.

"I do not mind killing a man in battle," Gian said, "where he is doing his best to kill me. But poison is a coward's weapon."

"Not even that," said Bellini. "*I* am a coward, and I don't mind admitting it, but that does not mean I am also a fool. The sultan is safe from me."

~ ~ ~

The lord of Rimini (and San Florian) was in a bad mood.

Not, reflected Filippo Cacciote, that this was in any way unusual. However, he had exerted himself to calm Malatesta by using the slow, deliberate speech that usually controlled Malatesta's excesses by reinforcing the spell of compulsion —and this time it had not worked. Was there a time limit to the spell? It had been some months now; perhaps he needed to repeat it.

When he had a chance.

Boredom and discomfort in the Rocca had prompted Roberto Malatesta to move his personal household down to the Palazzo Rinaldi in the center of the city for a while. After all, the city was most surely pacified –no one grumbled, did they? –and he had left most of his soldiers to guard the Rocca, taking only his personal guard down to the palazzo. Cacciote had endeavoured to dissuade him, even going so far as to remind him that the previous Count of San Florian had met his death precisely by leaving the safety of the Rocca to spend an evening in this beautifully decorated city house.

"Girolamo Rinaldi was an idiot," Malatesta said. "The whole city was inflamed over the new taxes he had announced; what did he think would happen? No one," he said complacently, "complains about *my* rule."

That might have been because they were satisfied by a lord who, although he did nothing for the city, was too lazy to bother with raising taxes. Or the spate of public hangings right after Malatesta took control might have had something to do with the seeming quiescence of San Florian.

Unfortunately, another complaint occurred to Malatesta at the same time Cacciote thought of it. "My worthless servants let Tommaso Peruzzi get away, and to this day I've had no hint of where he is hiding! Also Piero Giacomini, but he's just a useless scholar. But I *want* Peruzzi!"

"Most likely he is far away by now and will never dare to trouble you again."

"Unless," said Malatesta darkly, "there are traitors in the town, hiding him and secretly working to put the widow back in power. If only I had got her, that would not be a problem any longer. But what good are my soldiers? I send them on the simplest of errands, and what do they do? I knew that woman was in Venice, I even knew that she was making an exhibition of herself at a mountebank's booth in the Piazza San Marco, and they still couldn't find her! Instead they startled her into fleeing, and came home after a month of searching to confess that they have no idea where she has gone. Any idiot should have been able to knock her on the head, throw her over a horse and bring her back."

"That might," said Cacciote, "be slightly difficult in the middle of a great city."

"Nonsense, mage. You know nothing of these matters. In Venice they fish bodies out of the canals every day and feel that's enough to worry about. A body that did *not* wind up in a canal would not interest them in the slightest. And now," Malatesta said, "you cannot even tell me where she fled to!"

Cacciote's improvised pendulum swung reliably south and east these days; the trouble was, it kept going right to the bottom of his carefully drawn map, where there was nothing but the sea. Cacciote was reasonably sure that the countess of San Florian was not in the middle of the ocean, and completely certain that Malatesta would not believe she was.

"I have waited too long," Malatesta declared now. "Mage, I do not care how much of your time and energy it uses up; you must make me a *good* enchantment, one that will force the widow to return and submit herself to me."

He raised a hand to stop Cacciote's response. "No excuses! You can have gold to work with, you can use the pearls from that wedding dress we found in a chest full of mugwort and wormwood leaves, you can collect all the materials you want... but you shall raise a demon to bring her back!"

"Calling demons is forbidden..." Cacciote began.

"As if you had not done so a dozen times already, for lesser magics!" Malatesta scoffed. "You can shrive yourself after it is done –I don't care how many Aves and Paternosters you have to say!"

Of course he wouldn't. He wasn't going to be the one with his aching knees on the cold stone floor of the chapel.

But once you got involved with really powerful demons, having to say penance for a month thereafter in a cold chapel was actually one of the better possible outcomes. It meant you were still alive. Besides, how was Malatesta to know what he actually did? He had been able to fool him with shows of colored flame and singing bottles before now.

The trouble was, neither flames nor bottles could possibly be taken for a nobly-born young woman. And Malatesta had actually seen Caterina, so it wouldn't help to dress up a village girl. He was actually going to have to send a demon to fetch Caterina herself. He would just have to be extremely careful with the protective circle and the other necessary diagrams.

"And I shall be with you and watching everything you do," Malatesta said, "until you succeed. I have had enough of telling my servants what to do and having them to report failure to me. You will get me the woman, and you will do it within the week —see, I'm very reasonable, you have time to send for any special materials you need."

And time to escape? Cacciote wondered. He had told the Turks of his success in the matter of San Florian months ago. Perhaps by now they had freed his son; perhaps, even now, Andrea was making his way home on an Italian ship.

But a glance in his mirror, once he had regained the privacy of his tower room in the Rocca, showed nothing new. Andrea was in one of Topkapi's palace rooms, pouring sherbet for the sultan and yawning surreptitiously behind his hand. Filippo hastily put the mirror away for fear of distracting his son. He did not know what the Grand Turk did to servants who spilled sherbet on him.

～～～

Aysin Hatun was indeed ill —very ill. Receiving Caterina in her private apartments, she sent her maidservants away before undoing the buttons at the waist of her velvet gown, opening it and raising up the fine pleated shirt below it. The canker in her breast looked as terrible as Gian's description of the sultan's ulcer.

"My brother has spared no expense in searching for a cure. I have drunk ground pearls and *aurum potabile*, and he has sent to Venice for genuine theriac, and I have applied a plaster of mummy dust from Egypt," Aysin Hatun said, "but all to no avail. It keeps growing! And so, when I heard that the Italian physician who travels with you had cured the sultan's grievous ulcer —"

The hope in her eyes almost broke Caterina's heart.

"My lady," she said, "All that Gian applied to the sultan's leg was an herbal poultice intended to relieve the pain. He —we —have never seen a mere paste of bugloss work such a cure before! I will be happy to prepare another such dressing if you wish to try it. But I must warn you that we believe the sultan's cure was not due to the medicine, but to a miracle from God."

Aysin Hatun sighed and let her fine pleated shirt fall back over the ravaged breast. "For pain, we have opium," she said.

"I could pray for you…"

"It is a long time since I have heard Christian prayers… Perhaps we may pray together," said Aysin Hatun. "When I was young and unhappy in my marriage, it seemed no great thing to me to put off my religion along with my husband, and to become a Turk like my brother. But lately I have been thinking of the past. You are recently come from Venice, I understand. Is it still…"

Caterina confirmed that the Rialto bridge was still the home of the finest shops in Europe, that the front of the Basilica San Marco was still brilliant with mosaics and gold tile, that the bronze horses from Constantinople still looked out over the piazza, and that the Grand Canal still shimmered in the sun like finely pleated green taffeta. News still passed magically through the city from women gossiping across the wells in the *campi* and boatmen navigating the canals and apprentice boys selling their masters' news for half of a hot pie. Mountebanks and rope dancers and snake handlers still entertained in the Piazza San Marco, and the *meretrici* in their high-heeled shoes, with the little bells tinkling in their hair, still displayed themselves there. And Aysin heard her with bright eyes and some refreshment of spirit.

"I am either both Venetian and Turk, or neither," she said finally, "and it does not please me that the two countries I love best should tear one another apart in war. If the sultan and the grand vizier knew what I am about to tell you, I would be a dead woman today. But since I may very soon be dead in any case, that need not weigh heavily with us. Tomorrow, or the next day, the army marches. I have seen the maps and the plans of campaign. If you will tell Venice what I know, the Most Serene City will be on guard… I would not die easily if I knew that Venice had suffered the fate of Christian Constantinople, and that I might have prevented it."

Aysin Hatun had not, of course, been able to take away copies of the maps. But she had an excellent memory, and on a piece of white silk she reproduced what she had seen in lines drawn with a solution of alum. Caterina drew in her breath as she finally understood the importance of San Florian to the

Turks, and the reasons behind her troubles in her own city became clear.

Those faint lines faded and then disappeared entirely as the solution dried. "Rub the surface of the cloth with coal dust and you will see the white lines again," she told Caterina.

"Oh. We only use alum to fix our dyes. We use lemon juice on paper for secret messages," Caterina commented.

"A most inferior method. Do you think no one will wonder at it, if you try to walk out of here with a blank sheet of paper in your hand? Whereas the silk can pass as a sample that you are taking back to Galata to match with that in your trade goods. Besides," Aysin Hatun said, "everybody knows the technique of tormenting paper with fire to make the letters appear. No blank paper would be allowed out of the palace without first being gently heated in a warming-pan –and then neither the maps nor you would ever leave the seraglio, child!"

She rolled up the silk, tied it with a length of green ribbon and placed it among several similar rolls that had already been prepared. "There! Take all of these, but remember that it is the one tied with green that holds the secrets. And now," Aysin Hatun said, "perhaps God will be pleased with me for remembering the land of my birth, and perhaps He will hear our prayers."

# ~CHAPTER THIRTY-THREE~

*Western Europe had a potential fifth column in Constantinople in the European colony, and European diplomats, in Galata. It was a source not only of information and profit to, but also of intrigues against, the Exalted State. Within days of the entry of the Sultan, the former Genoese podestà wrote from Galata to Genoa that he hoped 'Constantinople will be the beginning of his ruin.' Venice made fourteen attempts to poison the Sultan.*

-Mansel, <u>Constantinople: City of the World's Desire</u>

~ ~ ~

The Lord of the Horizons and Sultan of the Two Seas was in a towering rage. "I am surrounded by traitors and incompetents!" he shouted when Gentile Bellini whipped off the covering cloth to display his nearly finished mural of the conquest of Constantinople. He squinted at the rightmost panel, where a triumphant Turk held up a severed head by the hair. "And I do not know which is worse! Can you not see what is wrong with that picture, Italian? No? Then I shall instruct you later —unless it is you who are to poison me first!"

"*I?*" Gentile Bellini made, Gian thought, a fairly good show of horrified innocence and surprise, considering how calmly he had been discussing just that possibility only yesterday.

"Or perhaps it is you!" Mehmed whirled and pointed at Gian. "All I know is that my Grand Vizier has uncovered a plot against my life. He has discovered that the Venetians have sent someone to poison me. Is it you, physician? Or you, painter? Or have I to look into the privacy of my very bedchamber?" Now the accusing finger pointed at Andrea.

"The sultan has no need to fear poison," said Hamideddin al-Lari calmly. "Only a fool would attempt to poison someone who eats off celadon plates and bears the shavings of a unicorn's horn on his person."

"I am also," the sultan said darkly, "surrounded by fools!"

Hamideddin managed to sketch a graceful, yet humble bow without actually rising to his feet. "Naturally to one so brilliant and learned as the Kayser-i-Rum, all others appear slow-witted and foolish. But I think in this matter –"

"I do not pay you to think!" the sultan erupted. A slow smile curved his lips. "I have thought enough for both of us. How do I know the assassin is a Venetian? He could be a Persian in the pay of Venice. Strip off your clothes! You too, painter. And you!" He pointed back at Gian. "All three of you!"

"We are going to the hammam," he announced. "And you may leave your clothing here, every stitch that you were wearing."

Somewhat bemused, Gian complied. He had no objection to making use of the sultan's luxurious baths. But why the sudden announcement, and the insistence on seeing all of them leave their clothing here to march through the palace mother-naked?

Gentile Bellini had been standing on a bench, the better to point out the fine points at the very top of the mural. He stumbled, getting down, and gripped Andrea's shoulder for a moment before recovering his balance.

On Gian's previous visit to the hammam, the sultan and his companions had undressed in the first of the three rooms of the hammam proper, where there were benches on which to leave their folded clothes and hooks for hanging garments discreetly placed between the pearl-encrusted golden hangings that covered the walls. Walking naked through the sarai was unusual and unnerving, and after seeing the smiles that twitched the lips of the palace servants they passed, Gian kept his gaze and his thoughts firmly fixed on the luxurious décor of the rooms they went through. Caterina would be interested to hear about this part of the palace…

The pride of the marble-lined central room was the fountain of warm water that fell from the wall at its far side. Gian stretched luxuriously under the warm, scented fountain and reflected that his native land could well benefit from certain Turkish customs. This was far better than a hasty dip in a bucket of nice, fresh cold water straight from the well!

On the other hand, he had never been concerned that his quick wash in a bucket of cold water was merely the preliminary to a summary execution.

Like Gian, Bellini, Hamideddin and the sultan all took seats against the far wall, where the warm water could run over their bodies. There must have been slaves stoking a boiler underneath the room, for when the sultan issued a command the heat of the falling water increased until it was almost painful and the room filled with steam. The gold pipes that ran through the room poured hot water into marble basins decorated with mosaics until the rising steam blotted out the colorful images.

"This opens the pores," the sultan instructed them. He had said that last time too. "After the pores of the skin are thoroughly open and cleansed, we shall pass into the warm room, for it is dangerous to lower the temperature of the body too quickly. The dangers of the hammam are few and well known. Those of the court are much, much worse."

Gian wondered how long they would have to sit here and listen to the sultan's speech.

"How long do we stay here?" he whispered to Hamideddin.

"I suspect, until our clothes have been thoroughly searched and every seam cut open," Hamideddin murmured in reply.

"There are a thousand ways for a sultan to die," the sultan went on, looking at each of them in turn with bright, suspicious eyes, "by treachery, by the bowstring, by the knife, by poison…"

Gian decided that he was tired of this game. "How fortunate, then, that the Emperor of the Two Continents has loyal servants with whom to relax in the hammam! For surely he would not expose himself to attack by allowing someone he did not trust completely to partake of this luxury with him!"

"Your Turkish has improved, but not your wits, Italian!" the sultan snapped. "We are surrounded by my slaves of the bath, any one of whom would die to protect me from an attack!"

After his midnight meeting with Andrea, Gian could not help but wonder exactly how devoted the sultan's other slaves were. But he had enough tact to let the subject drop.

After they had sat in the perfumed steam for so long that Gian had a raging thirst and an incipient headache, a palace servant came in and murmured something to the sultan.

"I knew it!" exclaimed the sultan. "There was nothing untoward to be found in your clothing or slippers! By Allah, despite the grand vizier's warnings, I can trust you foreign infidels better than my own servants! It is the tragedy of a sultan's existence that he is surrounded by those he cannot trust, and so I have to import men from distant lands to serve me, men who know nothing of the currents of treachery and deception within the palace. You, Persian, and you two, Italians, cannot even conceive of the complexity of palace life, and so you are much less to be feared than those who have grown up in my service. Come now to the outer room; you shall enjoy cooling sherbets while the slaves fetch new clothes for each of you –my gift to you!" He waved his arms grandly.

"The sultan's generosity is beyond praise!" Hamideddin responded immediately.

"And well-timed, since, in all probability, our old clothes have been wrecked by the search," he added in a cautious undertone when he and Gian were the last to leave the hot room.

After cooling down in the warm room and then nibbling on slices of snow-chilled melon in the outer room, Gian and the others put on their fine new apparel and returned to the divan.

"I hardly dare to open my paints," said Gentile Bellini, "for fear of staining these magnificent garments!"

"All the better," said the sultan. "You need to stop painting until you understand your subject better." He pointed at the last addition to the painting. "When a head is cut off, it does not look like that –as if it were still perfectly fitted to the body. The muscles of the neck contract."

"I have never been told of such a thing," Bellini argued, "and I have spoken with many soldiers."

Gian had a feeling that the sultan was right. There *was* something odd about the appearance of the head. But he had never stopped in the middle of a fight to consider the anatomy lessons being strewn around him, and so he could not verify the sultan's assertion.

"You need to see an example! Boy, call in a slave!" The sultan tried to stand, swayed, caught Andrea's elbow and managed to pull himself upright without quite unbalancing Andrea. He grabbed the boy's full sleeve to steady himself.

A small blue bottle fell out of the sleeve and onto the flowered carpet.

Everybody in the room froze. The sultan's countenance blackened. "Poison!" he barked. He drew his curved sword and used it to point at the next closest person to him, who happened to be Gentile Bellini. "Pick that up. Tell me what it smells like."

"Essence of scorpions," Bellini pronounced immediately, "and henbane. A most powerful poison."

Andrea fell to his knees. "Not mine —it was not mine, Lord! Some enemy put it in my sleeve! I beg of you, by Allah the most merciful..." The sultan's face turned to stone as he looked down at Andrea. "I shall not require another slave for this demonstration after all, boy. Not after this betrayal of one who has been kindness itself to you!"

Before any of the shocked onlookers could move to intercept him, the sultan gripped Andrea's fair hair and pulled his head up. With his other hand, and with all the force of his warrior's arm, he swung his naked blade across and through the boy's neck. The headless body collapsed with a great spurt of blood, soaking into the carpet and filling all the room with a hot, metallic smell.

"You see," said the sultan, holding up Andrea's head, "the muscles of the neck contract as soon as the head is severed. Take that for today's anatomy lesson, painter."

~ ~ ~

Roberto Malatesta was not pleased at having to return to the Rocca, but Filippo Cacciote flatly refused to attempt a major conjuration in one of the pleasant rooms of the Palazzo Revere, with their high arched windows and their hanging curtains where doors should be and their colonnaded antechambers where anyone could linger inconspicuously. The only room that could be properly closed off was the one that had been the lord and lady's bedchamber, and the smashed door leading to that room had never been repaired.

"I do not see why you are so insistent upon privacy," Malatesta grumbled. "Everybody knows that you are my court necromancer."

"Court *mage*," Cacciote said. "If I am widely known to deal with demons, the inquisitors will become interested in me. And being imprisoned by the Church would impair my ability to serve you. Also, there is grave danger to anyone who might walk in on us in the middle of the great work. That is why we are using this tower room in the Rocca with its bar across the door –it is for the safety of your people. We shall be protected as long as we stay within the perimeter I shall draw, but a servant or courtier casually entering the room would immediately become the prey of Sobedon."

"Sobedon –is that the name of the demon who will bring the widow to me?"

"This conjuration requires *three* demons," said Cacciote. "Sobedon, Badalam and Berith. I shall bind and require them to bring you the woman immediately." He had already done most of the necessary and unpleasant preparatory work. Creating parchment from the skin of a female dog that had been in heat had been the worst task; or perhaps it had been tearing the white dove apart with his teeth to get the blood with which he traced the image of a woman on the parchment and wrote certain words of compulsion across her genitals. When he searched Caterina's rooms in the palazzo, he had been lucky enough to find a broken ivory comb –the sort of thing that a lady would throw away, but that a serving girl might pick up and safe for her own use. Only, this one had fallen unregarded into a coffer of winter clothes in the ruined bedchamber, and there were still long reddish-brown hairs tangled in the fine teeth. These he had carefully stitched into the parchment image, so that there might be no mistake as to what woman he demanded of the demons.

Now there was nothing left but to trace the diagrams, say the words, and resist any tricks from the demons, who would of course try to get him to step out of the protective circle. And he would have to be sure that Malatesta, who was clearly not very bright, also did not fall for the demons' ruses. Without the lord of Rimini, he could not control San Florian; he had learned that lesson when Malatesta got himself trapped in the illusory castle. And it was absolutely necessary to keep control of San Florian until the Turks freed Andrea... Probably they would bring him with them when they finally landed in Italy and marched to San Florian. That would be a great day, when he was reunited with his fine, handsome, clever son, his hope for the future. The Turks would probably be grateful enough to make him rich as well as freeing Andrea, and then he would make a grand marriage for the boy and see his grandchildren heirs to one of the noble houses of the land.

Dealing with demons was a very small price to pay for the joy that awaited him.

Thinking of that reunion, Cacciote went through the preliminary steps of tracing the summoning diagrams and the defensive boundaries without a single misstep, without even having to consult his book. He seemed to be living in a different space, a bright and open place where he could not make an error; even the words of the incantation rolled flawlessly off his tongue, forming their perfect shapes in the air of the room, floating like flames into the three corners where the three demons would stand.

This time the demons chose to become visible as shapes of fire; one had to look closely to see that no smoke arose from these apparent flames. Malatesta jogged Cacciote's elbow and the mage almost made the fatal mistake of pausing his incantation to snap at him for the interruption.

"I say," Malatesta whispered when Cacciote finished with the long, rolling, mysterious phrases that had summoned the demons, "they aren't really fire, are they? I mean, it won't do me any good if they burn her up. I need a living woman to marry, or at least, the body of a dead one to show her supporters that it's time to give up hope."

"They will deliver her into this circle," Cacciote said, indicating the triple lines marking off the safe space in the center of the room.

"Willlll weeeeee?" whispered one of the tongues of flame.

"Shallllll weeeee?" hissed another.

Cacciote unrolled the parchment with its drawing of a naked woman. "I conjure and command you by…"

Incredibly, the living flames dared to interrupt him.

"Before you command us, mage, think well whom you serve."

"He cannot give you what you desire."

"No man living can do that now."

"Silence!" Cacciote shouted. "I conjure and…"

"Look in your mirror first," whispered a blue-tipped flame.

"Look to your son," hissed a writhing orange tongue of fire.

"Sssssee what your sssservice earnsssss," taunted the third and greatest flame, rising and whirling around the ceiling of the room.

Shaken, Cacciote found his fingers reaching, almost without his volition, for the cold curved surface of the Turkish mirror. As he drew it forth, Roberto Malatesta gave a cry of surprise. "What is that? What room is it?"

It was the sultan's divan, with its wall painting of soldiers in battle. Cacciote had seen the progress of the mural during his checks on Andrea. Now it was almost finished, with all lines leading to the painted figure of the mounted man in Turkish dress who triumphantly brandished a severed head.

Below that image of violence frozen in time, a dark hand tangled itself in his son's fair hair and pulled up his head. A bright curved sword flashed through Andrea's bare neck and his body toppled forward, spurting blood. The sultan held the sightless head up above the body on the carpet.

"No!" Cacciote howled. "No! I have been cheated!"

"Who cares? Finish your work!" Malatesta snarled.

"Oh, it is finished," Cacciote said from the despair that engulfed him. To have gone through all these months of treachery and necromancy, only to see his son dead at the sultan's feet! "All my work in this world is finished." Gripping Malatesta's arm, he dragged him forward across the boundary lines that kept the demons from feeding upon them.

"You can't do this!" Malatesta shouted as the smokeless flames swooped down upon them. "You said I should not die until three days after you!"

Cacciote, already burning, gave him a ghastly smile through which the demonic flames flickered. "I lied!"

~~~

"We are leaving *now*," Gian told Caterina when he finally made it back to Galata.

She frowned. "Messer Gritti wants –"

"To hell with what Gritti wants! We have given him all the information he needs; he knows now where the Turk plans to attack, and how." The combination of Aysin Hatun's map and Andrea Cacciote's story had made it perfectly clear. The Turks meant to land at Rimini, far enough south that they need not expect to be intercepted by Venetian galleys. They would march inland and use San Florian, that all but impregnable city, as the staging point for their armies; then they would attack Venice from a direction she was not expecting –from the southwest. The Turkish army would never even see the might of Venice's navy; by the time Venice recognized the danger and redeployed her galleys, the Turk would be over her walls.

Or such was the plan. If Gian and Caterina left for Venice immediately, they would be able to lay out all this information before the Ten in time for Venice to guard herself against the attack. And the prickling at the back of Gian's neck left him sure that they had no time to spare. Whatever might happen next in Constantinople, they would be better away from it.

"First the puppet master was murdered," Gian said, "and now, today, the sultan has just beheaded a boy slave of his on the mere suspicion that the boy intended poisoning him. The man is going mad, and I do not propose to wait until he lops off my head and takes you into his seraglio."

"I do not think," Caterina demurred, "that the Grand Turk has any interest in me, or that he even knows of my existence."

"The sultan knows more than we guessed," said Gian. "His spy service is at least as good as that of Venice."

But the sultan had not known –had he? that the little blue bottle had been in Gentile Bellini's possession before it somehow wound up in Andrea Cacciote's sleeve. And in the shocking aftermath of the beheading, Gian had not betrayed the little Italian artist. If it had been a matter of saving the boy, would he have spoken up? Probably —but in the event, there had not been time. And afterwards, what good would it have done to get another Italian killed over Battista Gritti's clumsy poison plot?

But why had Bellini brought the bottle, if he did not intend to use it? Perhaps Gian should have raised that question, but he had been too shocked at the time to think clearly. Now he wondered if the sultan might not still be at risk of poisoning, if Bellini might be suborned into making a second attempt. Well, if so, that would make the Venetians happy, would it not? And despite his distaste for poison as a weapon, surely it was not his job to warn the sultan at the expense of his own countrymen.

Caterina interrupted his moral quandary. "We should at least tell Battista Gritti that you are leaving."

"*We* are leaving," Gian insisted. The prickling of his luck-angel was becoming positively painful. "You can't stay here alone. As for the *bailo*, he's out, and I don't plan to wait for his return. I do not even want to take the time to pack," Gian said. "Just get your jewels, and we will casually stroll down to the waterfront and trade sapphires or rubies for fast passage to Venice."

But before Caterina came back down the stairs, the Venetian *bailo's* house was surrounded by armed men.

"The Lord of the Two Seas marches to war," announced a tall janissary, "and his personal physicians accompany him. Pack up your nostrums, Frank, and come with us!"

Gian glanced up the stairs to where Caterina stood, trying urgently to send a message: *go back quietly, don't let them see you.*

Instead she came down until, standing on the second step above the floor, she looked the tall janissary in the eyes. "I go with —with my husband."

"You can try," the janissary said. "But the army has no provision for fine ladies. I do not think you will like life on the march."

Caterina didn't back down. "That is my problem, not yours!"

Gian rather thought it was going to be his problem. But what would he have had her do? Staying in Galata without him to look after her, staying under the dubious protection of a Venetian *bailo* who did not care whom he sacrificed in the interests of the Most Serene City, did not seem to be any safer than following him along the army's line of march.

There were, in short, no good solutions. Except to have left half an hour earlier, and to be at this moment aboard a slim-lined brigantine making her way to Venice as fast as possible. *That* would have been a good solution.

# ~CHAPTER THIRTY-FOUR~

*When you wish to become invisible, first, under a waxing moon on a Wednesday, in the first hour of the day, having remained chaste for three days beforehand, and with cut hair and beard, and dressed in white, in a secret place outside of town, under a clear sky, on level ground, trace a circle such as appears here, with a magnificent sword, writing these names —Fyriel, Mememil, Berith, Taraor — and everything shown along with them.*
  *-Caterina Rinaldi's Book of Secrets*

~ ~ ~

The confirmation of the alum deposits east of San Florian aroused intense interest in that city's neighbors.

After the Ottoman conquest of Constantinople, the alum of Anatolia had passed into Turkish hands, and the Venetians had controlled that trade to the great benefit of their own dye houses. The discovery of alum near Tolfa, in an area under Papal control, had most regrettably disrupted the Venetian monopoly. San Florian's alum, once the city was naturally and rightfully allied to Venice, would restore the proper order of things, and someone should be sent immediately to explain this to the townsfolk.

Rome's analysis of the situation was the same, only with a slightly different emphasis. The expense of the Turkish trade and the failure of the Volterra alum mines had left Rome with a virtual monopoly on the precious mordant, an arrangement which clearly was God's intention. This troublesome little city of San Florian had recently sued for Roman protection, but then it had not seemed worth the trouble. Now, the pope had a different view of the matter, and his legate would make it clear to whoever was in charge of the city.

In Florence, Lorenzo de' Medici saw an opportunity to repeat his treatment of Volterra, only without repeating the mistakes of that adventure. He was willing to grant, now, that he might have overreacted to the Volterrans' request for better terms on the lease of their alum mines. He probably should not have sacked the city. It might have made his army happy, but sacking a city was always a net loss, as the conquerors never gained as much in loot as they could have collected in taxes from a prospering city. What made the whole matter worse was that the alum supplies at Volterra were becoming increasingly hard to retrieve; in fact, if the pope chose to lower the price of alum from Tolfa, the Medici would be operating the Volterra mines at a net loss. *Another* net loss. As a banker, Lorenzo found the prospect extremely painful.

This time he would be patient, tactful and peaceable... as long as those fellows in San Florian didn't make the mistake of trying to betray him with Venice or Rome! He would personally make them understand that Florence was San Florian's natural protector and ally... as soon as he could figure out whom to treat with. There did not seem to be anybody at all in charge of the city at present.

"I do not understand how this has come about," he grumbled to Paolo Uberti, whom he had sent to make preliminary inquiries.

"It is rather confusing," Uberti agreed. "Until recently the pope's nephew Girolamo Rinaldi held the city, which would not have been good for our prospects. Last year there was a small rebellion, quickly put down, but Girolamo was killed in the fighting. Somehow, possibly through witchcraft, his widow got back control of the castle and the city. She sent her son to be fostered at Urbino and proclaimed herself regent."

"So we have to deal with the widow of the pope's nephew?"

"No, my lord. Subsequently, Roberto Malatesta of Rimini took the city. He advanced a dual claim to it, first by right of inheritance from his father, and second by right of marriage to the widow. However, the Contessa fled the city before he could marry her, so matters were… well, undecided… until recently, when Malatesta himself died."

"Who killed him?"

Uberti shrugged. "The official story is that he died of a lingering cough."

Lorenzo's fingers flickered unobtrusively as he checked his arithmetic. "This was Sigismondo the Poisoner's bastard son? He could not have been much over forty. It seems unlikely that a mere cough would kill him."

"The alternative story, I am afraid, is even less likely. The common people claim he was carried away by fiery demons. I, personally, do not believe his sins were *that* bad. Most likely he was assassinated by someone secretly working for the Contessa."

"So we're back to dealing with her."

"Except," said Uberti apologetically, "that no one seems to have the least idea where she is."

~ ~ ~

To Gian and Caterina, unwilling witnesses, the setting forth of the sultan's army was as if an entire city had gone on the march. Janissaries, green-turbaned emirs, singing and dancing dervishes passed in cavalcade, each group bearing its particular banners and insignia. They themselves were in the midst of the sultan's personal household, preceded by the green banner of the Prophet, surrounded by the household cavalry on gold-caparisoned horses, followed by the Grand Vizier and his cavalry. It was an excellent vantage point for observing the massed power of the Turkish army.

It was not such a good location from which to make a quiet and tactful departure.

"Tonight," Gian said under his breath as their part of the column finally began to move. "We shall get away tonight."

He said the same thing for three succeeding days, during which there was never a chance for both Caterina and him to disappear inconspicuously. If Caterina was free to ride beside Hamideddin al-Lari and begin learning Persian, it was because Gian had been called to hear the sultan's list of complaints and to reassure him that the ulcer on his leg showed no sign of recurring. If Hamideddin, instead of Gian, was waiting on the sultan, Caterina was occupied with the women of low degree who followed the army, the dancers and singing girls and camp followers. For the army's nightly camp was the center of every imaginable entertainment: tightrope walkers, jugglers, ballad singers and ragged men with dancing bears all vied for the coins in the purses of the marching soldiers.

"It is too bad that Dottore Foscari did not come with us," Caterina commented during a rare quiet moment. "He would have loved all this –and he would have made a fortune from it."

"And maybe, between sword swallowers and snake handlers, he could have found a way to make us disappear," Gian said sourly. "I don't suppose your Book of Secrets has a recipe for invisibility?"

"It does," said Caterina, "but it requires us to dress in white, go to a clear piece of ground, and kneel to the four quarters while chanting certain invocations that will raise the spirits who can aid us. I suspect our companions would notice. Also, it must be done on a Wednesday under a waxing moon, which will not happen for three weeks."

Gian snorted. "No, I don't think we can wait that long. Don't undress tonight. I am going to steal a couple of horses and get us back to Galata if it's the last thing I do. I *refuse*," he said grimly, "to get myself killed fighting on the wrong side, for the Turks against Christendom."

But that night the sultan was troubled by insomnia, and required that Gian stay by his side all night to discuss the possible significance of his evil dreams and his upset stomach. The stomach pains grew worse through the night, and the next day the army did not march. Sipahis and archers and janissaries, horses and camp cooks and camp-followers all waited upon the sultan's return to health. Gian and Hamideddin consulted, worriedly; Ismail, the sultan's personal dervish, redoubled his chantings of the Koran. Nothing, neither purgatives nor emetics nor cupping nor massage, reduced the cramping pain in the sultan's belly.

"If nothing else, he must rest before this writhing in pain exhausts him," Gian decided in an hour when Hamideddin was catching a much-needed nap.

From his boxes of nostrums he prepared a spiced drink of wine mixed with Venice's greatest medicine, authentic theriac, to ease the sultan's pain so that he could sleep.

"I do not use opium," the sultan said when offered the wine. "It has turned my older son into a lazy coward who would rather write poetry than conquer a new world."

Gian reflected briefly that he personally, not to mention the rest of Christendom, would be delighted to see the Turks led by a poetry-loving man of peace. But he assured the sultan that there was no opium in the potion. There couldn't have been very much in any case; theriac had so many ingredients, from saffron and rhubarb to iris root and valerian, that no single ingredient could dominate. And he had only mixed a drachm of theriac into the wine; even if half of the medicine was opium, the sultan would barely consume enough to allow him to sleep.

Subsequently Gian decided that there must have been no opium at all in the theriac that da Treviso had supplied him, for the sultan's pain grew worse and sleep was as distant as ever. He was relieved when the sultan snapped at him to go away and quit bothering him with taking his pulse and looking at his urine. Dervish Ismail, he said, would bring him the comforts of religion, for it was clear that only Allah could relieve his sufferings.

But, like Hamideddin, Gian was required to remain within call. So he and Caterina tried to sleep in their small tent while the dervish chanted from the Koran and fed the sultan more bits of paper with holy words upon them.

If the sultan had not been so extremely ill, Ismail would have gloated at having put the physicians out of their place and getting this chance to show what Allah alone could do. But as the hours passed, he began to feel that Allah could use a little human help. He began to wrap his scraps of sacred writing around little pellets made of opium and rosewater. Allah would forgive him for giving the Lord of the Horizons just a little opium, just enough to let him sleep. The total could not amount to more than three-quarters of a drachm; no danger in that, no danger at all.

"Shut up and get out!" the sultan snapped when Ismail started for the tenth time to recite al-Fatiha, the very first and holiest sura of the Koran.

Ismail bowed very low. "My lord will surely sleep now," he said.

But less than an hour later, the sultan was seized with a new set of griping pains. Hamideddin al-Lari felt his patient's galloping pulse and was severely worried. Nothing they had done yet had eased the sultan significantly. And the last physician to attend a man before his death was often accused of having caused that death. Even at the cost of lying to his patient, he *must* calm the sultan down and at least alleviate the symptoms which made him cry out and clutch his belly. A little more than half a drachm of opium, mixed with honey, would not harm a man of the sultan's size –and it might save Hamideddin's life. He added some pungent spices to disguise the taste and told the sultan it was an electuary formulated by Rhazes.

It seemed to be a success. Retreating from the royal tent, Hamideddin put his head into the little tent shared by Gian and Caterina and told them the good news: "The sultan sleeps!"

Gian and Caterina consulted in whispers and decided to leave very early in the morning. Right now there were torches burning all around the sultan's tent and among his household cavalry and servants; right now, some irrational person in the sultan's household might well think that a physician who was attempting to leave the camp in secret was guilty of malpractice. By dawn the sultan would have slept for several hours. He would be in a better mood, and his household would not be so suspicious and on edge.

Caterina actually fell asleep, her head on Gian's shoulder, while he cradled her and waited for the dawn to free them. In the grief and fear and hurry of this march to war, there was no room left in him for sensual temptation; he might have been her brother.

At any rate, there *should* have been no temptation. And he applied himself seriously to the task of feeling like her brother... even while wondering if Gian-Maria Neroni might aspire to the hand of a noble lady who was infinitely above Gian Bracciaforte. Not, he reminded himself, that there was any chance of his being able to resume his name, retrieve his estates, and take his place in society. He had no reason at all to suppose that Lorenzo the Magnificent was any less angry with the Neroni family than he had been when they tried to murder his father.

But a man could dream…

Those dreams were rudely interrupted when a janissary pushed his way into the tent. "We are leaving," he said. "Quiet! We must not wake the camp."

Gian privately resolved to shout as loudly as he could rather than letting this soldier drag them off to some unknown fate. "Why? Where are we going?"

"The sultan's gout is much worse. He is returning to Constantinople. And you two are going with him."

"Gout! He was not suffering from gout."

"Karamanli Pasha himself told us. I am no doctor, to contradict the Grand Vizier. I was told to get you two and the Persian to join the caravan."

"Should we help prepare the sultan for the journey?"

"No! He does not need you now."

It was a strange, silent, midnight departure. Gian deduced that the sultan was certainly not better, because it seemed that he had been put into the royal carriage while he and Caterina were bundling up their few possessions. The sultan's horse was led behind the carriage while a small group of advisors and soldiers followed on horseback. Gian managed to maneuver so that he and Caterina were riding next to Hamideddin al-Lari.

"What happened?" he whispered.

Hamideddin shrugged. "I do not know, but I do not think it is good. Why the silence and secrecy?"

There was no obvious answer then, but one suggested itself when, an hour after leaving the camp, the royal carriage got two wheels into a rut, swayed, jolted, almost fell over, and was shoved back upright by the shoulders of a dozen janissaries.

Hamideddin and Gian looked at each other. That evening, the sultan had screamed with pain when anyone so much as brushed against him. Now, after that dreadful jolting, no sound came from the carriage. Hamideddin spurred his horse forward and demanded to see his patient. Gian joined him.

"I suppose it can do no harm… now that you cannot spread the news," said the janissary in charge of the group. "You physicians will answer for what you have done when we reach the capital!"

The body in the royal carriage was cold and growing stiff.

"*Bismillahi rahmani rahim*," Hamideddin whispered.

Gian crossed himself.

"Where is the dervish?" Hamideddin asked.

"You were the last to attend him," the janissary pointed out to Hamideddin.

Hamideddin pulled his robe around his shoulders and shivered in the chill of the dawning day.

"Where is Ozman Kapikulu?" Gian asked.

"He is too busy to attend to you now. The Grand Vizier has orders for him."

~~~

Nesri, one of the sultan's favored chroniclers, had marched and camped quite close to the sultan, although not within the inner circle surrounded by the sultan's personal guard. That evening he had considered himself fortunate to find a grassy hollow where he could wrap up in his blanket, cover himself with a rug, and sleep without being bothered by the snores and twitching of the other mid-level officials in the tent they shared. But before dawn, other sounds first entered his dreams and then disturbed his sleep. He dreamed first that he was a creaking wheel rolling along a rutted road. Then, as if that were not bad enough, he dreamed that he was riding a spirited horse that jumped, startled, at a fluttering black thing and threw him off. And then the fluttering black thing had blown over his face and it was not a blanket but silence, darkness, death... With a strangled cry of terror Nesri flung out his arm, sat up and... felt like a very great fool, because the thing over his face actually had been his blanket; he must have pulled it up in his sleep against the early morning chill.

And yet, something was very strange. Had he gone blind? No, in the dim pre-dawn light he could see the grass waving around him, behind him the tents of the army, and in front of him...

Nothing. The imperial tent had disappeared. The imperial carriage that had followed the tent all the way from Constantinople, while the sultan rode ahead of it on his white horse, had also disappeared, as had all the rest of the sultan's personal entourage. Where the heart of the empire had been the night before, now there was nothing but a few flattened circles in the grass of the meadow.

# ~CHAPTER THIRTY-FIVE~

*La Grande Aquila é morta!*

~ ~ ~

They were nearing Constantinople when Ozman Kapikulu came to Gian and Caterina's tent at dusk. He slipped in noiselessly as a shadow and held a finger to his lips. "You need to leave now," he said in a cautious undertone.

"We will be only too happy to do so," Gian answered in the same low, barely audible tones, "but would it not be easier to disappear into Constantinople, once we reach the city?"

Ozman shook his head violently. "No! When we enter the city, it will be impossible to conceal the sultan's death any longer. And who will bear the blame, if not his physicians?"

"The Dervish Ismail?" Gian suggested.

Another shake of the head. "He is revered as a very holy man. Also, he did not march with us; he is with the main body of the army. You and the Persian, though, are easy to identify in our little group. The people will be distraught to learn of the sultan's death. My own janissaries are, I think, under my control, but the ones who were left to guard Constantinople may rise up. I cannot guarantee your safety in Constantinople. But I have procured a small boat which can take you to Galata. Once there, it is to be hoped that your *bailo* Battista Gritti will waste no time in sending you to Venice. It is not – the Sublime Porte will not, you understand, pursue you. It is only the hysteria

269

of the crowds and the common soldiers that you have to fear."

"Was that why the Grand Vizier insisted on this secrecy? To put off the moment when the people would learn of the sultan's death?"

Ozman gave him a thin smile. "Not entirely. Karamanli Pasha wishes the attack on Venice to proceed. If the next sultan is the older son, Bayezid, there will be no war and there may be a complete change of government; the Grand Vizier could find himself replaced by a Sufi Dervish, for Bayezid is very religious."

"Oh? The sultan said he was an opium addict."

"The sultan is given to exaggeration. It is true that Bayezid takes opium occasionally; he also writes poetry and studies the philosophy of the Sufis. My late master considered all three of these interests unsuitable for a sultan; others of us are not so certain. In any case, if the younger son, Djem, reaches Constantinople first and proclaims himself sultan, Karamanli Pasha will retain his position and the war will proceed. And since Djem is in Konya, closer to the capital than Bayezid is in Amasya, and since the Grand Vizier sent three messengers to apprise him of the sultan's death even before we left camp, he hopes to discover a *fait accompli* in the capital already."

"But what do you think?"

Ozman's smile broadened. "I think that Karamanli Pasha has forgotten that Mara Despina Hatun, who favors Bayezid, is my patroness, and that Bayezid's son-in-law is Agha of the janissaries, and that no messengers will reach Konya without his approval. Meanwhile, the Agha has surely learned what news the messengers carried, and he will have informed his father-in-law of the sultan's death. But Bayezid will not have had time to reach Constantinople yet, and the city is likely to be a bad place for foreigners – particularly those who waited on the sultan in his last days. Hence, the boat. And we have wasted enough time already; come with me now."

"Wait!" said Caterina at the opening of the tent. "What about Hamideddin al-Lari?"

Ozman shrugged. "Yes, he will likely be accused of poisoning the sultan. I cannot protect everybody."

"But could he not come with us?"

Ozman frowned. "It is a very small boat, chosen to slip inconspicuously past the shore guards. It will not be a comfortable journey for three passengers."

But Gian sided with Caterina, feeling that being cramped for a short while in a small boat was less uncomfortable than leaving a man he knew and liked to be torn apart by a hysterical mob.

~ ~ ~

The reaction of Constantinople to the sultan's death was even worse than Ozman had foreseen. Shortly after the Grand Vizier's group reached Topkapi, the palace janissaries forced open the inner gate of the serai. At the sight of the sultan's dead body they declared that he had been poisoned and cried out for vengeance. When they were unable to find the sultan's two personal physicians, they turned their desire for revenge on the Grand Vizier himself. Before the city was restored to order, the janissaries paraded Karamanli Pasha's head on a lance around the city. "Karamanli desired high position, and behold, we have raised him above all others!" they shouted. Then they turned over their copper cooking kettles and drummed on them. As long as the savage, metallic drumbeat shook the city, the common people took it as license to revenge themselves on the enemies of the sultan. But who exactly were those, apart from the physicians who had vanished after poisoning their lord? Well, Jews and Christians would do as substitutes, and they had fine houses and shops full of good things. Not to mention covert taverns whose supplies of wine fueled further rioting.

The three messengers sent to Djem in Konya were, as Ozman predicted, arrested before they could deliver the news; those sent by the Agha of janissaries to the sultan's older son were more fortunate. When Bayezid arrived in Constantinople with four thousand horsemen, he was able to proclaim himself sultan with little opposition. The janissaries were compensated for the loss of a war with generous cash payments. This was to become a custom, and to be a recurring drain on the treasury each time a sultan died; but Bayezid could not be expected to think of everything.

~ ~ ~

The fastest brigantine that could make the passage from Galata to Venice was not fast enough for Gian. Despite Ozman's reassurances, he was not at all sure that the Turks would not pursue the men who were so widely believed to have poisoned the sultan. What made matters even worse, in his opinion, was that Battista Gritti shared that belief. He had congratulated Gian warmly on carrying out his mission and had promised to give him full credit in the dispatches he was sending to Venice immediately, even before he arranged for Gian and Caterina's passage.

"Please," Gian said. "You have told me that the Turks read all your letters. If they read that I carried out a Venetian plot to kill the sultan, they will assuredly try to capture me."

"Oh, they cannot keep up with the ship I shall send you on," Gritti said.

"And they will renew the war with Venice," Gian pointed out. "And they will probably also have you killed, for having made the poisoning plan in the first place."

Gritti looked thoughtful and eventually agreed that it would be better to write no dispatches at all, but to send one of his staff with a memorized message.

Hamideddin al-Lari was too depressed to worry about being captured and executed by the Turks. He had left his native land to serve the sultan, but that had been a considerable promotion. And he had always hoped that some day, when the sultan wanted a younger physician, he would be granted an honorable retirement and a pension sufficient for him to set up as a great man in his home town of Lari.

Now he was going even farther from Persia, and with no position awaiting him at the end of the journey. Worse, he was going into a land of infidels, pork-eaters and wine-swillers, where no muezzin called out the hours of prayer. What was he to do in such a place?

"Whatever you do," Gian said unsympathetically, "it will be preferable to being torn apart by the mob. Did you hear what they did to Karamanli Pasha before they struck off his head and put it on a lance?"

Hamideddin turned pale green. It might have been the effect of the waves that were beginning to force a nasty, lopsided rolling motion on the brigantine. "I heard," he said faintly.

~ ~ ~

Gian and Caterina had planned to enter Venice quietly, probably taking refuge at Agostino Foscari's House of the Crocodile until they could find out something about the situation in San Florian. There was nothing to be gained in advertising their presence in Venice while Malatesta still held San Florian.

Uberto Feo, Gritti's man, almost spoiled that plan before the brigantine was even tied up at the quai. Leaping ashore, he shouted at the top of his voice, "*La Grande Aquila é morta!*"

Gasps from the boatmen, the wharf workers waiting to unload cargo, the merchants waiting to evaluate their shipments to and from Constantinople and Alexandria, London and the Low Countries.

"The Great Eagle?" asked a merchant who prided himself on not listening to common slang.

"It is another name for the Grand Turk," kindly explained his neighbor.

"*Dead?*"

In no time at all a crowd gathered and Uberto amplified his announcement. "Yes, the Great Eagle is dead, and here is the man who killed him!" He made a sweeping gesture behind him.

The crowd murmured in confusion. Uberto looked back and was surprised to find that the hero had disappeared. Instead of standing up proudly to receive the thanks of a grateful city, Gian had stepped from one narrow boat to another and now was leading his woman and that Persian infidel along the quai, away from the brigantine that had brought them safely home. Well, so much for those idiots. He did not in the least object to taking all the credit and all the praise.

"I must inform the Ten!" he announced grandly.

Another murmur. "They are in council," said a merchant who had pushed his way to the front.

"With the Doge," another added.

"About the war!"

"Then," said Uberto, "I shall have the happiness of informing them there is to be no war!"

The crowd cheered. Carried on the shoulders of two sturdy wharfmen, Uberto reached the Doge's palace in a whirlwind of shouts, songs of praise, and yet more cheering.

Safe in the House of the Crocodile, Gian and Caterina sank into Foscari's two best chairs while Hamideddin prowled around the front room, investigating the bundles of herbs, the boxes and bottles of medicines, and the curiosities displayed on the walls. Gian noticed that the spiny fish skeleton had been replaced by that of a winged serpent with long, dripping fangs. The label below it read "Draco alata," and would have been more convincing had the wires holding the wings to the serpent body not been quite so visible.

To their great relief, Dottore Foscari was again in Venice, and as soon as one of his house servants brought the news of Gian's return he closed down his stage in the Piazza and hurried home to greet his young friend.

"And the Contessa has come back too? Excellent, excellent! You will have many tales of the Turk's lands, I hope? Those will make good hearing in the Piazza!"

"I do not know if I dare appear publicly," Gian said. "If you remember, just before da Treviso forced us to go to Turkey, that accursed Malatesta had tracked Caterina to this house. We probably ought not to have come here at all, but I did not know where else to go."

"Ah. As usual, you have not heard the latest news. Malatesta is gone —some say a natural death, some that he was burned up by demons. I am inclined to favor the latter story, for the mage has also disappeared and there were apparently no bodies to bury. Most likely the mage was working a conjuration and made some minor error which allowed a demon to get past his circles of protection."

"No body? Perhaps it is a trick —perhaps he is still alive and in hiding, waiting to get his hands on Caterina?"

Foscari shook his head. "Why should he play such a trick, when he had no way to know that she was about to come back? And your city councilors, Contessa, are meeting regularly in the Palazzo Rinaldi. If he were alive,

Malatesta would never countenance such a show of insurgency. No, you may take it that he and his court mage are both truly dead, whether by demons or some other cause. And there is a great deal of excitement here in Venice about some mineral discoveries or other in San Florian. You had best present yourselves at the Ca' d'Oro immediately; the word is that Ottavio Contarini himself is going to San Florian to treat with the council. He is one of the Ten now, you know."

"That should make Lucrezia happy," commented Caterina as they made their way to the Ca d'Oro.

"Do you suppose she has gone back to him?"

"I suppose that depends on how long since he was elected to the Ten, and whether she has heard the news yet."

# ~CHAPTER THIRTY-SIX~

*Volterra possessed mines of alum, a mineral indispensable for drapers, and Florence had taken these mines on lease. When the lease fell due for renewal, the Volterrans asked for a higher rent, which led to disputes and finally to a withdrawal of the concession. Lorenzo would tolerate no such solution; and on Volterra's rebelling, he let loose a condottiere who, despite his relative mildness, was unable to prevent the sack of the town. There were murders and hangings, and houses burned to the ground.*

  *- Lucas-Dubreton: Daily Life in Florence in the Time of the Medici*

                     ~~~

Caterina was surprised by the warmth of their welcome in Contarini's palazzo. It might have helped that Hamideddin al-Lari had been invited to stay with Dottore Foscari and look over Foscari's translation of al-Razi; the two men had been deep into a reasonably polite dispute about the interpretation of certain Arabic terms when Gian and Caterina took their departure. (Gian, the cynic, remarked that he wanted to be out of the House of the Crocodile before the scholars began throwing skeletons at one another.)

But Ottavio Contarini seemed really pleased at their arrival, and wanted to have a banquet in their honor that very night. Gian suggested that getting to San Florian was more urgent than socializing with the leaders of Venice; Contarini brushed that trivial objection aside. Caterina listened to the discussion and tried a different approach to avoid the banquet, pleading exhaustion after the sea journey, her lack of any dress suitable for such an honor, and the impossibility of dressing herself appropriately without a maid.

A maidservant Contarini could supply, but even he could not get one of the dresses Lucrezia had left altered to fit a shorter, slimmer woman in two hours; his draper's eye saw that immediately, and he conceded the force of Caterina's argument.

"I should like to know why he listened to you and not to me," Gian grumbled. Contarini had, tactfully, assigned them two separate bedrooms. But he had, perhaps even more tactfully, chosen two adjoining bedrooms with a connecting door between them. Not that Gian intended to use that convenience for anything more than *talking*.

Caterina giggled. Her spirits had been improving ever since she set foot on the beautiful and, well, reasonably solid land of Venice. "My poor captain. You are not used to a woman's arguments being heard more favorably than your own, are you? Ottavio Contarini is, as Lucrezia told us, first, last and always a merchant. You spoke of soldiers and capturing the Rocca; he has no desire to lead a military force, even if one could be assembled. Also, he does not believe that violence will be necessary –I pray he is right about that!"

"He believes that because it is what he wishes to believe," Gian said gloomily. "He will probably go right on believing it right up until one of Malatesta's loyal men skewers him on a spear."

Caterina paused in shaking out the few garments she had been able to bring with her. "I do not think," she said, "that Roberto Malatesta was such a man as to inspire loyalty after his death. In any case, his son is not old enough to pursue that or any other war."

"Why did you not point that out to Contarini, instead of twittering about clothes and maidservants?"

"You *have* met Lucrezia, have you not?"

Gian groaned assent.

"And Contarini is still madly in love with her?"

Even while greeting them and rejoicing over the sultan's death, Ottavio Contarini had mentioned his dear Lucrezia and the sufferings she must have undergone. He nodded, but warily, because he could not quite see where Caterina was going with this.

"So," Caterina said with satisfaction, "what he is used to is what I gave him –a woman who thinks of nothing else but appearance and dress. And since he was doubtless used to giving in to Lucrezia on such matters, he simply treated me as if I were Lucrezia. *And*," she added, "over a small private dinner I can do what would have been difficult to do in the formality of a banquet: I can convince him that his dear Lucrezia is desperately desirous of being reunited with him and that his best course is to set out immediately." Caterina stopped talking for a moment; she had to sit perfectly still while the maidservant provided by Contarini carefully removed the wisp of a veil fastened over her coiled braids and began drawing out the hairpins that held them in place.

"That pretty story will come to grief as soon as they see each other again," Gian pointed out.

Caterina looked up at him. "But by then," she said cheerfully, "we shall be in San Florian again, and I shall be in possession of the Rocca –assuming Piero and Tommaso have not made a *complete* muddle of the Council –and Ottavio Contarini's relationship with his wife will no longer be my problem! Now go away, Gian. Sofia here wishes to comb out my braids, and it really is not proper for you to be watching my toilette."

Gian retreated with two unpalatable facts to gnaw on: Caterina really was a better negotiator than he was, and her mere captain of the guard had no business living on intimate terms with her now that they were not running away or hiding or otherwise constrained. Not, he thought with regret, that there had ever been that much intimacy. In the elaborate dance of privacy and not-looking that they had conducted throughout their travels, although he had seen her hair down when she acted in Foscari's appalling drama, he had never been privileged to see her combing out the shining braids. There was something about a woman combing her hair, transforming those tightly coiled braids into a cloak that framed her face and her white shoulders…

He almost wished somebody would attack them; with a sword in his hand, at least he knew who he was.

Gian Bracciaforte. Gian of the Strong Arm.

Peasant's son, risen thus far and no farther through his military skills.

Anything that might hint at a different origin was buried more than ten years back, in the blood-soaked soil of the Neroni estates in Florence, and had best stay buried lest he be sent to join the bones of his father.

~~~

In the event, two full days elapsed before the Contarini party set out for Venice. Gian wanted to grumble that it was all Caterina's fault for convincing Ottavio that she was a fragile female who had to be given every comfort, but that did not comport with the facts. Contarini was extremely busy during those days. Messengers came and went between the Ca' d'Oro and San Florian, and since the master of the house was usually out on business, Gian was able to pick up a good idea of their news while he offered them refreshment. Not that there was much news to be had.

"Your city council is still meeting," he reported to Caterina, "only now that they know you are coming back, they have moved from the Palazzo Michele back to the great hall in the Palazzo Rinaldi. Tommaso holds the Rocca with a handful of volunteers, we shall have to get professionals from somewhere. Malatesta sent my men to Rimini, but I think they will return when they know you are back; that's a start. Meanwhile, Piero says he is very busy talking to somebody from the Vatican about mineral rights."

"That must be a mistake," Caterina said. "San Florian has no gold or silver. Not even copper! Piero once told me that the red soil in the south pastures is a sign of iron, but that there was not enough to be worth the expense of extracting it."

"Probably a mistake," Gian agreed. "More likely the Vatican representative is trying to set a base price for this year's wool clip."

"Then we had better get back there at once! Piero is sure to be cheated."

"He is?"

Caterina gave Gian a stern look. "Piero is the only man I know who is worse than you at negotiating."

"I shall speak to Contarini again," Gian said, "and try to hurry him up a bit. Perhaps he can represent you in the negotiations. Where is he today?"

Caterina shrugged. "He does not tell *me* where he goes, but he is either meeting with the rest of the Ten or attending to business at his dye houses."

"So he tells you what he's been doing when he gets home?"

"I don't think he believes a woman would be able to comprehend men's business. But when he's been with the Ten, there are black ink stains on his fingers. When he's been to the dye houses, his hands are... more colorful."

To their relief, the news that a representative of the Vatican had reached San Florian imbued Ottavio Contarini with a sense of urgency. He heard the news in late evening after a long day at the dye houses and ordered a departure at first light the next morning, ignoring the wails of protest from servants who could not possibly be ready in time, from apprentices who could not possibly continue the complex processes of dyeing without guidance, and even from Sofia, who could not finish stitching the you-know-whats on the you-know-what-I-mean in less than a day and a half. He told the servants that this was their chance to make up for a week of idleness during which he had been too busy to ask them to do anything at all, and told the apprentices that this was why he paid an arm and a leg for master dyers to supervise the work. Sofia, who had made the last and least comprehensible complaint, was told that she could either finish her job that night or work on it in the Contessa's carriage.

"I do not require a carriage," Caterina said on hearing this. "I can ride. Truly, Messer Contarini, I would *rather* ride!" This close to her home, it would be intolerable to be held down to the slow pace of a carriage lurching over an uneven road.

Contarini looked not at her, but at Silvia. "You heard. Finish it tonight – keep all the other women in my service up to help with the work if you must –but have it packed by daylight!"

Whatever it was, it must have been either packed or abandoned by the time Caterina came downstairs in the morning, for the procession of horses and pack-mules was ready to set off.

Traveling this road with a wealthy merchant was rather different from their previous experience of a midnight flight. There was no question of making the journey in a single day; Contarini decreed that men and horses required a night's rest in mid-journey to recover from the ordeal of plodding along a minor road in good weather. There was no attempt at secrecy; instead, messengers were sent ahead to insure appropriate hospitality at their all-too-frequent rest stops. And instead of pressing two ill-fed horses to their best speed, the procession moved at the speed of the slowest animals. Those were usually the pack mules, which carried what Caterina thought an obscene amount of luggage for the three of them, even adding a secretary, an accountant, and their personal servants. She entertained herself by imagining how Contarini would have fared if, like herself, he had been forced to escape his house in the middle of the night with nothing but the clothes he had on, and to ride double behind his castellan until two horses could be stolen. She did not think he would enjoy the experience.

It was not until noon on the second day that she learned what the you-know-what-I-mean was and why it had taken so long to sew on all the you-know-whats. They were so close to San Florian that Caterina felt as if they were almost there. The rolling hills rising to the mountains, the black earth of the cultivated fields, even the wild brambles and spikes of grass that edged the fields were all familiar, dear and sweet to her. Caterina was already straining her eyes to pick out the peak of the Rocca when the riders ahead of her turned aside.

"We will pause here," Contarini pronounced in front of a country house. "The family will bring refreshments to us in the courtyard while you, Madonna, prepare yourself for the triumphal entry."

Triumphal entry? All Caterina was hoping for was to get into the city without violence, assert control over the castle and then, once again, to set to work repairing her little world. Maybe Contarini thought her too dirty from the morning's travel? Her braids were springing loose from their tight coils? She put a hand to her head and reassured herself that this, at least, was not the case. But at Contarini's urging she returned the greetings of their slightly surprised hosts and followed a servant upstairs to a sparsely furnished bedchamber. Behind her Sofia toiled up the stairs with a bag that she had been guarding with anxious care ever since their departure.

As Caterina sat down on the bed, Sofia upended the bag beside her.

Billows of emerald-green silk enveloped Caterina. Too surprised to speak, she put up one hand to shield her face while Sofia shook out the dress and mourned over the inevitable wrinkles. "We shall have to wait a few hours while I press the fabric," she complained.

"Is that —for me —to wear?" Caterina could hardly believe it. Where and how had Ottavio Contarini come up with this extravagant garment?

"Well, it certainly isn't for me!" Sofia said with a cackle, holding up the dress so that Caterina could see how its narrow waist revealed her own more generous build.

"Then never mind the wrinkles. I don't."

As soon as Caterina put off her travel-stained outer dress, Sofia held it up against the new dress and congratulated herself on the success of her alterations. "It wasn't easy to cut this down, you know. The lady Lucrezia always wanted her dresses as full and sumptuous as we could make them."

Catherine's lips twitched. So she was to enter San Florian wearing one of Lucrezia's dresses! No doubt Lucrezia would raise the roof if she recognized the dress —and it was a very memorable one, with a broad twelve inches of floral embroidery around the waist, little figures of gold flowers with pearl centers. As Sofia laced on the matching sleeves, slashed to reveal semi-transparent white silk puffs embroidered with gilt thread, Caterina saw that the motifs of gold flowers and pearls were repeated around the edges of each slash in the deep green sleeves.

"The pearls were from a necklace," Sofia volunteered. "Messer Contarini felt that for the Contessa, something richer than mere embroidery was required."

So those dozens of pearls had been the you-know-whats that Sofia had complained took so long to sew on. And when —if —Lucrezia returned to the Ca' d'Oro, she would discover that an extremely expensive necklace was missing. Caterina privately vowed not to leave the safety of the Rocca until that discovery was over.

"Now for the jewels," Sofia prompted.

Caterina picked up the emerald brooch which, at Gian's behest, she had been wearing daily. Sofia shook her head. "The green of those emeralds clashes with the green of the dress," she said. "Look how much yellower they are! If you wear *that* with *this* dress, people will think they are fakes –quartz colored with verdigris, perhaps."

Now that Caterina looked at the brooch carefully, it seemed quite possible to her that the "emeralds" were really glass or quartz, colored by some alchemical process. That would be a surprise to Gian!

"Besides," Sofia said, "if my lady will forgive my saying so, that is quite the ugliest brooch I have ever seen."

Caterina had to agree with that. Whoever had thought that a gaping demon face with emeralds for eyes and teeth was a desirable embellishment for a lady? The designer must have been crazy, or at least seriously emotionally disturbed.

The more conventional ruby tiara, necklace and earrings met with Sofia's approval. The tiara seemed a bit excessive to Caterina, but Sofia pointed out that it would anchor the veil over the top and back of her head quite firmly, which was not a trivial consideration when my lady was riding all over the country without so much as a hat to protect her complexion.

There were more surprises waiting for Catherine when they reached the north gate of the city. Children were lined up on either side of the road, and the dusty road itself was all but covered with green branches and flowers. The hedgerows and the palazzo gardens must have been stripped bare!

The children were singing something, or rather, they were singing three somethings; a hymn of praise fought for supremacy with a children's counting-out rhyme and a third song which, in Caterina's opinion, nobody under twelve ought to know. Fortunately the children did not seem to understand the bawdy puns.

Most of the children were empty-handed, but a few who had been prudent enough to hang on to their flowers threw them at Caterina. She ducked a long, thorny branch that sailed over her head without, thank the Virgin, getting entangled in her veil; sat up again, waved graciously from side to side, smiled at the children and mouthed her thanks for the welcome.

Then Piero Giacomini, riding astride a bony grey mare which Caterina recognized as the extremely calm horse the stable master used for children under the age of five, with his robe hitched up on either side to show wrinkled hose borrowed from a larger man, rode through the north gate to greet her, and Caterina forgot all about the singing and the bombardment with flowers and branches. She was *home*.

"Our distinguished guests were persuaded to await you at the Palazzo," Piero said by way of greeting. "Tommaso said that your homecoming was San Florian's affair and that diplomacy could wait on the joy of the people."

Distinguished guests?

"Is all this because of the death of the sultan?" But no, that did not make sense. Venice and, reportedly, Rome had gone mad over the news, with nightly fireworks and cannon fire, dancing in the streets and, so one heard, even more passionate celebrations in the houses. But San Florian had not been hysterical about the sultan's threats; the people of San Florian tended to consider anything that happened more than ten leagues away as foreign affairs with no relevance to them.

"No. It's about *you*, Contessa."

"Me?" She was glad Ottavio Contarini had thought of the green silk dress. It would have been quite wrong to ride through all this cheering and acclaim, not to mention the shower of white blossoms and green branches, in a travel-stained dress that was limp from being washed in sea water during her voyage.

"They are happy to see you back." Piero paused. "Especially after the Malatesta. I have to admit that some of their joy is due to his death. Father Benvenuto was quite firm about *not* celebrating the death of a ruler, particularly one that had been whisked away by demons. He said it was tantamount to praising the demons... well, anyway. They are more than ready to submit themselves to their proper ruler. Although it might be wise to bring Ercole back here for a few days, to emphasize that you are acting as regent to the heir...well, we can discuss that later. Right now you had best decide how to greet your distinguished guests. If I might offer a word of warning: do *not* promise anything, no matter what they say."

"Who are they, and what are you afraid they'll say?"

Piero looked surprised. "What, did Messer Contarini not tell you?"

"He does not approve of women discussing politics," Caterina said demurely, mentally adding *and neither would I, if I were married to Lucrezia.* "He is, of course, eager to be reunited with his beloved wife —unless the demons carried her away too?"

"Oh, no, Lucrezia is quite safe."

Caterina felt real, honest relief. Mixed with, to be absolutely honest, just the smallest twinge of disappointment. *Of course I did not want Lucrezia to be the prey of demons. I am not a monster.*

*The possibility did cross your mind,* her conscience retorted. *You had better get yourself to confession before that thought grows and takes over your heart.*

"The visitors?" she prompted Piero.

"Ottavio Contarini, of course. Bishop Visconti, acting for the Pope," Piero said, "and even better…"

He paused as if to tease her. But who could possibly be visiting in San Florian who outranked a Papal Legate? The Pope? But then he would not have sent Visconti. Catherine shook her head in real bewilderment. "You will have to tell me, for I cannot guess."

"Il Magnifico himself," Piero announced proudly. "Lorenzo de' Medici."

That was more alarming than reassuring.

"Was he planning to lay claim to San Florian if I did not come back?"

Piero shook his head. "Not if we can come to an agreement on mineral rights."

If she had not been mounted on Contarini's rather skittish white mare, Caterina would have thrown her hands up. "San Florian has no minerals! God's eyebrows, if there were gold or silver or even copper in these hills, do you not think Girolamo would have extracted the metals and turned them into yet more paintings and statues and Venetian glass and Belgian tapestries? Or put them around the neck of his mistress?"

"You think too narrowly." Piero grinned. "I said *mineral* rights, not *metal* rights. It happens that the mountains around San Florian are rich in a mineral that certain people value more than gold —or rather, that can be turned into gold in the right hands. And *I* discovered it!"

"You have been out on the mountainside, prospecting for this valuable mineral?" Caterina's eyebrows went up. She could not see her awkward, scholarly councillor in that role.

"Actually," Piero said, "I was trying to find out why Maso Trevi's sheep were committing suicide at the high end of the east pasture. And the answer was…" He paused to build up suspense. "Alum!"

"Alum," Caterina repeated.

"Not just alum. *Lots* of alum. Potential alum, anyway. Alum-bearing rocks just sticking out of the ground. They taste salty, you know, that's what led the sheep to them," Piero added parenthetically before returning to his main theme. "Alum-bearing rocks *under* the ground. Half a mountain of such rocks, at a minimum, and my cousin from Tolfa thinks there is much, much more to be found."

# ~CHAPTER THIRTY-SEVEN~

*One of the intimate friends of Tommaso Soderini, reminding him of the advice he had given, asked him what he thought of the taking of Volterra; to which he replied, "To me the place seems rather lost than won; for had it been received on equitable terms, advantage and security would have been the result; but having to retain it by force it will in critical junctures, occasion weakness and anxiety, and in times of peace, injury and expense."*

*-Machiavelli, History of Florence*

~ ~ ~

Caterina looked down and picked up a fold of her dark green skirt. She was no dyer, but her best guess at how much alum had been necessary to fix that color was somewhere in the area of "lots and lots." And even in San Florian, one heard of the dyers' complaints. When alum came only from Anatolia and Venice had a monopoly of the trade, they had accused Venice of price-gouging and of trying to put all other dyers out of business. Then when the discovery of alum in Tolfa had broken the Venetian monopoly, they had complained because the alum profits from Tolfa only sent more money into the Pope's already swollen treasury. And when alum deposits were found around Volterra –

Caterina gasped. "Piero! The Medici is here to conquer San Florian! Look at what he did to Volterra!" Lorenzo de' Medici had hired the Montefeltro condottieri to take Volterra when he was dissatisfied with the terms of trade they offered, and he had allowed the condottieri to sack the city even though it had surrendered. Volterra had still not recovered from that orgy of destruction eight years ago.

"No, look at what the sack of Volterra did to his reputation and Montefeltro's," Piero said soothingly. "It was years before anybody trusted Florence enough to make another trade deal with them, and Montefeltro's reputation as an honorable condottiere was sunk for even more years. This time he has not come with Montefeltro's condottieri, but with only a small personal guard. I believe him when he says he desires only peaceful trade between our cities."

"Yes, but *you* believed Rospo Forza when he said that a hair from a horse's tail, put into a bottle of water and buried in a dung heap for three days, would turn into a serpent!" Caterina retorted, recalling that great disappointment of her childhood.

"So did you!"

"No, I didn't! I only said we should try it and see what happened!"

"Very well, you will of course make your own judgment of Lorenzo," Piero said stiffly. "It will not be my fault if you start seeing serpents where there are only the rear ends of horses."

A few feet further on he relented.

"In any case, Bishop Visconti is here to make the case for Rome. And if I am not mistaken, Venice has sent the only member of the Ten who is an expert on dye works. Lorenzo de' Medici will not have things all his own way as he did with Volterra."

Caterina tortured herself the rest of the way to the Palazzo Rinaldi with visions of three competing armies descending on San Florian and reducing the city to rubble. After all, there might be valuable alum beneath the ruins...

They were within sight of the open palazzo doors when a figure in pale blue silk came running out to greet them. She ran right past Caterina and stretched out her arms to Ottavio Contarini. "Oh, my dear, dear husband, you have come for me at last! Oh, Ottavio, it has been *terrible* here, but I could not leave San Florian after that Caterina abandoned her responsibilities..."

"Sh, sh, sh." Ottavio swung down from his horse, took Lucrezia in his arms and muffled whatever else she had been going to say against his broad, velvet-clad shoulder. "I am here to take care of you, my dear, and everything will be all right."

Lucrezia pulled away just enough to look at him, her eyes shining, and Caterina began to feel some hope for this marriage –and, possibly more to the point, hope that Lucrezia would return to Venice with Contarini when he left. *Maybe her experience with Roberto Malatesta has taught her the benefits of being married to a good and decent man.*

That part of her mind which did not seem to be under the control of her conscience added *Let's hope she does not tell him too many details about her time with Malatesta, or he'll never take her back.*

Another unkind thought to add in to her eventual confession to Father Benvenuto. It was certainly much easier to practice charity when one didn't have Lucrezia as the subject.

But in the next few minutes, Lucrezia lost all importance in her mind – and even, it seemed, in Contarini's. For as she received the greetings of Bishop Visconti and Lorenzo de' Medici, Contarini shouldered his way into the group. *He is determined that Venice should have its chance at our alum mines, isn't he? Even Lucrezia takes second place to alum.* She felt slightly more sympathetic to Lucrezia's complaints about Ottavio.

But where was Lucrezia? She seemed to have disappeared just when some new pages, unfamiliar to her, were bringing out dishes and setting them on the long tables in the hall. Somebody had ordered those tables set up; somebody else had seen to the preparation of dishes suitable to a banquet. The floor was uncarpeted, but no one would notice as they walked over green leaves mixed with sweet herbs that added their scent to the savory smells escaping from the dishes on the tables. The bare spots on the walls were covered with the same fabrics that Caterina had used to decorate the hall when Roberto Malatesta dined there –all except a certain sky-blue silk that, now she thought of it, just matched the color of Lucrezia's dress. Well, if she was responsible for producing this banquet, she had more than earned it.

*Tomaselli* of liver with raisins and cheese, roast capons decorated with orange segments, salads of radish and rampion, plates of roasted eel with wedges of lemon, fried marzipan pastries… Caterina lost count of the dishes, but there were certainly enough to feed her visitors and the members of the council, the important merchants of the city and… far, far away, nearly at the end of the table, the captain of her personal guard. She resolved to think up some promotion that would allow his being seated nearer her. Though it was hard to think of any title which would put him higher than a papal legate and the head of a neighboring state. Even Ottavio Contarini had been forced to mention, several times, that he was a member of the Ten and the official representative of Venice before the councilors shifted down the table to make room for him.

When the three peacocks with gold-dusted feathers were carried in, there was no more possible doubt as to who had arranged this feast. The only surprise was that Lucrezia was overseeing the work of the kitchens instead of coming out and taking her proper place beside her husband, where she could flirt with Caterina's noble visitors and receive their compliments on the banquet with becoming modesty.

That happened with the final course, an offering of sugar castles filled with sweet minced meat and meringue sailing ships with a cargo of sugared almonds. As the guests amused themselves by storming the castles and capturing the ships, Lucrezia slipped into the dining room and stood behind Ottavio, who promptly moved up the bench to make room for his wife.

For once, Caterina did not envy Lucrezia's golden beauty. With the confidence given her by the rubies and the emerald-green dress, she felt fully worthy of her place at the head of the high table.

What she did envy, quietly, was Lucrezia's ability to spend most of a prolonged banquet in the kitchens without getting a single stain, not even a water spot, on that pale blue silk.

"We must have a private chat later," Bishop Visconti told her as the feasting came to an end. "As this city was originally the gift of the Pope to your husband, there can of course be no question of who should manage the little deposits of alum recently discovered, but it is best to have everything clearly documented."

"Now that the house of Rinaldi is allied with the house of Contarini,"

Ottavio murmured in her other ear, "we really should have a private family meeting about your future plans. You can trust me to look after your interests."

Lorenzo de' Medici leaned back slightly, stretched out his legs under the table, and –purely accidentally –kicked Ottavio Contarini hard enough to make the merchant wince. "*I* do not insist on a solitary meeting," he said, without bothering to lower his voice. "In fact, I think there should be witnesses to any agreement that may be drawn up. Perhaps the Contessa would like to be attended by her accountant and the captain of her personal guard?"

The other two envoys looked affronted, but neither argued. And so, while the other dinner guests were somnolently digesting that magnificent meal, and slowly departing as the effects of the generous wine servings wore off, Caterina met in an upstairs room with the three envoys on one side of the table and herself, flanked by Piero and Gian, on the other side.

Ottavio Contarini was the first to mention numbers. Piero scribbled something on the paper in front of him, then looked at Caterina and shook his head.

"Venice takes a paternal interest in the affairs of San Florian," Contarini said, glaring at Piero, "and will see that you are not cheated by any unscrupulous speculators. You should be *particularly* wary of those who cloak their dealings in the righteousness of Holy Church."

Bishop Visconti took advantage of the momentary shocked silence to remind Caterina again that San Florian had been the Pope's gift to her late husband.

"Indeed it was," Caterina agreed with a sweet smile, "and you may be sure I also remember when I desperately needed Rome's help to combat the Borghini uprising. Your plan was for me to be forced into marriage with Domenico Borghini and to give him title to the city, was it not? And I do not believe that your plan accounted for how long I might hope to live after that."

Bishop Visconti's face, already somewhat flushed from overindulgence at the banquet, began to turn a dark purple.

"Bishop! Are you choking?" Lorenzo was out of his chair in an instant, pounding the bishop on the back until he coughed violently. "There," the Medici said sweetly, "all better now? Have a drink of wine, Your Excellency."

He remained standing, dominating the room. "Although San Florian will be justly compensated for all the alum we take," he said, as though the issue were already decided, "there are other factors than mere monetary ones to be considered here. I have been discussing those other issues with my man Paolo Uberti…"

A clamor of metal and shouts arose through the window that overlooked the Piazza, and Lorenzo paused until he could be heard again. In that pause, Gian Bracciaforte set his jaw and unobtrusively dropped his right hand below the table. Caterina would have wagered any sum that it was resting on the hilt of his sword. Would Lorenzo de' Medici dare to bring up the Neroni conspiracy?

The shouting died down, but there was a very firm knock on the door.

"Contessa," Tomasso Peruzzi called, "you will want to receive this visitor."

Contarini, being nearest the door, opened it.

A man of middle age and slightly more than medium height, with a broken nose and a patch over his right eye, strolled into the room. He had the slight swagger common to men who spent more time on horseback than on chairs, but he was sumptuously dressed in red velvet.

Gian shot to his feet; after a moment, Piero followed suit. Caterina and Bishop Visconti retained their seats. Visconti's face was going purple again.

"So, banker," the bishop growled at Lorenzo, "up to your old tricks again? Do you think you can frighten the Contessa into giving up by the threat of sacking her city?"

"I have no contract with Federico da Montefeltro," Lorenzo protested, "nor did I ask him to come here!"

Caterina looked at the new arrival with renewed interest. This was the first time she had seen the man to whom she had entrusted her son. Despite his battered appearance, she was prepared to like him. His one remaining eye took in the room without any hint of despising the simple furnishing, and the lines at the corners of his mouth suggested someone who laughed freely and often.

"You expect us to believe that?" Visconti said incredulously. "Why else – unless he seeks the alum rights for himself –"

"I have come," Federico da Montefeltro interrupted him, "to safeguard the interests of my foster-son, Ercole Rinaldi, the heir to San Florian."

At this moment there was a shout from outside, the sound of a slap, and the outcry of a very young voice. Ercole himself darted into the room, narrowly evading the hand of a young man who was reaching for his collar.

"Mama, mama, I am very nearly a soldier now!" he announced, ignoring the trivial concerns of his elders. "I can ride, and hold a sword, and two times in a row I lanced the straw man in the tourney practice! Also I know Greek and Latin now, and I can add up accounts nearly as well as Piero does, for my tutor said so!"

"Did he indeed?" Caterina asked, hugging her son. "But I think he does not know Piero?"

Ercole squirmed in her embrace. "Well, he said that no accountant in living memory had ever produced columns of figures quite like mine, which is nearly the same thing, is it not?"

Caterina controlled her expression. "Perhaps you can tell me something about your classical learning. What have you been reading in Greek?"

"Alpha. Beta. Gamma. Um…"

"Delta?" suggested Gian, his lips twitching.

"Oh, yes. Delta, Epsilon…"

He stalled again, and Caterina took pity on him. "And Latin?"

Ercole posed, chest out like a strutting bantam.

"Arma virumque cano, Troiae qui primus ab oris
Italiam fato profugus Lavinaque venit… and I know lots more!"

"Then you shall tell it to me later," Caterina promised, "but now you must go with your tutor, for we are working here to keep your city safe for you."

Feet dragging, Ercole left the room with the young man who had failed to catch him. Before the door swung shut, they heard his voice on the stairs,

"Actually I only know two more lines. Do you think you can teach me some more before Mama's meeting is finished?"

"You see that the boy does well?" Montefeltro inquired with a hint of anxiety.

"The boy does very well," Caterina said warmly. "I do not think I could have placed him better. But now, about the future of San Florian…"

"San Florian will, of course, remain an independent state," Montefeltro pronounced. "It is my duty to see to that." He fixed each of the envoys in turn with a piercing glance from his left eye. "And I have brought my condottieri with me, just in case there is any argument."

Bishop Visconti and Ottavio Contarini could not agree quickly enough that their interests in San Florian were purely commercial. Montefeltro eyed Lorenzo de' Medici.

"No other place has sent the head of the state to negotiate a *purely commercial* transaction," he observed.

"No one but I could make the offer which I am empowered to make," Lorenzo answered calmly. "I have been told by Uberti that you have a member of the house of Neroni in your service, Contessa. Not that I needed to be told, having seen him." He nodded to Gian. "You are the image of your uncle Dietisalvi, Gian-Maria."

"And he remains in my service!" flashed Caterina.

"That," said Lorenzo imperturbably, "is entirely up to him." He looked at Gian again. "You need not ever have fled, you know. Did you imagine I would hold a boy of sixteen responsible for the plots of his elders? But once you disappeared, well, I could hardly keep the Neroni estates forever, for fear of being accused of orchestrating the plot for my personal benefit —oh, yes, there are people who think like that. I am afraid that there is no reversing the gift of the town house to Paolo Uberti. However, I am not satisfied with his management of the country estates. He is a townsman through and through, and thinks a good estate with a vineyard will keep producing even though nobody but hired servants looks after it. I have *missed* the wine from those grapes… In short, I can offer you the Neroni country estate, several years of hard work restoring it to its former glory, and the right to bear your own name unafraid of retaliation."

Gian's face flushed, but to Caterina's surprise he did not close with the offer immediately. His eyes sought hers before he replied to the ruler of Florence. *Would you?* they asked.

And hers answered *Yes.*

"You and the Contessa would have to divide your time between San Florian and the Neroni vineyards," Lorenzo said, as though their marriage were already a settled thing. "I do not think that will be any great hardship, as they are so close together."

Caterina's heart was singing, and she could not make herself concentrate on dates and numbers and contracts. And she noticed that Gian was looking half stunned and half foolish —except when he looked at her. Then he simply looked happy.

"Piero," she said, "you will represent my interests in this contract?"

Piero nodded. "I have some preliminary figures here…"

"Then let us sit down with the accountant, and make sure that Florence's terms with San Florian are acceptable to the Contessa," said Lorenzo.

# Afterword

The number of writers to whose research I am indebted is too long to list here. It will be obvious to anyone familiar with Elizabeth Lev's The Tigress of Forli that certain incidents in Caterina Rinaldi's life are remarkably similar to those in the life of Caterina Sforza Riario de' Medici, but my Caterina is in no way intended as a faithful portrait of that lady; to do that I'd need to write three volumes instead of just one.

For Renaissance magic I have relied on some primary sources, such as translations of Alessio Piemontese and Albertus Magnus; these are supplemented with secondary sources, of which Kieckhefer's Forbidden Rites and Skemer's Binding Words were particularly useful. Gentilcore's Medical Charlatanism in Early Modern Italy and Eamon's The Professor of Secrets were valuable sources for the culture of popular medicine in the period. Wexler's Toxicology in the Middle Ages and Renaissance was an extremely useful view of an age in which poisons –real or imagined –played so great a part. For the general relations between Turkey and Europe, Goodwin's Lords of the Horizons and Creasy's The Crescent in the West furnished a starting point; for more detail on Mehmed II, I am indebted to Freely's The Grand Turk and Babinger's Mehmed the Conqueror and his Time.

Readers who are intimately familiar with the sequence of Turkish operations against Italy in 1479-1481 will observe that events in the book are not precisely in line with the accepted chronology. I apologize to both of you.

And while I'm at it, I owe an apology to Roberto Malatesta, who certainly never tried to conquer the totally fictional town of San Florian and who was probably not nearly as unpleasant as the character I have drawn here. As far as I know, it has never actually been proved that he poisoned his stepmother and half-brothers.

# Also by Margaret Ball:

**Regency Fantasy series:**

Salt Magic: Regency Magic Book 1

*A beautiful young widow with a deadly secret… monsters (and other creatures) from the depths of the sea… An accusation of murder… and six aunts telling her what to do, as if Sabira doesn't have enough problems already!*

Tangled Magic: Regency Magic Book 2

*Elspet's special brand of embroidery can help with everything from her sister's illness to getting dance partners. But is it enough to disentangle the problem of a sham engagement to the man whose love she wants?*

**Applied Topology series:**

A Pocketful of Stars: Applied Topology Book 1

*A quiet math major has to fight in the magical realm for her life and those of her friends after the CIA decides to make use of her paranormal abilities.*

An Opening in the Air: Applied Topology Book 2

*When a rival mage attacks, Thalia needs wits as well as magic to save the Center for Applied Topology. And the defense may cost her the man she loves.*

An Annoyance of Grackles: Applied Topology Book 3

*It's bad enough when a rival mage tries to destroy you. When he turns out to be a god, that's worse. And when the god teams up with the most notorious contract bomber in America? If Thalia can't outwit the duo, she may wind up scattered across the campus in tiny pieces.*

A Tapestry of Fire: Applied Topology Book 4

*Saving her best friend from life as a fish is difficult. Rescuing the man she loves from a past era of fire and fury ought to be impossible, so it may take Thalia a little longer.*

A Creature of Smokeless Flame: Applied Topology Book 5

*When CIA officers' children are kidnapped for revenge, Thalia and her colleagues follow the trail across the continents to an African terrorists' camp whose leader has the help of his own personal genie.*

A Revolution of Rubies: Applied Topology Book 6

*When the CIA sends Thalia and her colleagues abroad, they should have realized the diplomatic consequences could be explosive. Can Thalia stop the revolutionaries in Central Asia before all of Taklanistan is under water?*

A Child of Magic: Applied Topology Book 7

*When their son Aleksi is kidnapped, Thalia and Lensky are left wondering if the reason is ransom (bad) or revenge (worse). It'll take all Thalia's genius for applied topology (aka magic) to retrieve their baby - and she has yet to discover the consequences of having used applied topology (aka magic) while she was pregnant...*

**Harmony series:**

Insurgents

*The colony world of Harmony established its own separate colony to which everybody who disagreed with the government was banished. Now they're surprised that the exiles want to run their own country.*

Awakening

*Being a good citizen was never easy. It got harder when Devra realized that it was incompatible with being a decent human being.*

Survivors

*The pampered life of a holostar is no preparation for surviving the collapse of a country.*

**Earlier books:**

www.ingramcontent.com/pod-product-compliance
Lightning Source LLC
Chambersburg PA
CBHW050319200626

46808CB00023BA/1521